SPECTATOR SPORT

JAMES ALEXANDER THOM

D1157333

AN AUTHORS GUILD BACKINPRINT.COM EDITION

Spectator Sport

AN AUTHORS GUILD BACKINPRINT.COM EDITION

Published by iUniverse.com, Inc.

For information address:
iUniverse.com, Inc.
5220 S 16th, Ste. 200
Lincoln, NE 68512
www.iuniverse.com

Originally published by Avon Books

ISBN: 0-595-13345-2

Printed in the United States of America

AUTHOR'S NOTE

When I started writing this novel in 1973, I was not so much inspired as reacting. Like most Americans, I had been watching the pointless horror of the Vietnam War through TV and print film imagery—years of hi-tech death from which we could not avert our eyes, even though we felt we should.

I was in the crowd at the Indianapolis Motor Speedway during parts of the ill-fated 1973 race, not far from the first-lap wreck that sent fire and junk into the stands, injuring race fans. The subsequent stupefying, repetitive film coverage and endless replays of that accident, and others in the following two days, were so much like Vietnam's morbid photo-voyeurism that I began to perceive it as a kind of national sickness. Americans were being mesmerized by intimate events—dying, sex acts, grief—that customarily had taken place offstage and in privacy.

Another demoralizing aspect of the Vietnam conflict had been its enormous waste, of lives, materiel and cultures. Here in America, the automobile was the symbol of wastefulness on a comparable scale, and auto racing glorified it.

In those three days in May 1973, all those things became one for me, and a kind of malaise I had to write out of my system. If I had any notion that a book would help cure the sickness, I was wrong, of course. Now, more than a quarter of a century later, war, waste, voyeurism and vicarious peril, on TV and computer screens, are presented as art forms. I've survived that malaise, but believe that my message about it is still valid, and that is why this Backinprint.com edition is being published now.

Since the original publication of *Spectator Sport*, two of the major non-fiction characters in the book have died: Anton "Tony"

Hulman, owner of the Indianapolis Motor Speedway; and the famous "Voice of the 500," Sid Collins, who helped me immensely with the book by providing his tapes of the three-day event and authorizing unlimited quotation from them. The race was the big thing in Sid's life and he knew that the book I was preparing to write would not flatter it, but he helped me anyway. That kindness gave me my only good memory of the 1973 race, and I appreciate him for it.

James Alexander Thom
Bloomington, Indiana
May 2000

The 57th Indianapolis Race was the longest and shortest "500" run to date. It started on Monday and ended on Wednesday after 332 miles had been run. You can imagine there were lots of stories in between times.

—Carl Hungness, racing publisher

The race fan has to be an unusual breed.

—Sid Collins

PART I

May 28, 1973

AT five o'clock on the wet and windy morning of Memorial Day, an aerial bomb exploded over a residential neighborhood four miles northwest of downtown Indianapolis.

It was followed by an outburst of rebel yells and wild laughter, the grinding of hundreds of automobile starters, and the forward surge of an enormous mob in the predawn gloom. The bomb was the signal that the gates of the Indianapolis Motor Speedway were opening to let in the thousands of auto-racing fans who were gathered on the streets and lots and fields surrounding the Speedway grounds.

In the damp semidarkness, the inrush built up. It was as if a vacuum chamber suddenly had been punctured and was sucking in everything around it. Cars and pedestrians poured in through the gates in a great, noisy welter: headlights, honking horns, roaring engines, shouts, whistles, running feet.

The influx was most frenetic in the south end of the grounds, where the race fans were entering from West Sixteenth Street, thronging through the tunnel under the racetrack's south straightaway and making their famous headlong dash for the coveted infield parking spaces near the first turn in the southwest corner of the grounds. Automobiles roared, spun wheels, slithered, threw mud, honked, and sped toward that southwest corner. Drivers bluffed, charged each other, chickened out, cursed. A few bumpers were banged and fenders scraped.

One of the first cars to slide to a stop on the wet grass in this preferred section was a white Chevrolet with red racing stripes painted from front to rear on the driver's side.

3

It sat for a moment, its exhaust pipes burbling in a deep tone; then the engine was revved once and shut off. The rear of the car was elevated, and the rear wheels were outfitted with wide tires on massive, gleaming steel hubs. Lettering on the rear of the car labeled it HEAVY CHEVY. The driver, a jowly young man with greasy brown hair and the prolapsed abdomen of a glutton, climbed out of his car, reached into the back seat to lift out a Styrofoam cooler, and waddled hurriedly away to the wire fence. There he planted his feet wide apart and waited. His companion, a gaunt young woman with pink plastic rollers in her hair and wearing patchwork blue jeans, unloaded from the car a clear plastic tarpaulin, a blanket, and a white plastic tote bag. Balancing the load, she came to where he waited. They arranged their paraphernalia into a square and floored it with the tarp. Their homestead thus staked out, they rolled themselves into the blanket, took long pulls from a pint bottle of orange-flavored vodka to stave off the damp chill, and lay there waiting for daylight. All around them, with yells, curses, laughter, squalling of children, beat of radio rock music, and slamming of car doors, other arrivals claimed ground along the fence.

As the dawn lightened, the youth gazed through the fence and across the track, his head propped on the heel of his hand.

"C'n you see them marks on th' wall?" he said to her after a while.

"What marks?"

"Them there." He pointed and gravely nodded. She craned about and saw the black smudges on the low concrete retaining wall. "That there's where Pollard hit th' wall Qualification Day," he said. "I saw it from right here. It was really somethin'. I'm not shittin' you, I saw the whole thing."

"So'd I say you didn't?"

He grunted and lit a cigarette, and as he lit it, he remembered seeing it happen to Pollard. More than two weeks ago it had happened, but he could remember so clearly seeing it: Pollard practicing early in the morning before the start of the time trials, the copper-and-white race car whining into the first turn, then suddenly, with no evident cause, darting to the right, hitting the concrete wall with a thump felt through the ground, then tumbling along the south straightaway, flying to pieces, finally stopping right side up in the second turn, a wheelless hulk, the air around it turbulent with the colorless burning of methanol, Pollard slumped in the cockpit with his arms hanging out, being cooked alive in the innocent sunlight of a May morning.

The fat youth remembered this as he looked down his nose at the flame of his lighter.

Here in the first turn is where so much of the action is, he knew. Here where they swing into the turn after gunning it more than two hundred miles an hour down the main straightaway past the big grandstands. That's why he made sure he never got muscled out of a good spot on the fence here.

He never got muscled out of anything when he was behind the wheel. He always got away first when a stoplight changed. He was always first out of the drive-in theater after a show, or first into a parking space when one opened up. His driving had gotten him into trouble a few times. Once several years ago while racing a Corvette across West Twenty-fifth Street, less than a mile from this Speedway, in fact, he remembered, he had hit and killed a little boy on a tricycle. He didn't like to remember that. It had cost him his driver's license for a while, and that had really been rough. Six whole months without wheels! Fortunately, he had had a good lawyer.

But Jesus. After all, what th' hell can you do when some brat suddenly rides a goddamn tricycle across an intersection just when you're haulin' ass against some jerk who's tryin' to outrun you in a Corvette?

The fat youth sucked his cigarette, squinted, and with thick, chewed finger-ends scratched at his chest, vacantly clawing the front of his cotton T-shirt on which was lettered the motto:

RACING IS FUN

A telephone rang in the city room of the *Indianapolis News* at three minutes after five. A reporter with puffy, early-morning eyes leaned back from his typewriter, sucked his lungs full of cigarette smoke, carefully pressed the cigarette into the notch on the rim of his ashtray, and reached slowly, reluctantly, for the phone. Deliberate though he was, nobody else was beating him to it. He glanced around the cramped, fluorescent-lit room where other reporters and editors milled about in their shirt-sleeves among desks heaped high with paper. Before him on the desk was this morning's edition of the *Indianapolis Star,* the city's morning daily, sister paper of the *News.*

WEATHER THREATENS "500" RACE
SHOWERS, WINDS ARE FORECAST

On the right side of the *Star*'s front page was a dramatic two-column photograph of a gray tornado funnel probing down from black clouds, its lower end touching the earth beyond silhouetted trees and utility poles, dwarfing a small white house in the foreground.

AT LEAST 4 TORNADOES
SLAM ACROSS STATE;
GREENWOOD HIT HARD

The reporter lifted the phone out of its cradle. He expected the call to be some suburban area stringer correspondent with a tiresome detailed listing of local tornado damages. *"News* city desk," he said.

A deep, authoritarian voice came through the receiver: "This is Senator Barry Goldwater."

The reporter's indolent spirits snapped to attention. Here was he, on one end of a telephone connection; on the other end was Barry Goldwater. "How's the weather there?" asked the familiar voice. "Is the race still on? I've heard out here it's been postponed." He wanted to know, he said, because he would be flying to Indianapolis for the race if it was still scheduled.

The reporter assured the senator that the race had not been postponed. He was smiling when he turned back to his typewriter. A United States senator, once a presidential nominee, had asked him for information, and he had been able to provide it, and on the authority of that information

the senator would go to an airfield and get into the cockpit
of a jet plane and fly to Indianapolis to attend what was
known as the Greatest Spectacle in Racing, the Indianapolis "500." The reporter felt good, felt wide-awake.
Times like this he understood why he liked being a
newspaperman. Maybe he was just an anonymous person
with a meager salary and a rather ordinary personal life.
But he was on the very perimeters of important happenings, and his life brushed now and then against the elbows
of famous lives.

"Hey," he shouted. "Guess what race fan I just talked
to!"

In another part of the *News* city room, a rewrite man
walked toward his desk, carrying a mug of hot coffee in
his right hand and a new package of cigarettes in his left.
In far corners, telephone bells clamored for attention.

The rewrite man felt a certain dread, but also a certain
excitement. Race Day was always a backbreaker. The
volume and the urgency of the data that would be coming
over his phone and through his typewriter today would be
staggering. There would be an air of haste and pressure,
a daylong frenzy, because of the magnitude of the event
and the detailed coverage the Indianapolis papers always
granted to it and to all its peripheral ceremonies and
problems. On Race Day there was potentially a great
sense of accomplishment for the hardworking news and
sports staff. If all went right, the complete race story could
be in print and on the streets even before the mob of fans
vacated the Speedway. He remembered how amazed he
had always been as a young race spectator to drive out of
the Speedway shortly after the finish of the race and find
newsboys already walking between the lanes of traffic,
hawking editions headlined with the winner's name.
Until he had become a reporter he had marveled that
newspapers could possibly be written, printed, and transported so quickly.

Theoretically, it could be done more easily every year.
The race cars were now so fast that they could, barring
wrecks, spins, and other delays, complete the five hundred
miles in less than three hours, instead of late afternoon

after deadlines. And in recent years the crowds had become so much bigger, the traffic so much more congested, that the fans were still sitting in traffic jams long after the Victory edition reached the streets.

The rewrite man was seated at his desk now, stripping cellophane to open his cigarette pack. With his thumbnail he laid back the foil, tapped the pack on the heel of his hand, and drew out a cigarette. He struck a jet of flame on his plastic disposable lighter, applied it, and drew in the harsh, satisfying smoke. "Hey," somebody was yelling across the room, "guess what race fan I just talked to! Barry Goldwater!"

"Can you do a graf on that?" called an editor.

The rewrite man picked up his long steel shears and dragged the morning *Star* toward him on the desk. He leafed through it quickly, clipping out anything he might want to save for reference during his day's efforts, including maps and charts.

WAYS TO GET TO TRACK—
BETTER LOOK AT THIS

He glanced at photos of two celebrities he had seen in person in yesterday's Festival Parade. The parade always passed down Pennsylvania Street, directly below the windows of the city room, and he always brought his family down to watch it from the newspaper office. There were photos of Burgess Meredith and Jackie Cooper, perched on the seat backs of Cadillac Eldorado official pace car convertibles.

The rewrite man lingered over the editorial page, smoking his cigarette and sipping his coffee, enjoying the few minutes of what would probably be his only lull in the day.

"GENTLEMEN, START . . . ."

Ray Harroun, winner of the first 500-Mile Race at the Indianapolis Motor Speedway in 1911, roared to victory in his Marmon Wasp at a blazing 74.59-mph average.

Grandma, whizzing en route to the shopping center in her new hardtop, wouldn't give a second thought to equaling that on the interstate, very likely.

From the society page he clipped an article naming race-car sponsors attending the race. Then he looked, bemused, for a moment at two rows of photographs of race drivers' wives. How like ordinary people they look, he thought. No different from the brides usually lined up for display on this page. But how ordinary could they actually be, being the wives of race drivers? Seems they should look different somehow.

SKY FROWNS, CLOWNS, SOUNDS ABOUND

THOUSANDS OF FEET MARCH PAST CROWD

RAINDROPS

MAJORETTE BATTLES BALLOON

Those were headlines on a full page of photos from yesterday's parade. Among them was a photo of a youthful dark-haired squinting man and a tense-faced blond beauty sitting together on the reviewing stand:

MAYOR LUGAR AND QUEEN CYNTHIA

The rewrite man folded the paper now. From the front page he clipped the Race Scorecard, a quarter-page chart of car numbers, drivers, qualifying speeds, sponsors. He admired the ominous photo of the tornado. A twister, he thought, is about the only nonrace topic that could find a spot on the front page of an Indianapolis newspaper on Race Day. Then from the bottom of the page he made one final clipping:

ORDER OF THE DAY
(Eastern Standard Time)

5:00 A.M.—Salute bombs, gates open.
8:30 A.M.—Race cars pushed to respective pits.

9:30 A.M.—Spectacle of bands featuring the Purdue University Band and bands representing the fifty states of the United States.

10:00 A.M.—"On the Banks of the Wabash," by Purdue University Band. All cars pushed to starting positions on track.

10:02 A.M.—Celebrity Caravan moves through north end of pits onto track.

10:30 A.M.—Track inspection.

10:40 A.M.—The National Anthem.

10:45 A.M.—"Taps."

10:50 A.M.—"Back Home Again in Indiana," by Jim Nabors.

10:53 A.M.—"Gentlemen, Start Your Engines," by Tony Hulman.

10:54 A.M.—Start of the parade lap and pace lap.

11:00 A.M.—Start of race.

The rewrite man placed the schedule on the corner of his desk and laid his wristwatch upon it as a paperweight. Beside it he placed another sheet upon which were typed phone numbers of the police traffic-control center at the Speedway, the Speedway field hospital, pressroom, Speedway Motel, Speedway office, United States Automobile Club, and various law-enforcement agencies, ambulance services, and hospital emergency rooms. He dropped the butchered newspaper into the dented metal wastebasket at his feet, ground out his cigarette stub, made a sandwich of paper and carbon paper, tapped its ends flush on the leaf of his typewriter table, and fed it under the platen of his typewriter.

Okay. Ready as I'll ever be.

Much of the traffic approaching the Speedway from the west found its way across Twenty-fifth Street, passing the one-story brick home of Mr. and Mrs. Nicholas Alef in the town of Speedway. Their modest house was only a half mile from the west side of the racetrack. Across the street from Nick and Becky Alef's house was a vast field, owned by Speedway owner Tony Hulman. In the few days before the race every year, that field was a favorite encampment for early-arriving race fans from distant parts of the country. It was a sprawling mass of cars, vans, tents, trailers, recreational vehicles, and overloaded station wagons, many of whose occupants spent their days and nights shouting, playing loud music, and wandering the neighborhood in boozy aimlessness.

Because of the proximity of that field, the Alefs had deadbolt locks on their doors and at night drew down their window blinds and closed the heavy lined drapes throughout the house to filter out as much noise as possible. They turned on the window air conditioners in their bedroom and the bedroom of their son, David. The hum of the air conditioners helped a little to obliterate the noises from outside.

Nick Alef was awakened in the darkness by automobile horns and the thunder of passing motorcycles. He cursed them under his breath.

Nick was at once aware of several things that complicated his awakening. It was going to be a rough, frantic, busy day.

First, as always, there would be his habitual two-and-a-half-mile morning run, which would be unusually difficult today because of the Race Day traffic and crowds around the neighborhood and because, as he was now reminded by a caustic eructation, he had a hangover.

After running, he would have to get his cameras and films together and go to the Speedway, where he would be covering the main straightaway, as he had done for four years now, as a hired Race Day photographer for the wire service and free-lance photojournalist for several news and sports magazines.

And he had promised his son that he would take him to a movie in the evening.

It would be a hectic day, in which it would be almost impossible for him to arrange the one project that he really wanted to do: the pictorial feature on Diana Scheckley.

The thought of all that lay ahead made him want to hide like an ostrich under his pillow and emerge tomorrow. But he had to work the race. Money was scarce in the Alef household. To cover the race, and cover it well, was an economic necessity. It was a part of their seemingly endless game of survival.

Becky didn't stir when he eased out of bed. He groped to the bathroom door, went in, shut it, and turned on the light. A glimpse in the mirror at the puffed eyes, the mussed, short black beard, and the graying hair flattened to his temples by sleep made him avert his face. He wasn't ready for that much reality yet. His head hurt, and his insides felt raw and sour. Standing naked, he brushed his teeth and combed his hair and beard. He turned this way and that before the mirror, checking his sinewy, hairy torso for any signs of fat or age. He was pleased. To be in such fine condition at thirty-eight years of age was gratifying. Little else about Nick's present personal circumstances was so good. Thus he drove himself hard to keep himself tough and trim. Most of the journalists his age were securely employed by newspapers or broadcasting stations, with wages and fringe benefits, with several years toward retirement pensions, and with at least a few hundred dollars saved, but most of them were potbellied, short-winded, and sallow. Nick Alef was the opposite. He had left the newspaper six years ago to become a freelance writer and photojournalist, and his physical fitness by now was about the only asset he had left. Nick did almost everything that can be done with cameras and typewriters, but the few payment checks he did bring in each year were already committed to overdue bills. When he resigned from the newspaper he had felt confident and eager to do the finest, most creative and original kinds of work for the loftiest markets. But over the years he had learned to adjust his sights lower and lower.

Packed in a filing cabinet in his basement office was a huge accumulation of manuscripts, scenarios, synopses, and portfolios that he had created with incandescent soul until futility and rejection had dried him up.

So now Nick Alef made audiovisual materials, brochures, slides, and public-service films, wrote speeches, publicity, slogans, and insurance company commercials, and photographed machines, buildings, sporting events, ribbon-cuttings, and ground-breakings—and, occasionally, naked women. Now and then if he was lucky he would sell a few news photos or candid celebrity shots with captions and, in May, would serve as one of the hundreds of hired lenses at the Speedway.

He gazed now at the gray eyes looking back at him from the mirror. A slanting smile changed his visage from his benign look to his cynical look.

"Flack,'" he whispered at the face in the mirror.

"Hurry up in there," Becky said beyond the door. So. She was up.

"Wife of flack," he whispered. He reached for his sweat suit, which hung, pungent and wrinkled, on the back of the door, and pulled it on.

"Surely you're not running this morning," Becky said as he yielded the bathroom to her.

"I run every morning."

"You're almost forty years old. You had a quart of whiskey last night, and your lungs are black with nicotine. You'll kill yourself."

"Running when you have a hangover is the highest order of self-discipline," he said. He sat on the edge of the bed and tied his running shoes.

"Where's all that self-discipline when you should be at the typewriter?" she uttered through the closing bathroom door as her last words.

"My dear," he said to the door, "writing flack calls for more self-discipline than even I have. It's like shoveling horseshit. No. Bullshit, I mean." There was no reply from within. "Remember the formula," he cried as he went down the hall toward the front door. "P.R. equals B.S.!"

He stooped on his way out of the front door and, picking up the newspaper, looked at the headline:

WEATHER THREATENS "500" RACE

He threw the paper inside and shut the door. The wind was cool and humid. Streetlights were still on. There was a great movement of people and vehicles in the gloom, as if a city were being evacuated. He walked out to the street, taking deep breaths and waving his arms; then he turned west and stepped into a loose, reaching stride, running on the balls of his feet, dodging among startled race fans going the other way on the sidewalk. Usually he ran a measured course on the grassy field, but that was impossible now because of the encampment of race fans. And the street was solid with creeping cars, each sitting in the headlamp glow of the one behind.

Nick Alef always felt heavy and awkward the first two blocks, and would think of Becky's warnings about his age. But then he would find the rhythm—three steps while inhaling, three while exhaling—and his feet and legs would begin to feel like lively springs; the flowing morning air would seem to sweep the residue out of his lungs and blow the miasma of old disappointments and worries out of his head. The pedestrians, cars, and houses dropped behind him one by one, the cool wind blew, his breath sighed in and out on three-count cadences, and his muscles warmed to their work. Running was the closest thing to happiness Nick Alef had known in the last five years. He did it well for someone his age, and it was one of the few pure and simple things in his life and probably the only thing he did that was good for him. When his physical body ran and his spirits went freely along, he knew he was real and alive, and he was aware that to be alive is a miracle. When he was at the typewriter or behind a camera tripod taking industrial stills or talking with clients about public relations and statistics and capital and profits and quotas and corporate objectives, nothing was real and he was not alive.

He ran eight blocks, turned down another residential street, and ran five blocks that way. There was heavy traffic even here. Reaching the corner, he whirled around and started to return. He had held a fast pace in the first half of his measured distance, and now his body had reached that stage where it gladly would have stopped to rest. The breathing was painful and his leg muscles burned; his heart hammered fast and sweat was starting to drench his suit and sting his eyes. But when his body was tired of running, his will was only half-through, and it would force the body to make the return run without resting. And so the return run would be an agony in his body and a fierce joy in his head, and he knew he was truly alive.

In, two-three; out, two-three. In, two-three; out, two-three. Running is like making love, he thought; then a man is alive, too. I mean, when the love is deep and simple and not cluttered with psychological baggage like guilts and blames and regrets and resentments.

Katherine, he thought suddenly. He had not thought of Katherine for a long time. He thought of her now because of what he had been thinking about love. Ten years ago; three days with Katherine. It glowed misty and voluptuous in the murky background of his memory, a poignant, shameless secret growing in beauty like a pearl. Becky had never learned of it and thus had never been hurt by it. Nick's one regret about those few days was that they could never be repeated in his life. During those few days with Katherine, he had been supremely alive. He had not seen her nor heard from her since. Now and then he would think of her while he was alone and running.

In, two-three; out, two-three. In, two-three; out, two-three. He was drawing near his house now, and the exertion was no longer painful. His lungs and legs felt inexhaustible. Sometimes this happened at the end of the second mile. In, two-three; out, two-three. Easy. Feel like I could do five miles this morning. Like I did the year I quit smoking. Should quit again. Can't, though. It's a part of that unreal P.R. and B.S. at the typewriter. In, two-three; out, two-three. In, two-three; out, two-three.

Suddenly, a hundred yards from home, under a streetlight that was just blinking off in the lightening gray of day, Nick's eye fell on a storm sewer drain. He had trained himself not to think of it when he saw the drain, but this morning he thought of it.

He remembered his son Timmy lying there on the gray pavement smeared with his own red blood. It was the place where, three years ago, a hot-rodder had hit Timmy Alef's tricycle and dragged him along Twenty-fifth Street under the wheels. Keep running, Nick thought. But he had slowed to a halt, soles flapping, and he stood there gasping for breath, pouring sweat, remembering Timmy's blood trickling in a slow, thin red line into that storm drain. Race fans walking by with coolers and folding chairs looked curiously at this tall, bearded man in his sweat-darkened gym suit, panting and gazing at a place in the street.

Then Nick plodded the rest of the way home, chest heaving, sweat chilling on his face and neck, heart thudding fast. He didn't go in right away. It alarmed Becky too much when he came in heaving and flushed. Beside a small maple tree in his front yard there was a limestone bench; he sat down on it and leaned back against the tree trunk and waited for his heart to slow down. He was at the age when modern men are told to worry about their hearts, and he always audited his carefully after a hard run.

A life is such an intricacy, he thought; such a delicately balanced thing. It's rugged, but it's fragile. It's the only significant thing in the universe. It dies out in a flash or a slow leak.

But it's so cheap.

The speeder who killed Timmy had been charged with reckless homicide. That had been reduced to involuntary manslaughter. Childslaughter, Nick thought. The sentence had been suspended. Within six months the hot-rodder had gotten his license back and was still-drag-racing around town.

Nick often wondered what he would do if he came face-to-face with that driver.

The marriage had worsened since Timmy's death. Nick felt that he should spend more time with Davey, who was like a lost half of something since his twin brother's death, but there never seemed to be enough time, and the few outings they did have usually ended in squabbles. Becky didn't want to have another child because she felt she was past the age for easy childbearing and also because she was not altogether sure the marriage would last.

He wasn't quite sure it would last, either. Sometimes he hoped it wouldn't. It had become little more than a bad habit.

But how in hell do you get out, he wondered. It takes money to get out of a marriage. His desire to be rid of Becky and start life out again cleanly existed in him like a dull ache, but he had an array of excuses for not getting on with it. Lack of money was his main excuse. You can't start a good new life if you start it as a financial cripple, he thought.

Anyway, I'd need something or somebody better to go on to, he thought. You don't make a move like that to get *away* from something; you do it to go on *to* something. But he had given up hope of finding something to go on to. Everything he looked at faded into a gray dead end.

They had never spoken of divorce. She was an erstwhile Catholic but perhaps still had the Catholic attitude toward it. Nick had never been a Catholic—he defined himself, when asked, as a "devout Christo-Judaic Muslim Hindu"—and he had never mentioned divorce because he had never been quite ready to bear the emotional upheaval even of discussing it.

Nick had a vague understanding that his marriage had gone bad because his career had gone bad. He did not understand why the career had gone bad. He thought he saw the world more clearly than most people seemed to see it, felt things more acutely than most people, and could express it with more eloquence and wit than most can. But it seemed that nobody placed any monetary value on his rare soul and intellect. He could not quite understand why, after such a promising start, he remained at this age a mere flack, slowly losing headway on a treadmill of mortgage payments and small debts, unable even to afford repairs on his aged Volvo, which sat dormant in his garage. He was a loser who should have been a winner. It had been years since he had put a virgin sheet of paper into his typewriter and started to type a story, his soul full of hope and inspiration, or had sat in a restaurant for unclocked hours writing in a notebook. His creativity had etiolated inside him. He had simply decided one day to withhold his gift from an unappreciative world, and the decision had given him a delicious, bittersweet sense of righteousness and relief. There would be no more of his original ideas and powerful projects for them to toss back in his face. He hadn't told anybody he was giving it up. He'd just say his other work kept him away from it. He could foresee himself shrinking into oblivion, with inane slogans and commercial copy hissing out of him like a slow leak. It made no difference to anyone.

Well, anyway, he thought, sitting under the maple tree growing chilly in his damp sweat suit, there aren't many men my age who can put in a run like that in sixteen minutes. And it sure cures a hangover.

He sighed. Maybe the photo project with Diana Scheckley will change my luck, he thought. It could open some doors. It could be the better thing I could go on to.

And just in its own right, four or five thousand dollars would help.

If, he thought. If I can get her to go along with it.

But it's a natural. It's made to order. It's one of my better ideas. One of my more saleable ideas lately. He had been thinking about it for weeks, ever since Diana was selected as a "500" Festival Princess. Once the idea had hit him, he had started getting close to her: flattering her with his camera and with his words, ignoring the "500" Queen to pay attention to Diana, being as charming and witty as he knew how, giving her free prints of the most complimentary photos. And he could tell that she was beginning to respond. She grew a little gay and flustered when he came around. She seemed to think of him now as her own special photographer. Yesterday during the Festival Parade downtown, he had intercepted her at three different points along the route. He had had to run his legs off to accomplish that, but she had noticed.

Yes, Diana, he thought, I am your own special photographer. You watch and see.

He thought these things as he sat on his limestone bench watching the endless river of race fans flow toward the Speedway, filling the air with their hubbub.

While Nick was outside, Becky was going through the house gathering up drinking glasses they had left sitting in various rooms the night before. In passing, she eased open the door to Davey's bedroom; he was still asleep. She returned to the master bedroom and went quickly through Nick's pants pockets and jacket pockets. She found nothing unusual. No notes or phone numbers. But she had sensed Nick's preoccupation with something the last few weeks, and late yesterday afternoon, while mending the ripped-out seat of a pair of Davey's denims and desultorily watching the taped telecast of the downtown "500" Festival Parade, she had seen something that might have been a clue. She had watched the parade go endlessly across the screen under an ominous sky while winds tugged at skirts and guidons; she had seen hats tumbling through the air and the Shriners' horses shying and prancing, and parts of a float being blown off; she had seen the celebrities and the former prisoners of war riding in their places of honor in Cadillac Eldorado pace car convertibles.

And then there had been that unexpected glimpse of her husband, Nick, trotting alongside one of the vehicles with his cameras, talking and smiling up to a blond girl, all charm and attentiveness.

It's just part of his job, she had advised herself. Be glad he's doing *something*. But it was the way they were looking at each other. And they seemed to be talking as if they knew each other. It had been just a glimpse. But it had been enough to strike a note of warning in her intuition.

Becky glanced at herself in the hall mirror as she passed it. She was a nucleus of bright color in the shabby house, wearing a loose robe of velour printed in red and gold flowers. Her luxuriant brown hair was neatly pulled back and fastened tightly with a barrette, and she wore a pale shade of lipstick. Regardless of how things were around the Alef household, Becky always tried to look the best she could. It was a point of pride, one of the few she had left. And she never wanted Nicky to cite personal slovenliness as a complaint against her. In Becky's mind, grooming was the last redoubt to stand off the admission of personal failure. She had grown up in a poor family, but her mother had always told her, "Once you go to pot on the outside, you're done for on the inside."

She looked out the front window. There he sat, on his bench in the damp air, that bench they had brought back in the car trunk years ago from an outing in the limestone country in the southern part of the state. Back when they had outings.

Something's really on his mind, she thought. And it's not his work. Something personal. She picked up the newspaper from the vestibule as she went into the kitchen.

WEATHER THREATENS "500" RACE

She put the glasses in the dishwasher, then put on the kettle for instant coffee. Then she opened the basement door and went to check into his darkroom. The darkroom door was ajar. She turned on the light and glanced through the clammy, cluttered room with its black-painted walls and ceiling, its hoses, its hypo and developer tanks in the shallow steel sinks, always crusty with dried white chemicals, strips of 35-millimeter film clipped to an overhead wire, with clamps weighting the lower ends to keep them from coiling up. Stacks of black-and-yellow boxes of photographic paper. Camera magazines and *Playboy, Penthouse, Gallery,* and *Oui* magazines stacked on a chair in the corner near the enlarger.

Thumbtacked on a corkboard wall panel were black-and-white prints Becky had not seen before: poses of a brunette girl, naked. Pretty and shapely, flat-bellied, no sag in the breasts. Becky grimaced when she saw them. She could envision Nicky taking those photos, arranging the poses, touching the naked skin to adjust a limb, flattering, taking his time, coaxing her to stretch, arch, and sprawl, shooting up four or five rolls of film, then probably. . . .

Becky had her own memory of all this, of how he and his camera and his intense praise could seduce one out of her clothes, make it seem excusable, even thrilling, to be showing oneself naked. He had persuaded her once before their marriage.

She went forward to look more closely. One of the photos had been taken outdoors. The girl embraced a sycamore trunk, her face turned left. She appeared to be sixteen or seventeen. A serene and perfect profile. Another was an indoor photograph. The girl sat on a sofa facing the camera, leaning against the flower-patterned back, her lips parted slightly in a travesty of desire, her bare young breasts thrust forward, her pubic hair a small triangle. How young! The girl's nipples were tiny, pale. But from this close Becky could see the roughness of acne over the cheekbones, and something about the teeth in that slightly opened mouth: braces? Dear God, is he picking them up off the school playgrounds now? Oh, Jesus, Nicky. But she felt better in a way. Those imperfections meant Nicky wouldn't have become involved with this model. He was put off by physical imperfection.

The kettle was whistling on the stove. He should lock this door so Davey won't see such pictures, she thought angrily. She snapped the padlock as she left the darkroom

and plodded, heartsick, up the basement stairs, thinking of
Nicky's perpetual search for surface perfection: for the
perfect face, the perfect body, the perfect landscape, the
unblemished image. It seemed as if photography had made
him that way. When he was first and foremost a writer, he
wasn't so superficial. Now it's just the image, the look of
a thing, she thought.

She remembered when, in the joy of her pregnancy,
she had become aware that Nicky didn't like to look at
her anymore. She remembered that he would only make
love to her in the dark after Davey and Timmy were
born and the stretch marks had appeared. Every day for
years, Becky had done a hundred sit-ups, always with
Nicky in mind. But the marks remained, and she knew
they troubled him. And she resented him for that; he
seemed to forget that his desires had caused them. She
poured boiling water over the dark powder in the cup and
stirred it with a spoon. How perfect she had looked, for a
few brief years. . . . But to remember that was too painful. She turned her attention instead to the paper, to her
coffee, to a morning cigarette at the dinette table under
the hanging lamp. Not to think, not to brood, not to regret
—that was the only way to get through a day. She
smoked and sipped and read about the parade she had
watched last evening on television.

FESTIVAL PARADE THRILLS 300,000
AS STORM CLOUDS HOLD PUNCHES

Air Force Colonel James H. Kasler of Indianapolis,
former POW and the parade grand marshal, drew a
standing ovation from raincoated parade fans as he
passed the reviewing stands, followed by Cadillac Eldorado pace cars carrying eleven more Hoosier
POWs.

There were photographs of a small gathering at the
memorial service for war dead at the Indiana War Memorial. The Festival Parade and the race always drew a
quarter of a million people or more, while the memorial

ceremony attracted only one or two hundred. Nick and Becky used to grow indignant about people's sense of values, and once their consciences had even driven them to attend the service. But as the years and bills accumulated and they became preoccupied with the business of survival, they had stopped worrying about such things.

In ads and photographs on page after page of the newspaper there was the checkered flag, symbol of victory in the auto race. Checkered flags everywhere.

INDY "500" RACE SPECIALS FROM MOTOROLA

GOODYEAR STEELGARD RADIALS TO SET PACE AT INDY "500" RACE

PRERACE GALA REFLECTS EXCITEMENT OF SEASON

Along a part of the parade route, even the streets were carpeted from curb to curb in black-and-white checkered carpeting.

Becky thought again of the parade and of Nick traipsing along beside that beauty queen. And she remembered other disturbing things over the last few years: telephone numbers written in matchbooks, lipstick on a handkerchief, and once a pair of trousers stuffed in a closet, with something dried on them, like semen. He had exploded with indignation when she had confronted him with those. "It's hypo from the darkroom," he had shouted. "What do you expect a photographer to have on his goddamn pants?"

Now Becky heard the front door open and close, heard his footsteps, heard him open the basement door.

"Do you want some coffee?"

"Not yet," he replied from the basement stairwell. "Got some work to do before I go to the track."

She shrugged and turned back to the paper. Be nice if we could have a cup of coffee together some morning, she thought. There are things we need to talk about. He knows that, she thought. That's precisely why he won't ever sit down to talk.

TV MOVIES

9:00 A.M. (4)—"Roar of the Crowd" (1953), with Howard Duff and Helene Stanley. Race driver promises his girl he'll quit racing after he has one chance at the Indianapolis "500."

A loud knocking at the front door startled Becky. She jumped up from her chair.

At the door was a heavy man, vaguely familiar, wearing a white cap with a checkered flag on it. Becky remembered: people from Arizona who last year had parked their car in the Alefs' yard because it was easier than driving into and out of the Speedway. Davey had made eighteen dollars last year by advertising the lawn as a parking lot. Got to get him up, she thought. Parking attendant is his job. She took the man's three dollars and watched sadly as his tires cut deep ruts in the rain-softened turf.

Mrs. Plew next door had already sent her little entrepreneurs out. They were carrying cardboard signs:

> Parking All Day
> Easy Walk to Track
> Free Lemonade After
> the Race

Becky opened the basement door and called down, "The ground's awfully soft. Do you want people parking in the yard today or not?"

His voice came up. "Whatever you think."

Oh, shit, she thought. Can't you even give a thing like that a little of your attention? Goddamn you, Nicky, why are you always drifting around just out of reach? Why are you always sulking around about how hard being poor is and never talking to me? And going out in the woods on spring days to take pictures of naked girls? Goddamn Casanova, I wish you were dead, she thought. No, I don't wish.

Yes, by God, I do wish.

Sometimes.

*　　*　　*

In the basement, Nick finished loading in bags all the camera equipment and film he would need at the Speedway during the day. Then he went to his desk, which was a nest of carelessly stacked papers covered with dust and cigarette ashes, to get a couple of notebooks and felt-tipped pens. He sat down on the dirty pillow in his swivel chair and pulled open a bottom drawer that was his supply cache. In the typewriter was a sheet of paper upon which he had typed a few words of a speech about no-fault automobile insurance. He was doing it for the president of an insurance company, one of his public-relations clients, and was a week past the deadline for completing it. He always seemed to be at least a week behind on everything, and Becky was always letting him know it.

Taped on the wall above his head was a bumper sticker, white letters on green vinyl, with a safety slogan that had won a national award for him:

Unsafe Cars Are Recalled by Their Maker.
So Are Unsafe Drivers.

Under it, lettered by hand, were two of his facetious safety slogans, which he had made up one day when he was particularly sick of safety slogans:

Be Safe.
Don't Pick Your Nose While Walking in the Dark.

And:

Caution: The Surgeon General Has Determined
That Motorcycle Riding Causes Cancer
of the Crotch.

Also tacked up was a large sheet of butcher paper upon which he had brush-painted neatly a maxim that seemed to sum up the world as he had perceived it of late:

Indifference
is the
Invincible Giant of the
World.
　　　　　—Ouida

He heard footsteps on the basement stairs. He saw Becky coming toward him under the glare of the bare ceiling bulb. She had his coffee mug in one hand and her own cup and saucer in the other.

"Thanks," he said. She sat down on a stool by the typewriter table, put down her cup and saucer, and got cigarettes out of the pocket of her robe. They lit up and sipped their coffee. The damp basement air was cold about their ankles. She peered about.

Come on, he thought. Out with it.

"That no-fault speech isn't done *yet?*"

"No."

"Wasn't it supposed to be?"

"Yes."

"You're going to lose that whole account," she said, shaking her head.

"What a heartrending tragedy that would be."

"We can't afford to lose any more accounts, Nicky."

He blew out a sigh. "When I think what I could be doing at this typewriter besides this crapola—"

"If you'd just let me help—"

"I know you can write. But this speech is a bunch of legalese and technical insurance jargon. You don't know what they want."

"Why won't you ever admit that you need help? Even when you're behind on everything?"

"I don't need help! How can you help me write, anyway? Sit down at the typewriter beside me like playing 'Chopsticks'?"

"How about letting me go to the Speedway with you today as your assistant, like in the old days when you loved me?"

"What do you mean, when I— I still love you. But it's too complicated, having an assistant."

"It didn't used to be."

"Well, I don't want you to get hurt."

"I won't get hurt. I'll stay in the background and hold the equipment and take the notes while you get up close and risk getting trampled by the majorettes."

"Very funny." He bent to the drawer and made an elaborate production out of selecting the right notebooks.

But she didn't go away. She sucked coffee over the edge of her cup with a noise that irritated him.

"Nicholas?"

"Rebecca?"

"I think you should keep your darkroom locked so Davey can't see those filthy magazines."

"If he didn't see them here, he'd see them at the drugstore. What difference does it make?"

"And those girlie photos you took."

"What girlie photos I took?"

"The nudies you've got tacked up in there."

"I didn't take those."

"Then why're they in your darkroom?"

"I developed and printed them for Doug Randolph 'cause he was afraid to send them to a lab."

"You want me to believe that?"

"Suit yourself. I'm indifferent to your credulity."

"I know you are. Unfortunately." She shook her head. "You know, it's a big mistake for a man to be indifferent to his wife."

"Thanks for the marital counseling. Jesus, Becky, I'm not indifferent to *you.* I just want to be left alone right now. You know I get edgy on Race Day."

"A day like any other day. Nicholas?"

He leaned back in his chair with an exaggerated look of patience exhausted. "What?"

"Why must you take nude girlie pictures?"

"Because you're always telling me about the money we need, and, as I've explained so often before, magazines will pay for picture stories of naked girls even when they won't pay for any other kind of pictures or stories."

"How would you like it if I took pictures of naked men?"

"Well, how's the pay?"

"You wouldn't like it."

"Who knows? Maybe I'd be your first model. All eight inches of me. Or is it eight and a half? I forget."

"I've forgotten, too. More like three and a half, I think it was."

He laughed in spite of himself. "We'll have to do something to refresh your memory."

"Yes. If you can ever work me into the schedule."

"What's that supposed to mean?"

"If you don't know, never mind."

"No, what *is* that supposed to mean?"

"Nothing. But you should have finished that speech last night. Instead of developing pictures. For your friends, as you say. How much is your 'friend' paying you?"

"Nothing. But—"

"Or how much did you pay her?"

"Her who? I told you, I didn't take those."

"Your sweat suit smells. And you look awful."

"I sweated in it, damn it. If you don't like it, get upwind. Like upstairs. And who cares how I look in the privacy of my own office? What privacy there is, I mean."

"I care! I have to look at you. Remember me?" Her voice was taking on that high, bitchy pitch she hated, and rather than hear herself that way, she got up and started for the stairs. "One warning you forgot to give me, Mother," she said loudly enough for him to hear as she went up the steps. "Never marry a stinking literary genius. They get pitiful mean when they're frustrated."

He sat scowling for a while. Then he raised his right arm and put his nose to the underarm of his shirt, and grimaced. Maybe if you'd wash this once in a—

The door at the top of the stairs opened again. "Nicholas!"

"Yes, Rebecca."

"This antique dishwasher of ours is on the blink again!"

He hoisted himself wearily out of his chair.

Give me something to go on to, Lord. *Something.*

He thought of Diana Scheckley again as he started up the stairs. Such a classy one, he thought.

He had real qualms about asking her.

Half an hour later, Nick was lying on the kitchen floor cursing, still straining to detach a tiny fastener deep in the dishwasher. Usually he was able to prolong the life of the machine by adjusting that part. "I could say plenty about the myth of laborsaving devices," he growled. "You could have washed the dishes by hand five times while I've been laboring over this piece of junk."

"For God's sake, then, forget it and call the repair-man," Becky said wearily. "Maybe we can find one who'll work on credit."

"It's Race Day. All the repairmen in the entire Mid-west are doubtless on their way to the goddamned In-dianapolis Motor Speedway, where I should be by now instead of under this marvel of American industrial in-genuity," he said to her under his armpit.

"Then get off the floor and call one tomorrow," she sighed. "Spare me your profane and sarcastic mouth-ings."

He grinned into the floor despite his anger. She could, he had to admit, smart off with style. Ferociously he tweaked the stubborn clip. "There, damn you! Ah! I think I've just saved us twenty dollars on a house call. Does that redeem me a little in your eyes, my dear?"

"A little. Now if you'd just finish writing that speech and earn us a few hundred for a new one—"

"I'm doing all the work I can handle, damnit. I can't make any more money. Nick Alef, free-lance, is a losing proposition."

"If you'd go out and call on your clients—if you'd get projects done on time, you'd make a go of it."

"I don't have time to go out and make calls! There are a thousand details to every project!" he exclaimed, getting up and closing the machine.

"If you'd let me handle some of the paperwork, then. I *was* a P.R. woman once, remember?"

"God, don't talk like you're proud of it."

She folded her arms over her breast and sighed, staring at him. "Then I guess there's nothing for me to do but go back to work full-time at the ad agency."

"Well, now. There's an idea!" He said it dispiritedly, with a weak, feigned tone of enthusiasm. It really would help, of course. But it was an admission that he couldn't even make a flack agency go. They had often talked of it as a last resort. And now they had reached it. Nick turned away from her so she couldn't see the shame he thought must be showing in his face. "God, I got to get in the shower and get myself over to that damned race-track!"

Diana Scheckley, he thought. You've got to help get me out of this.

The kitchen of the Rumples' house on North Crittenden Avenue was full of light, warmth, and savory aromas. Ella Rumple was wrapping the last piece of fried chicken in foil, and Gerald was packing the foil packages into their yellow picnic basket. The basket was full of chicken, bread-and-butter sandwiches, celery with cream cheese filling, and deviled egg halves pinned together with toothpicks.

Gerald and Ella Rumple were both forty-one, with kindly, handsome features, clear eyes, and clear skin. Both were perfectly groomed, their coloring healthy. But their pleasant faces had a tight-skinned, swollen look, as if they had been stung by some giant bee and puffed up; Gerald weighed 250 pounds and Ella 210, despite their short stature.

As Gerald closed the lid of the basket and got ready to take it out to the car, the telephone rang. "Who would that be at this hour?" asked Ella. "Would you get it, please, darlin'? My hands are greasy."

"Hello?"

"Jerry! Glad I caught you before you left the house. This is Gene Roepke."

"Gene! Hey, where you callin' from? You sound like you're in the middle of the Dan Ryan Expressway!"

"No, I'm here in Indy. In a phone booth a couple miles from the Speedway. We're stopped in traffic, and I saw this booth here and I said to Ruthie, 'Honey, you scoot over here and hold the wheel a minute while I go over and give ol' Jerry and Ella a call.' "

Gerald grinned. "You ding-a-ling. What if the traffic starts moving and she leaves you stranded beside the road?"

"Shoot. I could walk to the Speedway quicker'n that traffic could go three blocks. Hey, you're goin' to the race, aren't you?"

"We always do."

"So're we. Got tickets up in the fourth turn this time."

"Good place. Lots of action up there. We're in our usual. Tower Terrace, down by the pylon."

"Good. Well, hey, listen. What Ruthie and I were wondering was, why don't we all get together after the race for a good steak dinner before we drive back up to Chicago?"

"Sounds all right. Let me check with the boss. Hon, the Roepkes are in town for the race, and they want to have dinner with us afterward."

"You mean—"

"Dinner out. Steak."

"Terrific!"

"Okay, Gene. Ella says she wouldn't think of missing you guys while you're in town. Where and when?"

"How about six or so—just to be on the safe side—at the Speedway Motel. The lounge, okay?"

"Sounds great. See you then. The kids with you?"

"Nope. But they send their love. Well, traffic's moving a little. Ruthie's about a block down the street now. Guess I'll amble along and catch up with her."

"You better. See you at six. We'll hold a table if we get there earlier. So long." Gerald shook his head, amused at the vision of Gene Roepke plodding alongside a traffic jam with that splayfooted gait of his, the handsome, kindly gray head thrust forward on the long neck. Gene had been Indianapolis district sales manager for a carpet mill firm that Gerald had worked for until he and Ella had established their own E & G Carpet Care Company. Gene and Ruthie had moved away when Gene was promoted to a job in the regional office at Chicago, but they all got together once or twice a year, and almost every Race Day. One of the ties that still bound them was that the Rumples were godparents of the Roepkes' son and daughter, Allan and Janet. Having no children of their own, the Rumples doted like grandparents on Allan and Janet whenever they went to Chicago for trade fairs or other business.

"Well," Gerald said, rubbing his fat hands together, "that was good timing, eh? Ten more minutes and we'd've been gone, huh, dumplin'?" They pressed their great soft bodies together in a high-spirited hug, and Gerald started lugging their paraphernalia out the side

door to the car, whistling. Race Day was the greatest day
of their year.

Werner Dold was awakened when his pilot's voice
spoke his name through the intercom. He drew his thumb
and middle finger together over his eyelids as if pinching
away sleep, and was alert at once. Leaning forward toward the intercom speaker, he glanced out the small
round window by his right shoulder. Below, city lights
gleamed feebly in the dawning grayness and a dark river
curved among them. Now and then the lights would fade
or vanish under wisps of cloud that scudded below the
plane; then they would reappear. Dold pressed a button
on the bulkhead and spoke.

"Did you call, Harold?"

"Yes, sir. We're over Indianapolis now. The airfield
says Dr. Upton is waiting there already."

"Fine. I think I'll come forward, Harold."

"Very good, sir."

Werner Dold hoisted his thick body out of the high-
backed seat. He turned to speak to Kitty, his wife, but
she was asleep, lying supine on the rear seat that extended the width of the cabin. Her head was propped on
a pillow. A copy of *Cosmopolitan* lay in the aisle where
it had slipped from her hand. He studied her for a moment, this actress he had married two years ago to
everybody's surprise, including his own. She was thirty-two,
exactly half his age, radiantly tanned by a recent stay in
Miami. She was dressed in white slacks and belted tunic,
and her toenails were painted orange. On the arm of the
seat before her was draped her white fur jacket. She was
artificially blond, and her eyes were of a hazel so light
they appeared, in bright light, to be almost gold. Fre-
quently he would pause and wonder why he had become
so instantly magnetized by her, and he believed it was,
as she called it, her color scheme. She had not been much
of an actress, but she was quick-minded and practical,
understood Werner's needs, and was, of course, most
decorative. He had met her while she was playing the
lead in a comedy at a civic theater that his foundation
supported. In general, Werner Dold was quite pleased

with his wife, but sometimes suspected she could bear watching. And he preferred not to think much about the series of films she had starred in during the mid-1960s. Fortunately, few people in the Dolds' social set had ever seen those movies. If Werner had seen them in time, he might have been hesitant about marrying her. But all in all, he did not feel that he had married badly. Kitty pleased him in many ways, and his affection for her had become gradually deeper and more complex.

He stooped now and went through the small forward door into the cockpit, where the thrumming of engines was louder. He preferred to keep this older, slower, prop-driven plane; he had a secret fear that jets were always on the verge of exploding.

Dials glowed pale radium-green on the black instrument panel, and the little indicator lights burned vigilantly like emeralds. The windshield showed shifting patterns of murk and mist and a dark plain without horizons. Balancing stiff-armed, he lowered himself with a grunt into the copilot seat and drew the safety harness across his body.

"Good little nap, Harold. Very smooth trip."

"We're lucky. Came around a lot of rough stuff, but not through any." After a pause, the pilot went on, "I've never understood how those little half-hour naps can do you any good, sir, if you don't mind my saying so. Me, if I go to sleep for less than six hours, I wake up all groggy. I'm better off staying awake."

Werner Dold rubbed his hand over his hairless scalp, looking out and down at the flat terrain and the rows of streetlights that seemed to drift slowly backward under the plane. "You don't say. I would've thought anyone who had been a military pilot would be a master at cat-napping."

"Not me. I don't know how you do it."

The pilot's admiring tone pleased Dold. He smiled and gazed into the turbid distance. "Thomas Edison worked day and night," he said, "but he had a cot in his laboratory, and any time he had a spare minute, he could lie down, throw everything out of his mind, and get a few minutes' restful sleep. I've tried to emulate that, with some success. It just requires mental conditioning. And a clear conscience."

Harold turned his face away and grinned. Scarcely a day went by in which his employer did not compare one or another of his own traits with traits of Edison or some other famous and successful man. Sometimes Thomas Watson. Sometimes Bertrand Russell. Sometimes Cornelius Vanderbilt. Names the pilot vaguely remembered from history or bookracks. Mr. Dold constantly read biography on the plane. One day several months ago while waiting at Meigs Airport in Chicago for Mr. Dold to return from a board meeting, Harold had picked up a biography of Henry Ford that his employer had left lying in the passenger salon. He had found many sentences underlined, and a day or two later he had heard Mr. Dold say something about himself, something very similar to an underlined passage in the book. Harold had assimilated that quietly into his impressions of Mr. Dold. From what Harold knew, Mr. Dold seemed to be as wealthy and successful as any of the people whose biographies he read, and if he was not famous, it was only because he seemed to try never to publicize himself. He was a billionaire, with a great deal of power, and so he very well might compare himself with other wealthy and powerful men. Still, it had amused Harold.

The pilot had been amused a bit also when Mr. Dold had married this actress. In layovers between flights, Harold had seen two of her films, in which she was a hip private detective who used karate and could not keep her clothes on. Even to Harold, who had no pretensions to taste, those movies had seemed ridiculous, and he doubted that Mr. Dold knew of them.

Mr. Dold now was silently studying the lights below, this tycoon with no hair and no eyebrows, wearing a fine cream-colored suit, white shoes, a white silk shirt, and a blue, polka-dotted silk neck scarf instead of a tie. Harold glanced at him out of the corner of his eye. By observing and overhearing, he had managed to develop a broad and sketchy picture of Mr. Dold's empire, and it was more than Harold cared to ponder.

For a rich man, he was certainly an easy man to talk to, Harold thought, although anything he talked about was always right off the surface and didn't reveal much about what he was thinking or feeling down deep. But Harold could understand that, as he himself kept a pretty private soul.

"My Lord," Werner Dold now said over the drone of the engines. "Look at that mess around the racetrack."

They were swinging near the Speedway as they made their approach to the airfield, and from this altitude they could see the lights of tens of thousands of automobiles lining the streets and roads everywhere within miles of the track. Like gold and rubies trickling toward a center were the headlights and taillights of the most incredible number of cars Harold had ever seen in one place. Though from his seat in the sky he had become accustomed to the impression that America is dominated by automobiles, Harold had never seen jams like these at the Indianapolis Speedway.

"Look," Werner Dold said, "they're lined up clear out on the interstates. They're predicting half a million people will be at that race today, Harold. Can you imagine half a million? You know what kind of a figure that is?"

"No, sir," said Harold, who sometimes had tried to envision Mr. Dold's fortune. "I can't think in those terms."

"That many people in about a square mile. Makes quite a crowd, eh?"

"Kind of crowded up here, too, sir," Harold remarked above the noises from the radio. The tower was issuing landing instructions in croaking, harried succession. Small aircraft were lining up in the ragged gray morning sky, waiting to descend in single file upon the airfield. Hundreds of other private planes would be landing all morning at large and small airstrips near Indianapolis: Wier Cook, Shank, Sky Harbor, Metropolitan. Many of the racing people—builders, fans, car owners, sponsors, drivers, mechanics—flew about the country in their own planes. It was the only way they could cover the racing circuit in all the corners of a broad land.

A rush of faucal noises came out of the radio receiver, punctuated by bursts of static as tower and pilots switched receivers in and out. Harold said something inaudible into the mouthpiece and then replaced it on its bracket. "Might as well relax," he said. "There's a waiting line to land."

"Mm. Then maybe we shouldn't feel too smug about those traffic jams down there, eh, Harold? Ha-ha." Dold's laugh was nervous. He always became edgy about landing delays.

It grew lighter as they cruised and banked and waited in the sky, but it was obvious there would be no significant improvement in the weather within the next few hours.

"Wouldn't it be something if the race were rained out," Dold mused aloud. "Think of all those rainchecks." He inclined his gaze toward the Speedway below, where now the two-and-a-half-mile track could be seen with its great tiers of grandstands, its soaring Paddock, its towers, terraces, and buildings, its observation suites, garages, parapets, walks, tunnels, parking lots and meadows, trees and fences and golf course—all now being invaded by an ant army of automobiles.

That this was in the midst of a residential section of a city was to Werner Dold a most remarkable fact. A sporting event of such magnitude, alleged to be the biggest in the world, making so much noise and creating such stupendous traffic problems year after year, might be expected to exist in a vast open area somewhere beyond the suburbs, instead. When it was built, before World War I, he knew, it had been only a field on the outskirts of the city, laid out with a dirt track for the infant sport of motorcar racing. In the intervening six decades, though, the growing city had engulfed the track and spread its boundaries miles beyond. Now the Speedway, and the town of Speedway beside it, were more like a specialized unique neighborhood within the sprawling city than something apart from it.

"It won't get rained out," Harold said. "They say Tony Hulman's got a special arrangement with the good Lord about it."

Dold smiled at the legend, and thought of Hulman, the Speedway owner: the pleasant, country-boy face, the wavy brown hair, the ingenuous grin, teeth going dull with age like piano keys, the simple shyness, the fashionable but comfortably worn clothes. A Terre Haute millionaire with the look of a trusting handyman; modest, polite, and generous.

As the plane made slithering, air-cushioned lurches in the morning wind, Werner Dold recalled the most recent time he had seen Tony Hulman. It had been a strange moment, just five days ago, in the ballroom of the Indianapolis Athletic Club at the American Red Ball Transit Company's annual cocktail buffet and Eddie Sachs Sportsmanship Award Party, one of the most ostentatious of the many private events of the week-long "500" Festival social whirl. It was an evening when socialites, editors, announcers, sportsmen, and businessmen dressed up to go and drink, chat, and mingle with famous race-driving heroes. For an hour or so, hundreds of people had milled about in the ballroom, lining up at the free bars and drifting into and out of little galaxies of people around this or that driver, chattering, swirling ice in highball glasses, balancing paper plates from which they speared Swedish meatballs, egg rolls, scallops, and canapés with decorated toothpicks.

When the guests were summoned to gather around the stage for the Eddie Sachs Sportsmanship Award ceremony, Tony Hulman had been called upon to make appropriate remarks and had shambled shyly to the dais to drawl his customary sentiments: platitudes playing out like line off a reel, sentences winding down in mid-thought, and new ones starting, never to be finished, humorous digressions that never returned. No one knew what Hulman had said, nor did it matter; it was not what he said but the fact that he was speaking at this festival event that mattered; everyone had heard everything he always said year after year. Flushing under his tan, then, he had turned away from the microphone and ambled happily off the dais, his eyes glinting from the richness of his feelings, followed by polite and affectionate applause. It was the routine. Tony Hulman's one memorable line was the one he uttered every Race Day morning, his famous, hair-raising command to thirty-three tense race drivers:

Gentlemen, start your engines!

The party hosts had then introduced onstage the race drivers, some of whom were missing bits and pieces of themselves, pieces that had been burned or torn off in races past. There had been an awkward moment when Merle Bettenhausen, with an artificial right arm, had tried to shake hands with Mel Kenyon, whose left arm was a burn-shrunk stump. Bettenhausen's arm had been torn off just below the shoulder in a Michigan crash the year before. Dold remembered Kenyon in particular: the brownish-pink burn scar of his lower face, part of the tip of his nose gone, but above, the kindly eyes and boyish, curly dark hair. Dold knew that Kenyon was a modest, gentle man whose religious convictions had been solidified by a narrow triumph over death, and who now wrote religious poems and sometimes gave printed copies of them to people as other drivers gave autographs. Seeing the camaraderie of these survivors in a glittering ballroom full of laughing cocktail drinkers had seemed to Dold at once touching and grotesque.

Turning then to put his plate down on a littered bus tray, he had noticed Tony Hulman sitting at a nearby table, close to the stage. The others at the table were watching the stage, but Hulman was not looking at it. His eyes were floorward; his aging, sun-browned face was vacant of expression, looking tired or withdrawn, as if in some grim reverie. Dold had looked intently at this man, this central personage in a million-dollar race and a festival of Mardi Gras proportions, this internationally renowned sportsman now sitting unnoticed, preoccupied, or spiritually blank, and had wondered, What can the man be thinking? What an advantage it would be to know what he's thinking.

And at that moment, as if feeling Dold's gaze, Hulman had suddenly looked up from his trance, straight into his watching eyes, and had smiled his bashful smile at him and nodded. Werner Dold had thought then, He's seen me a few times, and he's trying to attach a name to my face. Or maybe he just knows that I've been kibitzing on his reverie.

And with a strange twinge almost like shame, as when one is caught gazing on another's nakedness, Dold had returned the nod and looked quickly back to the stage where Mel Kenyon was accepting the sportsmanship award. And Dold had thought then that he felt Tony Hulman gazing in turn at him.

Now the pilot picked up the radio handset to reply to another burst of instructions from the tower. He hung it up again, made a wide turn, and began a descent toward the airstrip, watching with swiveling head for other craft. He knew he was going to have his hands full for a few seconds now, landing in this wind. But Harold was thinking, even as he concentrated on the landing, watching the gray runway rise whizzing up to meet them: Reason he comes here every year is 'cause he's watching for a ripe time to make an offer for that Speedway. He knows old Tony can't live forever. That's what he's thinking about, I'd bet my ass on it.

"Right on the button, Harold," Dold exclaimed as the feathering props beat a fluttering backstroke in the air to slow the rolling plane. "Damned good landing! Now, let's just park this thing and go find Doc Upton and go to the races, eh? Ha-ha! Thanks for a nice trip, Harold!" As Dold left the cockpit and went back into the cabin, Harold glanced through the door and saw that Kitty Dold was sitting up, apparently awakened by the landing, and was combing her hair.

The one thing about Werner Dold that irritated the pilot was that he could never hide his relief upon reaching terra firma. After all these years of flying together, too. Harold was a professional and was insulted by this. But the pay and the working conditions were, of course, just great. "You're welcome, Mr. Dold," he said in a voice sounding full of pleasure.

Dr. Noble Upton climbed out of his Continental Mark IV when he saw Werner Dold's familiar pewter-colored plane taxi into view around the edge of a hangar. The airport was filling up like a parking lot with incoming planes. The deep tones of their engines pervaded the morning. Two or three were taxiing or landing at any moment. The doctor's gray hair ruffled in the wind. He went around to open the door for Mrs. Upton, but she shook her head. He knew. She was afraid the wind would disturb her hairdo. He walked away from the car, pursing and unpursing his lips, breathing the heavy huffs of the very fat. He shook his head and smiled at the sight of the two-engine plane. He liked to kid his friend about his planes, calling them "sky yachts." In retort, Werner would call Doc Upton's Mark IV a "land yacht."

Werner Dold's annual visits to Indianapolis had begun after World War II. He would come out several times each May during the race season. Anonymously, he would patrol the social events, the time trials, and the race, always watching and calculating. He would go to functions where Speedway owner Hulman was present, but would take pains to avoid meeting him. As far as Doc Upton knew, the two had never been introduced.

For years, Dr. Upton had been Dold's host and confidant during these visits. Now that Werner had married, Mrs. Upton had been drafted as companion for Kitty Dold. Doc knew his wife didn't like it; privately she referred to Kitty as "that young golddigger," and he could only try to imagine what Kitty privately called his wife. But for their husbands' sakes, they always gushed politely and made shopping tours together.

Doc could remember clearly Werner's first visit to the Speedway right after the end of the war. It had been closed for the duration, and there was talk of turning the place into a housing development. Prewar racer Wilbur Shaw had been trying to round up investors to save it. On five successive days Werner and Doc had wandered around that ghost town of a racetrack while Werner pondered on it. It easily could have been he instead of Tony Hulman who had bought the Speedway from Captain Eddie Rickenbacker at that time. He could have bought it quite cheaply. It had become a run-down, weed-grown place full of rotting wooden buildings and rickety bleachers, with grass sprouting between the bricks of the track and weeds flourishing in its fields, haunted by the glories of pioneer motorcar racers: Ray Harroun . . . Jules Goux . . . Rene Thomas . . . Gaston Chevrolet . . . Pete De Paolo . . . Billy Arnold . . . Wilbur Shaw . . .

Then, after those five days of prowling and pondering, Dold had finally run his hand over his scalp (he had had short, wavy brown hair then, before illness caused him to lose it all) and decided no, he wasn't going to buy the track. He just hadn't had the same conviction Hulman had had about its future.

That was just as well, Doc thought now as he watched the pilot help Werner and Kitty climb down from the plane. Not believing in it the way Hulman did, Werner never would have put as much of his money or personal attention into the Speedway as Hulman had. Consequently, it could not have become what it was now. Who could have foreseen the symbiosis that had developed between this Speedway and the city of Indianapolis? Who would have suspected that a staid, sober Midwestern state capital like Indianapolis would have put up with the perennial disruption and congestion created by such an event? Only some local tycoon like Tony Hulman, someone who didn't seem to know any better, that's who, Doc thought. Then by being so nutty about it and loving it and promoting it and plowing so much of the gate money back into seating and buildings and facilities, Tony had made it so economically respectable he had also brought it to social respectability. City leaders realized it gave their plain and serious city a dash of world renown, and that there was money to be made on its fringes. Doc Upton, who had watched this phenomenon evolve, knew that by now Indianapolis would do almost anything in its power to advance and nurture its 500-Mile Race, and gratefully endure its problems, noise, traffic. Monumental Babbitism, that was Doc Upton's term for it, but he was circumspect about saying it.

Werner Dold, this portly, powerful, hairless man in the cream-colored suit now coming toward him across the windswept apron with a flashy plaything of a wife on his arm, had had too much sense to buy the track then, or too little vision. But he'd sure like to have it now. Who knows, Doc thought. Maybe this will be the year it looks right to him and he'll go to Hulman and offer to start purchase negotiations. Would that ever make news in this old town!

"Hi, Werner! Glad to see that old sky yacht of yours made it again!"

Mrs. Upton reluctantly got out of the car, forced her socialite-matron smile, and gave Kitty the obligatory hug, which was returned in like spirit. Harold put the luggage in the trunk of the Continental, received a few last instructions from his employer, then went away to the airport office to make service and fueling arrangements for the plane.

The four then settled themselves in the car, the wives in the back seat, and started down the long road leading away from the airport. Doc Upton cleared his throat. "Read where you, uhm, your foundation donated a new cardiology wing to a hospital in Cleveland."

Werner Dold ducked his head as if embarrassed. "Well, yes."

"Oh, did you!" Mrs. Upton trilled from behind.

"And also established a big ambulatory care clinic over near Hartford," Doc added.

"Uhm."

"Oh, you dear man!" Mrs. Upton exclaimed, stifling a yawn.

"All in one week I read about that," said Doc. "What is all this, Werner?"

"Well. People do things like that."

"Sure, God love 'em. But isn't it, uhm, sort of a departure for you? Your name cut in stone, on bronze door plaques, all that?"

"And on a theater," Kitty reminded them. Mrs. Upton looked out the window and rolled her eyes.

"Well, it isn't for the name, you know. I just thought a little of my money could do some good there, you know. And of course the foundation's good for my tax situation."

"Hell, I'm happy to see it," Doc said, suddenly laughing to dispel the obvious embarrassment. "Just thought maybe if I got a word in, you might spread some of that stuff out our way, eh? Ha-ha!"

"Just let us know what you need."

Suddenly Doc Upton understood. It was indeed for the name. Werner Dold, who had built up his financial empire for decades with the least possible amount of publicity, was approaching old age as possibly the country's most obscure billionaire. There were television actors, sportsmen, even mechanics passing through this airport right now who were more familiar to the public than Werner Dold. Even Werner's own wife was.

Doc Upton put some things together in his mind while

he was nosing his big car into the creeping flow of Speedway-bound traffic: certain conversations, the sudden rush of philanthropic gifts, the recent marriage to a glamorous young woman, the constant reading of biographies, and this renewed interest in the Speedway— Of course it's for the name, he thought. Old Croesus realizes he's mortal and is afraid of leaving no traces.

Doc glanced in the rearview mirror at Kitty, who was gazing abstractedly at the traffic alongside. He thought Werner had shown a terrible lack of judgment in marrying someone of her background. Doc knew of her films. But he had never said anything about that to Werner. He could kid Werner unmercifully about anything—anything except what was really important to him. And apparently Kitty was really important to him.

The two girls edged away from the dining hall and down a short flight of concrete steps to a double steel door. They had gambled on the chance that there would be no one guarding the door, and they were right.

Not really knowing whether it would be locked or not, Renee walked confidently to it and put her hands on the latching bar. She tried not to show any doubt because Puggles was scared half to death.

Renee glanced back toward the dining hall. No one was following them. Beyond the walls there was the hum of voices and an occasional long, clashing sound as silverware was dumped in trays. She pressed down on the bar. It yielded. She leaned her weight against the door, and it opened. A breath of wet, cool air touched her face, and she could smell fresh-cut grass, like a whiff of freedom. "See?" she whispered triumphantly. She jerked her head toward the gray outdoors. Eyes wide, Puggles hesitated. Once they were outside that door, it would mean they had willfully walked away from their group, and it would be impossible to convince anybody that they weren't making a break for it. "Come on," whispered Renee urgently. Puggles moved out then, and Renee followed and closed the door behind them.

It would have been nice if it were darker. They would just have to brave it and stroll across the grounds and

hope no one would see them. High inside with fear and
daring and anger, they walked across the wet grass toward the fence, being careful not to hurry because hurrying people in this place would attract the eye. The frayed
cuffs of their bell-bottom jeans swished around their ankles, growing wet from the grass. Renee, with long,
straight blond hair, narrow features, and bluish eyesockets, walked slightly in advance. Puggles had a fuller face
and figure. Her hair was brown and hung in frizzy waves
from a part in the middle of her scalp. Her face was
broad, with puffy, little-girl features.

The girls knew enough about each other. They had the
empathy of losers.

At fifteen, Renee was an accomplished runaway. She
had been running away from home for three years, and
now she was getting away from the Indiana Girls' School
for the second time in six months. She had been caught in
raids in the pads of drug users three times and finally
been locked up here. She had only tried drugs. She wasn't
really a user. She didn't really care that much about
them. She didn't care much about anything. She was just
listless and sick of life. "Pa fucked me when I was eight.
With his hand over my mouth so I couldn't hardly
breathe," she would recount. "After that, I promised I
wouldn't yell, so he didn't try to smother me after that.
He'd just fuck me when there wasn't anybody else at
home. What could I do? I told Mom once, but she just
whipped me for lying. She knew it was going on, but she'd
just cry and never admit it."

Puggles thought her mother was crazy, too. Her mother
had always told Puggles she would end up as a whore.
Puggles hated her mother for her cruelties and her
preaching tantrums. At the age of twelve Puggles had discovered that the one thing that would upset her mother
the most was to go away for a few nights and then come
back and tell her mother she had had sex with a boy. So
Puggles had started doing that every time the going got
rough at home. At first it had been a lie about having sex
with the boys, but before long it had become true.

Now Puggles looked very scared because this was the
first time she had ever dared to run away.

They came to a place where a depression had been

formed under a corner of the fence, hidden by shrubbery. Erosion had washed out the place. They got muddy seats scooting under. Then they walked fast along a side road, looking back once in a while at the dark shapes of the buildings and the outside lights growing wan as daylight came on. Before long they were close to the highway. It was filled with cars going east toward Indianapolis, almost bumper to bumper. Renee had picked today because the holiday meant the surveillance in the school would be lighter, but especially because it would be so much easier for a pair of walkaways to disappear into the city with all these race fans coming into town.

Renee was excited by this freedom now. But she knew they really weren't in the clear yet. A sheriff's deputy or a state trooper or even some employee of the school could come along the highway and spot them yet.

But she knew, too, that she and Puggles wouldn't have to wait long for a ride. Not with all the guys driving into town for the race.

They walked up on the shoulder of the highway and stood there with the wet wind blowing in their faces. They faced the endless string of headlights and stuck their thumbs out.

Side by side in the front seat of their blue 1972 Chevrolet Impala stopped in westbound traffic on Thirtieth Street sat Gerald and Ella Rumple. The car engine idled; the well-tuned vehicle barely trembled. Gerald's right wrist rested on the top of the steering wheel, his left arm rested on the sill of the open window, and his right foot held down the brake pedal. Occupying the back seat were the yellow picnic basket, a drink cooler, a blanket, and two umbrellas rolled up, lying side by side, one black, one transparent.

"We'll have to remember to leave by the Sixteenth Street exit after the race," Ella said, "since we're meeting Gene and Ruthie."

"Yeah. Be sure and remind me." He chuckled. "But we have to get there before we worry about leaving."

Ella loosed an exasperated little sigh and craned to try to see if any traffic was moving ahead.

"I think we should have waited till later and let some of this traffic thin out before we left home."

Gerald removed his hand from the top of the steering wheel and gently patted her enormous thigh. "We tried that last year, and ended up in traffic just this bad, remember? Only in broad daylight, and it was hotter than blazes and we got in too late to see the marching bands." He knew she couldn't argue with that. They had attended the last fifteen races. Each year they had tried a different time and route of approach, but never had they been able to avoid these great jams in which the traffic crept forward at the rate of a glacier or ground to a total halt for long periods, as it had now.

Gerald looked up at the dark clouds rolling eastward, blown ragged by the wind. He looked down at dark rainwater in a chuckhole between his car and a station wagon in the next lane. The station wagon was rusty, mudstreaked, and full of the indistinct dark forms of people and piled paraphernalia. From its open windows came pulsating rock music, shrill laughter, and ugly outbursts of arguing. Gerald rolled his window partway up against the unpleasantness, put his hand atop the steering wheel again, and began drumming rapidly upon it with his fingertips.

"Anyway," he went on, "this isn't the bad part. Getting out of the track after the race is the bad part." The year before, it had taken them longer—three and a half hours —to drive five hundred yards out of the infield parking area than it had taken the race cars to go the five hundred miles of the race. But Gerald Rumple was patient. They loved the race so much that to them the traffic jams were worth it, as long as their car didn't get dented in the crush, or overheat and stall. At least it shouldn't overheat this kind of a morning, Gerald thought. Thank God for small favors.

He heard a clank outside the car and looked out his window. Somebody had dropped an empty beer can from the window of the station wagon to the street. Hamm's. It rolled a few inches on the pavement and stopped. "Look at those litterbugs," he said tersely, in a tone as close as his voice ever came to expressing anger. But he didn't get out to pick up the beer can or say anything to the people in the station wagon, or even look or scowl at them. He only stared straight ahead and drummed his fingers. The people in the station wagon looked like the kind of people who might pile out of their vehicle and give you a hard time or even start a fight if you looked at them critically, Gerald thought. He always felt relatively safe in a car as long as the doors were locked and the windows up, and he didn't aggravate anybody by staring at them. He and Ella had to drive through a black neighborhood every day to go to their E & G Carpet Care Company. They were very careful and would never look directly at the face of a black man on a curb or in a car. Gerald didn't like trouble of any kind.

Just then, with a rusty screech, the near front door of the station wagon opened and a tall young person with frazzled shoulder-length yellow hair and wearing faded Levi pants and jacket lurched out. Gerald couldn't discern immediately whether it was a boy or girl, but instinctively checked his door latch button with his elbow to be sure it was down, then again looked straight ahead.

"What is he *doing!*" Ella exclaimed.

Gerald looked out the window again. He saw now that the young creature was a boy. He was standing in the angle of the open car door, grinning and urinating into the water-filled chuckhole while shrieks of laughter spilled out of the station wagon. Gerald's face flamed with indignation, and he rolled his window the rest of the way up to shut out the musical splashing.

Someone doing that right in the middle of a traffic jam almost in broad daylight!

"Why isn't there ever a policeman around?" Ella snapped, looking in the other direction.

"I sure don't know, dear," he said in a quavering voice through compressed lips. "But I wish this traffic would get moving. At least our lane or theirs!"

Except for some of the people it attracted, Ella Rumple loved everything about the "500" even more than Gerald did. She loved all the festivities throughout the month of May and all the good it did for Indianapolis's economy and image, and she loved being able to see the famous people and the famous drivers so close up—sometimes just a few feet away through a fence. For her it was the best part of the year.

Some years the race was completed with nobody badly hurt or killed, and she liked that. She enjoyed talking effusively and thankfully about how safe it had been. But sometimes terrible things did happen right close by. When Eddie Sachs and Dave McDonald were killed in 1964, it was right in front of the Rumples. That had been awful. Ella liked to tell about it whenever anyone would listen. "That Eddie Sachs was such a nice man," she would say, giving people the impression that she had known him personally. "A Danny Thomas sort of person, kind of homely and smiley. And he was just down there being burned up, and we couldn't do anything about it but just stand there helpless and watch with the smoke getting in our nose, and all the screaming and screaming just going on and on all around." She would tell it, her voice quavering. Ella and Gerald also had been witnesses when the pace car crashed into a photographers' stand at the start of the 1971 race. She liked to tell about the horror of that, too, about all those people hurt and strewn around all over, writhing in pain on the ground. "At the Speedway you can just feel it in the crowd when something happens, even if you don't see it yourself," she would say, "and your heart sort of jumps, and you get shivers all over— that's what I mean about feeling it even if you don't actually see it—and you just automatically face that way yourself, even though you know very well you wouldn't want to see anything bad."

Ella could also recite all the current speed records set at the Speedway, and loved to do so. "By the way," she would add, "there was one other record set there at the track last year, though I shouldn't brag about it, and I'm not: Gerald and I between us ate twenty-four pieces of fried chicken—all breasts—and a dozen deviled eggs. That's four more breasts and two more eggs than we've ever eaten on any day at the track. We just get famished out there in the open air and all the excitement!"

Lloyd Skirvin had it all the way to the floorboards, and they were doing about 110 down the country road toward Indianapolis. Gravel rattled like shot in the fenders. The body of the Mercury shuddered and squeaked as it tore over the uneven road. Now and then the tires would lose their grip on the road surface, but Lloyd would get it out of its sideslip, not by braking but by stomping more heavily on the gas and steering in the direction of the skid. That was the difference between Lloyd Skirvin and the average guy behind the wheel. The average guy would get scared and try to slow down until he got it under control. But Lloyd Skirvin was known around racetracks in the South and Southeast as one who never got scared. His way of getting out of a spin or squeeze of any kind was more power. On the front fenders of his muscled-up white Merc was painted in purple:

Movin' Mutha

That was Lloyd Skirvin. In his opinion, the main thing he was, was a movin' mutha. He gave a rebel yell every time he recovered it like that, his mouth open so wide his hard jaw muscles and the corded muscles in his neck stood out under the fatless brown skin.

And Billy Joe ("Worms") Marshall, beside him on the front seat, would giggle excitedly at the humor of it because to Worms Marshall everything Lloyd Skirvin did was either funny or brave or both. He had even thought it was funny three years ago when Lloyd nicknamed him "Worms." Now to be riding flat-out down a dirt road with Lloyd Skirvin at the wheel was almost unbearably funny and exciting, and especially so because they were on their way to this big-ass race in Indianapolis, the real big-time run of them all, and by God, Lloyd had told him, there'd be more cars and cunt than he'd ever saw in his whole life.

Where the gravel road intersected with the asphalt highway leading east to Indianapolis, Lloyd Skirvin didn't even stop for the red sign. He downshifted to fifty or so approaching the intersection, sitting tense in the seat with his dirty tan fist clutching the taped steering wheel with bulging knuckles. He spotted a gap between two cars eastbound on the highway; he gunned it across the westbound lane and swerved hard left into that gap, the two right wheels going off the far side of the pavement for a moment. The undercarriage pounded and groaned as the wheels thudded through the ruts, but Lloyd got back on the pavement in a second without losing any speed at all. The driver behind reacted by hitting his horn. Lloyd answered by glancing deadpan into the rearview mirror, raising his left arm outside the window and giving him the up-yours sign. Worms thought that really was clever, and giggled until he almost choked.

Now Lloyd was running right on the rear bumper of the car ahead, a station wagon whose rear window was lined with the faces of wide-eyed, grinning children. Lloyd hung on that bumper for a minute or so, running high and noisy in third gear, looking at the pale young faces. Now he gave the kids the finger sign, too, grinning at their hilarity. "Them little boogers know what it means," he remarked, and Worms whinnied with laughter and bobbed his shaggy round head.

Then the driver of the station wagon began flashing his brakelights, warning Skirvin to quit tailgating.

"Git movin', y'dumb shit," Lloyd muttered. Then he stepped on it and roared around the station wagon in a surge of power, quickly wedging his way back into the right lane just as an oncoming car began swaying in a panic maneuver.

Worms Marshall felt his heart pounding. He wouldn't have had the nerve to pass just then like that. *Man, you have to admit ol' Lloyd can really herd a car along!*

Traffic was getting dense now. Slowing down, then moving, stringing out, closing up. Blinking taillights as far ahead as you could see. No more chances to pass. Just had to creep along. Listen to the radio. "Close to You," it sang. There was a news broadcast describing traffic jams developing everywhere within miles of the Speedway, as thousands headed this morning toward the Greatest Spectacle in Racing. Hard-faced Lloyd bobbed his head in time to the music that came on after the news. His eyelids were narrowed, his gaze piercing the distance, as if for an opening in traffic. Now and then he would draw his lips thin and twitch his head sideways and hitch up his shoulders. Or take his driving hand off the steering wheel, clench a tight fist and rotate it on the wrist, mak-

ing the tendons in his forearm ripple. Worms admired
that. His own arms were covered with fat, and you
couldn't see any muscles. They smoked and drank morning beer and edged the car slowly along the road through
the dew-damp suburban flatland. Morning was lightening
ahead.

INDIANA GIRLS' SCHOOL

The tail pipe burbled. The powerhouse under the hood
rolled smoothly through its cycles. Lloyd and Worms got
antsy when they had to sit in traffic. This mutha was built
to moooove. You could feel that through your seat and
through your fingers on the wheel and your boots on the
floorboards, that trembling, rumbling power waiting to
go. This movin' mutha was too good to creep in traffic
jams. "Shit," Lloyd would hiss now and then through
clenched teeth.

Now he shook his head and clucked his tongue in the
left side of his mouth, and turned a grin on Worms. "Hey,
ol' buddy. Y'gittin' horny?"

Worms whinnied. "Y'all better b'lieve it. I'm *always*
horny."

"I b'lieve it. Like I come inta th' drugstore yesterday,
and there you's standing at the panty-hose rack with a
big hard-on."

Worms snickered through his nose and blushed.
"Were'n', neither!"

"Shit, you weren't." Lloyd knew this pleased his simple-
headed buddy. Only thing Worms could laugh about concerning himself was his horniness. He liked being called
"Ol' Everready" and "Stud Boar." He liked it when Lloyd
Skirvin would point a thumb at him and say, "Ol' Stud
Boar here got hisself a bad back lyin' in bed thinkin'
'bout nooky an' sprained his sackerilliack." Then he'd
punch Worms hard on the shoulder affectionately, and
Worms would just glow with pride. Nobody'd ever been
so good to him before. Especially not anybody as great
as Lloyd Skirvin.

Lloyd was a good ol' boy. Goin' on twenty-five he was,
and Worms was twenty-three. They had been all over the
dirt-track stock-car circuit for three years now. Lloyd

drove, and Worms was mechanic. They went from track to track, from six-dollar motels to the trailer homes of distant kinfolk in various towns, from junkyard to parts shop. Between races they could always find work in garages and filling stations. They always had enough bread in their jeans for gas and beer and car parts and tires and race entry fees, for hamburgers and corn dogs and Cokes and whiskey, and now and then for a good twenty-five-dollar piece of tail if there wasn't any free stuff available, which was seldom. And every once in a while ol' Lloyd'd outrun everything on the track and pick up a couple hundred or even a thousand in prize money, and then they'd go into Cincinnati or Memphis or Charlotte or whatever place was nearby and get themselves a big steak and then head off to Ruby's or Michelle's or some other studio for a massage with all the extras.

This was the first time they had ever gotten near Indy at "500" time. Lloyd claimed he was sort of halfway interested in seeing the big race just because he never had before. But he pretended to have nothing but scorn for this kind of a race. Hundred-thousand-dollar cars on a satin-smooth oval track, all big, easy left turns—what could be easier? "Like t' lead some of them fancy Yankee bastards over some of th' tracks I've ran on, huh, Worms?" he'd say.

"By God! By God, Lloyd, yeah, tha'd be a sight t' see, I swear to God!" Worms would answer.

"Hey, Stud Boar, you see what I see?" said Lloyd suddenly, craning upward. "Lookit that young stuff jus' a-standin' on th' berm a-waitin' f'r us."

"Eeeeaaaaahoooo! Mutha dawg!"

Lloyd brought the big Mercury nose-down to a halt right in front of the two hitchhiking girls, the bosomy brown-haired one and the lean, yellow-haired one. The girls looked a little fearful. The morning wasn't bright yet, and they peered into the shadowy car trying to see what the faces of the two men were like.

"Come on, honey," Worms called, swinging the door open. The girls looked at each other, evidently deciding they should take any ride they could get. They came closer to the side of the Mercury. The cars ahead were moving, and the ones behind were starting to sound their horns. "Where you gals goin'?" Worms said.

"Where *you* goin'?" asked the blond girl.

"We're goin' t' th' Speedway."

"Fantastic. Come on, Pug."

Worms pulled the seat forward so the girls could stoop and climb into the back. "You can jus' move them six-packs down on th' floor an' make y'se'f some room," Worms directed, as Lloyd laid down rubber to catch up with the traffic. "This here's Lloyd Skirvin—maybe you heard of him—and I'm Billy Joe Marshall, but folks call me Worms." He was turned around toward them, with his arm along the top of the seat back.

The girls giggled. Clearly they were awed by the situation: in a car with two cool-looking older guys, six-packs of beer piled around them, the exciting surge of power and noise as the car leaped ahead with screaming tires, the buildings of the Girls' School dropping away behind them. And a name like Worms.

"I'm—uh—Renee Krebs and this is Mary Puggliacco. We call her Puggles."

"You gals wanta go t' th' race?"

Renee smiled. She couldn't have asked for a better deal. They'd be lost to the world in there all day and could do anything they wanted, and these two guys looked like they were good for anything.

"Sounds great to us," she said.

And Puggles was thinking, *Wow! Wouldn't Mom just shit her britches!*

Mrs. Olive Canfield, behind the wheel of her rusting little Falcon, suddenly realized she was trapped. A graying widow in a pink counter clerk's uniform, she had set out at 5:30 A.M. to go to work in the Westside bakery shop where she had been employed for almost two years. Because it was Race Day, she had been careful to take a route that would skirt the Speedway by a couple of miles.

Only when the lane of traffic she was in was waved down a side street toward the south by traffic police did she realize that a couple of miles had not been a wide enough detour.

"Oh, hell's bells," she muttered. The traffic rolled forward slowly. She was not alarmed, only annoyed. Surely she would be able to turn off when she reached Thirty-fourth Street, and then could continue west from there to the bakery. But this might make her late and keep her from getting the bakery open and ready for business on time.

Mrs. Canfield switched on her right-turn signal and watched in the rearview mirror for an opportunity to get into the right lane. But the traffic in that lane was speeding up now, and cars were tearing past on her right, almost on each other's bumpers. She didn't have the nerve to swing out into that kind of a stream. And apparently nobody over there was going to heed her signal and make room for her to cross over.

Preoccupied with watching the mirror, she barely perceived in the corner of her eye a brightening of taillights a few yards ahead of her. Reflexively, she stamped her foot on the brake pedal. Her car screeched to a stop inches from the one ahead. She braced herself at the sound of squealing tires behind her, anticipating a crunching jolt from the rear.

Amazingly, there was no crash. She heard a succession of panic stops behind her, but no collisions.

The car ahead began to move now. Heart pounding, cold pricklings running down her skin, she moved her foot to the gas pedal to follow. There was no response. Her abrupt stop had killed the engine. Flustered, she jerked the transmission lever into neutral and put her left foot on the brake and her right one on the gas pedal. Already a chorus of horns was beginning to bleat behind her, and somebody was yelling in an incredibly loud voice, "Move it, bitch!"

Careful, she told herself. What you don't need right now is to flood it.

In a moment she had the car running again, and accelerated to catch up with the traffic. Instead, she had to hit the brake again because during her pause a dozen cars from the right lane had swooped into the space in front of her and stopped. Again she killed the motor. Again the clamor of horns and curses. That right lane, meanwhile, was full of cars roaring past again.

Almost to Thirty-fourth Street now and afraid to plunge over into the right lane, she began to grow concerned. If she didn't get out of this at Thirty-fourth Street, she might be trapped in it until Thirtieth Street—a notorious traffic trap on Race Day—and her chances of getting off there would be even slimmer. Bracing herself, she flipped on the right-turn signal, glanced in the mirror, stepped on the gas, and swung praying out into a gap ahead of a looming glare of headlights. Tires squealed and a horn bellowed behind her, but there was no impact.

Thank God I made it, she thought. Now almost upon the Thirty-fourth Street intersection, she was just about to steer right around the corner and be on her way, when a policeman appeared in the path of her car, throwing gestures at her, signaling for her to turn east. As she braked to avoid hitting the policeman, another file of cars broke out from behind and began to storm around still farther to the right—clear off the right side of the street they were, on the shoulder, blocking her last chance to turn right at this corner.

Now Olive Canfield was angry. If that's the way you're going to be about it, she thought, it's your problem to get me out of this mess. She bit her lips, held the pedal down, and began blasting her horn at the policeman. She wanted him to come around to the side of the car, hear her explanation, and lead her out of the trap.

But his gestures only became more violent, his manner almost apoplectic. Her determination quailed, but she kept honking the horn. Other drivers, in the lanes to left and right, were now making all manner of maneuvers to get around this clot in the stream, and soon the entire intersection was snarled with cars sitting at all angles, horns blaring. A nightmare. The policeman started here and there, waving his arms, blowing a whistle, turning every few seconds to shoot murderous glances at her and try to wave her to the left. Finally his chest swelled up and he charged to her open window and, in the din of car horns, began yelling at her, spraying saliva, words that she couldn't understand over the noise.

"I WANT TO GO RIGHT!" she cried. "I want to go that way! I have to!" She jabbed her finger toward West

Thirty-fourth. "HELP ME TURN RIGHT, PLLLLEE-
EEEASE!"

"YEOWRGH!" the policeman bellowed, thrusting his
face toward hers, reaching in and jerking the steering
wheel to the left while pointing eastward with his other
hand, as if he simply could not comprehend that someone
would want to go in another direction on Race Day.

The last of Mrs. Canfield's resolve caved in, and she
nodded weakly. Evidently it was not to be her fate to escape at Thirty-fourth Street. The policeman withdrew
from her side and leaped heroically back into the mass of
traffic. It took him several minutes of violent pantomime
to dissolve the knot of automobiles. The traffic really began to move only when two more officers arrived, their
white crash helmets going this way and that in the intersection.

Weak from the experience, Mrs. Canfield allowed herself to be herded along Thirty-fourth Street in the direction opposite her intentions, knowing that she would have
to try again to break out as soon as her nerve was
restored. If she didn't open the bakery on schedule, she
could very well be fired. And she couldn't afford that.
This is simply asinine, she kept saying over and over in
her mind. Surely a body can go the other way if she needs
to go the other way. I have rights, too!

Clifford Cole and his family were in their new Ford
heading out of Kokomo by 6:00 A.M., on the way to
their first 500-Mile Race. They drove eastward through
a residential area of large old white frame houses
and streets flanked by huge maple trees, and then
rolled through the deserted downtown section, stopping
now and then at the command of traffic lights and waiting until the green signals glowed and gave them permission to proceed.

Clifford Cole had lived all his life in and around
Kokomo, and his parents had always lived there, and his
grandparents. The town had changed a lot in his forty-
five years. He could remember when the downtown area
was busy with streetcars and shoppers. When he and
Marjorie were courting, there had been a variety of

places downtown where they could eat or get a soda or go to the theater. Then a bypass had been built to run highway traffic past the east side of town, and before long, much of the town's business had moved out to set up along the bypass, putting up neon lights and huge signs to catch the eye of passing motorists. Now it was hard for his parents or anyone without a car to go any-place in Kokomo, and there was very little to do down-town anymore.

As he turned south onto U.S. 31 now, Cliff Cole ob-served the endless array of neon signs, plastic flags, drive-ins, and road signs.

HAPPY MOTORING! HUMBLE

On the right side of the highway was a long, low, blue-and-white building.

CHRYSLER CORP.
TRANSMISSION PLANT

It's a shame, he thought, that everything's all arranged to cater to them that have cars and to hell with them that don't. Like my folks.

BIG WHEEL

But then, on the other hand, if it weren't for cars I wouldn't have a job and neither would many of the peo-ple I know.

SUNOCO
STANDARD
SHELL
MARATHON

The Coles were going to their first 500-Mile Race be-cause their youngest child, Kevin, had a passion for speed. Kevin had made up his mind that he wanted to attend some of the racing events in Indianapolis on the Memorial Day weekend. He had wanted to see the motorcycle and sprint-car races at the State Fairgrounds and the races at Indianapolis Raceway Park and then the "500" and had been disappointed that they were going only to the "500." Although Kevin was the baby of the family, they all functioned very much according to his wishes, and he had been astounded when all his tantrums earned him only one race out of the many they could have gone to see.

Little, wiry, good-looking, aged twelve, Kevin knew how to manipulate his parents to make them do what he wished, and they scarcely realized the extent of his control over them.

Kevin had been a speed demon for as long as his family could remember. Neither Keith, now fourteen, nor Pam, sixteen, had been interested in cars beyond the normal adolescent impatience to be old enough to use the family auto. But Kevin was different. He had browbeaten his parents into buying a Go-Kart for him when he was eight, and he had roared around their neighborhood for many months in that, becoming a notorious community hazard and hurting various pedestrians below the knees. The Kokomo police would come to the Cole home on Sunday mornings and make Mr. and Mrs. Cole take the Go-Kart away from Kevin under threat of arrest, because Kevin liked to run it around the big parking lot next to the Methodist Church, making it impossible for the Methodists to hear the sermons.

When he was ten and a half, Kevin had set out to get a Honda trail bike by his eleventh birthday, and so subtly had he brought it off that his father actually believed it had been his own idea to surprise Kevin with it. From that day on, Kevin could be seen going through lawns and down alleys, wearing a white crash helmet, terrorizing slow dogs. He was not supposed to ride it in the streets because he was too young to have a license, but now and then the police would bring him back from the other side of town. His parents would then ground him for a month, but usually he could contrive to be back on the bike within a week.

Kevin spent most of his allowance on hot-rod, drag-racing, and dirt-bike magazines. All his conversation was about hemis, blower drive kits, mags, spacer plates, chromed headers, cowls, grill shells, dynos, superlifters, front-end spoilers, sneaker pipes, manifolds, rocker arms, posi-units, and street/strip cams. No one else in the family had the slightest comprehension of this language, and Kevin suffered their ignorance with exasperated snobbery. Right now he was thinking championship race cars, his face set with concentration. He wanted the long drive to Indianapolis to be over with, so he could see and hear the big cars. Everything else was just a pain in the neck, as far as he was concerned. Eyes narrowed, Kevin Cole was thinking of speed.

FORD   MERCURY   LINCOLN
WE REALLY DEAL

"Hey, Pam," said Keith. "Lookit that smashed dog!"

"Yeck," she replied, shutting her eyes.

Cliff Cole was not a slow driver. He kept the speedometer needle at sixty-five to seventy. But even at seventy miles an hour, he found he was being passed every few seconds by other cars heading for Indianapolis. Some of them appeared to be going eighty or ninety. Cliff would draw back the corner of his mouth and make a rueful clucking sound and shake his head at their stupidity. Cliff had never been in an automobile accident and did not intend to be—especially with this wonderful family of his depending on him for their safety.

EAT 2,000 FEET

Now and then he cast a sidelong look at Marjorie sitting beside him, and felt proud and lucky. People said sincerely that they couldn't believe she could have children aged up to sixteen. She was still a fine-looking, youthful, confident, healthy woman. No gray in her hair yet, and "just the littlest bit of double under her chin," as Cliff always phrased it.

She could still get into a summer pantsuit and look as good as most eighteen-year-olds.

Before long the kids began getting restless from riding, and a bit wound up. Kevin was calling Pam "Bumps" just under his breath, referring to her bosom. He thought his parents couldn't hear him. His usual tactic was to keep muttering "Bumps" until she yelled at him or slapped. But with that incredible hearing of hers, Mrs. Cole heard.

"Okay. Knock it off back there before it gets óut of hand."

They were on a two-lane road now, going through rich farmland—gentle, rolling terrain. Everything was green and growing lush because of the rain they'd had all spring. Morning light reflected from standing water in the fields and ditches as they sped by.

"Let's play something," Kevin said. "Can anybody say, real fast, 'Peter Piper picked a peck of pickled peppers'? Come on, Bumps, let's hear—"

"Mom, you heard that!"

"Okay, Kevvie. One more time—"

"I'm sorry. It just slipped out. Come on, Pammy, real fast, say it: 'Peter Piper picked a—' "

"I know how it goes. 'PeterPiperpickedapackapicka—' No, wait. 'PeterPiperpickapeckapipplepeck—' Now, wait. Uhm, 'Peter Piper picked a peck of pickled peppers. A peck of pickled peppers did Peter Piper pi—' "

"Well, sure, that slow. No wonder," Kevin taunted.

"Here. Let me," Keith popped in. " 'PeterPiper pickedapecka-pimpled-peckers!' "

Screams of laughter erupted in the back seat, and Marjorie Cole bit her lips to keep from laughing with them.

"Keith, you did that on purpose," yelled Kevin, laughing his nasty, snorting laugh. Pam was red-faced and laughing behind her hands. Cliff Cole was watching in the rearview mirror, and even he couldn't keep from grinning.

"Who me?" Keith acted innocent.

"How about this one, then," Kevin led them on. " 'One smart feller, and he felt smart; two smart fellers, and they felt smart; three fart smellers and—' "

More pandemonium. Keith fell over laughing, and Kevin was snorting and whooping, and Pam was making squeals and embarrassed noises and telling Kevin not to laugh at his own bloopers, especially ones he did on purpose. So now it was Kevin's turn to act righteously indignant and pretend he hadn't said it on purpose. "All I said was," he snickered, " 'Three smart fellers and they smelt fart—' " And then they were off again in gales of red-faced hilarity.

"ALL RIGHT!" their mother yelled like a thunderclap. "SILENCE!"

It worked. They didn't mess with that tone of voice. It was her end-of-the-road voice. She wouldn't stand for hysterical silliness or naughty stuff, no matter how much fun. She still remembered her own strict upbringing as the daughter of a wealthy farmer near Kokomo.

So for a few miles more it remained quiet in the back seat. They were getting near Indianapolis. Cliff Cole could see the haze over the city. Before long, he figured, they should come to the Outer Loop; they would get on it and swing around to the Westside of the city and cut in toward the Speedway. Suddenly, from the back seat, Kevin complained, "Dad, they're talking about me!"

Cliff Cole hadn't heard a word. But he glanced in the mirror and there the older children were, going on a mile a minute in sign language. Cliff could only grin and shake his head.

"Just don't worry about it, Kevvie," said Marjorie Cole. "If you don't want to hear what they're saying, just don't look."

"How does it look to you so far, Chief?" a reporter asked.

Deputy Police Chief Raymond Strattan looked exasperated. His eyes and mouth were hard slits. "I've been on traffic for twenty-three years, and this looks like it'll be the worst day I ever had. We've got six hundred and eighty-five officers detailed to this traffic, but the way it's building up already, I'm not sure that'll be half enough." Telephones clamored in the background in the Speedway traffic command post, and there was a babble of voices. The traffic chief's face hinted at his impatience to get back to the task at hand.

"Are there any unusual traffic patterns or circumstances making it worse this year than usual?" persisted the reporter. The Indianapolis race crowds were legendary in their ability to dream up new approaches and throw off every kind of planning the traffic detail had done.

"Just that this has got to be the biggest crowd ever. The people who waited till the last minute to head for the track are jamming up behind those that can't get into the infield." Even while speaking, the chief was signaling something to a nearby policeman.

"Any other—"

"Look," said Strattan. "Just yesterday my people had to handle a crowd of three hundred and fifty thousand at the parade, and today we've got one that big or bigger. What's the problem? Just too many people and too many cars. Isn't that always the problem?"

By eight o'clock, Olive Canfield had been herded along in the traffic to a point on Thirtieth Street where traffic was being funneled into several lanes that led off the street and south through a field to the Speedway. There had been no opportunity to get out of the mess, and she was thoroughly disgusted. If she didn't lose her job at the bakery over this, she would be surprised.

All about stood city police and state troopers, waving the rivers of converging cars into the approach lanes. Horns honked incessantly. Here and there were automobiles that had become trapped in mud when their drivers had tried to detour around the slow-moving lanes. Their motors strained, and their rear wheels burred and slithered in the ooze. Olive Canfield felt no sympathy. Those drivers had come to this place of their own free will, and it was just their kind of impatient, aggressive driving that, two or three times already, had cut off her chances of escaping from the Speedway-bound traffic. Serves them right, she thought. But, never having been a spiteful woman, she was ashamed of the uncharitable thought.

About three car-lengths ahead there was a state police officer who looked familiar. Mrs. Canfield suddenly recognized the calm and intelligent-looking face: he was a middle-aged trooper who was a regular neighborhood patron of the bakery. He always got a dozen cinnamon twists. She felt a surge of hope. This might be the person who would listen to her and understand her plight, stop some traffic and help her get her car turned around and out of this terrible jam. Why, he could even help her explain later to the bakery owner, Mr. Sanders, and thus maybe save her job, she realized. Suddenly her spirits began to lift; she almost wept with relief. The trooper's kind, strong face now loomed like a beacon before her. A few feet more and she would be close enough to summon him and explain to him that she was supposed to have opened the bakery an hour ago. Come on, come on, she silently urged the traffic.

Another thing was needling her anxiety: Mrs. Canfield customarily had three cups of coffee each morning before driving to the bakery, and the rest room was her first stop when she arrived there. By now, she was long past that point in the morning and was suffering, in addition to her frustration and anger, a very acute need that made her shiver now and then and tighten muscles and press her knees together.

Traffic in the lanes on both sides was moving slowly, but hers was stopped dead and she could not get an inch closer to that magnificent familiar state police officer ahead. "Come on, come on," she now muttered aloud. To be so close to help and yet. . . .

Suddenly her line of traffic began to move, and she felt a powerful surge of hope. But at the moment her car began to move forward, the trooper turned his head toward something in the distance and then strode off in that direction, disappearing among the cars. Oh, God, she thought. And though by nature too timid to be a horn-blower, she suddenly started pressing frantically on the horn button in hopes of calling him back.

But of course not, she realized. She was only one horn-honker among hundreds, and no police officer in this mess was paying any attention to any honking horn.

I've got to stop here, she thought, or I'll never be able to turn around even if I do get help. She was getting into what seemed to be the very throat of the funnel now. She decided to put on the brake and wait for a policeman to come. Even if one came at her enraged, she had to get a policeman to help her. But she was intimidated immediately by the deafening chorus of horns that now opened up behind her.

She moved forward now, starting to sob. She hated this noise, this helplessness, this feeling of being a twig in a torrent; she hated this dirty, tire-tracked, oily mud and gravel she was driving through, the tire-flattened drinking cups, straws, soft-drink cans, newspapers, candy and gum wrappers, cigarette butts, and sodden facial tissues that were strewn everywhere; it was the kind of ugly waste that perpetually accumulated in the little parking lot in front of the bakery shop, making it look so ugly she would feel compelled to go out and sweep it at least twice a day, even though that wasn't her responsibility. Mrs. Canfield hated untidiness and disorder and loud noise, and now the whole world around her was untidy, disorderly, and noisy.

Now there seemed to be no more policemen; most of them had been stationed back by the street, and the people directing traffic now in this field were civilians wearing caps or sun helmets with insignia designating them as Speedway employees. They stood at intervals along the traffic lanes, some of them waving the cars along, some tweeting on whistles, some talking on walkie-talkies, others stopping the cars and checking something—taking tickets, evidently.

Tickets!

I don't have a ticket or any money, so they'll have to turn me back now!

Again, hope welled up in Mrs. Canfield. She stopped her car now beside a Speedway man who was obviously a ticket official. He was looking down at her from under the dark oval brim of his helmet. He had a broad, plain face and horn-rimmed glasses and was not at all intimidating. Confident now, Mrs. Canfield looked straight in his eyes and said, "I don't have a ticket and I don't have any money and I got here by accident, and so you'll just have to help me turn around and get out, do you understand?"

The ticket man, showing no expression, blinked at her a few times while somewhere in his brain the data of her plight were processed. Then, without a word, he dipped his head and waved his left arm toward the Speedway, indicating that she should go on.

"I most certainly will not! I am not going any farther into that awful place! I'm late for work, and I have to get out of here!" She crossed her arms over her bosom.

Horns began to sound louder behind her. The Speedway man's face grew red, and his eyes widened. "Ma'am," he said, "you'll just have to move on. There's nothing I can do to help you."

"Well, then, who can, sir?" she demanded. "Somebody has to be in charge here!"

The din of horns grew louder, and there were derisive voices shouting profanities.

"Ma'am, you better move it, or God help you," yelled the Speedway man.

Defiantly, Mrs Canfield reached to the dashboard and switched off the ignition, put the gear lever in park position, and refolded her arms. She set her jaw and looked straight ahead. "I'll just wait here for the man in charge, thank you," she said. Gooseflesh rose on her legs. It was hard to be defiant while needing so badly to pee. Cars were moving by in the adjacent lanes, and now Mrs. Canfield could hear behind her more voices raised in fury. The Speedway man was livid now, was waving furiously with his left arm. "I'll wait here," she repeated, "for the man in charge."

"Lady, damnit, there ain't no man in charge!" He pointed back. *"They're* in charge now, ma'am, and you better get your ass in gear or—"

"I won't have that kind of lang—" But she glanced into the rearview mirror, and suddenly she went cold with horror.

Car doors were flying open. From the cars blocked behind her emerged men and women, their faces contorted with rage, clenched fists upraised. Large men with beer bottles in their fists were advancing on her car, and some of the women were screaming filthy words through their bared teeth. Suddenly Mrs. Canfield felt a fear that she had felt only once before in her sixty years, once when the bakery shop was being robbed by a yellow-eyed gunman: a fear that she was actually going to be killed.

With a despairing little cry she turned on the ignition, jerked the shift lever, and pulled away just as the first of her pursuers reached the car. Something hard, a thrown rock or bottle, banged the roof of her car. She drove ahead, sobbing, nearly blinded by tears, her heart pounding, toward the traffic tunnel ahead. And now, surmounting even her anger and her fear, was a strange new shame:

In her fright she had wet the car seat.

Gerald Rumple peered up at the clouds for the hundredth time this morning. When he looked back to the road, the cars ahead had moved a few feet, and he accelerated quickly in order to catch up before other cars darted over from another lane. Ella looked up briefly from the newspaper and then returned to it.

Johnny Rutherford will lead the pack from the starting line when Starter Pat Vidan waves the green flag after a parade lap and a pace lap to set up positioning for the field that averaged 192.329 miles an hour during qualification. Rutherford is expected to hold the No. 1 spot going into the first turn at the beginning of the 200-lap race that will pay a purse of more than $1 million for the third consecutive year....

With five former Indianapolis winners in the field —another record for the 57th "500"—the chase for the front of the pack should be spectacular....

Mario Andretti, the '69 winner, will be sixth in the field. Al Unser (1970, '71) will be eighth, and three-time winner A. J. Foyt (1961, '64, '65) will be making the farthest-back start in his Indianapolis experience—23d.

"Let's see your boy Foyt take *this* race," Gerald taunted.

"He'll make it, just don't you worry. How many times have we seen him come shooting out of the back of the pack?" Ella gave a smug smile. She had full confidence in her favorite. Admittedly, he had lost some races here since 1967, but in Ella's opinion there was nobody who could outdrive him if he didn't have mechanical troubles. "When A.J. wants a win as bad as he wants his fourth '500,' nothing's going to hold him back."

"Hunh-uh. Except middle age, maybe."

"Ha! Middle age? He's just in his prime!" She gave Gerald a haughty smile. He grinned at her and patted her on the fat, dimpled cheek. They had been having this same argument, with variations, for more than a decade. She always rooted for A.J. And Gerald, even if he didn't have a particular favorite, would argue against A.J. just to keep it going. Childless, they spent all their time almost exclusively with each other, both at work and at home ("Who else would have us?" they'd always say, laughing), and their teasing routines kept them communicating, kept them interested, kept them fond. They could get a whole month or more of teasing and good-humored contention out of the "500" season.

"Gerald, darn it!" she exclaimed suddenly, startling him. "Look, you went and let that car in ahead of us! Gerald, I swear I could just kill you! Won't you *ever* assert yourself in traffic? You always let the other driver muscle in!"

This stung him more than she could know. He was all too aware that he was not an aggressive, quick, or bold man, as he supposed she or any woman would, deep in her heart, long for. He sighed. "Oh, Ella. You think one place in line is worth a dented fender? An insurance claim? I don't want a wreck and a hassle here. We'd *never* get to the race that way!"

"Nobody's going to hit you, Gerald; they'll just back down!"

"Well, I'm sorry, then! Maybe I'm just not a charger like your dear A.J.!"

She tightened up suddenly. He saw that his tone of voice had brought tears to her eyes. She hurt easily, too, he knew, because she knew she certainly was not the kind of woman a man's dreams are made of, either. "I'm sorry," he said. He put his right hand on the car seat between them. After an appropriate pause, she put hers on top of it.

"I'm sorry, too," she said. She patted his hand, and then he patted hers.

"Sure don't like fighting," he said, looking at her and smiling tenderly. His throat constricted with an unexpectedly powerful surge of poignancy.

"Neither do I, Jerry. And we sure don't want a silly argument to spoil the best day of our year, do we?"

"Sure don't," he chuckled, happy again. "All you have to do, Dumplin', is realize that I'm always right, and quit fighting it."

"Oh, is that so—"

1973 INDIANAPOLIS
500-MILE RACE
SOUVENIR EDITION

In the back seat of the Cole family car, now stopped dead in traffic on Twenty-fifth Street within sight of the great grandstands, Kevin, Keith, and Pam Cole were looking at the colorful special section that Kevin had saved from the Saturday *Star*. On the cover was a design suggesting the Speedway's symbol, the wheel with golden wings. Under that were pictures of three race cars, and under them seven signal flags.

Kevin gazed with concentration at the low, wedgelike shapes of the pictured race cars and gnawed the nail of his left index finger.

Keith looked at his little brother. Sometimes he fancied he could hear pistons running in the cylinders of Kevin's skull.

Cliff Cole turned off the engine of the car.

"Whyja do that, Dad?" Kevin piped up.

"No sense burnin' gas just sittin' here, son."

"But the line might start moving and you wouldn't be started."

"This line isn't going to be moving for a while."

It didn't look as if it would. The street was packed with stopped automobiles, a mass of vehicles extending all the way ahead to the huge gray grandstands. In lawns along the right side of the street there were parked automobiles. Most of the open field on the left side of the street was filled with automobiles also, and with parked camper trucks, buses, vans, and some tents. Along both sides of the street straggled hundreds of fans who evidently had parked farther back and were walking the rest of the distance to the track. They looked like a mass of refugees, carrying boxes, chairs, bags, coolers, binoculars, tarpaulins, cushions, bottles, camp stoves, pennants, cases of beer, bags of potato chips, shoes, sweaters, balloons. As they moved they shed cans and wrappers and peelings, drinking straws, plastic cups, half-eaten buns, cigarette butts, and chicken bones, all of which were soon mashed into the muddy shoulder of the street by the feet of others who followed. A motorcycle wove slowly forward among the pedestrians, emitting crepitant bursts of sound as its driver, an enormous girl with great swaying breasts, twisted the throttle. On the back of her T-shirt was printed:

FCK—THE ONLY THING MISSING IS U

On the other side of the street a thin teenage boy swung along on crutches, a muddy cast on one foot, a floppy-brimmed hat on his head, and a plastic bag full of pink ham hanging from his belt.

Pam, her face full of boredom, looked down at the souvenir edition on Kevin's lap. "What icky-looking cars," she commented.

"Like heck!"

"They are. Those silly fin things on them. They look like they're trying to look like spaceships or something."

"Fins? Ha-ha! *Fins?* Ha-ha-ha! Listen to her! Fins!" Kevin squinted up his eyes as if in pain and slapped himself on the forehead. "Those aren't fins; those are wings!"

"Oooh! You mean those cars fly?"

"Those aren't for flying, dumb-dumb, they're to *keep* them from flying. The wind going back over them presses the car down, see, like it weighed more, so there's more friction and it holds the track better. When they're going that fast, you *have* to design them like that! My gosh, Pam!"

"Well, why don't they just go slower and save all that trouble?"

Kevin's face twisted up in an exaggerated expression of dazed disbelief, and his voice came out an agonized squeak. "How can you be so dumb? *The whole point is to go faster!*"

"Go where faster?" She was smiling demurely at her little brother as she asked it.

"Around the track," he croaked, sliding down in the seat, crossing his eyes, sticking his tongue out of the corner of his mouth, and letting his head fall sideways like a cartoon character stunned by a blow.

"Around the track?" she responded. "Around the track, eh? Oh, yes. Hmm. Faster around and around the track, you say. Ah, yes, my dear Watson, *now* it all makes sense. Around and around the track. Hmm." She pointed her forefinger at her temple and made a circular motion.

"Pam," Kevin said, now straining up toward her and, like a serpent at her ear, hissing, "Your—brains—are—all—in—your—boobs."

"Mom! Did you hear what he said?"

"I always hear everything, darlings," said Mrs. Cole. "Now all of you, stop that unpleasantness. This is exasperating enough without your help."

"Tell you what I've got half a mind to do," said Mr. Cole, "is just pull up in one of these yards along here where they're parking cars, and just hoof it the rest of the way, like those folks, 'stead of trying to take the car on in there."

"Aw, Dad, y'mean *walk?*" Kevin pronounced the word as if he were speaking of the most loathsome form of human activity.

"Sure. Our seats are on this side of the track. I bet if we parked inside the grounds we'd have to walk this far, anyway, and still get hung up in traffic. Yep. I bet we'd get on the way home quicker, too, after the race is over if we did park out here."

"Look," said Pam. "There's a yard that says parking all day for four dollars and free lemonade after the race! How about that one, Daddy?"

Kevin was now watching the children who carried the signs along the side of the street. "Man!" he exclaimed. "Wouldn't it be neat to live this close to the Speedway and park cars in your yard? Like that Corvette! Man! Look!"

"Place next door says three dollars," remarked Mr. Cole. "And looks like they got a space left right alongside the street. Keith, you hop out and run up there and tell

them to hold that place till we can get the car up there."
He started the engine.

"But Dad, the other place has free lemonade," complained Kevin.

"It's not free, it's the difference of that extra dollar," Keith said, climbing out of the right side of the car. And, looking very businesslike, he went ahead alongside the street. He stopped and talked to a thin, dark-haired boy in front of a brick house. They had a long discussion, with much nodding and waving of arms, and finally a handshake. Then Keith came back. Bending down to his mother's open window, he told them officiously:

"I've reserved the place for us. It's ours, for three dollars."

"Great work, son," said Clifford Cole, smiling at Marjorie.

"You didn't let me finish, Dad. Included in that three dollars I talked him into giving us Cokes after the race."

"Oh, Keith, you didn't!" exclaimed Mrs. Cole. "Why, his mother might not—"

"It's all set up, Mom. Don't worry about it. Besides, I saw his mother standing in the front door and she looked real nice. She was real pretty, Mom. I bet you'll like her."

"That's just fine, son," Clifford Cole said. "You did real well for us. I think you're pretty darn smart."

"I bet I could've got it for two dollars," muttered Kevin.

A wave of yelling and clapping swept through the crowd in the grandstands when the first of the great race cars were rolled out from the mouth of Gasoline Alley into the pit area. Whistling and scatterings of applause swelled and diminished as the colorful vehicles emerged one by one into plain view. The crowd, which had been walking, sitting, and huddling in the gray chill all morning, seemed to take heart from the appearance of the fabulous machines. One at a time, driverless, gleaming with chrome and stainless steel and brilliant enameled paint jobs, they were maneuvered to their respective pit areas by the white-clad mechanics and pit crewmen, who constantly guided and caressed the vehicles with the palms of their hands.

Nick Alef, with his cameras and camera bags hanging
heavily on his shoulder, took up a position on an abut-
ment that, augmented by his stature, allowed him to aim
his camera down over the heads of the crewmen, photographers, and onlookers who were pressing around each
emerging race car. From up here his camera could take
in the wide, squat contours, the frail-looking struts and
steering linkages and wings, the manifolds like exposed
intestines, the gleaming, snail-shaped turbochargers, and
peer down into the narrow cockpits with their round-
knobbed shifting levers, clusters of dials, and tiny, padded
steering wheels.

Spectators in the high seats nearby stared expressionless down into these intriguing confines. They mused over
the dark, stitched, padded, high-backed seats, reminiscent
somehow of the astronauts' couches in spaceships. Fascinated, they stared down in. Some of them, probably,
were wondering how it would be to sit strapped low into
this tight, custom-tailored tub of a cockpit four or five
inches above pavement, sandwiched between bladders of
ultravolatile fuel, thrust forward along a narrow asphalt
track at more than two hundred miles an hour by a
yowling, hot, thousand-horsepower superengine, in com-
petitive traffic with thirty-two similar machines. Nick was
sure some of them were thinking such thoughts, because
he, even after years of filming the 500-Mile Race, still
thought of it each time he looked into a race car's cockpit.

It's so easy to visualize yourself in there, he thought,
because we all drive automobiles every day. and we know
how it feels to steer and brake and we know the pleasure
of power accelerating. Anybody can relate to the man in
that seat. It's not something like a bullfight or a boxing
match or a pro football game or a moon mission that
you've never tried yourself. This is simply something you
know you could do yourself if you had some practice and
lots of guts.

Sometimes, when he looked into a cockpit, what he felt
was fear. Even though he knew he would never be in it,
still there was a nameless fear evoked by that formfitting
cockpit down into which he now gazed.

Nick descended and walked through the short tunnel to

the walkway behind the Tower Terrace. The pavement of the wide walkway was already covered with a mush of dirty mud, tracked along it by the thousands of fans who strolled gawking, or hurried anxiously, looking for their seating sections, for rest rooms, for souvenir shops and hot-dog stands. Overhead, the sky was still gray and threatening.

Nick watched the river of people go by, and many of them watched him. His stature and dark good looks and his conspicuous cameras drew admiring and curious looks. He was aware of this attention. He knew what kind of a figure he cut, and though he tried not to succumb to the stirrings of narcissism, he was often troubled in public by a sense of embarrassment, of role-playing. Sometimes he would surprise himself posing, with an intense look in his eyes, a sort of far-seeing squint, glancing rapidly about as if scouting for some serious something worthy of being photographed, some pictorial quality ordinary men might not recognize, his jaw clenched, jaw muscles working, and his lips drawn thin and serious, perhaps stroking his short beard. He knew from his mirror that this way he looked best, looked most manly, most knowing, most commanding, most like a keen, coldly professional news photographer might be expected to look. A coy and deep-breathing girl had told him once that he looked like the sort of a man who reads *Playboy*, and even while holding back a laugh of ridicule, he had felt a blush of vanity.

Nick's eyes sorted swiftly among the passing faces. He did enjoy the attention of women, the language of eyes. He knew how to connect with the pretty eyes that glanced at him, and how to hold such glimpses, just perceptibly smiling, until the pretty eyes dropped or turned away or transmitted something to him. Though he deplored it mentally as a silly game of vanity, it somehow soothed a tickle of emptiness somewhere not too deep inside him. He understood that his ego needed it these days; it was something like getting a check for a submitted photo essay. Occasionally he would play out a glance-game just to see how far it would go.

A stunningly formed girl with straight black hair passed before him, and he caught her glancing at him out of the corner of her eye. He showed her a candid and friendly look, but she faced the other way and went on.

From the other direction came one with masses of auburn curls and a pretty, lewd face. Under a transparent raincoat was revealed a loose mesh shirt, the ruddy nipples of her wobbling breasts showing through. Nick tried to watch both the breasts and the eyes. She was lighting a cigarette as she went, and did not notice him, to his disappointment. And he ridiculed himself for the sense of disappointment. He watched her pass and go on, the frayed cuffs on her bell-bottoms dragging in the mud, the soles of her bare feet black with dirt. Girls like that, he had found, could be coaxed easily into posing naked. They were true exhibitionists, but usually had little real physical grace.

What a contrast, he thought, to Diana Scheckley. He knew intuitively that she would have grace before the camera. She has the body of a thoroughbred, he thought.

Before long now, he thought, Diana should arrive at the track to take her place in the Celebrity Caravan. He glanced at his watch. It was 9:05 now. Farther up the track, he could hear the band instruments blaring and whistling, tuning up for the parade down the mainstretch, which then would be followed by the Celebrity Caravan touring the track in the Cadillac convertibles. He would try to catch her a few minutes before the caravan formed up. With Diana, his game of eye contact had been for a purpose. He had started it with her at the beauty contest in March. Like all the contestants, she had expected to be chosen the Festival Queen, and she had suffered a humbling letdown when Cynthia Foster was chosen instead. But when everyone else's attention had moved on to the new Queen, Nick had continued to stay by Diana Scheckley with his cameras and glances and his flattery. "Those judges must be blind," he had said. "If I'd been the judge, you'd be the Queen." "Thanks," she had replied, raising a hand to sweep her long, honey-colored hair back from her cheek, "I needed that."

He had continued his homage to her at the "500" Festival Mayor's Breakfast in April; then, three days ago, at the Mechanics' Banquet in the Convention-Exposition Center; again, two days ago, at the Queen's Ball in the same place; and, finally, just yesterday when, during the downtown parade, he had maneuvered to make their paths cross so often. He had let his camera dote on her at each encounter. And she had noticed. She had begun watching for him, too. She would say bright and silly statements in which there seemed to be suggested meanings. Diana Scheckley: a spoiled, rich college girl getting high on adulation. Usually with her was her festival sponsor, Harry Kuntz of the manufacturing Kuntzes, whom Nick had met from time to time over the years and considered a pompous prig.

Nick had first seen Diana Scheckley several summers ago. He had not known her name then. At the age of sixteen or so, she had been a lifeguard at a Northside swimming club of which the Alef family were members. Many times that summer he had observed her in a clinging, brick-red tank suit, ambling about the pool's edge, stooping, bending, always moving provocatively, always seeming to watch to see who might be watching her. On many a morning that summer he had lain prone in the sunlight, covered with suntan oil, watching this girl parade about in the revealing swimsuit, the soft white cotyledons of her buttocks showing beneath the taut seams of the suit. He could recall even now the glinting gold fuzz on her brown thighs, the beaded water droplets on her lotioned shoulders. He could remember her with the shapely arms upraised, revealing white, shaved armpits, the uplifting breasts; he could remember her combing long wet blond hair back in the sunlight, her lips holding a row of bobby pins, her blue-gray eyes scanning the sunbathers, ever conscious of their gaze. She had made that lifeguarding job in the glare of day a perpetual intimate toilette, before the furtive eyes of scores of married voyeurs. Nick remembered all that, and he remembered his own longings, his inflamed fantasies, his yearning loins pressed against the sun-hot concrete of the pool's edge, while his wife, Becky, sat beside him on a towel reading a novel, growing pink with sunburn, and Davey and Timmy played in the pool nearby.

It was because he remembered her exhibitionistic self-awareness at the swim club that Nick Alef had singled her out from among the other thirty-two contestants and begun cultivating her attentions. Now the time was right. Today, somehow, he would have to ask her, and he would have to ask her right.

Somewhere in Gasoline Alley a piercing whistle was blown between someone's fingers. A child whined his desire for a coney. And radios throbbed and wailed, radios carried by the ambling young, radios thumping funky rock, transistor radios frantic with the trucking drive of Nashville guitars: highway music, roadside café blues music, heartsick lonely music to drive by, No-Doz long-distance-hauling music, the throttle music of a motoring people.

The international flags along the back of the Tower Terrace fluttered in the wet wind. Concessionaires hawked hot dogs and soft drinks and checkered flag souvenirs. The passing people shed laughter and litter and gripes and disconnected fragments of talk. "They gone from a five-cell fuel system to four cells in them McLarens," said a passing voice. Nearby, surging in the wind, was the huge inverted bag holding the hundreds of multicolored helium-filled balloons that would be released just before the race to float away over the city. The bag strained like something alive against its anchor ropes, which were staked into the ground. Feet splatted in puddles and shuffled on the muddy pavement. Now and then, applause would ripple somewhere in the distant bleachers. The public-address system spread the throaty echo of incoherent announcements over the vast compound. And always in the background were the susurrus of moving traffic, bleat of car horns, whoop and wail of distant sirens, and drone of airplane engines. For a moment the whistling whine of a descending jetliner sliced through all the other sounds and then was absorbed by them.

Nick, slowly following a race car, made his way now through the streams of shuffling people to the pit area. Several hundred people were milling about in the pit lanes now. Half of them seemed to be photographers, and the other half wore the billed caps, the bright, insignia-studded windbreaker jackets of officials and quasi-officials or the coverall suits of mechanics and technicians. The bleachers and the soaring grandstands appeared now to be perhaps half-filled, all aisles and stairways clogged with slow lines of brightly dressed people. Their myriad voices blended in a pervasive, buzzing shush. Along every walkway a river of people flowed in slow, half-aimless currents such as one sees along a carnival midway.

The main straightaway lay like a long, paved valley floor between the grandstands and Paddock on the outside and the tiers of seats in the Tower Terrace inside. Dominating the Terrace was the Tower, a modern building looking much like the control tower of a metropolitan airport. Its various floors glowed with electric light, and, inside, people could be seen moving about: newsmen, broadcasters, photographers, officials, timers and scorers, celebrities and special guests. The infield at the south end of the grounds was now completely full of people, literally acres of people shoulder to shoulder, a living carpet of humanity.

As he always did here, Nick now felt the peculiar premonitory excitement of the arena, the stadium sense. Unthinkingly, he perceived the Speedway as a vast bowl around him, an enormous shallow Coliseum brimming with impending spectacle. The vastness of it was awesome even for someone who had been here year after year.

Here within his own sensate and man-size dimensions he stood, his big body feeling, despite his slight hangover, strong and significant, the center of his universe, the familiar weight of the photographic equipment on his shoulder, the taste of breakfast egg still in his mouth, his stomach full, pulse beating, packed full of the importance of his own concerns. At the far end of the straightaway were thousands of persons equally man-size and important but so diminished by distance that they appeared no larger than the sand grains cemented into this concrete wall beside him. And for just an instant he had the disturbing realization that, seen by those at that distant end of the stretch, he, too, was just a grain, just a speck of color. He blinked. The thousands of individuals in the distance, each wearing a color, each a soul full of personality, blended to a blue-gray mass, like the inked color-dots that make up the masses of form in a four-color photoprint. Yet each of those faraway light-points was a personage like himself; each was the center of a universe, feeling, thinking, breathing, desiring, worrying like himself. . . .

He turned away from it and shook his head. That happened to him sometimes, here or in football stadiums, wherever great crowds were, and it disturbed him somehow, momentarily made him feel insignificant. And Nicholas Alef, probably more than the average man, was terrified by the feeling of insignificance.

Once already this month, Nick's delicate sense of self-confidence had been almost devastated. On May 12, the first day of qualifications for the race, Art Pollard had been killed right in front of him, and he had failed to film it. Damn, damn, damn, he thought now for the hundredth time. Did I ever blow it. He had missed the opportunity to get the best movie footage of the wreck. If only he had had his camera ready and had filmed it as clearly as his mind remembered it!

There was no excuse for not having had his camera ready. He had just been gabbing over the fence with a cute little Michigan State coed with a compact figure and wondrous eyes, trying to persuade her to pose for him later on, pose for pay. Just for a few minutes he had talked to her, there by the infield fence where everything had seemed so mundane, so familiar; a picnic atmosphere, it had been: short green grass underfoot, hazy blue spring morning sky overhead. Brightly dressed people sitting, standing, moving, and talking all around, waiting for the time trials to begin, occupied with little ordinary things: unfolding lawn chairs, shaking gravel out of a tennis shoe, prying the cap from a Coke, ripping open a plastic bag of ice cubes. Mothers cooing to crying babies, Frisbees spinning through the air, beer can tabs snapping, sun-browned, shapely legs going by. A timeless time in which one is expecting nothing of oneself, one of those spaces between the ticks of the clock . . .

He and the coed had just paused in their conversation to wait for the yowl of a practicing race car to pass by, when right behind him there had been two loud sounds, separate and distinct but simultaneous: the sharp report of a heavy object hitting a hard surface and an exploding *whooosh!* No sound of a skid preceding it, just that jarring *crack-whooosh!* He had spun around, seeing first the black marks on the wall; by the time his eye had caught up with the hurtling car, it had spun into the grass inside the track, dug into the ground, and started flipping along the south straightaway, its right wheels off, the air full of chunks. The copper-and-white car, deteriorating, had bounced and tumbled for a quarter of a mile before coming to rest, right side up, a shapeless hulk, in the second turn, flickering with orange flames. So clearly now Nick could remember Pollard slumped in the car, his arms hanging out of the cockpit, not moving but seeming to quiver in the waves of heat. Nick remembered spectators pressing forward against the fence.

Only then had he thought of his camera and realized what he had missed filming. Shaken by his own stupidity, he had fumbled in trying to get the camera ready, and by the time he had it operating and trained, the emergency trucks had arrived. Mortified, he had filmed only the aftermath: the firefighters advancing with the nozzles of their extinguishers spewing white foam on the burning hulk; a gray-and-white column of smoke and fumes piling up toward the sun, and the silhouettes of firefighters and rescuers in their moonwalker suits moving busily back and forth. Nick had gotten some dramatic footage of that, and of the spectators ganging on the fence, their mouths open, trying to comprehend the incomprehensible fact that right there before them in the sunlight a man was dying. But he had totally missed his chance to film the crash itself, and had gone around disgusted with his unprofessionalism ever since. And now he vowed, never again will I let one like that catch me unaware. Maybe you don't have any control over chance. Maybe you can't know where to be, but there's always the chance that it's going to happen right in front of you, and you'd better be ready to do the right thing because it doesn't take much fumbling or waiting around to fuck up a perfect chance.

Nick had lost confidence in his writing ability over the last few years, but he had clung to his faith in himself as a lensman. He couldn't afford to lose that faith.

He made his way now slowly through the dense crowd in the pits. Between bodies he glimpsed the low, gleaming, knee-high race cars: the polished red of the STP Team cars, the Aztec orange of the Foyt racers, and the others, the whites and golds and blues and yellows. Over and around each car now hovered the crewmen in their clean uniforms, studying, tending, inspecting, fiddling with the beloved machines, looking like surgeons and their aides around operating tables. Stout, florid men in bright sport coats and white shoes, ascots and rakish hats, posed in clusters here and there for photographers. Nick recognized many of them as aging "500" winners and car owners and sponsors. Some of them spoke to him by name. He replied to them by name when he could remember their names. He wished he could remember names better. It was the mark of a good reporter to have names on the tip of the tongue, and Nick was sometimes dismayed by the vagueness and abstractedness of his mind, which would remember only what and whom he was interested in particularly.

The Tower Terrace crowd behind the fence kibitzed hungrily on all this esoteric activity in the pits. They gazed down from their seats, many through binoculars, studying the big cars and the celebrities, or hung on the fence watching from the closest possible vantage points the technical preparations being done by the teams of mechanics. Nick had wandered and filmed in these pits for years, and was known and greeted by drivers and mechanics and car owners and USAC officials. They were friendly and open with him. They considered him a man's man. He had learned more than he really cared to know about their world of machinery and money, so that he could talk with them knowledgeably and do his job well. In their estimation, Nick Alef belonged. In his estimation, somehow, he never quite did. He didn't know all he should know or care all he should care. He was haunted by a notion that his mingling here was just another game, just another role.

Musing thus now, he continued northward, pausing now and then to photograph some of the incongruous clowning that the drivers so often did to amuse themselves or, more likely, to ease their own tension. Sometimes it was hard to keep in mind that these goofy, boyish, profane men were about to go out and gamble with fortune and death for the next three or four hours.

"Whaddya say, Nick?" said someone passing in silvery coveralls. Nick turned.

"Hiya, Gordy." It was Gordon Johncock, a bantam

racing driver with wavy brown-blond hair. "Hey, best of luck," Nick called. He didn't really expect Johncock to do much in the race; he was not one of the charismatic drivers. He was a veteran big-car racer who lived in a nearby small Indiana town. Johncock raised his stubby hand in acknowledgment and was engulfed in the crowd.

Now a big, broad-shouldered, long-haired, short-nosed young man in driver's coveralls was edging past. Nick stuck out his right hand to him. "Hey, Salt, lots of luck, huh?"

"Thanks, Nick," David Walther replied, gripping with a big, warm hand and moving on. Walther was a speed-boat racer as well as an automobile racer. This was his second year as an entrant in the Indianapolis "500," and though bad luck had kept him from achieving anything at Indy so far, some were saying he might be watched as a real star in the making. Such facts and impressions Nick Alef managed to retain for the sake of his job.

The air was full of the talking of thousands of voices. Nick raised his head to sniff the damp-laden wind and almost stumbled over somebody's industrial photographer who, equipped with an expensive Hasselblad, knelt as if praying beside a gold-and-white race car, leaning forward slowly until his camera was focused point-blank upon the logo of its sponsor.

At least, Nick thought, I'm not that much of a prostitute. Yet. Or am I?

Everywhere there were logos, decals, each symbolizing invested money. On cars, on crash helmets, on jackets, on walls, on coveralls, on caps: *Goodyear. Marlboro. Olsonite. Gulf. STP. Sunoco DX. Monroe. Viceroy. Sugarripe. Firestone. Champion. Castrol. Premier. Valvoline. Norton. Gatorade. Samsonite. Purolator. Ashland.*

Smells in the cool, damp air: Rubber's dense odor from the high stacks of racing tires near the fence. Petroleum grease. Sweet pipe tobacco, after-shave. Scent of fried chicken and of hot dogs. The warm, coppery scent of electric motors. Fuel fumes, the ammoniac stink of an unwashed body, or an exhalation of a breath rank with onion or gin. And from the cars, the varied smells of unnameable chemicals: absorbents, cleaning compounds, adhesives, waxes, additives, solvents. And now and then from somewhere a fart or a breath of perfume.

In a running commentary of controlled excitement, pregnant with anticipation, the voice of track announcer Tom Carnegie echoed between the stands. Somewhere in the distance a tuba burped, and a flute noodled up and down the scale. The bands were forming up for the parade around the track; that meant that Diana would be up there somewhere by now. Nick pressed on in that direction. He stopped once to get some shots of comedians Joey Bishop and Dick Martin, who were displaying serious interest in somebody's race car. Overhead, helicopter blades beat the air, and applause for something pattered somewhere nearby. But now the sounds of the musical instruments pulled Nick most strongly. Where the bands were forming there would be majorettes to photograph; there would be Purdue's voluptuous Golden Girl in her skintight short suit of sequins; there would be youngsters photogenic in band uniforms; there would be celebrities and bagpipers and midgets and clowns. And there would be Diana Scheckley, the—

Nick felt a hand on his arm; there was a chunky young man with gnomish features, wearing the uniform of a racing mechanic. Vaguely Nick remembered; it was someone he had talked to at the Mechanics' Banquet the other night, and also last week at an all-night booze party in an apartment complex near the Speedway. "How you doin' there, Mr. Alef?" said the oafish, grinning face.

"Pretty good, thanks," Nick replied. He was ransacking his brain for the mechanic's name. Some stooge on one of the big racing teams. This was not an important man in any sense, and Nick had not liked him well enough, apparently, to take note of his name. "How's yourself?" he added, wanting to move along.

The mechanic didn't seem to want to move along. He stood in front of Nick with an uncertain smile on his face, as if waiting for Nick to say something, or as if he were about to say something himself. Impatient, but not wanting to be rude, Nick hesitated, thinking how odd this was; usually at this stage of Race Day the mechanics were too busy to spare a minute.

"You remember me, don't you?" said the mechanic, evidently wanting only to be recognized.

"Sure I remember you. Glad to see you survived that party!"

The young man laughed, a hard, wicked chuckle. Nick recalled now that he had stood talking about something at some length with this youth late in the evening of the banquet, while waiting for Diana Scheckley to return from the ladies' room, and that they had laughed together about something at the apartment party. Both times, unfortunately, Nick had been very full of highballs, so he could not recall what they had said. He could remember only the repulsive features swimming before his eyes.

"So how's it going?" said the mechanic. "Your—uh—project?"

"Project?"

The face was leering now. "Yeah. The *Playboy* centerfold you was tellin' me about. With that Princess."

"Oh, that." Good God, that's what I was talking to this creep about, he thought.

"Yeah," said the round face. "That still on?"

"Uhm, yep. Far as I know," Nick said with a weak grin. "Still working on it." He wanted to get away from this person to whom he had said much more than he should have. He remembered now: drunk, and effusive with wishful thinking, he had talked about his idea as if Diana had already agreed to pose for him. But he hadn't even asked her yet.

This wasn't good. What if this creep had mentioned it to other mechanics, or to drivers? That kind of thing spreads fast in this racing fraternity, Nick thought. Was that why he had been greeted so smilingly by Johncock a moment ago? My God, he thought now. What if she hears about it from one of these grease monkeys, or from some cocky driver? Or already has? Then you can kiss that project good-bye, he told himself in disgust.

"Well, listen," the mechanic was saying. "You just let me know when, and I'll arrange for the car, y'hear?"

"Uhm, yeah, the car." In their conversation Nick had asked this mechanic to help him get access to a race car to pose her with in some private place. "Listen," he said now, taking a firm grip on the mechanic's biceps, "don't you say anything about this to anyone, promise? She's a well-raised girl, you know. She's not some go-go or massage parlor slut, you know."

"Sure, I promise. You just let me know when."

"Sure will. Now I got to get to work. You, too, I'll bet. Keep that thing running today, huh? There'll be one driver counting on you."

"Try to, yeah. Hey, Mr. Alef, remember," the mechanic called after him as he walked away, "remember, I get to be there, right?"

"Right. See you."

Nick remembered that, too, and it was the worst part to remember. As compensation for setting up the place and the race car, the mechanic had asked to be allowed to be present during the posing. " 'Cause you can't just leave a seventy-five-thousand-dollar race car with strangers," the mechanic had explained.

Jesus! When will I learn not to talk with these shitheads when I've been drinking? Holy crap! he thought.

But on the other hand, it was some progress toward the technical side of the project. He hadn't thought enough about how to get the car and the setting, and maybe in a way it was good that he had set the idea in motion in that creep's head. First, though, he thought, I've got to find a way to talk her into it. He knew that no matter what he had to do to arrange it, he couldn't let this chance slip by. Nude models were easily available, for a price. He had hired go-go girls and prostitutes and exotic dancers to pose for nude photo spreads, which the men's magazines would buy and then publish with a lot of phony text calling them concert violinists or sky divers or nuclear physicists or Zen philosophers. Nick had sent nude photo features one after another to *Playboy,* and they had always come back. Some of them he had managed to sell later to the sleazier men's magazines for less money.

But this one was something else: a sure thing, a true "500" Festival Princess in an authentic auto-racing milieu in the so-called Speed Capital of the World, Indianapolis. Never had he come up with such a combination of beauty, big theme, and authenticity. In reverie he had already posed her for the feature photo: stark naked, posturing beside a championship race car, her fair, soft skin a vivid textural contrast to the hard bright enamel of the race car's shell—succulent flesh and costly machine. The race buff's dream come true. Hugh Hefner could never resist that combination, Nick Alef was sure of that. There would be a check in the mail for five thousand dollars. Godalmighty, could he use that! It would surely end forever Becky's complaints about his nude photography. He would have to pay Diana a thousand or maybe fifteen hundred out of it, of course, to make it worth her while.

And surely—and this would be the most important part—surely it would be a door-opener for him. She probably would emerge as Playmate of the Year, and that would be to his credit. Then he would be in with *Playboy*, right into that lucrative market, recognized, at last able to get out of the rut.

Diana, he thought, sucking air in between his clenched teeth as he made his way toward the sounds of the bands, Diana, you and I, we're going to do each other some good. All you have to do is say yes when I tell you what I've got in mind.

He remembered how she used to strut and flaunt it around the swimming pool those past summers, and he was sure she'd say yes. Yes, yes, let's do it, she would surely say.

From the milling masses, uniformed marching bands somehow were being organized, coalescing into neat ranks and files, and moving with precision and cadence one by one onto the smooth, wide ribbon of racetrack. With rattling and thumping drums each band turned south down the main straightaway, treading in place until interval was established, then striding off between the towering grandstands, led by high-strutting drum majors bedecked in comic-opera uniforms who with eloquent wrists poked six-foot batons into the air. Behind them came majorettes and twirlers, wearing only boots, sequined tights, cosmetics, gooseflesh, and toothpaste-ad smiles. Guidon bearers, their fists in cotton gloves, locked their staff ends into socketed trusses and braced against the tugging wind that made the banners flutter and crepitate. Then came the musicians, brilliant with spats, frogs, braids, and brass, each unit the finest battalion of pride and prestige its parent high school could afford to put into the field.

Harry Kuntz squinted and held the brim of his pearl-gray hat against the wind. He smiled in amusement as a passing unit of black bandsmen swung into a soul-rock version of "Washington Post March" and shuffled down the straightaway in a maneuver of precisely choreographed goofiness. Harry turned to the blond girl beside him to see if she, too, were amused. But Diana Scheckley's perfect face was set against the wind, her mascaraed eyelashes trembling. She held at her throat the tie straps of a clear plastic rain hood with which she was trying to keep her golden hairdo from blowing apart. With her other hand she tried to control the wind-whipped hem of her skirt.

"Isn't that funny?" Harry Kuntz said.

"What's funny?"

"The way they're playing that. Sousa would turn over in his—"

"I guess so. Oh, damnit."

"I beg your pardon, my dear?"

"Oh, this icky wind. It blew me upside down yesterday in the parade. And now again." She shut her lips firmly.

Harry's face flushed suddenly at a gallant notion. He unbuttoned his raincoat and spread it open to surround her, to harbor her inside with him.

Always trying, she thought with a small, wise smile. But she did let him draw her into the shelter. He was wide and tall and warm, and always smelled faintly of Aramis. Diana stood there in the lee of her sponsor, aware that he was gradually, insidiously, with seeming innocence, drawing her closer to his flank. She could hear his breathing change and knew that his heart would be racing now; he would be in a heady state. Dear old Harry, her festival sponsor, her father's boss and neighbor. Trapped within the propriety of his station, but with yearnings. When she was sixteen and seventeen she used to tease-test Harry—in swimming pools, in touch football games, at garden parties and debuts. By now she knew his affections were not strictly avuncular, and she was afraid to encourage him as she used to. Once, Diana had had an impulse to put her hand in his crotch to see if he would faint. Sometimes the impulse would recur and she would burst into laughter at the thought. And Harry, oblivious to the cause of her laughter, would smile in fond perplexity.

But most of her attention was somewhere else now. She scanned faces in the crowd. Many of them were familiar by now. Many were glamorous; many were important, like Harry, perennial members of the social group that coordinated and perpetuated the Festival events from year to year. Diana Scheckley was the fourth girl Harry Kuntz had sponsored in the Festival Queen competition in the last decade, and she presumed that he had lusted similarly for the others.

It was all harmless enough. It gave a girl a chance to meet exciting people and be treated royally. During the festival month she had met and talked with all the drivers, had dined and danced with some of them. She had been excited and vaguely troubled by their strange, controlled physical tension. She had heard some of them at times break into almost hysterical laughter at things that had seemed hardly funny at all to her. All in all, Diana did not care for them. They talked almost constantly of cars. They were frightening, somehow, in their attractive ways. She had picked one as her favorite: a tall, modest blond youth named Swede Savage. She was going to root for him.

But amid the swirl of celebrities and glittering personages she had met during the month of May, she had found herself becoming most aware of one man who was not wealthy or famous. He was a photographer who had begun getting near her. Nicholas Alef. There was something about his attentiveness, his way of appearing out of the crowd and paying attention to her at certain moments when she felt alone or intimidated, something she couldn't put out of her mind; there was, above all, something about his eyes and the way he looked at her. It was not the devoted-spaniel look of Harry Kuntz, nor was it the practiced sexual appraisal of some of the drivers, nor was it the jaded lechery evident in the eyes of some of the older movie and television stars. No, this man Alef somehow looked straight into her, made her feel uncovered, yet did not intimidate her. He was unusually handsome, and a big, well-formed man, true, but it was more than that. In Nick Alef's look there was projected something full of portent. When he looked at her, she felt the way she had felt on the beauty-contest stage in her bathing suit with the eyes of an entire audience upon her.

Huddled here now in the protection of Harry Kuntz's raincoat, Diana was watching for Alef. Between the grandstands, echoing tunes of the bands overlapped. One nearby was playing the "Colonel Bogey March," while another farther down the track was playing an unrecognizable fast march that penetrated the rhythm of the nearer band and transformed it into mere noise. And interwoven were the echoing noise of the track announcer describing the parade, the distant cheers and whistles, the nearby shouts of organizers marshaling the bands and caravans, and her plastic rain hood rustling as the wind buffeted it.

Then she saw Nick.

He had not seen her yet and was walking toward one of the bands that were forming up ahead. Afraid he might vanish into the crowd, she ducked suddenly out of the shelter of Harry Kuntz's raincoat.

"Where are you going?" Harry called.

"I'll be back in just a minute!" she called back.

"But the caravan will—"

Piddle on the caravan, she thought. She wove among the milling people, stopping every few steps to rise on tiptoe and watch for Nick's dark head standing up from the crowd. It was good that he was so tall. Men smiled at her, and familiar faces loomed before her, greeting her, but she only smiled and said "Hi" to them, and craned to look over the heads of the mob, and pushed and wedged her way toward him.

He had stopped near the front of one of the high school bands when she caught up with him. A cute red-haired majorette with blue Doris Day eyes and muscular legs was preening, trying to arrange her windblown hair while Nick adjusted lens settings. Diana came up behind him and spoke close into his ear.

"Are you going to waste film on a little mongrel like that?"

He turned to see her laughing, but with mock menace

in her eyes. "Hey!" he cried. "I've been looking for you!"

"Unh-hunh. I can see you were." She was holding the rain hat ties at her throat with one hand. Her lips were set, challenging, teasing, firm.

"Hey, what about me?" came the voice of the red-haired majorette. Her face was in a pout.

"Uhm, listen, honey, I'll catch you later—marching, huh? Strut down the mainstretch. I'll film you there, okay?" The girl gave an exaggerated grimace and shrug, and turned back to the band.

"Hey, you gorgeous Princess, I'm glad to see you."

"Me, too."

"What about this crowd, huh?" He looked about for someplace where they could get out of the jostling mass. He put a big hand on her arm and led her to a fence, and she was very aware of the touch. Drums were thumping rhythmically a few feet away, and a plane went over noisily. Now that she had found him, Diana felt happy and excited about the whole event, now loving even the windy turbulence that had been annoying her only moments before. "Think we'll ever see each other without a million people around?" he asked, drawing her up against a chain-mesh fence and blocking passersby from her with his broad back.

"I don't know. Would you like that?"

"Would I ever! Listen, Diana, I've got something I've got to talk to you about. It's terrific." He took a deep breath and shifted the weight of the camera bag on his shoulder. "Tonight after the race, can you get free for a drink?"

She had hoped to hear something like this. "I don't know. There's the Victory Banquet. I have to—"

"Before that, then?"

"Where?" she asked. She felt reckless. This man wore a wedding band, but she was heartened by his attentions; if he was married, that was something they could get to when he was ready to mention it.

"Can you get to the Speedway Motel about six-thirty? The Flag Room lounge. Right off the lobby."

"Yes. Yes, I can." She liked the pleasure that spread over his face when she said yes. "What's it about, the big thing you've got to talk to me about?" She said it that way with a suggestion of a naughty double entendre in her expression.

"It's about some modeling. Big money. National exposure. It's—" His face was growing tense; he paused. "I'll tell you about it then. Here comes your ubiquitous chaperone."

"Oh, God, yes."

Harry Kuntz, his smooth face showing its perpetual hurt perplexity, had seen them and was swimming toward them through the crowd. "Diana, my dear," he called, "we have to be in the cars right away!"

"See you at six-thirty," she said, moving away to meet Harry. Nick stood in the midst of the hubbub and watched them go until Diana looked back at him. He winked at her and made an okay sign with his hand. A renewed sense of confidence was welling up in him.

Two people out of all these hundreds of thousands, he thought, coming together and recognizing that something was meant to happen from it. By God, I think she recognizes it, too!

"My gosh, I can't believe this! This is fantastic!" Pam Cole squealed. They took their chairs a few feet from the retaining wall. They were sitting almost at track level. Built atop the eighteen-inch-high concrete wall was a wire fence, and only that fence separated the Cole family from the track and the passing bands. A section of brass went by, playing "Seventy-six Trombones," and the musicians were so close one could see the blemishes and fuzz on the young men's bellowing cheeks. Drumbeats echoed back and forth among the grandstands. Whistles shrilled, and hundreds of shoe soles scuffed cadence.

Most of the bands had already marched past. Moving slowly, the colorful train of musicians could be seen stretching for half a mile along the curving racetrack, through the first turn and along the short south straightaway, where they were lost to sight beyond the masses of people and vehicles in the infield.

Cliff Cole stepped close to the wall and looked up the main straightaway. He couldn't believe the scale of this place. "I never saw so many folks in one place in all my blessed days, Marj!"

"Dad, I wanta go up to the pits and see the cars!" cried Kevin. He was grimacing and squirming with impatience.

"You just stay right here with us. You'll see those cars soon enough. They'll be goin' right under your nose, and it won't be more'n an hour or so."

"I can't wait an hour!"

"Sure, you can."

"Please lemme go! Pleeeeease!"

"Kevvie, you'd just get mixed up in that crowd—or lost —and you wouldn't get back here for the start of the race," Cliff Cole said. "Just settle down."

Keith, meanwhile, had taken a quick survey of the place, then had turned his attention to some teenaged girls in nearby seats. He had already found out their first names and knew they were from a town called Wingate. A quiet, shy boy, Keith always surprised everybody by getting acquainted in a hurry with the nearest pretty girls. They were quipping with him and giggling to each other.

Just then an unhappy murmur swept through the crowd, and a general stirring. Cliff Cole knew what it was about: he had just felt the cold kiss of a raindrop on his cheek, and then several more, and he heard the drops pelting on the nylon of his jacket and saw them spotting the pavement of the racetrack beyond the wall. As far as the eye could see now, people in the stands and the infield were moving in agitation, raising newspapers, hats, umbrellas, and plastic tarps over their heads.

"Shit!"

"Goddamnit!"

"Oh, for cryin' out—"

"Hey, Tony! Forget to renew your contract with God?"

"Ha-ha-ha!"

Keith didn't mind it. The people from Wingate had a plastic sheet up, and the girls had let him come in under it with them.

But the crowd was not happy. When the racetrack got wet, they knew, it could mean long delays. These cars couldn't race on a wet track.

*   *   *

Gerald and Ella Rumple always bought three tickets to the race. They explained that they liked to have the extra seat to put their picnic basket on. Actually, they always put the picnic basket under the bench, and the two of them easily filled the three seats with their broad posteriors.

Gerald and Ella were now sitting in their three seats in the Tower Terrace section just behind the pits inside the track, near the south end of the straightaway. Ella's closed transparent umbrella leaned beside her, and Gerald's black umbrella leaned beside him, its handle hooked over the backrest of the bench. Gerald got two Cokes out of the Styrofoam cooler, closed it and shoved it back under the seat, and snapped the tabs off the cans, looking up and down the track with happy attention while Ella scanned the pit area carefully with the binoculars. She was looking for A. J. Foyt. She always liked to have at least one look at his healthy, dimpled face before he was hidden by his helmet. And when she saw him, she would always say with a squeal of delight, "There he is! Hey, A.J.!" and raise her fist in the air, and then smile at herself because it was so unusual for such a quiet person as herself to yell out in public. And Gerald would smile at her and shake his head.

But today she didn't yell when she found A.J.'s face in the glasses. She remembered the little outburst in the car earlier when Gerald had said with such unexpected rancor in his voice, *"Your dear A.J.!"* Now she almost yelled for A.J., but restrained herself, and felt somehow a little strange and sad.

But it would be a good day in spite of that, she knew. Race Day was always a good day for them. The sheer size of the Speedway and the presence of so many people was like a sustained electrical charge in the air, and she could feel her heart beating faster as the moments of the ceremony came up one by one. She always felt her soul grow big and proud when they played the National Anthem, and she got tears in her eyes when the brass of the Purdue band played "Taps" and its sad notes hung echoing in the air, and she grew weak in the knees when Tony Hulman gave over the loudspeaker the order for the drivers to start their engines. And shivers went all over her when the thirty-three powerful engines burst into snarling, whooping life and the smell of the exhaust fumes blew over the stands.

They sat now and waited, taking turns with the binoculars, watching the busy men in the pits, looking for famous faces. The blended voices of the thousands of fans in the great Paddock and grandstands across the track sounded like a waterfall, and the familiar rich voice of the track announcer on the public-address system walloped back and forth in the space, inflected with enthusiasm and excitement. The Rumples were always eager for the race to start, but it wasn't boring to wait, because there was always so much to see.

But now, just as these familiar procedures were progressing, the skies fulfilled their threat: a chilly rain began pelting down, advancing eastward over the track and through the infield, and thousands of voices wailed in protest. There was a great wave of movement in the grandstands as countless umbrellas bloomed, plastic tarps and ponchos were raised, and many of the fans left their seats and scurried for cover.

"Oh, Jerry. How could it?"

Gerald shook his round head and smiled ruefully, and they raised their umbrellas. Ella shivered at the unexpected chill, drew her coat tighter around her, and watched the racing team crewmen hurriedly drape tarpaulins over the parked race cars and then huddle under the coverings themselves. Some of the crewmen just stood there on the pavement, their hands in their pockets, shoulders hunched up, hair beginning to grow wet and hang limply down, and scowled up at the traitorous sky.

Soon the pavements were wet enough that the people could be seen standing on their own inverted reflections. It was not a hard rain, but it kept sifting down.

"Don't worry," Gerald said. "The day's young. There'll be plenty of time for the track to dry and the race to start. Let's just relax and have something to eat."

Ella smiled tenderly at him. The rain pattered on their umbrellas. "Let's do," she said. "A little food in me probably would warm me up. I love you, Gerald."

"Well, as you must know, I love you, too, Dumplin'."

She smiled as he dug into the picnic basket. "I did see

A.J.," she ventured to say after a while. "And he's getting a little heavy."

"Hm-hm," replied Gerald, tearing some white meat off the bone with his nice, even teeth.

In Lloyd Skirvin's Mercury, Worms Marshall finally got loose enough to make the remark he had been saving up throughout the sustained hilarity. Waiting until the girls' giggles had subsided after Lloyd's last quip, he waved his beer can and yelled, "Hey, ever'body! Let's all get nekkid an' jump in a pile!"

The giggles broke out again, and Puggles grew especially agitated. Her face flushed, and she seemed unable to control her outburst. She hid her face behind her forearm and laughed until it seemed she would choke. Soon she was sucking air in feeble little gasps that sounded like hiccups.

Lloyd Skirvin turned slowly in the front seat until he was facing Worms, his eyes half-closed and his face an expression of mock resignation. He looked at Worms for several seconds with that expression and then said, "Mr. Marshall, if brains was dynamite, you wouldn't have enough to blow your nose, now, would you?"

"No, but maybe you'd like to blow my nose. Or blow something!" Worms Marshall didn't usually have the boldness to throw that kind of crack at Lloyd, but he was feeling pretty gamy just about then.

Lloyd gave him a sly smile and then said, "Tell you what, ol' buddy. Betya I can deck ya and dick ya before you can throw me and blow me."

That one got the upper hand away from Worms again. The girls went hysterical. Worms just never could hold his own very long in matching wits with that ol' Lloyd Skirvin. That ol' Movin' Mutha.

Puggles had drunk three beers and was giggling. She had scooted far down in the back seat and had her feet up on the back of the driver seat, and she was giggling at some of the things Lloyd Skirvin and Worms Marshall said to each other. They were sitting in the car in the infield parking area, and the rain was pattering on the car roof. Their clothes had gotten damp when the rain pursued them back from the infield area to their parked car. Worms was in the back seat with her, grinning a goofy grin and studying the shape of her thighs in the tight jeans. Lloyd and Renee were in the front seat drinking beer. The car windows were fogged, and rainwater was trickling down the outside of the glass. In the car it smelled of beer, gasoline, sweat, and some of the older blended smells of a car that has been used and lived in, and the conversation soon turned to the subject of odors.

"Worms ain't really strong," Lloyd said back over his shoulder. "He just smells that way."

"Fuck you!" Worms rejoined, with his nasal laugh. And the girls giggled.

"That ol' Worms," Lloyd went on. "He smell like a chitlin' fart in a shut-up car."

They all got another big laugh out of that. Worms had a mouthful of beer, and when he laughed he spewed it out all over Puggles. She took a sip of her beer and squirted it on him through the little gap between her front teeth. They tussled a little; Worms got a quick feel of one of her breasts, and it felt good. For a moment it made him speechless and hot in the face.

"What really smells bad, though," Lloyd was saying, "is—did you ever smell a goober-paste fart?"

Renee was shaking with laughter, such a release of laughter that she was afraid she was going to start crying. She felt the crying building up in her and suddenly was so crushingly miserable that she had to hold her breath to keep from sobbing out loud. After a while it passed, and she was silly-happy again, and no one had even noticed. "Oh, wow," she cried. "What's a goober-paste fart, anyway?"

"You know goober paste," Lloyd said. "You dam-yankees call it peanut butter."

"An' it do make a helluva-smellin' fart!" Worms shouted.

They had been getting along just fine like this ever since the girls had climbed into the car out by the Girls' School. They were all having a great time getting acquainted. These two guys didn't seem to care what they said, and Puggles's lewd-sounding laugh encouraged them to keep a real routine going at latrine level. Outside, the rain was easing up. Now and then someone would pass outside the window, a dim, distorted shape, usually huddled under a tarp or poncho, feet slopping and squishing in the rain-soaked turf.

All at once Puggles thought of something she needed to do.

"Hey, I gotta go for a minute."

"Go the hell where?"

"Uhm, the john."

"It's rainin'."

"I gotta go, anyway. It isn't raining so hard now. I'm wet, anyhow. I'll put my jacket over my head." She was straining forward now, reaching for the door handle. Worms grabbed her shirttail and held her for a moment.

"You come back, y'heah?" It was almost like a command.

"Sure! I wouldn't miss it!" Worms let go, and she climbed out. "You wanna go?" she asked Renee.

"No."

Puggles slipped her nylon jacket off and draped it over her head like a hood, and set off in the direction of the Tower. She made her way among parked vehicles that stretched in all directions as far as she could see. From within many of the cars came the muffled laughter, talk, and the cursing of people who were inside waiting out the rainshower. Here and there, other persons stalked about or hurried, many of them like herself shrouded against the rain, some simply going along sodden and stringy-haired, no longer fighting it. The air had grown chilly with the coming of the rain.

Puggles felt light-headed with the beer. She had never drunk beer in the morning before. And she had lain awake much of the previous night, unable to sleep because of the anxiety about running away. Now she walked toward the Tower, which seemed to be the central place where there would be toilets and telephones, and felt a curious dreaminess.

I ran away, she thought. How can I be walking around in plain sight in a crowded place like this?

It seemed she should be sneaking or hiding, but she knew in her mind that it wasn't necessary. It was that strange, loose-ends feeling she got sometimes. Often, in fact.

Nobody really gives a shit, she thought.

She had dimes in her pockets. She had made sure she had dimes. She was now coming near a long, high concrete structure. There were all kinds of flags along the top of it. In the rainy air she could smell meat cooking. She walked along a muddy pavement and kept watching for something, the thing for which she really had left the car. Then she found it:

PHONE

They finally waved Olive Canfield's car into a rank of cars that were being parked in a muddy meadow. She couldn't go any farther forward; the parked cars made a solid wall ahead of her. And she couldn't turn around and start back out because cars were still crowding in behind her.

At least, thank God, she could stop. She didn't want to be here, but the relentless crowding and honking had quit and she could turn off the car engine. The windshield wipers were moaning and clicking rhythmically, wiping away the rain that had started a few minutes earlier. When she switched off the ignition key, they stopped. She let her head drop back against the seat back, shut her eyes and let her mouth fall open, and took several long, deep breaths and waited for her heart to slow down. Rain drummed on the roof.

Never had she been through such a frustrating, intimidating experience. It seemed like another world she had started out from early this morning, on her way to work; it seemed like something that had happened ages ago. It seemed that she had been reincarnated into this automotive hell and had lived this whole present life carried along in a creeping mass of cars. She let out one long, shuddering breath, choked back an almost overwhelming desire to weep, and then got a Kleenex out of her handbag.

After a while, the rain eased off. People afoot were streaming past her car, carrying baskets and coolers, cameras and chairs. A woman walked in front of the car, her enormous hams working in tight-stretched black pants.

With her was a gaunt man wearing a hat covered with Budweiser labels. Everyone was moving in what Mrs. Canfield, in her disoriented state, felt was a westward direction.

All she knew was that she was inside the oval of the track now, and it would take her forever to get out. There was no use trying to drive out while traffic was still coming in. All she could do, she decided, was to find a telephone and call the bakery and tell her employer what had happened, and then come back and try to drive the car out after the rest of the crowd had stopped coming in.

She blew her nose in the tissue and unlatched the car door. And as she moved in the car seat, she felt the wetness, remembering with shame what she had done.

Using all the rest of the facial tissues out of her purse, she dried the seat as well as she could. If people saw her from behind, they would just have to think she had sat down on a rain-wet bleacher seat or something.

Shaky and weak, Mrs. Canfield got out of the car, pushed down the door latch button, and shut the door. She started across the field, following the moving mass of people. Her feet slid and sank in the trampled mud, and before long her shoes were wet and caked with the dark goo. She couldn't worry about a little mud. Her primary concern was getting to a phone. But she would have to keep her bearings so that she would be able to find her way back to her car. She made a mental note that it was three rows in front of a van that had lounge chairs set up on top and flew a Confederate flag, visible from anywhere in the infield. Then she slopped on. A damp wind was blowing, chilly now with a lingering drizzle of rain.

At last Mrs. Canfield arrived, breathing heavily, at a place where the muddy footpath gave onto a sidewalk leading among hedges and buildings. The people moving along this sidewalk seemed cleaner, better dressed, more civilized than the ones who had crowded the infield, and Mrs. Canfield felt a little less intimidated. She looked at the ordinary faces passing. She couldn't believe that people like this had been leaping from their cars to attack her simply because she had slowed their progress in traffic. It's incredible, she thought. What gets into people when they're in cars?

Suddenly she saw the sign that said PHONE. Her heart jumped up. She hurried toward it. Then stopped short. There was a line of ten or twelve persons lined up to use it.

Oh, dear God.

But she realized there would be just as many people at any other pay phone in a place where there were so many thousands of people.

Resigned, miserable, she took her place at the end of the line behind an unkempt adolescent girl in damp blue jeans with a wet jacket draped over her head. The girl turned and looked at her with dead eyes, and Mrs. Canfield could smell beer on the girl's breath.

Good God, she thought. What is this world coming to? And she began waiting.

Puggles had to stand in line for quite a while to get her turn at the phone. There were lines of people at the phone booths and at the concession stands and at the rest rooms. People were standing in the drizzle everywhere, waiting while other people walked past on their way from somewhere to somewhere, peering out from under the edges of whatever they wore over their heads for shelter. Behind Puggles there was an elderly woman in a pink waitress dress, looking very uptight.

Finally Puggles got into the phone booth. She dropped in her dime and dialed the familiar number. The mouthpiece of the phone smelled like onion. She looked around as the phone rang. Everything was gray except the colors of people's clothes constantly going by. Rain hissed on the roof of the booth.

"Hello?" said a spiritless woman's voice.

Puggles didn't say anything. She waited a few seconds.

"Hello?" said the woman again, a slight edge of anxiety now audible in her voice.

Puggles waited a moment longer. Then she said, "Hi, Mom."

There was a caught breath, then a pause. "Mary?"

"Yeah, Mom."

"Aren't you at the—the—the school?" It always shook

her mother up to have to speak of the place. Puggles smiled at that.

"No."

"You aren't?" The tone of alarm was stronger.

"I walked away, Mom."

"Oh, God, Mary! Why do you keep doing these things to me?"

Puggles smiled. She had known she would hear that.

"Haven't they even called you from the school, Mom?"

"No, they haven't yet, Mary, but—"

Nobody really gives a shit.

"Well, I'm okay, Mom. I just wanted to call and tell you I'm okay."

"What do you mean okay! Where are you?" The voice was getting frantic. "Mary, are you with anybody? Tell me!"

"I'm with some friends. 'Bye, Mom, I've gotta go."

"Wait! Honey, are you with boys?"

Puggles smiled, looking at the mouthpiece of the phone.

"Not boys, Mom," she said. "Men."

"Mary! Mary! Please, wait! Why do you do these things to—"

Puggles hung the phone up. Now she felt better.

The young girl with the beery breath hung up the phone with a little smile on her mouth, and Olive Canfield was glad she had made her call so brief.

Her wet clothing feeling icy where it touched her skin, Mrs. Canfield handled her dime and the telephone dial with shivery fingers. Mr. Sanders, the bakeshop owner, answered in an unpleasant voice, and in her mind Mrs. Canfield could see him scowling over the rims of his little steel spectacles, his flushed, round face waiting for an explanation.

"Mr. Sanders, I'm sorry I didn't get the shop opened this—"

"Why in hell aren't you here? Did I say we were going to be closed today?"

"No, you didn't, Mr. Sanders. I tried to come in, but I—"

"I don't want any excuses! This place has to open on time or there's not enough time for the mixing and the baking! Do you realize the trouble you've caused by not being here to open?" Her mind's eye saw the stainless-steel machinery in the bakeshop kitchen, the machinery with its temperature gauges and switches. It ran their lives: Mr. Sanders's life, and hers, and the lives of the other people who worked for the bakery. Things had to be done at particular times, no matter how annoying it might be for the people.

Mr. Sanders's voice had fallen still, and she realized he had said or asked something and was waiting for her answer.

"Mr. Sanders, I got caught in the Race Day traffic and they wouldn't give me any chance to turn around and now I'm in the Speedway and—" She paused, almost crying, having reminded herself again of the ordeal.

There was a long pause, then he said, "Then why in hell are you talking to me on this telephone, I ask you, instead of driving back out of that Speedway and getting here to work? You like your job, Mrs. Canfield?"

"Of course I like it. I just—I just thought I'd better call you and explain—"

"Explanations I don't need. I need you here."

"It will take me awhile to get back out of here, Mr. San—"

"It better not!" he yelled, and the receiver banged down in her ear.

Seldom had Olive Canfield been chewed out in her life. She had always conducted herself in such a way that she would not give people cause to raise their voices at her. When it did happen, she became intimidated and her heart speeded up and she had to sit for a minute or two to get hold of herself or she could not go on. She paused now, with her fingertips pressed on her eyelids.

But suddenly she was jolted out of it by angry voices. She opened her eyes and looked up, and there were many faces yelling at her.

Of course. She had forgotten: there were people standing in line in the drizzle waiting for the telephone while here she was not even using it. Suddenly flustered and full of apologies, Mrs. Canfield left the booth, went with bent

head past the people waiting in line, trying not to hear
their ugly mutterings, and headed back toward her car.

Gerald and Ella Rumple knew what to do when
everything else failed: eat. They sat under Ella's umbrella,
huddling together for warmth, and made a picnic. They
cleaned the bones of about a third of the chicken in their
basket, and each had two deviled eggs. They munched and
watched the crowd and the cars. Half of the race cars
were on the track in their starting positions. The others
were in the pits. All the cars were covered with water-
proof shrouds of various colors. One could see only their
wheels: the wide black tires, the steel hubs. Under some
of the tarps, crew members sat on the pavement leaning
with their backs against their beloved cars and gazing
dolefully out at the wet pavement. The cars looked like
enormous Frankenstein creations full of still, dormant
power and needing to be unveiled and brought to life by
their creators. The announcer was still talking, and in the
distance there were band instruments playing in the rain.
   A young couple sitting in front of the Rumples had
been caught without umbrellas, and Gerald had looked
at their wet hair and felt sorry for them and wished he
had a tarp to share with them. He had given them his
umbrella. Gerald wondered what it would be like to have
a grown son and daughter-in-law or a daughter and son-
in-law who could come to the races with them and sit here
near them, smiling and giggling and touching each other
and enjoying even a rainy day in the bleachers. As usual,
the thought of the children they didn't have left Gerald
with a vague sadness. He thought fondly of Allan and
Janet Roepke, then sighed, edged closer to Ella, and
peeled the foil off another piece of chicken. It was
a breast, so he wrapped it again and rummaged until he
found a thigh. The young couple opened a bottle of cham-
pagne. They laughed as the cork popped out, arced
through the air, and bounced off an umbrella down in the
front row. They offered the first two glasses to Gerald
and Ella, and in return accepted two pieces of Ella's
chicken.
   After a while, Ella shuddered and said she needed to

go to the bathroom. Asking the young people to guard their things, they made their way down the concrete steps and back through the milling, squinting, damp crowd of fans in Gasoline Alley to the rest rooms behind the stands.

Mud had been tracked into the men's room, and there were paper towels and ribbons of sodden toilet paper underfoot. There was a constant salvo of flushing as men milled in and out. Gerald never could urinate when there were people standing alongside at the urinal troughs, so he waited until one of the doorless toilet stalls was vacant, and went in to use it. It had stopped up and was full to the brim with an evil-looking stew of paper and excrement. Gerald couldn't look as he urinated into it. He washed his hands. He went back outside and waited for Ella at the door of the women's rest room. The rain had stopped. A small boy slopped past wearing a profuse set of goose pimples and a T-shirt with the message:

I'M A LITTLE RACE DRIVER

Gerald's clothes were damp, and he shivered. A dirty youth with long hair and a headband went by, holding onto a stiff, straight leash with a dog collar on the end of it, holding the collar a few inches above the sidewalk so that he appeared to be leading an invisible dog. Gerald grinned at the sight. The youth paused in front of him and squeezed a rubber bulb that made the collar squirt a small stream of water onto Gerald's foot. Then he walked on, led by his invisible but obviously relieved dog.

Finally Ella emerged from the ladies' room, looked up at the wet gray sky, and joined Gerald under the umbrella. "Thought you'd fallen in," he said. "What took you so long?"

She rolled her eyes and made an expression of ruefulness on her fat face. "You ever try to pull up wet panty hose?"

"We've had chances over the years to fill in because of delays in the race," said the voice of Sid Collins on the radio. For a quarter of a century he had been broadcasting the Indianapolis "500" to audiences around the world

on the Indianapolis Motor Speedway Network. *"Unfortunately, back in 1964 when it was stopped for the first time in its history—in 1966 for the first-lap accident, another hour and a half, and then in 1970, we had some rain, as you may recall, about thirty minutes or so, as we thought we might have for today—and then Jim Malloy unfortunately hit the wall coming out of turn four as they came down on the pace lap to take the green flag—so at that time we had further time to chat."*

Nick Alef stalked in the waiting crowd with his telephoto lens. A red-haired girl with long, suntanned legs, wearing a miniskirt and a rain jacket with a Champion Spark Plug decal on the back, was making her way up the steps of the Tower Terrace. Nick aimed up from the pit area, got her in his sights, and followed her like a sniper. He filmed as fast as the camera would advance, and on the fifth frame something fortuitous happened: a fat man in an aisle seat, wearing a saggy yellow rain hat, turned as she climbed past him, stuck the point of his furled umbrella under the rear hem of her skirt, and raised it a few inches, peering at her exposed backside for a moment. There was the merest wisp of white panties between her untanned buttocks.

Ha! Perfect! Nick thought. The girl went on up the aisle, unaware that her posterior had been recorded for posterity. Nick wrote in his notebook: *5/28/*A.M. *Rl. 6. #21. T.T. lecher. buns. Ntl. Enq?*

Gazing around then after that concentration, his perception of the vast, wet, rushing, murmuring spaciousness suddenly swelled, as when one emerges from dense undergrowth to find oneself at the brink of a broad valley. This sense of expansion, following so quickly his focused attention upon the girl's fundament, seemed deliciously absurd. It was the kind of exhilarating absurdity he used to feel years ago before his mind grew benumbed by reality, by disappointments.

And now Nick thought, as if he were receiving some vision: A quarter of a million people sitting in the rain looking at a wet street that goes nowhere.

He turned, his gaze sweeping the hundreds of acres of

shivering, gray-faced people, and wagged his head in almost delirious appreciation.

What an epic sight gag! he thought.

He started laughing.

Some wet people went by. They looked at him. They looked at each other.

They shrugged.

The rain slackened off.

The Celebrity Caravan, made up of Cadillac Eldorado convertibles carrying people of various degrees of national or local renown, set off around the track. It made three-fourths of a lap and then had to stop because some of the race cars were still lined up above the starting line.

After the race cars were moved off, wrecker trucks began pulling out onto the track and running fast laps in twos and threes to speed the drying of the track.

Nick Alef was standing at trackside when an announcer buttonholed Senator Barry Goldwater for a few remarks. Nick took pictures of the Arizona senator, his wisps of silver hair blowing in the wind, grinning his tight slash of a grin.

"I've been threatening to do a little sun dance around out here," Goldwater said as the trucks swished by. "And if I could find a snake, I'd do it."

Renee was tired. She had lain awake almost all the previous night thinking of their impending escape from the Girls' School, and it had been a long, hilarious morning in the car with Puggles and Lloyd and Worms. She had drunk five beers, had staggered away twice to a crowded outhouse in the infield to pee, and had gotten lost both times, wandering almost a half hour in the mud and grass among cars and people with rain sifting down on her. Now it was warm and dry in the car, and the beer had made her mind fuzzy. She closed her eyes. Worms and Lloyd were making jokes now and then, and occasionally Puggles would start giggling, but mostly they just listened to the radio and grew sleepy. Renee opened her eyes and vaguely saw Lloyd—lean, hard Lloyd with his mean half smile—propped up against the door with his arm over the steering wheel, looking her over. She tried to smile at him, then shut her eyes again and let the radio talk fill up her head.

"Let's see if Chuck Marlowe is still standing by in the pit area."

"Right, we are, Sid. We're underneath a plastic tarpaulin ourselves and watching the crews move cars around in these pits, and the crew of Lee Kunsman is sheltered under the airfoils, or the wing, on the rear of car number sixteen—a couple of others under plastic tarpaulins—and, uh, for the most part the activity has subsided here—a little bit of laughing and releasing of tensions, and watching the skies, too. Bob Harkey is standing under an umbrella—he's offered it to Mel Kenyon, so they're standing there laughing and kidding among themselves. So the tension's not quite as high as it was a few moments ago."

Renee half-opened her eyes one more time, vaguely saw the grayness and the rain-streaked windows and the dark forms of the dashboard and Lloyd Skirvin through her woozy senses. Then she shut her eyes one more time and went to sleep, not even aware that Lloyd's right hand was on her thigh.

Nick Alef took a few photos of Mel Kenyon and Bob Harkey—both very durable Speedway veterans—and then saw that Kenyon was smiling at him, a gentle, amused smile such as a minister might give while shaking hands with his flock after Sunday morning service. "You'll break your camera, friend," Kenyon said. The driver didn't know Nick's name, Nick was sure, but whenever they met, Kenyon was pleasant to him and called him "friend." Kenyon was nice to everybody. He was unusual among drivers. He was never arrogant, never boisterous; he never posed as a stud. He just seemed always to appreciate anything and everything. Kenyon was not a robust-looking man. His eyes, despite their fine, crinkled smile lines, were faintly ringed with the darkness of one who has suffered long illness or pain. But even his eyes, and the burn scars that mottled his features, failed to dim his pleasant, naive-looking boyishness. It seemed almost outlandish in this milieu, but Kenyon radiated what his admirers knew was the spiritual peacefulness of religious faith. Nick Alef, cynic though he had come to be, always felt a little envious of it; then he would feel embarrassed for having envied. He felt that he could have it himself just by saying the words of acceptance down inside himself, but he had never been quite able to say those words in his adult life. They seemed too corny.

"Well, good luck out there today," Nick said. "If they ever get it started."

"Luck?" Kenyon replied, nodding and grinning. "Sure. God willing."

He'd always do that to you. Bring God into it. Apparently, he believed God was riding with him; he gave God credit for his three USAC Midget Championships and for bringing him out alive when he was critically burned in a wreck at Langhorne, Pennsylvania, in 1965. Kenyon talked about his faith and wrote verses about it. On a pink card among his memorabilia in a drawer at home, Nick Alef had a verse Kenyon had given him once at a party. It was called "Practice and Qualification," and it read:

> Throttle, Torque, and Traction, friend,
>   Will set you on the pole.
> They're an added blessing
>   Everywhere you go.
> It would help an awful lot
>   If you would make just one pit stop
> And ask the Lord to share
>   Everything He's got.
> Patience can be yours, you know.
>   Courtesy to others show.
> You can even smile
>   When friends go by.
> Pleasure's tach goes out of sight
>   When everything is set up right.
> Because you know He is The Way
>   The Truth—The Life.

Nick thought he understood what was so strange about Kenyon. Kenyon was in the hero business, but, unlike heroes, he didn't try to upstage God.

Heroes have to be heroes on their own, Nick mused. If men perform heroism for God, they're not heroes, they're saints and martyrs.

Nick remembered something from his own novel, *Hubris*. His protagonist, a hero, had reflected on this very thing, and had penned a verse:

> Ashamed to kneel,
> afraid to die,
> his universe within his eye,
> wee man hurls pride
> into the face
> of God, eternity, and space.

"Well, then," he said to Kenyon, who stood smiling at him in the damp air in an arena among hundreds of thousands of impatient people, *"God willing,* you'll have luck."

Kenyon nodded, still smiling, and they went their separate ways.

Gene and Ruthie Roepke, of Northside Chicago, were staying dry in their seats near the outside of the fourth turn. Gene Roepke was a man of foresight and always had everything one might need when leaving home. He and Ruthie were snug inside rain suits with hoods.

Gene and Ruthie didn't talk much to each other except when they were with their children or with friends. It was not because of any shortcoming in their marriage; they just didn't have much to talk about, or much desire to talk. Ruthie was involved in women's clubs, and Gene's mind was always full of the problems and statistics of the carpet industry, so the two of them were quiet and self-contained together. They became loquacious only when dining and partying with old, familiar friends, such as the Rumples in Indianapolis.

Just now, Gene was watching the continuous procession of trucks and wreckers going around and around the racecourse, trying to help dry the moisture on it.

Hope this quits and dries off pretty soon, he thought. This is an awful lot of people to be wasting so much time.

"It's going to be impossible to get in touch with Gerald and Ella and change our dinner plans if this gets delayed too long," he said.

"Give me the glasses," Ruthie said. "I want to see if I can see them."

He gave the binoculars to her. "You'll never spot them in this crowd. Even as big as they are."

"Oh, now, that's not nice to say about your friends," she said, raising the glasses and aiming off in the direction of the Tower Terrace.

"I meant it in a nice way." That was one reason why Gene preferred not to talk a whole lot with Ruthie. He'd always have to mean things in certain ways.

She scanned the Tower Terrace slowly, methodically. The place where she knew the Rumples would be seated was about half a mile away. And the sloping stands were alive with people, as dense as the pile of a carpet. Most were under umbrellas or other makeshift shelters, so she gave it up and put the glasses in her lap. She sighed. "Wish the kids were here."

"Yeah. Or us there."

"That would be even better." Ruthie was getting very tired of this.

"Well, shit," a woman's voice said loudly beside Ruthie. " 'Scuse my language," the woman said when they turned to look at her. She was tall and solid, with gray-brown hair and a gap where one of her big front teeth was missing. "I just get all hyped up for this goddamn thing, and I hate it when I have to sit on my butt and wait."

Gene and Ruthie nodded.

"I'm Ivy Yarbrough," the woman said.

"Gene Roepke. And this is my wife, Ruthie."

"Hope I don't shock you," Ivy Yarbrough said. "I'm just excitable."

"It's okay."

"Sure. You'll get used to me before the day's over. HEY! Let's get go-ing! Let's get go-ing!"

A slight, sharp-eyed old man in a checkered cap sat in the driver's seat of an ancient Delage race car. Around him stood several of the race drivers, looking at him, smiling, laughing, pretending to talk with him. The old man looked from one to another of the photographers who stood crowded in front of the car, and smiled. Now and then he would look at the race drivers and say something in French, and they would pretend they understood him and laugh, and then the old man would laugh and look at the cameras again. A handsome, stocky, nattily dressed old man with a suntanned face moved close to the old Frenchman's left and grinned for the lensmen. Nick Alef shot a couple of frames, then backed out of the crowd and wrote in his notebook: *Rl. 20. 5/28. 1914 winner Rene Thomas & 1925 winner Pete DePaolo. Posed. Vestiges past glories. Try Star-News and racing pubs.*

A great shudder passed through Nick. The water from the wet pavements had finally seeped through his shoes, and his socks were wet. The shoulders and sleeves of his corduroy jacket were wet from the rain, and so was his hair. The wind felt icy. It seemed like anything but a spring day.

Come on, damnit, he thought. Enough is enough.

"The sky looks a little bit darker now, unfortunately. Mr. and Mrs. Edward Cole—he's president of General Motors Corporation, honorary starter for this year's race, and Mrs. Cole, Dollie Cole, will be riding in the pace car— Raymond Firestone, chairman of the board of Firestone Tire and Rubber Company, is honorary— honorary steward this year, he's been a referee— The last woman chosen to fill an honorary position for any Indianapolis 500-Mile Race was the late Amelia Earhart, internationally famous aviatrix—she was an honorary referee here in 1935— It was at ten-forty this morning that Harlan Fengler told the fourteen drivers with their cars on the track to move them back to the pits so the Speedway trucks and firefighting vehicles could run around and help dry the surface, and that's what's going on right now. Now stay tuned for the Greatest Spectacle in Racing."

*   *   *

Nick Alef paused near one of the Cadillacs. He cupped his hands expertly around a match to shield it from the wind and lit a cigarette.

Beside the car a young Air Force captain stood alone, his downcast eyes and troubled expression apparently discouraging anyone from approaching him. Nick had seen him in the parade the day before; he was one of the recently liberated prisoners of war. Obviously, he was a bewildered and disturbed man. He was very lean, and his hair was blond, fine and wavy. His chin was narrow and cleanly sculpted, his delicately shaped mouth seemed infirm, and his eyes were deep, frightened, vulnerable-looking, like the eyes of a cornered small woods mammal of some kind. Some quality in his face held Nick's attention and drew it away from the surrounding noisy activities.

Nick studied the man's campaign ribbons and deduced that this had been a combat airman, probably one of those who had streaked through the Vietnamese skies in the intricate cockpits of million-dollar flying machines, touching electronic triggers to dump bombs, bullets, and fire on people on the ground.

And then suddenly, Nick imagined, something had gone wrong and the flying weapon had disintegrated against a mountainside or on a forest floor, and its young, clean-shaven, skillful operator had drifted to earth on a parachute to find his own sensitive body abruptly involved in a new, very personal, and very carnal kind of a war, a flesh-and-blood, eye-to-eye war instead of a remote-controlled-machine war.

Nick looked at the withdrawn young airman and remembered his own involvement in that flesh-and-technology war when, in the mid-1960s, he had been in South Vietnam for many months as a photographer for the Associated Press. He remembered the humid, lush green, the paddies stinking with sun-ripened corpses, the scorched, pulverized landscapes, red blood on yellow dirt, the stunned and burned faces of childish-looking soldiers and aged-looking children. He remembered the shrill, nonhuman sounds of long-distance death in the air: jet planes, missiles, artillery shells, bullets—all dispensed by such technicians as this frail-looking young captain in his smart-looking blue uniform. And Nick also remembered how he had watched the whole war through the view-finder of a camera. He remembered taking photographs from ten feet away as a bound prisoner was shot through the head with a pistol; he remembered taking pictures as men's glistening intestines slid out onto the ground. The Vietnam War for him had been a series of ghastly images, the capturing of instants of incomprehensible mayhem.

He remembered, too, his first evening at home after his return to the United States; he remembered lying naked in bed with Becky after intercourse, watching the Vietnam War on the "Late News" and thinking for the first time how odd it was that such bloody images were being produced as a show—that was the word that had come to his mind: a *show*—brought to the great American television audience through the courtesy of finance companies, potato-chip manufacturers, muffler shops, and cosmetics makers.

And the show had been so well produced over the long years, Nick mused, that the television watchers had seen the faraway events even more clearly than the people who had been there actually doing it and getting it done to them.

But of course, he thought. You don't see something clearly if you're inside it.

That first evening at home had been the occasion that stretched Nick's sense of the absurd so far that it had never really snapped back to its original delightful dimensions.

Nick studied the young officer, who was still not aware that he was being watched so thoughtfully. Imagine, Nick thought, going through however many years of the very serious business of being a prisoner of war in North Vietnam and then coming back and immediately being paraded around as a part of this big sight gag. Seems like that would be a hard transition to make, he thought.

He dropped his cigarette on the ground, where it soaked up rainwater and hissed out.

I don't blame you for looking so bewildered, buddy, he thought.

*   *   *

Most of the people in the seats near the Cole family had remained there when the rain started. Even with tarps and umbrellas it was impossible to remain completely dry. Wind blew the chilly rain under those coverings. Cliff Cole held Marjorie in the crook of his left arm to keep her warm, and held the umbrella up with his right hand. The right sleeve of his jacket was soaked, and he shivered as if it were a November day instead of late May.

"Hooo, boy!" Marjorie said with a big sigh. "What funsies. I could skin that Kevin for getting us into this mess."

"Well, now, Kevin didn't—isn't entirely—"

"Sure he is. And you always go along with it."

"I?"

"Never mind. I guess we both do. Where is he now? Can you see him?"

"He went up toward the pits there when they started moving the rest of the cars off the track. Wanted to see them move. Even at a creep he wants to see them move."

"I wouldn't mind a little moving myself," she said. "Myself out of here and into a warm car going home to Kokomo."

It was hard to hear because a fleet of some eighty or ninety wreckers was going around and around the track at high speeds, trying to blow some of the wetness off the track. The race fans had begun cheering some of the trucks as if this were the race. Laughter went up when a garbage truck roared by and swung into the first turn. In lulls Cliff Cole could hear snatches of Sid Collins's famous Memorial Day "500" broadcast from a nearby radio. Collins had come on the air before the rain started and had been ad-libbing race lore and gabbing with other announcers and with racing celebrities in a valiant effort to keep his millions of listeners entertained during the delay. The broadcast was punctuated every few minutes with commercials for frankfurters and for STP Oil Treatment additive and Cadillac cars.

"ONE FOR THE MONEY, TWO FOR THE SHOW . . . STP."

Cliff Cole and millions of others listening to the radio learned that rain had postponed the race for two days in

1915, and for two hours in 1931, and had closed it down after 400 miles in 1926, and after 345 miles in 1950. They soaked up this data, which had been culled from somewhere in the vast archives of "500" history.

"It may be possible to start this race pretty much on time," opined one of the radio voices.

On time, my butt, thought Cliff Cole.

"We'll say 'when,' not 'if,' " another radio voice said encouragingly.

"We'll get a race in today, I'm sure of that," said the famous radio voice of Collins.

Then, during a station break, just after all the announcers had talked about how quickly the track was drying, Cliff Cole felt raindrops on his hand again. A collective groan went up all around as the new sprinkle turned into another downpour.

"Honey," Marjorie implored, "why don't you just send Pam or Keith to find Kevin and let's go home."

"No, wait. This may not last long."

"I may not, either," snapped Marjorie, drawing a little away from him. "You're as bad as Kevin. You actually *want* to see this dumb thing, don't you?"

"Well, not all that much. But by the time we found Kevin this rain'd probably by over with, anyway, and—"

"Never mind, *never mind.*"

Werner Dold stood at the window of his VIP suite and gazed out at the damp asphalt of the racetrack's second turn. Every few seconds, trucks roared through the turn below the balcony and up the backstretch, their tires hissing. Beyond the track and the green grass was a huge fenced-in field of people waiting under any kind of rain cover they could improvise. They looked like a nation of hobos. On the outside of the asphalt racecourse, hundreds of yards of towering grandstands curved away to the west and north, also filled with people huddled against the rain. Doc Upton stood beside Werner, and behind them their wives were talking and dropping ice cubes into glasses.

"What you ought to do, Werner, is investigate a newer racetrack. Like the one at Ontario, California."

"Why do you say that?" Werner Dold knew Doc was wrong, but he believed that an intelligent man should listen carefully to all sides of an argument. Many of the world's most successful men listened with special attention to their adversaries' rationales, or at least claimed in their autobiographies to have done so.

"Well," said Doc, "this place is obsolete. Its configuration hasn't changed since 1911. You know that. And at the speeds they run now— But the main thing—from your standpoint—is that it's landlocked. There's no room to solve the traffic and parking problems. You saw the mess we came through to get here. It just gets worse every year. You've seen the Ontario track, how much safer, how much roomier it is. And goddamnit"—he laughed—"it doesn't rain there."

Werner took the highball Kitty had brought to him, kissed her on the forehead, and smiled. "That's how little you understand about racing, Nobe. And race fans."

"How in hell can you say that? I haven't missed a race since 1936. And I've been on the '500' Festival Committee—"

"I know all that. But you and your Festival people. Your social set. You watch the race from a VIP suite like this, sipping highballs. Sure, the way you watch a race, you *would* appreciate Ontario. But I've got it in my mind that for the ordinary race fan, Ontario's too sanitary."

"What's this 'too sanitary'?" To Doc Upton, "sanitary" was a good word—nothing could be too sanitary.

"I think a race fan wants to be close down where he can see all the details. He wants to hear the drivers and mechanics talk, feel the vibrations, smell the fuel and rubber and all that. When a car crashes, he wants to be close enough to breathe the smoke and see the driver die."

"Oh, Gawd," Kitty said, making a face and turning away toward a chair. "Yuck."

"That's a whole lot different from just watching it with your eyes," Werner went on. "You might as well just watch it on a screen if *seeing* is all you want. Admit it, now. Just watching a race is boring. I've seen you. You start talking about other things, you mix drinks. You only turn your attention back to the track for the finish.

Or for accidents. No, Nobe, if I ever buy a track, it'll be this one. This is the one that brings the fans in by the hundreds of thousands, because they can get right close to it."

"Well, I'll tell you," Doc Upton said after a while. "Maybe you and your garden-variety race fans do need to get down to the midst of it, and smell and taste and feel it, as you say. As for me, I get enough real-life groping and sniffing around in people's viscera. So when I go out for a day at the races, I'll just watch from a nice, clean, high place, if it's all the same to you."

"I just wish you'd buy it or not buy it," Kitty said. "You don't take ten minutes to decide anything else. You've been talking about this thing since before we got married." Werner didn't answer but continued to sweep his eyes back and forth over the crowd. Doc looked at him and imagined he could hear Werner's brain calculating profits at so many dollars' admission a head.

"Kitty, my deah," Mrs. Upton drawled elegantly, "it's such a pity you were in Florida and missed all the festival parties and things. Oh! Such a season!"

"It must have been just gala-gala," Kitty said, scarcely disguising the mockery. Werner turned his head and aimed a slight warning frown at her. She saw it and amended her tone. "I am sorry I missed it all. But I did have a marvy time in Miami, so I'll survive."

"Oh, I'm sure you did. But you *must* let me show you some of Indianapolis while you're here."

"Love to, but we're only here for the day." She knows that, Kitty thought. That's why she offered.

"Well, if they don't get this race started, you won't be leaving today, will you, Werner?" said Doc.

"No, we'll stay for it."

"Well, listen, all," Kitty said, draining off her drink. "You must excuse me. I've got to go freshen up. Flying makes me feel so gritty." She went to the door and opened it. "I might take a nap. If the race ever starts, knock on the wall for me."

"If the race starts, you'll hear it easier than you'll hear a knock on the wall," Doc said.

Kitty blew a kiss around the room, looking wearily at the two stout men and the stout woman, and postponed a yawn until she was outside.

"Good-bye for now, dahling," came Mrs. Upton's voice through the closing door.

Locking herself into the adjacent suite, Kitty flung herself onto the bed and lay on her back for a few minutes, gazing at the ceiling. She had used all her wit to attain the condition of the idle rich, then had found to her great surprise that she didn't know how to handle indolence. Sometimes even shopping would pall on her, and she would nearly climb the walls for want of a purpose in life.

She sighed and got up. She drew the drapes slowly, looking out at the balcony with its chairs a few feet above the racetrack. She stripped off her clothes and threw them over a chair, went into the bathroom, and turned on the water in the tub. She tested it with her hand under the spigot, dribbled in some bath oil, then went back to the bed and stretched out on it to wait for the tub to fill. She examined her breasts with her hands, then stroked her flanks. She raised her legs, alternately, sticking them straight up and watching their smooth muscularity as she rotated each foot on its ankle.

Then she turned onto her side and lay with her head propped on her hand, thoughtful. She looked at the telephone on the bedside table, then stood up, walked around the room a couple of times, and suddenly sat down on the edge of the bed. She lifted the telephone directory out of its stand, opened it near the front, and lay down on her side again. She turned pages, then ran an orange-nailed finger down a column. She wasn't sure the name would be there. It had been so many years, and her own life had been so transient it was hard to imagine someone would still be in the same old city. . . .

There it was.

She read the name several times, while the bathwater roared.

There was nothing to do about it. She simply had had to look and see. That was all. She shut her eyes, shut the phone book, exhaled, and put the book back in its stand.

Then she turned the radio on and got into the bathtub.

Kitty couldn't figure out what was wrong today. She lay in the tub dry-eyed but feeling as if she wanted to cry.

She was not one who cried. She used her mind, not her feelings. There had been many men through her life in the last ten years, and not one of them had made her lose her head and cry. And she did not lose her head in passion. No matter what was going on with her body, no matter how much she enjoyed it, she always kept her head. Werner had said to her once, "Do you have any idea how disconcerting it is to a man that you have your eyes open while he's doing this to you?" She had smiled at him and closed her eyes. Since then she had made herself keep her eyes closed while Werner was doing it to her. But only her real eyes. The eye of her mind always stayed open. Kitty had a motto that she had never told to anyone:

Never let them fuck your brains.

You don't get a lead in movies or marry a billionaire by letting anybody fuck your brains. If you let them do that, they get what they want and you end up with nothing. She had seen it happen to too many chicks who let producers and agents and actors and whatnot fuck their brains.

Don't cry about men, and don't shut your eyes when they're doing it to you, she thought. She had made up a proverb about it:

Your brain is your survival kit.

And sometimes she thought of it this way:

Your brain is your survival, Kit.

The man who had taught her the pleasure of playing with words was also the only man who had ever fucked her brains.

Now that she had everything she had ever thought she wanted, she often caught herself thinking about that man. But here she was in his hometown, and there was nothing she could do about it.

Olive Canfield looked for the van with the lounge chairs on top and the Confederate flag, and when she saw it, she had little trouble locating the row where her car was parked. She went around to the driver's side and took hold of the door handle. It wouldn't open, and she remembered then that she had locked it.

She rummaged in her purse for the key, shivering. It wasn't there. She looked into the car. The keys were in the ignition.

Oh, no.

Barely hoping, she went around the car trying the doors. They were locked.

She tilted her head back, looking up at the overcast sky, shut her eyes, exhaled a long sigh through her nose, and tried to keep herself from screaming. She didn't scream. She stood there for a moment staring at the car with hatred blazing in her eyes. She put her purse on the hood of the car and started looking through it for something she could use to get the car open.

The only thing that looked as if it might work was a rat-tail comb. Standing in the mud, shuddering with chills, she tried to insert it past the edge of the vent window to move the latch. Immediately the tail of the comb snapped off. Darn! she thought.

A family went by, a man and woman and one adolescent girl. They were carrying a picnic basket. "Oh, sir," she called. "Wait!" They paused. "Listen," she said "Can you help me get my car window open? My keys are locked inside."

"Uhm, no. Look, uhm, we gotta get to our seats. Sorry."

"It would just take a minute! Don't you have a pocket-knife or something?"

"Uhm, no. I never carry a knife, ma'am." He started to turn away.

"Wait, wait! Maybe you have a knife or a fork or something in your picnic basket?"

"Well—" The man started to put the basket on the ground.

His wife snapped, "George, if you bend up my silver-ware—"

The man's face reddened. He said, "I'm sorry, lady, I don't think we can help you. Why'n'cha just break your window?" And the family moved away.

Why don't I break the window? she thought. Because I can't afford to have it replaced, that's why not. Especially now that I probably don't have a job anymore.

And she walked off through the mud again, hoping to find somebody who might have tools. Or even just a wire coat hanger. Be patient, Mr. Sanders, she thought. You may still see me today, you slave driver.

Olive saw a young, heavyset man standing between a pickup truck and a car, his back toward her. Maybe he has a tool, she thought. "Oh, sir, could you help me, please?" she said.

He turned his head toward her. "Yeah?" She gasped, averted her face, and put her hand over her eyes. He was making a foamy puddle in the mud before him.

"I'm sorry," she said. "I didn't realize—"

"Be right with ya, ma'am," he said, chuckling. "Okay, now, ma'am." He came toward her, zipping up his trousers. "What c'n I do fer ya?"

He had a round, loutish face, wet red lips, and red eruptions amid the black stubble of his neck. His long hair was dirty and greasy. His eyes looked red and glassy. She smelled beer.

But you can't be choosy, she told herself. So she explained to him the predicament of her locked car.

"Shoot-a-bug, ma'am. Ain't a car made, ol' Billy Joe Marshall cain't git into. Show me where."

He didn't go for the windows. Instead, he pulled a ring of strange-looking keys off a reel on his belt and inserted two or three of them in the door lock, humming and belching. In a moment the lock button popped up and he opened the door for her.

"Oh, my. You're good at that, aren't you?"

"Too good fer m'own good, used t' be. Why, I— Well, nev' mind that." He smiled a sloppy smile and shook his head.

"Well, I don't know how to thank you, Mr., uhm, Marshall, but here." She had taken a dollar out of her purse, and extended it to him. She hoped he wouldn't take it, because it was all she had with her, besides a few coins in her purse. But he took it. He stuck it in his pants pocket and walked away. "Y'all come t' th' right man, ma'am," he said over his shoulder.

It wasn't until she started to get into the car that Mrs. Canfield noticed what had happened while she was gone. She looked back; her mouth formed words but didn't say them; she dropped her head forward, stood with her cheek flat on the wet, cold roof of her car, and slowly pounded on the cartop with both fists.

Somebody had started another row of cars behind the row hers was parked in. She was hemmed in front and back, as well as on both sides, by parked, locked automobiles.

After a while she raised her head, got her purse off the car seat, slammed the car door shut so viciously she almost lost her footing in the mud, then stalked off again toward the Speedway buildings. As she went, it started raining again.

"So there I am, gittin' rid of some a this good ol' beer, when some lady comes up 'hind of me an' says, ' 'Scuse me, sir, but c'n you he'p me unlock my car?' So I turns aroun', still pissin' like a tall horse, an' I says, real polite-like, 'Billy Joe Marshall at y' service, ma'am, jus's soon as I git done drainin' m' radiator.' "

Puggles really went into hysterics.

Lloyd Skirvin grinned. Then he said, "Long's y'had it out, y'oughta gave 'er some *real* service, y'ol' Stud Boar."

"Ha-ha-hee! Like shit, man! If you'da saw 'er!"

"Saw 'er, shit, y'ol' Stud Boar. You'd put it in a gnat's ass if y' could find one little enough t' fit it."

"Sheee-hee-hee! Look who's talkin'! Ol' teenie-weenie hisself!"

"Oh, wow!" Puggles gasped, almost collapsing with laughter. "You dudes are unbelievable!"

"Yeah, we are," Lloyd said, grinning on one side of his mouth. He reached a sinewy arm over the back of the car seat and punched Worms on the knee with his fist. "Right, ol' Stud Boar?"

"Right on," Worms said, winking and clucking his tongue in the side of his mouth. "Un-fuckin'-believable."

In the pits near Johnny Rutherford's orange race car there was a discussion going on. Nick Alef stood on the retaining wall. He was too far away to hear it, but he wasn't interested in what they were saying, anyway. They were crew members and car designers, and the discussion was probably all technical. What Nick was interested in was Rutherford's face. Rutherford seemed to be half-listening to the discussion, but most of his facial expressions hinted that he was alone with deep thoughts. His brow was wrinkled, and he gazed at the ground or through people most of the time, his eyes dark slits. Once or twice he put his right hand on the back of his neck, shut his eyes and strained his head back against the hand, then slumped and gazed tiredly at the race car. His racing suit was covered with logos: *Gulf. Goodyear. Hinchman.* The suit had epaulets. On each epaulet was the word *Goodyear.* Nick used an entire roll of film getting telephoto close-ups of Rutherford's face, and the driver never was aware of it.

Nick wrote in his notebook: *Roll 25, all. 5/28. Johnny R. Soul hang'g out. Try a.m.s. motorsport mags.*

The sturdy, handsome Rutherford was a perennial favorite with a large proportion of the race fans, and this year, having won the pole position, he was the recipient of even more adulation than usual. He had been photographed and interviewed in such festival-flavored publicity stunts as a turtle race and as honorary conductor of the local symphony orchestra. Nick had been one of dozens of photographers who had filmed Rutherford waving the conductor's baton in a special festival concert. Interviewers had asked Rutherford what his musical qualifications were, and he had replied that he had been a cornet player in his high school band, then had admitted that the symphony orchestra had played its renditions without very much influence from his baton. Grinning, he had explained, "I just started 'em and stopped 'em."

Sportswriters and race fans, Nick had observed, enjoyed making much of any hobbies, avocations, or abilities these speed-obsessed race drivers had besides driving. Several years earlier, Nick had been pleasantly surprised to hear that Johnny Rutherford's favorite pastime was painting. What do you know, Nick had thought, a race driver with an aesthetic side. For some time Nick had wondered what sorts of landscapes or abstractions this affable Texan might paint. Eventually he had had an opportunity to see an exhibition of Rutherford's paintings.

They were all pictures of speeding race cars.

*   *   *

At 1:10 P.M. a ray of sunlight came down through the
clouds and vivified the enormous scene within the Speedway. A cheer went up from the crowd. The sunlight did
not last long enough to dry the chilly clothing of the spectators, but it did seem to warm their hopes. Gerald and
Ella Rumple turned their faces to each other and smiled.
Ella had the radio to her ear. "They're going to interview
Colonel Kasler," she said. Gerald leaned close, and, with
the radio between their heads, they listened.

"*—spent six and a half years as a prisoner of war and
really deserves and has received a tremendous ovation
upon his return from Hoosiers and others throughout the
world. First of all, Colonel, if I may once again publicly
welcome you back and say how pleased we are to have
you here with us.*"

"*Thank you, Sid. Uh, you don't know how pleased I
am to be here.*"

"*It must be a thrill now to know that this little microphone and that cord we're looking at reaches all the way
around the world. You told me that you had heard this
broadcast yourself in Thailand in 1966.*"

"*That's right. I heard the start of the race in '66 when
they had the big pileup—and I hope we won't repeat
that this year. I'm sure we won't—*"

Becky Alef was watching one of her favorite movies on
television. It was *Friendly Persuasion*. It had started just
a few minutes earlier. Gary Cooper's Southern Indiana
pioneer Quaker family had been getting ready to go to the
meeting house, when a commercial break came on and
Becky decided it would be a good time to make lunch for
herself and Davey.

She worked quickly in the kitchen, stacking lunch meat
and lettuce on brown bread and spreading mayonnaise,
pouring milk into two glasses, and spilling potato chips out
of a bag into a bowl. She split a dill pickle and put it on
the plates. Becky always felt guilty about watching daytime movies on television when she felt she should be
working somehow to alleviate their financial plight. But
now she had made her decision to go to work for the ad
agency, and Nick had finally acquiesced; and since that

hurdle had been overcome, she felt that she might as well enjoy what would probably be the last week of daytime leisure she would have for a while.

She wished Nick could have been here to see the movie with her. One of the first things she and Nick had discovered during their courtship was that both had seen it five times when it was released in 1956, and that both had laughed and cried at it; they had vowed that when and if they got married they would try to have a close, warm, lively relationship like that of the Birdwell family in the movie. She and Nick had put other things aside to see the movie again and again, every time it was shown on television. Today was the first time in their marriage they had missed seeing it together, except once while Nick was in Vietnam with the Associated Press.

It's a shame, she thought. We need to see it together now more than ever. It always does Nick so much good. He's always wished he could be a good, simple, strong man like Jess Birdwell and a good provider, but the world's different now, he says.

She sighed and started to the side door to call Davey in for lunch, but at that moment the door flew open and he came in. With a jolt, she remembered how he had burst in through that very door, face chalky, the day Timmy was killed in the street.

"I don't hear the race yet," he said.

"No. I guess it's still too wet. Here's your lunch." She felt chilled by the sudden, awful memory. "Come and eat by the TV with me. *Friendly Persuasion*'s on. Remember it?" She wanted somebody to watch it with her.

"Oh, yeah! The one where the little kid's always gettin' chased by a duck?"

"Yes. By a gander."

"Sure. I like that part. What're we eatin'?"

"Pressed ham." She carried her plate into the family room, where the music of the movie had started again.

"Wait," said Davey. "I'm gonna put some peanut butter on mine."

Davey came in and sat down beside her during the scene in which Jess Birdwell raced his buggy against another buggy along the sun-dappled country road. Davey took enormous mouthfuls of sandwich and forced the half-chewed mass down in strenuous swallows. "He's not s'posed to be racin' his horse 'cause it's Sunday, right?" he recalled.

"Right. So he's acting like he can't stop it, remember?"

"Yeah! Ha-ha." Davey, who hardly ever misbehaved, seemed to get real pleasure from seeing this adult movie character involved in rather boyish but harmless mischief. "You and Dad really like this, don't you?"

Sometimes Becky suspected that Davey enjoyed the movie primarily because he knew how much his parents enjoyed it. She gazed at him, at the clear olive skin, the dreamy gray eyes. To him, she suspected, their life was divided into two kinds of life: the present—this real, strained, and mundane time—and a kind of glowing, mythical time in the past when he had a brother named Timmy and his parents had been like these parents in the movie and they had all enjoyed things together.

The movie scene ended, and the commercials returned. Davey scooped a handful of crumbling potato chips into his mouth, saying, "Tell me—uhm—about the time we went down there."

"Well," she said, "we went down there lots of times, remember? Down near the Ohio River where that story took place."

"Timmy went with us, right?"

"Right. And remember you cranked water up out of a well and drank it out of a dipper?"

"Yeah. And what did we go there for?"

"You remember, don't you?"

"Yeah, but tell me."

"Your dad and I wanted to buy a farm there on the riverbank."

"Yeah. And live there. And he would write books."

"Yes." She sighed.

"Will we ever do that?"

"Do you still want to?"

"Could we have a horse?"

"I imagine."

"I wouldn't want a gander, though," he said, wincing and grinning. And then he seemed to return to the present world. "Sure hope Dad'll get home in time to take us to the movie," he said. "Think he will?"

"Honey, I know he intends to. And he will if he can.
But Race Day is one of his hardest days."

Davey slumped in the sofa and sucked brine out of his
dill pickle.

"Yeah," he said. "I know."

Olive Canfield slogged through the mud to the sidewalks, her lips set in a firm line. Then she marched along
the sidewalk toward the telephones. If Mr. Sanders tried
to chew her out this time, she wasn't going to take it. You
just better keep a civil tongue in your head this time, Mr.
Big Shot Baker, she thought.

But when she got to the phones there were about twenty
people waiting in line. She stood with her fists on her hips
for a minute, trying to decide whether to force or beg her
way in at the head of the line. She decided to try. When
she explained her predicament, an elderly gentleman let
her stand in front of him despite the protests of others behind him.

Inside the phone booth a black man was pounding the
telephone with the edge of his fist. Then he flung the door
open, nearly twisting it off its hinges. "Don't waste your
time, don't waste your dime," he announced as he came
out. "The muthafugga's out of order!" A chorus of curses
and sighs went up all along the line.

Olive Canfield turned slowly to the elderly man behind
her. Her eyelids were narrowed. "Excuse me, sir," she
said. "Do you have any idea where I might find Mr. Tony
Hulman?"

The man started to grin, thought better of it, and said
gravely, "Well, I suppose he's over there in the Tower.
Or near it."

"Thank you very much," she said.

And she stalked off that way with her hands made into
fists.

Shortly she came to an opening in the wall that looked
as if it might lead to the Tower. There were two men
standing there wearing Speedway hats. She started to go
through. One of the men stepped in front of her.

"Ticket, ma'am?"

She stopped and surveyed the man. "I don't have a ticket."

"You don't have a— Well, look, ma'am, you have to have a ticket to come to the race."

"I did not come to the race."

"Uh—what?"

"I did not come to the race. Now, will you kindly let me through?"

"I can't let you in without a ticket, ma'am."

"Is Mr. Hulman in there?"

"Who?"

"Mr. Hulman. You *do* know who Mr. Hulman is, I hope."

"You mean, *Mr.* Hulman?"

"I believe that's what I said, yes."

"Well, what about him?"

"I said, is he in there?"

"Well, I don't know. Somewhere, I suppose."

"Well, then, either let me in, or go see if he is. Will you, please?"

"Ma'am, I can't let you in. And I can't leave this gate. Who are you, anyway?"

"I am—I'm—" Say *something*, she thought. "I'm his mother." Oh, God, don't strike me down, she thought.

The man gave her a long, skeptical look. Then he looked at the other Speedway man, who was busy checking tickets of people who were going in through the gate. "Did you hear that, Frank?" he said.

"Yeah."

"What d'you make of it?"

"She isn't his mother," said the man called Frank. "He's older than she is."

"I thought so, too. Look, lady, do you take me for an idiot?"

"Well—"

"Now look. I don't know what your name is, but you better just move on. I swear, I've seen people do screwy things to get into this race, but—Mr. Hulman's *mother!*"

Olive Canfield by now was trembling with frustration. "Please, I am not trying to get into this race, I'm trying to get *out*. That's what I have to tell Mr. Hulman!"

"That doesn't make sense. Come on, lady. Beat it. You're interfering."

"*I'm* interfering? *I'm* interfering? Oh, hohohoho*ho!* Now you listen! This stupid Speedway is interfering with *my* whole *life!* What do you mean, I'm inter*fer*ing? Ooooooh! Ooooh, dear God in heaven!"

Apparently something in her voice got through to him. He put his forefinger to his lips for a moment, then pointed to the nearby Tower. "Look. You go to those steps there. Go up the steps. Talk to the people up there. But lady— *don't* tell them I sent you. Or I'll call you a liar."

"The skies are still pretty dark, no darker than they were, but then they're no lighter than they were— I think that the race fan, Fred, has to be a very unusual breed. Those three hundred thousand folks are sitting there in those stands, and if you look, you don't see any vacant spots. It looks as though someone had painted a picture, doesn't it?"

"Aaah, a race fan is a red-blooded American man or woman! And they love this business; they love speed; they love competition."

"We also see outside our booth Larry Bisceglia, who has been first in line at the Speedway gates for—this his twenty-fifth consecutive year. He arrives in mid-April. I think maybe the Guinness Book of Records should print that, because a quarter century as the first man in line for the 'Five Hundred'—sometimes sixty days ahead of time —is certainly a unique accomplishment. And yesterday at the drivers' meeting here, right down beneath this Tower, Larry Bisceglia received an award from Tony Hulman for being first in line for twenty-five consecutive years— A lot of applause out there as our special guest celebrities are going around in the beautiful Cadillac Eldorado convertibles."

Kevin Cole had worked his way through the crowd to the tunnel that went under the west side of the racetrack, and had squirmed among the people streaming through the tunnel to make his way to the fence behind the pit area. He was hanging onto the mesh fence, his fingers hooked through it, peering between the big fueling tanks at the nearest race cars, when word came that Harlan Fengler, the chief steward of the race, had given permission for the cars to be started and warmed up in the pits. Aswarm with mechanics, the first car started with a tremendous, gut-shaking *ffffrrrroooob-m, ffffrrrooooooob-m, frroooob-m,* just a few feet in front of Kevin. Nowhere in his boyhood of engine worship had he heard such overwhelming noise, and his heart leaped in response. Cheers and clapping swept through the stands just behind him, barely audible under the noise of the motor.

Then more engines were started up and down the pits area, their noise deafening. Exhaust smoke, smelling faintly like bananas, blew through the crowd and was in-haled like perfume. Kevin sniffed it and felt shaky and intoxicated. He heard and smelled and saw. He knew what was going on. The mechanics were putting warm-up spark plugs in the cars for the duration of this slow-running warm-up period. Kevin knew they would then replace them with racing plugs just before the start of the race. His heart slammed in his narrow chest, but his face didn't betray his excitement. He appeared as intent and know-ledgeable as any of the master mechanics working beyond the fence because he knew what was going on. He could feel in his fingertips the machined steel of engine parts instead of the fence wire he was actually clutching. And he was yearning toward the future.

Nick Alef had a moment of indecision as preparations began for the start of the race. He wasn't sure where to place himself.

He had been thinking a lot about covering the fourth turn. There was always a wind in that turn, and it was suspected that it had caused a lot of the many crashes there. He had heard some of the drivers say they parti-cularly dreaded that windy place now that their cars were all decked out with wings. Somebody at one of the parties had said those wings would make you take off if wind went under them instead of over them. A. J. Foyt had said he didn't like the wings at all. He had said the drivers were being used as guinea pigs for design, and that he would like to see the wings done away with so the drivers could just race. The wings, and that legendary wind, could mean some real action in the fourth turn. The papers and wire services and television people always had cameramen covering it like a rug.

Finally, though, Nick set off down the track for the first turn. The drivers ought to be really wound up from the rain and all the waiting, he reasoned, and they were aware the track wasn't all that hot and dry for good traction, so it might be a real skittish start when they got that green flag and tried to get good positions going into the first turn. Besides that, he thought, they fuck up the start about half the time now, and they're about due for that.

You never know where things are going to happen. Sometimes you just have to go by your gut feeling.

Renee came out of her sleep feeling a hand on her crotch and dreaming that it was her father again, sneaking into her bed. She gave a little frightened cry and opened her eyes and saw Lloyd Skirvin jerk his hand away. He was smiling his half-smile.

Her head ached, and she had an awful taste in her mouth and felt heavy as a log. She heard Puggles's giggling still going on in the back seat; there was some scuffling back there, and Worms guffawed. Lloyd lit two cigarettes, looking over his Zippo flame at her, and then gave her one of them. "Couldn't take 'at beer, hey?" he said. She shook her head and passed her hand over her eyes, then took a pull on the cigarette. The smoke seemed to dissolve the gummy feeling in her mouth. She didn't want to look at Lloyd because she was thinking of his hand on her crotch. She was aroused a little, but she was angry. That's no way to make it with me, buster, she thought. I've had too mucha bein' snuck up on in my sleep.

"I think they 'bout t' start that fuckin' race," Lloyd said, inclining his head toward the radio. "Whaddya say we git our asses out an' walk over t' th' first turn—maybe see 'em move them muthafuckin' race cars a lil' bit?"

The girls shared Puggles's lipstick, and they all got out and stood in the mud and stretched. The sky was still overcast, but the wind was dry and people were out from

under their ponchos and plastic sheets. Everywhere was
the rushing noise of thousands of voices talking at once,
and the echoing voice of the track announcer above it all.
As they picked their way among the people, lawn chairs,
cars, vans, soaked blankets, Styrofoam coolers, beer cans,
and mud-smeared newspapers, they heard the "Star-
Spangled Banner" begin playing in the distance. An old
man in a chair on the roof of a Ford hardtop got up
carefully and stood at attention, facing the music, but nobody else paid attention to it.

They walked through a line of trees and then had to
wade through about a half an acre of young people who
were lying about on the ground, so densely packed in that
their bodies were almost touching. Most of them were
filthy, their bodies and clothes black with mud. Some even
had mud caked in their hair and beards. Some slept, drool
running out of their open mouths. Others sat as if in a
trance, weaving, their eyes glazed. There was a stink of
tobacco and marijuana smoke, bodies, food, spilled beer,
farts, and vomit. Renee had heard about this area from a
girl in the Girls' School the day before. It had become
known as "the Snake Pit" over the years. She had heard
that pushers worked in there and that you could get just
about anything if you were careful. Many of the people
who came to the Speedway came to gaze at the Snake
Pit as well as the race itself. Policemen with clubs and
dogs patrolled the edges of it.

People were massed along the fence, but the four
managed to force their way up to the wire, mainly because Lloyd could outstare most of the men he pressed
upon or shouldered aside. Worms had referred to Lloyd
as a "mean mutha," and Renee was beginning to understand why. She was a little bit afraid of him. But on the
other hand, nothing really scared her too much anymore
because she had always been able to handle things that
happened to her. And being around Lloyd was beginning
to make her horny.

The place they got on the fence was just about as far
to the west as they could go. They were in a sea of people,
and all of them along the fence were standing up, looking
eager, as if expecting something to happen. Many had left
their blankets and cots and chairs behind them. There was

a grassy area in front of the fence, then a creek and a guardrail, more grass, and then the slightly banked pavement of the racetrack, with a low concrete wall on the other side of it and a wire fence with steel posts on top of that. There were bleachers full of people on the far side of the track. From a derrick, a platform hung high above the crowd with television cameras and men on it. The camera was aimed north, up the straightaway.

"Hot damn fuckin' mutha dawg," Worms exclaimed. "Lloyd, you ever seen so many folks at one race?"

"Wha'd I tell ya?"

"Man! With a crowd like this, couldn't you have a hell of a purse fer th' winner!"

"Man c'd git rich here in one day," Lloyd said.

"You ever win much money in races?" Renee asked.

"Listen," Worms said excitedly. "He ain't done bad, that ol' Movin' Mutha. Have y', Lloyd?"

"I ain't done bad."

Unblinking, Renee gazed at Lloyd for a moment. Lloyd read her expression. He liked it. It was that look women gave you when they thought about you racing a car and winning prize money.

"You ever been in a crash?" she said.

He snickered. "Couple."

"Yeah," Worms exclaimed. "Mos' th' time, though, th' crashes is b'hind of ol' Lloyd. Ain't they, Lloyd?"

"Yeah. I ain't got time for that kinda shit."

"Hee-hee! Y'ol' Movin' Mutha."

Renee continued to gaze at Lloyd, and he looked off at the track, aware of her eyes on him.

The last notes of the National Anthem trailed off in echoes and were washed over by a wave of cheers. Captain Carl George, USAF, had been standing at attention beside the Cadillac he had ridden in the Celebrity Caravan. He leaned against the car and watched the thousands of people in the grandstands begin seating themselves. The noise settled to a steady roaring that reminded him of river rapids he had heard once. When? It seemed as if that must have been in another life. Before the war. Before the prison in Nam. Before this.

Then he heard the first note of "Taps." It was being played on two, three, maybe more horns; he couldn't tell. But not on a single bugle as he had always heard it. "Day is done," he thought. "Gone the sun. . . ." His heart felt as if squeezed, and tears smarted on his eyelids. He hated it when this happened. He hated it when he felt this sentiment. He had always thought it was maudlin in circumstances like these. Since he had come back from Nam he had been having trouble with crying. Things that seemed to be just not quite right made him start crying, helplessly crying, and it had happened once or twice in public. He was afraid this not-quite-right "Taps" was going to make him cry with all these people around to see him.

The only time "Taps" had ever sounded just right was when he was twelve and his great-great-grandfather, a Civil War Veteran, had been buried at a military funeral. Ever since then, it had always sounded like an inept imitation of the real "Taps." This now sounded especially wrong because of the number of horns. But it made him feel that awful, hard-swallowing weakness. And now he had a strange feeling, as if he were hearing it from the other side, as if it had been played for his own funeral. There was a little whimpering sound starting in his throat. Of course, no one could hear it in all this hubbub, but he didn't want it to start, anyway. He bit the membrane inside his cheek until it bled, and got the awful feeling under control.

"What's that for?" asked one of the Festival Princesses nearby. "The drivers that get killed here?"

"No, dummy," said another Princess. "You know. Memorial Day."

"Oh, sure! How dumb! I forgot." The Princess slapped herself on the forehead and giggled.

Olive Canfield realized as soon as she got into the Tower that nobody there was going to be of any help to her. There were too many important-looking men walking around in expensive white-and-red checkered sport coats, wearing badges, and pretty women dazzling teeth and big bosoms. Telephones were ringing, messengers in Speedway hats were coming and going, and photographers were standing about, making people get into groups or shake hands. Olive saw faces she had seen on television and in magazines. These people were greeting each other and talking to each other, drinking, laughing, and handing each other notes.

Olive stood, damp, bedraggled, and bewildered, for a few minutes, looking for someone who might be inclined to help such a minor soul as herself, but saw no one she would even dare approach with her problem. A police officer with white hair and a lot of gold designs on his cap came pushing through the crowd. She stepped in front of him, her mouth open, but he looked through her, said, "Excuse me," and went past.

Several more people ignored her when she tried to get their attention. Then she saw a tall state police officer and went to him. "Please, sir, I need to see Mr. Hulman."

"Uhm, that's not my department, ma'am."

A man came by in a Speedway hat. "Could you take me to Mr. Hulman, please?" The man looked at her as if she were a curiosity.

"Lady, he's out there about to start the race. You probably couldn't talk to him now if you were his mother."

So Olive Canfield left the Tower. She wandered around for a few minutes looking for another telephone, but all the telephones were either out of order or had long lines of people. Another call to Mr. Sanders would be useless, anyway, she thought. And I don't think I could stand it. I don't even have the strength to talk back now.

She trudged along the sidewalks. A bugle was playing somewhere. A huge mass of colored balloons rose into the air and started drifting away.

If I were a balloon, I could get out of here, she thought.

And as she plodded toward her car in the parking field, her mind busily formulating the story she would have to tell Mr. Sanders when she saw him, a voice beyond the Tower was singing "Back Home Again in Indiana."

Sure, she thought. I wish I were back home again, period.

*   *   *

"Did you find him?" Marjorie Cole asked as Cliff came squeezing among the people and sat down beside her.

"Sure. I just went to where the starting line is. I knew he'd be there, and he was."

"And you didn't bring him back?"

"I couldn't get to him. But I waved him down this way, and he saw me, all right. He'll probably watch the start up there, and then he'll be down here to watch the action in the first turn."

"Cliff, you should've—"

"Marjorie!" Cliff seldom raised his voice. She shut her mouth. Bugles were playing 'Taps' over the public-address system. "Hon," he said, "you're a good mama. But now you're being unreasonable. How do you expect Kevvie to sit still for four hours in this place?" He grinned. "You're bein' like that time at Fort Lauderdale when you looked up from knittin' and yelled at Pam to stop tracking sand into the ocean."

"I still say I never did that. You made that up."

"No. Those were your yelling and worrying days. You don't have to be like that with the kids now."

"All right, all right. I just have a bad feeling about—"

"Listen," Cliff said, turning to face up the track. A rich voice was singing over the loudspeaker system, echoing majestically.

> *"Back home again, in Indiana,*
> *And it seems that I can see*
> *The gleaming candlelight*
> *Still burning bright*
> *Through the sycamores*
> *For me."*

"Who would've ever thought that Gomer Pyle could sing like that?" Cliff chuckled.

> *"The newmown hay*
> *Sends all its fragrance*
> *Through the hills I used to roam."*

Marjorie Cole remembered the smell of alfalfa hay. It had been so many years since she and Cliff had been in 4-H together, since they had smelled hay together. She remembered a time—she remembered the prickling of hay on her skin, Cliff's weight on her, the sun on her eyelids. . . . And now there was all this responsibility and the pressure of all this noise and all these people and this somehow terrible thing about Kevin and speed. It's so different what they want nowadays, she thought. You just don't know what to do about it.

> *"When I dream about*
> *The moonlight on the Wabash*
> *Then I long for my Indiana home!"*

"Can you see him?" Marjorie shouted over the applause.

"Not sure. I think that's him on that scaffold thing there in front of the—"

"I don't mean Gomer Pyle. I mean Kevin!"

"He'll be along."

Marjorie sighed and shook her head. She took one more quick survey of her family. Pam was here next to her, craning high in her seat, watching the huge cloud of balloons drift up eastward against the gray sky beyond the Tower Terrace. And Keith was still acting goofy and pompous by turns with the young girls he had met. But that Kevin. Damn him.

"LADIES AND GENTLEMEN, THE PRESIDENT OF THE INDIANAPOLIS MOTOR SPEEDWAY, MR. TONY HULMAN!"

"Here we go," Cliff said in an urgent voice, pressing his elbow against her arm.

Being strong, small, and pushy, Kevin Cole had been able to force his way among the hundreds of hips and torsos until he stood where he wanted to be for the start of the race: belly against the concrete retaining wall, scarcely ten feet, it seemed, from the nearest race car. His heart was hammering. He wanted to see A. J. Foyt; he wanted to see and hear Foyt's car start up. But there were too many mechanics and officials and other people milling around. He could see here a great black tire and steel wheel, there a tiny windscreen, a gleaming exhaust pipe, a wing, the helmeted head or silver-shrouded arm of a driver. But he couldn't make out Foyt exactly. So he reached up, clutched the mesh of the fence atop the wall, and hoisted himself up to stand on the wall so he could see over the people on the track. People yelled at him, but he ignored them. Up on a platform a man was singing a song. Kevin glanced up and down the track, trying to make out Foyt's famous orange V-8 Coyote. About a hundred feet down the track, down in the direction where his family was, there was the Cadillac pace car, with some men standing up in it and many people around it.

At that moment a big arm went around Kevin's waist, and he was plucked off the fence and roughly set upon the ground, his feet in a wet, yielding mass of wrappers and the remains of a Colonel Sanders lunchbox. He looked up and saw a big man with a Speedway hat and an orange plastic raincoat standing over him, scolding. Kevin had no time for that. He turned and faced the track again, but knew enough to stay down off the wall, at least until the guard left.

Now the tone of the crowd's babbling changed a little, growing a degree higher, and some of the people around the race cars hurried off the track. By each car now there was a man kneeling, holding an electrical tool. Kevin knew they were starters.

"LADIES AND GENTLEMEN, THE PRESIDENT OF THE INDIANAPOLIS MOTOR SPEEDWAY, MR. TONY HULMAN!"

There was a moment of strange, waiting silence, the thousands of people almost still.

Gerald and Ella Rumple could hardly stand this moment. The flags fluttered behind them. The balloons, thousands of them, rose and spread in the sky. The audience cheered Jim Nabors for his singing. Gerald and Ella stood pressed together, looking intently at the pace car that stood, white-and-gold, with its cargo of famous people, on the smooth, dark-gray paved surface of the track. Behind it were the ranks of wide, shovel-nosed race cars, poised in brilliantly colored, polished ranks. And everywhere, people waiting. Gerald held their transistor radio in one hand, and he and Ella leaned their heads together so they both could hear it. In a voice quaking with excitement, Luke Walton was announcing:

"Comes now the electric moment that removes an imminent thirty-day and four-hour suspense: the start of the race! For the past three hours—and plus—four, the two-and-a-half-mile oval has been abustle with celebri-tees from the show world, marching bands, and pageantree! Now the track has been cleared, and as thousands of multicolored balloons fill the Hoosier sky, the Magnificent Thirty-three are po-sitioned at the starting line in eleven tiers of threeee."

Throughout the vast scene, the track announcer's voice was building to a crescendo of excitement. Ella reached across with her right hand and clutched Gerald's right hand, and they squeezed their fat fingers together. Walton raved on in the little radio:

"We are standing in the pace car, some fifty feet in front of the field, at the py-lon, awaiting the signal that triggers the 'Five Hundred.' Once it is given, each man who handles the inertia starter on each car strives to have his engine operating before the others, because without viewing the instruments, the roar makes it difficult to know his own is running!"

Everyone was standing now, thousands of eyes focused on the dark ribbon of asphalt between the grandstands and the Tower Terrace. Gerald glanced at Ella; one year the excitement of this moment had made her faint, and it had required four spectators to lift her bulk out from between the seats.

"Now, the man whose trademark is a four-word communiqué: the president of the Indianapolis Motor Speedway, Mr. TONY HULMAN!"

"MR. TONY HULLLL-MAN!" the track announcer's voice echoed in the huge arena.

Holding his camera over his head, Nick Alef aimed it at the center of a densely packed group of people near the pace car, and began firing away. Eighty percent of these exposures would be of other upraised hands holding other cameras, he knew. But . . .

In the center of the crowd, visible now and then when photographers and broadcasters jostled each other aside, stood Tony Hulman, wearing a summer blazer with a great gold Speedway medallion under the left breast pocket. Pressing around him were intent men, thrusting candle-sized microphones toward his face. His left hand steadying an outstretched ABC Network mike, with another mike almost shoved in his mouth by an eager announcer, a long strand of graying brown hair blowing across his tanned forehead, Hulman frowned, took a deep breath, waved his right hand, and yelled:

"GENNA-MUN, START YOUREN-JUNS!"

The words, magnified, echoed among the grandstands; a mighty cheer went up; a thunder of engines erupted a few yards up the track.

And Nick Alef, accustomed though he was to it, cynical though he was about it, quailed under the power of the moment and felt a shiver run through his skin from one end of his long body to the other.

Gerald and Ella Rumple gripped their hands so hard they hurt, and Ella screamed with excitement. The thunderous roar from the cars shook the stands; a bluish haze rose above the track. The track announcer's voice, barely coherent above the roar, was naming the cars and drivers. *WOOOOOOOOOP-m, WOOOOOOOP-m, WOOOOOO-OP-m!*, the gunned engines bellowed. Starters scurried off the track, carrying and pulling their electrical equipment toward the pits.

Then the pace car and the bright race cars began to roll forward, and the cheering of the spectators surged up, even louder than the din of the engines.

Gerald and Ella leaned against each other weakly, smiling, as the ranks of cars went rumbling by. Ella raised a fist.

"GO GET 'EM, A.J.!" she screamed.

The air above the racetrack grew warm. Kevin Cole could feel it on his face and hands. His guts clenched up. In a lifetime spent with stereo earphones blasting into his skull and snarling motorcycles between his knees, he had never heard anything so loud.

The noise seemed to have a weight and force, and, although he was thrilled almost to a frenzy by it, Kevin felt a rare twinge of fear. His mouth hung open. He almost wanted to be with his family, close among them.

But only for a moment. He shut his mouth and tightened his jaw muscles and squinted through the fence and inhaled the pungent fumes. Everything was fine now. When the cars began surging forward with their terrible whooping of engines, Kevin was, except for his little physical body constrained behind a steel fence, riding with them.

"The beautiful white Cadillac Eldorado convertible with red-leather interior pulls away to pace the fifty-seventh running of the Indianapolis 'Five Hundred'! Jim Rathmann's at the wheel today. He drove in fourteen Memorial Day races, coming in second three times and winning it all in 1960. Riding with him are Speedway President Tony Hulman, Mrs. Edward M. Cole, wife of the president of General Motors, Astronaut Al Worden of Apollo Fifteen, Chris Schenkel, Bob Lund, general manager of Cadillac—This is the parade lap, the first of two scheduled laps prior to the start of the race."

"Here they come," said Doc Upton. He stood up and leaned on the balcony railing of Werner's VIP suite overlooking the second turn and south end of the back straightaway. Werner Dold stepped up beside him, twirling ice in a Beefeater martini. This was the first year of the new VIP suites, and Werner didn't know yet whether he liked them as well as the penthouse seats they had always used before. The pace car sped through the second turn, just a few feet below their balcony, and Dold had a moment to glimpse the smiling faces of the two people he recognized in it: Dollie Cole and Tony Hulman. Tony held a movie camera.

The thirty-three powerful vehicles, looking like baked-enamel toys, thundered by in ragged groups. The building vibrated. Werner Dold looked up the long back straightaway at the vanishing Cadillac convertible and thought.

Doc Upton was watching his profile.

In spite of herself, Marjorie Cole rose out of her chair when the engines roared to life. She didn't like this big, terrifying event; she was almost frantic for Kevin, who still hadn't appeared; she resented the crowding and the noise and the awful idea of people coming like this to watch danger. But she was so excited that somehow everything seemed all right, and she wanted to see it start.

And then they came. First the Cadillac whispered by, accelerating in the middle of the track, giving a glimpse of its glamorous-looking passengers, and then, right along the wall, so close it seemed she could have reached over and touched one were it not for the fence, the race cars began howling by, whipping her face with warm air and an acrid smell, the noise deafening, making her tremble inside. She felt she was being swallowed by noise. She wanted to tear away from the fence and run away and go home, but more than that, she wanted to see if she could stand to stay there until the last car had gone by.

Then the pack was out of sight beyond the first turn, the drone of their engines winding up in the distance, and a few slow starters shot howling through the turn to catch up. The track announcer was yelling through the loudspeakers, and the crowd was on its feet yelling its millions of encouragements.

Marjorie sagged weakly and started to turn back to her seat. But Cliff held her arm. "Watch up there," he yelled. "They'll be around again in a second!"

"Now as you hear the engines roar as they traverse the two-and-a-half-mile course, there is one driver missing: Art Pollard lost his life on the first day of the time trials here. To respectfully salute this highly respected gentleman of racing, and to in some small fashion include him in this lineup with his friends, here is the voice of one of his closest pals: pole-sitter Johnny Rutherford."

*"It's still hard to realize that Art Pollard's not going to
be with us here today. Art was a great man, a racer. We
all thought a great deal of him. He lived with the highest
principles and a great deal of dedication to the sport of
auto racing—and to the needs of others. Even though
Art isn't strapped into the cockpit of a racing car right
now, I feel that he is riding alongside in spirit."*

"Look!" Cliff yelled, pointing. Almost a mile up the
straightaway, the bright Cadillac had reappeared; a mere
dot, it swung through the turn at a high speed on the
ribbon of dark asphalt laid in a curve through the huge
bowl of people, and then it came toward them, growing
larger, and behind it the ranks of racing machines came,
orange, red, yellow, blue, trailing their mist of heat, now
coming faster. Marjorie's heart climbed into her throat;
she didn't know whether she could stand it again so close.
She crossed her fists over her bosom and stood braced
within herself that way as they plummeted by again in
neater rows, slamming the air with noise.

*"Bob Harkey has not been able to start; his car has
been pushed back to the pits— a very bad break for Bob
Harkey— Mike, have you picked them up? Please."*

*"Okay, Sid, thank you! The Cadillac pace car now
bringing them in perfect order by the turn here—the last
time, if all goes well, we'll see them in such perfect rows
—one long single file in a moment, those neat rows will
funnel down into! Johnny Rutherford trying to key the
pack, but he's got some pretty fast company alongside—
the winner of this race usually comes from the first three
rows! The Unser brothers, Mario Andretti, Mark Donohue have all been there before! They're by us in perfect
order, in the short chute now, into turn two, and in the
high-priced seats, Howdy Bell!"*

*"Ha-ha! Thank you very much, Mike! In perfect or-
der, as you pointed out! Of course we can see Rutherford, Unser, and Donohue in the front row! Even though
the sun isn't shining right now, the colors are still magnificent as they come through this number-two turn!*

Swede Savage, Bettenhausen, Andretti, Krisiloff in the red car, Al Unser red-and-white! Jimmy Caruthers in the twenty-one gold-and-white car, Peter Revson in the orange, Gordon Johncock in the Day-Glo red, and Bobby Allison in the beautiful blue machine! And Doug Zink should have them up the backstretch!"

"And we do have them, Howdy, as they move up the backstretch, the pace car picking up just a little bit of speed—the cars in the tail of the field now starting to pick up just a little momentum and get into shape! They're up in turn number three; here's Ron Carrell!"

"And thank you, Doug! That gorgeous Cadillac pace car is here! The pole-sitter! The front rows are by already! Billy Vukovich in his canary-yellow back in the pack and number two— Most unusual—and number— in row number eight, three-time winner and hard-charging A. J. Foyt in his Coyote Gilmore Special! Well, the moment of truth is just one—ah—one—one left turn away; to tell you about it, here's Jim Shelton in turn four!"

"Hey, this is a sight hard to describe, and it's a sight that'll make any heart beat faster."

"Your A.J.'ll never get up front in this field!" Gerald yelled at Ella.

The crowd was standing on tiptoes; all heads were turned toward the north turn as the cars came roaring into the mainstretch.

"Hey, they're comin' down that homestretch now! The orange McLaren is past us with Johnny Rutherford, and here to start this race, to call the start, is the voice of the 'Five Hundred,' SID COLLINS!"

The pace car swerved left off the track into the pit lane as if skipping out of harm's way; Pat Vidan at the starting line flourished his green bag, and the crowd screamed as if from one mighty throat.

"Now down the mainstretch for the world's fastest fly-ing start they come! The green flag is waved! AND THE 1973 INDIANAPOLIS FIVE-HUNDRED-MILE RACE IS ON! TURN NUMBER ONE, MIKE AHERN!"

The cars yowled in full acceleration now and were a blur as they rocketed down toward the first turn. Gerald could see little through the standing fans, only that there was a strange knot of cars in the sixth or seventh row.

"Yes, Sid! What a battle for the lead! It's Bobby Unser shutting off Johnny Rutherford in the turn! Then it's Mark Donohue and Mario Andretti! Unser leads."

Suddenly there was a great ball of flames where Gerald was looking, an orange flash of fire billowing through the fence and into the crowd beyond it, a thump, a squealing of rubber, a succession of impacts, and large chunks of something sailing down the track out of sight beyond the people in the turn. Oh, God, no, Gerald thought. He turned and looked at Ella.

"WE HAVE A TREMENDOUS CRASH HERE, GOING INTO THE NUMBER-ONE TURN, IN THE BACK OF THE PACK! MIKE, WE'LL TAKE IT BACK HERE ONCE AGAIN! THE RED FLAG IS OUT! THE RED FLAG IS OUT!"

Ella's face was chalky. Her hands were over her mouth. They began to shake. She took a deep breath.
"A.J.!" she shrieked.
Her eyes rolled up, and she fell sprawling among the seats, smashing their picnic basket flat.

Cliff and Marjorie and Pam Cole were holding hands as the race cars came accelerating down the track for the start. "This is it!" Cliff yelled over the swelling noise of desperately straining engines. Marjorie was wishing Kevin were there with his family for this moment. The leading cars rocketed past, mere blurs of color.

Suddenly Marjorie felt a bolt of terror as her husband's hand tightened on hers convulsively.

One of the race cars was rising off the track. It climbed over another car and came flipping through the air directly toward the place where she stood with her family.

There was no time to move or cry out. There wasn't even time to think. The bulk of the object was hurtling toward them, falling to pieces, snapping off fence posts in a tumult of banging, rending, and whining. Then something warm and wet splashed over her face and seared her lungs and she saw a wall of flame coming and then she knew nothing else.

No fair.

That was what Cliff Cole thought in that instant. No fair that a man should be given no time to shield his family or pray or even tell them good-bye. Just this great hard jagged thing coming suddenly through the air, this thoughtless machine. Something round and black and spinning struck the man beside Cliff, and the man's head snapped sideways. Cliff's hands and something in his lower body contracted, and then his insides seemed to fall out. A terrible heat enveloped him and his mind blanked out.

Pam saw it coming and dropped behind the wall screaming. She tried to pull her mother down. Then there was a powerful *whooosh,* a hot wind, and she couldn't breathe. She was suffocating. Her mother fell on top of her.

Keith Cole had been watching the lead cars go into the first turn when he heard a loud smash. He turned in an instant, saw a race car flipping by a few feet in front of him, followed by a white cloud. He lunged forward, wanting to be where his family was, but fell. There was a moment of ovenlike heat. People were diving for the ground everywhere, turning, falling, screaming. Tires were screeching, and metal was being torn. Lying on the ground, the taste of fuel in his mouth, he looked up and saw the girls from Wingate he had been talking to jump up screaming, their clothing ablaze. Two men were standing a few inches away from Keith, their hair and eyebrows disappearing in flames. People were trying to get away from each other and to each other. Keith tried to get up, but a fat boy had fallen on his legs and he couldn't move. Screaming kept up all around, terrifying, pulsating screams, and men's voices were bellowing in pain. Keith was afraid to look around now, fearful of seeing more people burning, afraid of seeing his own family burning. *Mom. Dad. Pammy.* And Kevin. Where's Kevin? A crazy thought came into his mind. *Kevvie, did you cause this?* And then he dismissed the thought, but it became hilarious to think that he had thought it. He started laughing; he couldn't keep from laughing. *Kevin, you little stinker, you did this!*

He lay there, growing weak with laughter, until somebody bent down and hit him in the face and told him to by God stop it.

Kevin had stood as close to the starting line as he could get. He watched the white-haired man twirl the green flag, saw the pace car dodge off into the north end of the pits.

"EEEEEEEEAAAAAAAA-Haaaaaa!" he shrilled as the race cars shot by him, shaking the air.

And then he saw something happening down the track, down toward where his family was. He heard a lot of bumping and saw a flash and some smoke.

He began shoving his way through the crowd in that direction, worming among the people who were pressing forward to see what had happened.

Oh, jeez, he thought. Is Mom going to be mad at me!

"HO-LEE FUCKIN' CHRIST!" Lloyd Skirvin yelped. A great trail of flame came pouring along the curve of the racetrack, and a big chunk of something resembling a race

car came spinning out of it and stopped at the inner edge
of the track, a man's feet sticking out of it, burning.
Wheels and jagged objects went careening and bouncing
along the track. More race cars emerged from the flames,
some going forward, some sideways, some backward,
sucking the flames along with them as they came. One
car spun out of the firestorm on brake-locked wheels and
slid sideways on the grass toward the crowded infield
fence, bringing smoke and flame with it. It stopped, and
its driver leaped out and ran back toward the flaming
wreck. The wall of fire suddenly faded and became dirty,
grayish-brown smoke. Inside the screen of smoke there
were the impacts of other cars hitting each other. People
with walkie-talkies, fire extinguishers, and cameras were
running toward the broken, burning car, which now appeared to be upside down, its front end gone. Lloyd stared
at the burning shoes, which were pointing toes-downward.
Then a cloud of white from a fire extinguisher hid it, and
wreckers and ambulances with flashing lights were stopping all around.

"Hot damn! Hot damn! Hot damn!" Worms was yelling, straining at the fence, his eyes popping. Puggles was
standing behind him with her face buried in his back, and
Renee stood nearby, bent forward, her fists jammed into
the crotch of her jeans, her mouth hanging open, staring
at the burning feet. A powerful thrill raced through
Lloyd's chest time after time, until he burst out in a shrill,
ululating yell: "YEEE-HI-YI-YI-YI-YI-YI-YI!"

Beyond the wall on the outside of the turn there were
thousands of faces gazing upon the strewn wreckage, most
of them appearing intent but calm, studying the scene with
the greatest interest.

Puggles had now dropped to all fours in the wet trash
on the ground beside the fence and was copiously throwing up among the Dixie cups and Kleenexes and plastic
straws.

And farther up the track, where the ball of flame had
appeared first, people were screaming and screaming.

Nick Alef had obtained a good, clear vantage point
near the scoring pylon, and that was where he was stand-

ing with his cameras ready when the distant green flag
swept through the air and the cars came stampeding down
the mainstretch. He got good footage as the leaders went
by him in shock waves of air, and he was about to turn
when he saw something developing in the back rows. He
couldn't tell just what it was, but he kept his camera
trained on it. There was a series of screeching, rending
sounds, and a blue race car was suddenly up in the air
on its side, spewing mist along the fence.

His legs twitched, wanting to run, but he gritted his
teeth and swung the camera as the disintegrating machine
went thudding past him at more than a hundred miles an
hour. Other photographers were scattering and diving,
but Nick remained afoot and followed the hurtling wreckage with his lens. A few yards beyond him the mist suddenly blazed yellow with a terrific *whoomp!*, and he felt a
blast of heat. The fiery cloud was clear across the track
and billowing through the crowd beyond the outside wall.
In a corner of his mind Nick was aware that maybe half a
dozen cars or more were flying blind into that inferno, and
he felt that, likely as not, some might start knocking each
other out of the track right where he stood. One car
planed along the low inside wall nearby, making a spray
of sparks and a sound like a buzz saw. Nick's heart sped,
but he kept shooting. The shattered hulk of the blue car
was several hundred feet past him now, spinning across
the pavement like a released balloon, flinging great, curving trails of flame. Across the track from him now, Nick
heard what sounded like ten thousand people screaming,
and he glanced and saw pandemonium there, thousands
of people moving behind a shimmering wall of smoke and
superheated air. The rest of the race cars had vanished
into the holocaust now, and he could hear them skidding
and running into each other. Aiming his camera for a few
seconds into the bedlam of spectators beyond the shattered fence, he turned then and joined an army of photographers and firefighters who were sprinting toward the
fire. All along the way he could hear the yelling and crying people in the stands. Got to come back and see how
bad it is in there, he thought. But he knew what his markets were and wanted to photograph the wrecks first. He
got as close as the heat would let him. There were several

race cars sitting on the track and on the grass, some of
them crumpled and bent, their drivers still in them or
scrambling out. The biggest part of the blue race car, its
rear wheels still on, lay upside down on the inside edge of
the track, burning. A driver in helmet and flame suit, evidently from one of the other stopped cars, was making
rushes at the car, grabbing it and trying in vain to turn it
right side up. He must think there's still somebody in
there, Nick thought. And then he saw a pair of legs sticking out of the hulk where the car's front end had been
sheared off. The feet were toe-down in a river of burning
fuel. Man, oh, man, he thought as he dodged in and out
to photograph the ghastly scene from all angles. Man, oh,
man, I think that's Walther!

Nick shivered. He remembered shaking hands with
Walther this morning. And wishing him luck.

Soon the scene was being blocked off by wreckers,
ambulances, rescuers, and extinguisher foam, so Nick
turned and started running back up the track toward the
screaming crowd where the fire had swept through. His
mouth was dry, and in his breathing passages as he panted
along the trackside there was the unmistakable clinging
stink of a fuel and car fire. Cameras and equipment
banging against his flanks, Nick began shooting through
the fence at the dazed fans as he went. He put away his
movie camera when it ran to the end of its film, and
started using his Minolta.

Soon he came to the place, a few yards south of the
pylon, where he had seen the flames sweep through the
crowd. Half the seats were empty. Chairs were overturned
and flattened. People were kneeling around other people
who sat or lay on the ground. There was a smell of burned
hair. Hundreds of people were coughing, crying, talking,
and yelling. Nick ran across the track. Just inside the wall
a man knelt with an unconscious woman's head resting on
his thigh. His face was dirty and tear-streaked, and he
was looking about desperately for help. Nick took three
photos of him through the fence before the man turned
his anguished face to him. "Please, can you get a doctor
here?"

Nick took one more photo of the man's haunted eyes.

"There'll be one here in a minute," he said, and moved on.

A few steps farther on, there was a group of people gathered around a girl who was lying on the ground wrapped in a blanket. She was moaning; her face was scorched and blistered, and much of the hair was gone from the front of her scalp. Nick took four photos of her and the stunned-looking people who waited around her. There was a mass of men and women making their way down from the high seats. They would study a victim through squinted eyes, biting their lips in concentration, then would move on and go to look at another victim.

Nick used three rolls of film here. He didn't concentrate as long as he could have on this scene. He didn't think there was much market for pictures of a grandstand in shambles with a few grisly skin-burns showing. But there were weeping and stunned faces, and one man who had been hit by something solid and was covering his face with a blood-soaked shirt. And soon there were white-clad ambulance attendants and nurses clambering through the mess with first-aid kits and oxygen. A stretcher was being carried toward an ambulance by medics. The person on the stretcher was wrapped to the mouth in a fresh white sheet, which stood out against the dirtiness and trash in the seating area. And standing on a chair, gravely looking down at the stretcher, was a small blond boy blowing a pink bubble of gum. On his T-shirt was printed:

I'm a Little Race Driver

Nick carefully composed and shot that one on color film.

Wonder what Diana would think of all this, he thought.

Werner Dold and Doc Upton were leaning on the balcony rail outside the suite, watching the leaders come through the first turn in a swift single file. "By God," Doc exclaimed, "that damned Unser's got in front of—ooop—Hey, what the hell's going on back there?"

Werner Dold stood on tiptoe and looked at the fire in the first turn. Well-dressed cocktail sippers all along the balconies were exclaiming and pointing. From this distance the fire looked no bigger than a bonfire among the vast acres of people. "Well," he replied, "if you were over there among the people instead of up here in a clean, high place, you'd know, wouldn't you, Nobe?"

"Hmmph." Doc Upton raised his binoculars and aimed them toward the fire.

"Sounds like they're stopping the race," said somebody on a nearby balcony. The cool wind brought faint sounds of screaming.

"If I'm not mistaken," Doc said, "something or other got up into the crowd there." He handed the glasses to Werner and pointed. Werner looked and saw the disorder and agitation in one section of the frontstretch seats, and then studied the smoke and fire and wreckage a little farther down the track. "Well," Doc said. "Another fucked-up start. More goddamned delay. More hurt people and bad publicity. Can't you see what you'd be getting into, Werner?"

"Certainly I see," said Werner, handing the binoculars back. "A gold mine."

A race driver with his helmet off ran through the grass holding a tire up and grinning. Some of the people along the infield fence cheered and laughed and clapped. The others continued to strain forward against the fence and watch in fascination as the wreckers and the men in fire-fighting clothes and coveralls worked to turn over the smoking chunk of car with the man's feet sticking out of it.

Renee stared. Her mind was full of unusual thoughts, and her knees were wobbly. She was trying to imagine what it would be like to be in there, burning. She had burned her arm once on steam from a teakettle, and she remembered how it had hurt so much it had made her sweat and get sick. She remembered the blisters and redness and skin coming away. I bet he's like that all over, she thought. Wow.

But no, he must be dead, the way he was banged around. And there couldn't be any air in there for him to breathe. So probably he can't feel the burns or anything.

Dead. Wow, she thought. Am I looking at a man dead but not in a funeral home? Jees.

But she kept remembering the steam burns on her arm, and imagined them so vividly that she twitched and began to feel them.

And as long as she felt the pain, it seemed that the man in the burning car must be alive.

"Well, it's almost incredible. You know, I try to keep the thought in mind, the things I'm going to talk about when the race starts, and look for certain things, one of which today, of course, would have been A. J. Foyt moving up from twenty-third. Another was, I was going to be happy to say that 'Salt' Walther had completed his first lap, because last year he did not complete any laps. It was a zero after his name because he didn't finish one lap in the race, and came in last. And once again, 'Salt' Walther, unable to complete even one lap, or even get into number one turn, which is a very bad break for the young man indeed— Preliminary report says that the cars were John Martin, car number eighty-nine; seventy-seven, 'Salt' Walther; number sixteen, Lee Kunzman; number thirty-five, Jim McElreath; number ninety-eight, Mike Mosley; and number sixty-two, Wally Dallenbach."

In their seats on the outside of the fourth turn, Gene and Ruthie Roepke took turns looking through Gene's binoculars down the mainstretch. The glasses drew up close the scene of the accident, but all they could see was a crowd of men and emergency vehicles and some white smoke rising: a silent, busy scene seemingly totally remote from the murmuring of the people here in the fourth turn. Next to them, the big woman who had been bellowing for Mario Andretti stood up on her seat with her hands on her hips and stared, silent, down the track.

The race cars that had escaped the pileup had come on around the track at reduced speed, their big engines rumbling slow and deep, and were being parked along the track in front of the Tower Terrace. Gene watched them for a little while and then gave the glasses to Ruthie.

"Really not much to see from way up here," he said. He sighed.

Then cheering went up all around, and he looked toward where people were pointing. In the north short straightaway a red race car came dragging slowly along on two wheels, under its own power, its left front and right rear wheel bent up. Gene saw the number, 35, and ran a finger down his chart. "McElreath," he said. The car limped through the turn and down into the pit lane as the crowd clapped. Gene turned and looked about at the spectators. Many of them were listening to radios they held beside their heads. Most had vacant stares and looked impatient. It's nice that McElreath drove on around so they could see something of the wreck, anyway, Gene thought. The fans get bored by delays.

"I think it's going to rain again," Ruthie said.

"Probably."

"Why don't we leave now?" she said.

"Leave?"

"And beat the crowd out. Look. People are leaving already. If it starts to rain now, there'll be a stampede. And a worse traffic jam getting out than last year."

"You're right," he said. "They'll never get this restarted today, probably, even if it doesn't rain. But still," he added while gathering their paraphernalia, "I hate to waste these tickets."

"Well, there's nothing we can do about that. Come on. Let's go get a table at the motel, and we can have a nice drink while we wait for Gerald and Ella."

"Now that sounds okay to me!"

Captain Carl George finally got his sobbing under control. He became aware of the sounds around him. He took his hands off the back of his head. His neck hurt because he had been pulling his head down so hard. Slowly he sat up, blinking. Some people were looking at him strangely, and they glanced away when he looked up. He tried not to meet anyone's eyes. He was ashamed of himself.

It was just the sight of that fire going into the crowd. He had been looking down that way through a pair of binoculars at the start of the race and had seen that fire go into all those people. It hadn't scared him, exactly; it had just made him unbearably sad, and his mind had gotten all mixed up and he had started crying. He felt that he should not have agreed to come and be a guest of honor at this festival and race. There were just too many things here that a man in his condition couldn't handle.

"*To the south pits—Lou Palmer.*"

"*Right. And standing alongside me is John Martin. Uh, you came through that mess, but the car itself is parked down here in the number-one turn. John, I don't know if you can tell any more than anyone else what did happen out there. First of all, how are you, man?*"

"*Well, I'm fine. I got pretty hot there for a while because of the—I run through a, uh, big flash fire, and it burned the paint off the nose of my car and stuff, but other'n that, uh, it's okay. What really messed me up, a wheel come flyin' through the air, and, uh, I thought it was gonna come in the cockpit with me. But I darted, and it caught the front of the car.*"

"*Right. Now you were far enough back in the grid that you really wouldn't've seen what began up in front, I guess.*"

"*No, I was accelerating. In fact, the car that was right in front of me—I was within about ten feet of him when, uh, when everything broke loose, and I just seen coil springs and tires ricocheting all over the place, and the fire was what I was afraid of, more'n anything.*"

"*You actually came right through it! We were watching you here. You picked up flame as you came through, and then pulled it real tight into the grass. Is that it?*"

"*Yeah, that's right. Uh, I locked the brakes up and tried to get the extinguisher goin', but I felt a lotta heat in the cockpit with me, but it flashed out, so it turned out pretty good, and I didn't get much damage, really. I was concerned about the car upside down over there, and I run down there and helped get it over. I don't know who it was, but it was pretty bad.*"

"*Okay. Thank you for stopping by. We're glad you're fine, and I'm sorry the race ends for you, I guess, at this point, but wait'll next year.*"

"Yeah. Well, I'd just like to tell everybody in Long Beach and all over the country that I'm fine, and we'll try it again next year."

"Lou, thank you. We're very happy to hear the voice of any of the men who were in the accident. . . . Johnny Martin, car eighty-nine, the Unsponsored Special, starting twenty-fourth position. A. J. Foyt, who started twenty-third, apparently was not involved, and that's quite unusual, but he maneuvered his way out of there."

When the reporters and announcers saw a dismounted race-car driver walking near the wreckage-strewn area, they rushed to surround him. With notebooks and microphones, tape recorders and cameras, they swarmed upon him until he had to come to a halt and talk. Nick Alef got in with a group that had just netted David Hobbs, a long-haired young man from Leamington, England, whose Carling Black Label car had come along the inside of the track just in time to be showered by flaming junk from the outside of the track. His sweat-damp hair hung over his right eye and over his ears; his narrow face looked perplexed and disgusted. He breathed with his mouth open as he listened to the reporters' questions.

"Well, the first thing that strikes me," he said in his British accent, "is how incredible it is that thirty-three of the supposed best drivers in the world can't even drive down the bloody straight."

The reporters asked him what he had done.

"I was just shifting gears and going rather slow when it all began. My car got pinned against the wall, and I hit the fire extinguisher and *au revoir*'d the scene."

Gerald and two other men hoisted Ella's limp body up on the bench. Gerald rubbed her wrists and lightly slapped her cheeks, trying to awaken her. Finally one of the other men, a lean fellow with a plaid sport coat and a trimmed gray mustache, gave a disgusted look, reached back to his seat, picked up a large waxed-paper cup of iced tea he had been drinking, and dumped it—ice, lemon slice, and all—in her face. She came around. Gerald looked at the man in astonishment. He appreciated the help, but somehow the sloshing of iced tea in this kind of a crisis seemed disrespectful and not very polite.

The man paid no attention. Abruptly, he picked up his raincoat and started to leave. "Revolting," he snapped.

"Wha—what?" asked Gerald, looking up from where he was bent over the awakening Ella, his hand cupping her jowls.

"This," snapped the man, waving his arm to indicate the whole Speedway. "That," he added, pointing across to the grandstands where ambulances were parked beside the wall and people in white were climbing among the overturned chairs and milling people. "Absolutely sickening. You'll never see me again at this—this Roman circus." And he turned abruptly and started down the steps.

"Suits us fine, ya prissy son of a bitch," someone nearby yelled after him. Gerald glowed inside with agreement. But he did feel somehow troubled, sort of ashamed, by the thin man's remark.

Ella looked up at Gerald, beseeching. "I'm sorry," she whimpered. "Is—is A.J.—?"

Aaaah, the hell with A.J., Gerald thought. But he didn't say it. "He's all right, dear," he said. "He got through it all right."

"I'm cold," she said with a shudder.

"It's the iced tea," Gerald said.

The reporters were congregating around drivers who had left the Walther crash behind them. Those drivers had driven their cars slowly around the track and parked them along the mainstretch above the starting line, and had gotten out to walk around and wait to see what would be decided next.

A. J. Foyt was out of his helmet and had donned a billed cap with GOODYEAR across the peak. There was a deep vertical frown line between his brows. He stood with his hands thrust in the pockets of his driving suit and glared around beyond the reporters, answering their questions curtly, as if it were an unpleasant obligation. Some writers and announcers fussed a lot about the Texan's arrogance and surliness. Some liked to bait him; others were afraid of his volatility. Nick Alef had never seen anything to like about Foyt. But, he thought, I guess lots of us would be that way if we were everybody's hero and had made a fortune into the bargain. Even the ones who knock him worship him, and he knows it.

Foyt had started the pace lap in row eight, two cars behind Walther, but had spurted out ahead of the holocaust, his car unscathed, and the reporters were trying to find out if he had seen what caused the accident.

"I dunno," he said. "All I know is, Salt wasn't accelerating very well. He went into the side of a car against the wall. I just scrunched down in the seat and stood on it. I wanted to get out of that mess."

Nick left while Foyt was talking with Chris Economaki of ABC Sports, who was so wired for sound with electronic earmuffs and antennas that he looked like a Martian in plaid pants.

Nick glanced at his watch and suddenly felt the pressure of time. There were only about three hours left before his date with Diana Scheckley at the Speedway Motel. The rain had really delayed everything. Better unload this film at the UPI office now, he thought, and pray they don't try to start the race again this afternoon. Don't see how they could. There won't be time to go home and develop any of the magazine stuff till after Diana. . . .

Then he remembered his promise to take Becky and Davey to a movie.

Oh, shit.

Well, he thought, that'll just have to wait. You can go to the movies anytime. Maybe the little guy'll forget about it. . . .

He visualized Davey's face then.

What the hell am I doing here, anyway, he wondered.

Marjorie woke up with a terrible burning sensation in her lungs. Her eyes stung when she tried to open them. She raised her hand.

"You're okay, honey; you're okay, Marjorie, my darling." It was Cliff speaking. She opened her eyes and saw his form vague above her, then had to shut them again because of the stinging. There was a frightening noise of people crying and yelling all about, and objects being lifted and thrown, and people trying to comfort other people with solicitous voices, like the time she had come out of the anesthesia too soon when Pammy was being born.

"My eyes—"

A thumb pried up her eyelid, and a pinpoint of bright light shone in. "Can you see the light?" said a voice from behind the light.

"Yes, but it hurts."

"Just fuel," said the voice, going away.

"You're okay, Marj, hon," Cliff said. His hand was stroking her cheek, and he was sliding his arm under her shoulders and starting to lift her from the ground.

"We're all okay, Mom," said Pammy's voice, that dear, sweet voice. "It's a miracle, but we're all okay." A flood of tears welled up in Marjorie, and she began sobbing uncontrollably; it hurt her lungs.

"Kevvie?" she gasped. "Is Kevvie here? My baby? Where's my baby boy?"

"Why, uhm—"

"WHERE'S KEVIN?"

"He's okay! He's okay! Darn it now, Marjorie. We know he's okay."

"WHERE IS HE?" She was trying to rise now. Everything ached.

"He just isn't back yet," Cliff said soothingly. "Now listen, we know he's okay. He was lucky he wasn't here—"

"HOW DO YOU KNOW HE'S OKAY?"

"I've been all over here," Keith's voice said. "I know he's not here. He wasn't here when it happened."

"Good God, somebody go find him! Ask the hospital or something! Find him and let's get out of this god-awful place! Let's find him and go home. Oh, God, Clifford, I want to go home!"

"Bob Forbes has Mike Hiss, who was also involved in the accident. Come in, Bob."

"Thank you, Sid. We've got Mike standing here. Mike, uh, what was your recollection of the wreck?"

"It's hard to say, Bob. The first thing I saw was a ball

of smoke. I thought perhaps somebody'd blown an engine. Then I saw 'Salt' hit the wall, and cars started spinning everywhere; pieces were flying all across the track, and I started slowing down as best I could. Then it was obvious I was gonna hit him, too. Uhmmm, Lee Kunzman was hit in front of me. He spun into the wall, came back across, and clipped me; and then somebody else hit me from the other side, and I got hit from two or three sides, so I don't —just don't know, y'know."

"Keith," said Cliff Cole, "You go on along the wall there and look for him. I'll meet you back here in ten minutes." They had left Pam with Marjorie.

"Where you going, Dad?"

"Uhm, I want to go under the grandstand and see if I can find him coming back that way."

"D'you really think he's okay, Dad?"

"Sure. He's okay. See you here in ten minutes. One of us'll find him by then." Keith turned and wandered up along the wall with his mouth hanging open—that habit he had when preoccupied that made him look far less intelligent than he really was. Cliff and Marjorie had never been able to figure out a way to cure him of it without hurting his feelings. But Cliff couldn't think about that now. He was worried about Kevin, though sure he hadn't been hurt in the crash. But there was something even more pressing. Cliff had an extreme discomfort and looked away whenever he thought he saw someone looking toward him. He needed to find a rest room and clean out his trousers.

Black clouds had been moving up from the west for several minutes. And then, while the wreckers and track crews were getting the race cars and pieces of race cars off the first turn and the ambulances were carrying injured race fans away from the wall in front of the grandstand, more rain came. It began pelting down. Umbrellas and tarps went up again throughout the bleachers, and thousands of voices murmured in complaint. The rainfall increased, and soon it was a deluge. Once again, the vast arena was dark gray and wet, lights gleaming only in the Tower and on the scoring pylon.

Many of the race fans stayed in their seats, as if thinking that this, too, would pass. But now lines of people were moving slowly like lava flows down the aisles of the sloping bleachers, through the gates and tunnels, and disgorging into the parking lots. Here people broke away from the shambling mass and sprinted through the rain and mud, heading for the places where they had parked their cars. Every second was crucial in this kind of exodus. To get one's car out of the rain-softened field and onto one of the paved exit roads ahead of the rest of the crowd was a triumph. To be caught in the glacier-slow, jammed masses of traffic trying to funnel onto those roads five minutes later was to be consigned to two, three, or even four hours of creeping, waiting, honking, cursing frustration.

As in most competitions, there were few winners and many losers. The swiftest few got to their cars, turned on motors and windshield wipers, accelerated up through the long rows of parked cars and sped onto the paved roads and through the tunnels, and were waved onto the uncrowded city streets away from the Speedway in minutes, whooping to one another in exhilaration. But behind them, at every aisle end, at every turnoff, at every place where at least two cars had to meet and only one could go first, the bottlenecks of losers began to form. Dozens, then hundreds, then thousands of automobiles backed up at the junctures. The enormous outflow of automobiles quickly congealed at every outlet.

And in a late-afternoon downpour, another legendary annual Indianapolis Motor Speedway traffic jam was under way.

Gerald and Ella Rumple, carrying their broken picnic basket between them, were shoved and jostled down the Tower Terrace aisle, along the pit fence, through the Gasoline Alley gate, and out onto the sidewalks leading to the infield parking area by the mob of impatient fans who wanted to escape in a hurry. The Rumples couldn't move fast. They plodded along, their two umbrellas up, their shoes and pant legs becoming soaked with rain and mud.

Gerald's face looked different. There was a strange expression on his mouth. It was a firm, angry line, but compounded by a pout. And in his puffy eyes there was a rare dark and resentful look. Ella glanced at him several times as they moved along. In all their years together, she had hardly ever seen him lose his equanimity. He's going to say something unpleasant pretty soon, she thought.

"Ella, I've been thinking something."

"Yes?"

"I've been wondering—I mean, well, I've been wondering if it's worth it."

"What?"

"Coming here."

"You mean to the race?"

"Yes, I mean—"

"You mean you're going to say we shouldn't come?"

"I'm just thinking out loud. I mean, what the heck are we here for, anyway? I mean, what is it we're here for? Did you ever really ask yourself what it is we come to see?"

"You know what we come to see. The excitement, the —the—I mean, to root for somebody. Oh, now, listen, Jerry. You know why I root for A.J. all the time. I'd just like to see him be the first four-time winner and then retire. He would, I bet—"

"I'm not talking about A.J., Ella. I'm talking about—" He tried to think of how he had felt when the man called it a Roman circus. It had made him feel that it was wrong to be here, but he didn't quite know how to say it to Ella. If he came right out with words like *blood* and *death* and *crashes,* she would jump all over him with protests and he would have to try to defend feelings he didn't even know how to articulate. "I—I just don't think we ought to come back," he said. "I mean," he added quickly to soften her reaction, "this year anyway. We saw the start. That's the exciting part. After that—" He didn't want to say it, but once or twice in past years both had admitted that it was boring to sit there for three hours watching the race cars go by. Even though they had bought stopwatches, and kept their speed charts up some years, there were times when they grew tired and restless on the hard seats, and perspired terribly, and had moments of excitement only when a car would spew smoke or flame, or the announcer would bring them to their feet by excitedly reporting a spin or a crash in this or that turn. And then there would be that strange relief when it was announced that the driver was all right. A relief, yet . . . "Ella," he said, squinting with the concentration of trying to phrase it right, "do you ever feel, uhm, wrong, sort of, about being here to watch the crashes?" He was certain what her outcry would be: that she didn't like to see crashes and hoped she never would see any. But she didn't say that. She didn't say anything. She just walked alongside him, huffing, her feet squishing in the wet grass. They were almost to their car now. He glanced at her profile and saw that there was some kind of unease in her mind, too. This might be the right time to say what he wanted to say. "Ella, honey, what would you say if I just threw away these tickets? Just this year's, I mean; then we could see whether—"

She looked at him, and though she didn't say okay, she didn't say no. Their eyes met, and he had the feeling that she, too, was remembering the ambulances and the stretcher-bearers over by the grandstands. After coming out of her swoon, she had looked over there often, even though it was something he knew she would try not even to see. They seemed to be having an understanding now, one of their special wordless understandings. Heartened by it, he clutched his umbrella against his chest with his forearm and, reaching with his fingers into his shirt pocket, drew out the tickets and dropped them on the ground.

Ella sighed. "To tell the truth, I don't think I could have faced another Speedway traffic jam tomorrow morning, anyway."

"Amen," he said, suddenly feeling good and light and happy with relief. "We're not even out of today's yet, for cryin' out loud."

As they approached the row where their car was parked, they had to keep stepping aside for people who came running past them in the rain and for cars that were pulling out and heading toward the road. "Look up there," Ella said.

There was an enormous knot of automobiles full of people building up at the exit from the parking field to the road. Horns were honking, and people were shouting. The mass of cars grew larger by the minute as drivers pulled out of their parking places and tried to get close to the road. Some cars were slithering and whining, their tires flattening the wet grass, tearing through and sinking into the mud. "Looks like we'll be awhile getting out," Gerald said. "Oh, shoot, Ella! Look at this!"

They had reached their car now, and they saw that another row of cars had been parked behind theirs. "Why do people do that?" Ella demanded. "Now we're blocked in."

With sighs, they began putting their gear into the back seat of the car. "At least we can get in out of the rain and wait," he said. "I've just about had it with rain for one day." He opened her door for her, shut it after her, then waddled around and got behind the wheel. He turned on the ignition, the windshield wipers, and the radio. There was nowhere they could go yet. And in a moment, their damp clothes and breath had fogged up the windshield. Rain was beating on the roof. Gerald turned on the circulation system. It sighed and began clearing the glass from the bottom up. Then a human shape materialized on the wet, misty glass beside him and rapped on the window. He rolled the window down a turn, saw that it was a woman's face, and rolled the glass the rest of the way down. The woman was haggard and squinting. Her graying hair hung wetly in strands, and her wet uniform dress sagged and clung to her body. Water was dripping from the end of her nose.

"Sir, this is my car here," she said, pointing over her shoulder to a rusty Falcon alongside the Rumples' Chevrolet. "I just wanted to tell you how lucky you are that you're not the people parked in that row behind us."

"Uhm, why?" Gerald said, with a puzzled half smile.

"Because I've been trapped in here all day long, and I probably would have killed you."

"Oh, yeah," he said, chuckling. "I know how you feel."

"No, I don't think you do. You see, I had no intention of coming here. I got caught in the traffic this morning, and now all day I've been trapped in this place! So you see, I'm not kidding. I'm not a violent person, mind you, but when those people come back—"

"Well, it should be soon now," Gerald said. "Lots of people are leaving the track."

"Is the race over?"

"No, it never really started."

"All this for nothing," the woman said, shaking her head. She turned away, her wet face set in eaglelike ferocity, and squished around to the far side of her car and got in. Gerald turned to Ella, chuckling low in his throat. Ella was sitting there laughing voicelessly. Then she began laughing out loud. Each one's mirth infected the other and soon they were both laughing and wheezing helplessly. When it died down they looked at each other and started again, and it was a long time before they could stop. Finally Gerald took a deep breath and exhaled through puffed cheeks.

"Hooo, my," he said, shaking his head.

"Oh, Gerald. I love you, honey."

"I love you, too, baby. I don't know. I just don't know. My, gosh, what're we gonna do for laughs if we stop coming out here?"

"We do have fun, don't we, honey?"

"Yeah, we sure do." He patted her shoulder. "My ittybitty buddy. Do we be bestest buddies?"

"We be bestest buddies." She sat slowly shaking her head, smiling. The rain had slowed. Car doors were slamming and motors were being started all around, but no one had come yet to the cars that had them blocked in. To the south, a helicopter rose out of the infield and fluttered off to the east. Gerald and Ella knew it was leaving the Speedway Emergency Hospital and going to Methodist Hospital, which had a heliport on its roof and was the place where seriously hurt Speedway accident victims were always taken. The Rumples wondered whether it was carrying Salt Walther or some of the race fans, but neither said anything about it to the other. After a while, Gerald turned up the car radio so he could hear it better.

"—to restart the race."

"I think, Fred, that the chances of having really gotten very far along with the race were rather slim, anyway,

*though, when the race did start. Looked as though per-
haps the rain could hold off for, well, let's say an hour
and a half, time to run those one hundred and one real
necessary laps. I personally favor the fact that, uh, the
race may be stopped today and continued at a later date,
because I like to see the full two hundred laps. How do
you think the drivers feel about that?"*

*"Well, I think the drivers would rather do that, too,
for a driver would feel rather squeamish in winning a
race and running it a short distance, or just fifty-one percent. He would rather feel that he has definitely won the
race had he gone the full five hundred miles, and this does
add to one's feeling and prestige in winning the race.
They have a tendency to feel sometimes that, uhm, it was
given to 'em, and they do not appreciate that. I wouldn't.
I'd like to go the full distance. That's for sure."*

"Honey——" Ella said.

"Yes, m' darlin'?"

"I was just wondering, my bestest buddy, if, uhm, you
might happen to know just where you, uhm, dropped
those tickets."

"Sort of," he said after a pause, looking at her. "Why
d'you ask?"

"Mmmmmm, I was just wondering. You know. I mean,
what if, uhmmm, say, tomorrow was a real nice day and
they did run the race again?" He didn't answer right
away. He looked out the window. Another helicopter was
taking off from the field hospital. "I mean," she went on,
"tomorrow being a workday, there probably wouldn't be as
much traffic in——"

"You'd like me to go back and see if I can find the
tickets, if I read you right?" he said.

"I mean, since we're just sitting here, anyway——"

Gerald reached back and got his umbrella. "I have to
admit," he said, "I was sorta thinking about those tickets
lying there on the ground myself. They might be a little
wet, but after all, they are rainchecks, aren't they? Ha-
ha-ha."

Ella sat in the car and waited after he trudged away.
People came and got into cars, but not the ones that
were blocking them.

The jam of cars trying to get onto the road had now

built up until it was backed up to the Rumples' car, and beyond. Ella listened to the rain on the roof and thought about the accident and about Gerald's silly jealousy of A.J. Sid Collins was talking on the radio, saying Salt Walther had been flown from the Speedway hospital to the Methodist Hospital. Then he stopped, and a commercial came on.

"Yeah, but there ain't nothing like Indy. You never heard so much yellin' and screamin'—and there's always more people than there's room—and more STP stickers than there are people—you never seen so many of those STP decals—y'know, one girl was wearing one on her— y'know, from dirt track t' brickyard, wherever there's racing, you'll find world-famous STP Oil Treatment and STP Gas Treatment! S—T—P IS THE RACER'S EDGE!"

In the Falcon parked alongside, the gray-haired woman was sitting still, waiting, her head leaning against the back of the seat. Funny woman, Ella thought. Imagine being mad enough to get out in the rain to tell us how mad she was. . . .

For once, Kevin Cole was up against people who were as pushy as he was. And there were thousands of them, and most of them were about twice his size. He would press and wriggle, then would come to an impenetrable crush of people, half of whom were straining to see what was happening in the distant first turn and half of whom were trying to get out of the grandstands and leave the Speedway. He would shove against the masses of flesh, umbrellas, beer coolers, cameras, and plastic paraphernalia, and try to wedge himself among them, only to be shoved back twice as far as he had gone forward. They were all wet from the rain and smelled. At one time he was trapped between two huge pairs of buttocks and thought the breath was going to be crushed out of him; only by administering a powerful goosing to the one in front did he manage to get enough pressure off for an instant to slip free. At another point he was socked in the right eye by the sharp elbow of a woman who was fighting her way through the crowd ahead of him. The blow made lights flash in his head and his nose run, and he was sure he would have a shiner from it. He had been in enough fistfights, football games, and hockey-rink melees to know it was that kind of a blow.

It seemed he had been struggling against this tidal wave of people for an hour since the crash, and he had gained only a few yards. He was too intent on his progress to listen to the track announcer, but occasionally he did hear snatches of the broadcast and was able to piece together in a part of his mind a general picture of the accident and its consequences.

Mom won't like that crash, he thought. She'll be wanting to go home, and she'll be mad at me for slowing them down if I don't get there.

Kevin considered himself a very cool character; in his twelve years he thought he had seen and experienced almost everything, and seldom worried or became scared. His Little League coach had once called him "Fearless," and he had so loved it that he had striven always to live up to it. But now that figurative rock of fearlessness at the core of him was beginning to crumble. He had never been this tired in his life, and he had never been so frustrated for so long. Problems just weren't supposed to last this long. Always before in his life there had been quick relief, quick comfort, quick triumph. A few minutes of being nasty or noisy always had made his family give in and do things his way; a few minutes of whining always earned him a candy bar or a bike or another half-hour extension of his bedtime; a few seconds dashing or pushing in a game resulted in a score at best, a penalty at worst. On television all problems were solved within half an hour; on television commercials all miseries and shortcomings were remedied in half a minute. He had been brought up on television and had learned in his family that he could make anything happen almost that quickly. It seemed to him the way life was and should be, and thus he had of course grown confident and fearless. But now for the first time he was up against indifference—indifference on a huge scale—and he was beginning to be shaken and disoriented by it. Suddenly he wanted to be with his family, with his mother, with those who cared about him, those he could control or dismiss as he chose. But he couldn't seem to get to them. Ordinarily a punch in the eye was something to be endured as a badge of honor; now it was something that watered and hurt and made him feel still more helpless. His feet had been stepped on, and he had been thumped and pushed from all sides, and down inside he quailed.

I'm not going to cry, he thought. I'll never do that. *Fearless. Fearless.* He repeated it several times and then plunged against another wall of adult bodies. Outa my way, Fatso. Get your big butt out of my way.

Right about here, Gerald thought. I know it was right about here. He stood under his umbrella and let his eyes sweep over the ground in widening semicircles. On the grass there were race programs, Kleenexes, cigarette packs, rain-soaked hot-dog buns, plastic spoons, brown paper bags, cardboard hats, little checkered Speedway souvenir flags, aluminum can tabs, beer bottles, soft-drink bottles, cigar butts, and little plastic catsup containers.

But no tickets.

He turned around and again searched widening arcs of ground. Napkins, jar lids, broken pieces of Styrofoam, torn envelopes, foil gum wrappers, a hubcap, a pencil, wisps of cellophane smeared with food, part of a shoelace, a hair roller, the paperback cover of *Future Shock*, matchbooks, a bottle of fingernail polish, and a chicken thighbone.

But no tickets.

Maybe a little farther back, he thought. He walked on toward the Tower Terrace slowly, scanning the ground. People hurrying the other way, toward the parking area, had to dodge around him. As they went, they shed more detritus: a cheap sandal with a broken strap, a popsicle stick, a race scorecard. A boy under an umbrella collided with Gerald's umbrella. He wore a T-shirt that said GET REALLY STONED—DRINK WET CEMENT. The boy mumbled an apology and hurried on.

Finally, Gerald knew he had come too far back. He turned and headed toward the car again, moving with the crowd now, still sweeping the ground with his gaze.

Oh, well, he thought. Maybe this means that we really shouldn't come back. He heard another helicopter and looked up to see it rise and head off eastward. Again he remembered the feeling he had had when the man had called it a Roman circus.

But still, he thought, it's a shame to let the tickets go to waste. Whatever possessed me to throw them away?

"He'll probably be there when we get back," Cliff Cole said.

"I sure hope so," Keith said. "You know, I'm gettin' worried. I mean, he can take care of himself, but he's just a little kid."

Kevin wasn't there when they got back. Marjorie's eyes widened in horror as she saw them coming back through the disordered seats without him. Cliff started reassuring her before she could say anything because he feared that in her state she might go all to pieces if she started.

"Okay, now, honey, it just means that he's in the crowd someplace. But he knows where we are. He can take care of himself—you know him. Now, come on, honey. Let's move up there under the roof out of the rain, and we can see him if he comes—I mean, when he comes."

To his surprise, she stayed calm. "All right, now," she said. "I know you think we should just wait for him. And I hope you're right, that he'll show up. But I can't just sit and wait. Cliff, we've got to go check the hospital—the police—*something!*"

"But if he came back here, we'd be gone."

"Keith could stay here."

"We shouldn't split the family up again, honey. That's what's—"

"Keith, you could wait here, couldn't you? Then we could set a time to meet at the car."

They decided that in this crowd it could take two or three hours to get around and check out every possible means of finding Kevin, and agreed to meet at the car by six o'clock at the latest. Cliff and Marjorie and Pam then started northward toward the tunnel through which they could go under the track to the Tower and the infield hospital. Keith watched them go in the rain. His mother kept dabbing at her eyes with a handkerchief. They had looked red and swollen, and he wondered whether it was from crying or from the fuel.

They had left Keith without any cover from the rain, but he found a piece of yellow plastic somebody had discarded. He raised it over his head, sat down in one of the empty seats, and began waiting.

More than half of the seats were empty now. The rain sifted down on the people who remained. They were all sheltered under one kind of cover or another. But in twos and threes and bigger groups, as the minutes wore on, they abandoned their seats. Some evidently were deciding that a restart was impossible now; others were simply getting up to try to find places out of the rain under the overhangs of the grandstands.

Keith thought back over the happenings of the last few hours. He thought of the parade and the great excitement of the start of the race. He remembered the girls from Wingate, who had been so cute and so nice to him. They had talked to him about basketball tournaments and bicycles and summers of swimming and just messing around. They had promised to write to him and he had promised to write to them, but then the accident had happened before they could write down addresses. He remembered the incredible sight of the race car flying through the air toward them, like something one sees in a nightmare but then wakes up from just in time not to die. And now here he was, all right, and that made it seem still more like a nightmare.

And he remembered the girls standing there with their clothes burning, and the people whose hair was burned off, and his mother and dad and Pam all in a heap on the ground. It was like a dream, and now he was sitting here like nothing, perfectly okay, in a big, gray, strange, and boring place, looking across the racetrack at a pole with lighted numbers on it, meaningless numbers to him, numbers reflecting off the rain-wet surface of the racetrack while the rain beat on the plastic over his head and drained off the edge to soak the knees of his trousers. The rain on his knees was uncomfortable and annoying and much more real than everything that had happened. Again he tried to see in his mind's eye the crashing car and the burning people, but. . . . He remembered something his dad had said a long time ago when the family had stayed up all night to watch the television transmission of the first men walking on the moon: "You just can't get your mind around it." That was the way it was now: he just couldn't get his mind around it. Instead, he tried to arrange the plastic so the rainwater wouldn't run onto his knees.

And after a while as he sat there waiting and people kept leaving, he started needing to pee. There were rest rooms under the grandstands, and he knew that he could get down there and back in just a few minutes. So he got up and went. And while he was gone, Kevin came to the seats, his hair and clothing soaking wet, his teeth chattering and lips blue as they were when he would go swimming and stay in too long. He went among the seats where his family had been, and looked about in all directions. His face crumpled up as if he were about to cry. But instead of crying, he suddenly gritted his teeth, kicked over a chair, made raging noises in his throat, picked up and flung some pieces of litter about, and then stamped off toward the exit.

Two minutes later, Keith returned from the rest room, sat down in a chair, and resumed his lookout.

"I think that we've probably, who broadcast this race, have done more time over an empty street than any broadcasters in the history of the world. Hours and hours and hours; the rain comes down harder.

"The tarps and the covers are covering the cars, and now the water is teeming, and I think anyone sitting in those stands now has to have more optimism than good judgment."

"Might I say something in regards to A. J. Foyt? You know, there's been a lotta comments made in regards to A. J. Foyt not wantin' to start in the back, and he has made that comment himself; he felt that starting back as far as he was, was a dangerous situation. I think after what you have seen happen here, after the start of the race, depicts quite well his expert thinking."

"Yeah; he just moved up considerably, too. Mark

Donohue predicted he'd be— A. J. Foyt would be fourth by the twenty-fifth lap."
"Well, Mark Donohue knows what he's talkin' about."

Still nobody had come to drive away the cars in front or back of theirs. The Rumples were disappointed that Gerald had been unable to retrieve their tickets, and now they were having a bad letdown feeling and simply wanted to get out of this sodden field and relax. And they were getting hungry again. Wheezing and straining, Gerald opened the damaged picnic basket. There was very little left, and rainwater had been leaking into the broken basket, making the meager remnants look even less appetizing. He sighed and replaced the basket in the back seat. Beyond the rain-flowing windshield they saw another helicopter rise and fly away. Throughout the parking field now, cars were bumper to bumper, only their windshield wipers moving. Drivers drummed on their steering wheels with their fingers and waited for opportunities to move a foot forward.

"Hey, bestest buddy," Gerald said. "I've got a brilliant idea. Why don't we just get under our little bumbershoots, and walk over there to the motel, and just have ourselves a nice little drink to warm our cockles while we wait for Gene and Ruth, instead of just sitting here in the middle of nowhere? Hm?"

"Wellllllllllll . . . I hate to get out in that rain again. But we sure aren't going anywhere for a while in this traffic. Bestest buddy, you is a genius."

In his state of mind, Kevin could only think that his family had gone off when the rain started and left him. He could imagine his mother saying angrily, "Well, let's just teach him a lesson. Let's just go to the car without him!"

Well, he thought, if that's the way they want to be, I'll show them. I can go faster than they can, and I'll get to the car first.

He was too furious to give any thought to the overturned chairs all about. It still hadn't occurred to him that his family might have been hurt or endangered here

when the cars crashed. Though he had noticed the
mangled fence a few yards up the track, his only thought
of it was a regret that he had not been close enough to see
it. Now he was bent only on showing them they shouldn't
treat him this way. After all, he had tried to get down
here in a hurry. Boy, if they only knew how he had
tried.

His spite gave him new energy, and he charged off for
the nearest exit. He knew where the car was in the people's yard, and he could get there before they did.

This was simply a race now, and Kevin was right at
home in a race.

In the Tower, Harry Kuntz smiled and maneuvered his
Princess, Diana Scheckley, from one group of celebrities
to another, lightly propelling her with a manicured hand
on the small of her back. They engaged in some commis-
eration about the rain and the crash with Burgess
Meredith, then moved in on a circle of businessmen and
sportsmen who surrounded Luci Arnaz. Again the talk
was the same, of the disappointment caused by weather
and the accident, and of the condition of the driver
Walther, who had been flown to Methodist Hospital with
burns over much of his face and body and possibly a back
injury, yet was, amazingly, still conscious. But Diana felt
Harry wasn't really very interested in the talk; he was,
instead, preening for these important people, and she was
a prop for his preening. Harry was noting with satisfaction that the men's attention strayed from the famous Miss
Arnaz to his Diana, who was in his opinion a far fresher,
more statuesque, and desirable beauty, and thus an excellent reflection upon him. She understood Harry Kuntz a
little better each day, and liked him less.

God, she thought. What a long day. She stole a glance
at her little wristwatch with the diamonds around the outside that Harry had given her as his festival protégée.
Harry noticed, as he noticed every move she made. "Getting tired, my dear?" he asked in her ear. She turned and
gave him a dazzling surface smile. "Just admiring my
beautiful watch," she replied softly, and then laughed in-

side at the expression of smugness that spread over his jowly face.

The problem, she thought, is going to be getting rid of Harry before six-thirty.

"We're staying on the air until we find out officially exactly what time the race is scheduled to start tomorrow morning. Or this afternoon, if that's the case, which Fred and I are thoroughly convinced will not be. But we'll have to find out what time it's on tomorrow morning so we can tell you what time we'll be on, which will be fifteen minutes prior to the dropping of the green flag. And just as rapidly as we learn that, we'll let you know and we will go off the air. And happily so, because we've been on the air here since, ah, ten-fifteen this morning. What is that? Ha-ha-ha. One, two, three—that's five and a half hours, right?"

"Ha-ha-ha. We could've run two five-hundred-mile races by now!"

"Five and a half hours, and we haven't started yet. So, Fred, it's nice visiting with you."

"Well, hey, Sid, it's nice visiting with you. But this rain is going to allow one thing to occur that will be beneficial to the competitors. Those cars that were bent up in the race, uh, the start of the race, that can be fixed overnight will be added to the lineup again tomorrow. If they were to restart right now, I'd say at least, oh, five of the cars would not be able to go. Five to six of them. However, this way we may be able to pick up a couple of the cars, to—adding to the field and the competition that is expected by the fans for the money they paid to see this race. And those guys will give it to 'em."

Kevin sprinted through the rain outside the Speedway, dodging among the slow-moving people. The people were going to their cars, which were parked everywhere outside the Speedway. Cars that had been parked inside the Speedway were coming slowly out of the gates, and state policemen in slickers and campaign hats were waving and blowing whistles, trying to guide a few lanes of those cars through the throng of pedestrians. The people were muddy up to their ankles. They shuffled along under umbrellas or held blankets and plastic sheets over their heads, and lugged coolers and baskets. Kevin dodged and pivoted among the people and the cars with all the skill he had learned on the football field, and in a few minutes reached Twenty-fifth Street, where he cut a corner and ran westward. When he got to the house where his dad's car was parked, the black-haired woman who lived there was standing on the front stoop under the little porch overhang with a worried look on her face, talking to a red-faced man with a long-billed cap on.

"I just can't help you right this minute," she was saying. "You'll have to wait till they come and move it. Wait. I think this is one of them. Is your family coming?" she called to Kevin as he went to his family's car and tried the door handle.

"Yeah, pretty soon, I guess."

"See?" the woman said to the man. "It shouldn't be but a minute."

"Well, they'd better hurry," the man said. "I've got a long way to go, and it's getting late. And look at that traffic." He pointed to the street, where cars were inching along bumper to bumper.

"I can't do anything about that, sir," the woman said.

"Well, it seems like when you let people park their cars in back of my car, you'd get their keys."

"People don't want to leave me their keys," she said. "And I don't want the responsibility of their keys, anyway."

"Well, then, why do you park cars here?"

The woman crossed her arms over her chest. "You asked me if you could park here, remember?" she said. "If you don't want to get in traffic and parking problems, it doesn't seem very smart to come to the Speedway."

"Yeah, yeah, yeah," the man retorted. He opened the door of his car, which was next to the house, and got in and started talking with two scowling women who were sitting inside.

The woman on the porch started to turn to go inside. Kevin called to her, "Hey, ma'am, can I have that Coke now?"

She turned and looked at him. "What Coke?" she said after a moment.

"Your kid said you'd give us Cokes if we parked here, remember?"

"Oh, yes. I'm afraid I do remember." She didn't look very happy about it. "Hold on. I'll get it."

When she went in, Kevin tried the other door handles. He was locked out. He began shivering.

The woman came back out onto the porch with a Coke can in her hand. She stood there for a minute looking at Kevin. Obviously she wasn't going to bring the Coke to him. "What's the matter?" she called. "Are you locked out?"

"Yeah."

The pretty woman got that expression that Kevin's mother often got when she knew she was going to have to do something she really didn't want to for some kid or other. "Come on in," she said. "You better wait where it's warm." Kevin went slowly toward the house, looking up the street for his family. "Here," said the woman, handing him the Coke can. "Heavens. You should have hot chocolate instead. You're soaked. Where's the rest of your family, anyway?"

"I ran. They'll be here after a bit."

"Let me get a blanket around you. You can watch TV with my Davey. 'Superman' is on. You like 'Superman'?"

" 'Tsokay."

"Wait," she said. She sighed, then waved her hand until the man in the other car rolled down his window. "Would you folks like to wait in the house?" she called.

"Lady, I just wanna get outa here!"

"Then sit there," the woman muttered, ushering Kevin in.

When Becky Alef had the chilled boy wrapped up and seated with Davey before the television set, she returned to the front door and gazed out at the huge exodus moving west on Twenty-fifth Street. She looked eastward for Nick or for the boy's family, but couldn't see them. The man and the two women, who were from Arizona, were sitting, sullen-looking, in their car. Becky, though feeling charitable under the influence of the movie she had just seen, was glad they hadn't come in when she invited them. The man in the car unwrapped and lit a cigar with jerky movements, and puffed on it. The women in the car with him made faces and waved their hands and talked at him vigorously. He rolled the car window down and threw the cigar into the yard. His face was redder than ever.

Come on, people, she thought. Come and get your kid out of here and move your car so these awful people can leave.

Come on, Nicky. The race is over. Surely you're done there now.

She didn't want to think about him lingering at the Speedway. If he stayed there long, she knew, she would start imagining things. About that blond girl.

Oh, come on, Becky Alef, she thought. Get hold of yourself and don't be so silly. He probably does still have valid things to do at the track.

He has valid things to do in his darkroom, too, she thought. He really ought to be here.

My God, she thought. I wish we could've bought that farm when we were trying to. I don't know how we could've made it down there, but it would have to be a better life than this.

Nicky, damnit, at least call and explain if you're going to be late. But by God, you better come home. Davey's counting on it, and he's about reached the point where he'll give up on you, too. You don't want that to happen. But you can't string a child along forever. Becky really was surprised at how frantic and irritated she was becoming.

Out in the yard a car horn began blowing. She looked. The man in the blocked car was hitting the horn button, making three long blasts at a time.

Stop that, she thought. What good does that do?

The horn blasts continued. She grimaced and put her hands over her ears. The noise drilled insistently into her anxiety and made it worse. Shut up, she thought. I have a small son who doesn't have tantrums like you.

The horn kept going, three bleats at a time.

Becky took a deep breath, set her jaw, and jerked the door open. She strode down from the porch into the rain. The man kept honking as she walked to the car. She rapped on the window with her wedding ring. He rolled the window down, glaring at her. She put her face down close to his, as if she were going to whisper to him.

"SHUT UP!" she screamed louder than she had ever screamed in her life. Then she turned and marched back into the house. There was no more honking.

She stood in the hallway, clenching her fists and trembling. She felt a little guilty about having screamed like that, even though it had stopped the awful honking. She thought she should go out and apologize, try a little friendly persuasion to make the man be patient with his plight.

She turned back to the door just in time to see the red-faced man drive his car in a tight turn all over her shrubs and flowers. He stopped, backed over her rock garden, shifted into forward gear again, then accelerated out of the yard, his spinning wheels digging deep, muddy ruts. The corner of his bumper knocked over Nick's limestone bench and broke it. Becky thought immediately of going after the obstreperous man for damages—but just as he steered his big car wildly onto the street, he hit the rear end of a Volkswagen camper that was swinging out from the field across the street. Some enormous bearded youths in black hats swarmed out of the vehicle and surrounded the car. The man in the car looked so terrified that Becky forgot about the damages and turned away from the door, feeling that justice had been, or would be, done.

Becky could hear Davey and the other boy. "What's your dad do?" Davey was asking.

"He's a race driver," the boy said. "What about yours?"

"He's a book writer."

"Huh. I'm glad mine's a race driver. That's what I'm gonna be," the boy said.

"We're gonna live on a farm," Davey said.

"A farm?" said the other boy. "Yuck."

"My dad's takin' us to a movie tonight," Davey said.

"My dad's gonna bring us back to the race tomorrow," the other boy said.

"We don't go to the race," Davey said. "Except my dad. He's an important photographer, and he takes pictures there."

"If I lived this close, I'd be there all the time."

"We'd rather go camping," said Davey. "We go all the time."

"You got a car?"

"Sure. It's in the garage. It's broke."

"Shoot. Bet I could fix it. What's the matter with it?"

"We dunno. It just won't start."

"Bet I could get it started. I know all about cars."

"You're not old enough to drive."

"Huh! Maybe I don't have a license, but I can drive cars. And fix 'em."

"Hey, Mom!" Davey called. "He thinks he can fix our car!"

Olive Canfield saw the fat man and woman poke their umbrellas out of the car, open them, then climb out, lock the car, and walk away.

Less than a minute later, two men and two women approached, walking abreast under one long sheet of white plastic. They went to the car that was parked directly in front of the car the fat man and woman had just left. One of the men unlocked the doors, the four got in, and the car edged forward into the line of creeping traffic. "Oh, no," Olive Canfield said aloud. "Oh, no, no, no, no, Lord, how could you?"

With that car gone, she saw, the fat people could have pulled out. If they had waited one minute longer, they could have been driving their car out now, which would have opened the space beside her so that she might have been able to maneuver her own car out from between the ones in front and in back of it. But the fat people hadn't waited that minute. They were gone, and she didn't know when they would be back, and she was still blocked in on four sides.

"Dear God. Tell me they've just gone to the bathroom. Tell me they'll be back in five minutes so they'll move their car and I can leave. I don't think I can stand any more of this."

It seemed absurd to be mentioning bathrooms and cars in a prayer to God.

But, she thought, it's just been an absurd day.

She sat. She waited. After another hour the traffic began moving out of the field a little. People came and got into cars all around and drove them away, but nobody came to the cars in front of hers, behind hers, or on either side. Now she was sitting in the center of a cluster of five cars, in a half-empty field.

It's almost quitting time at the bakery now, she thought. I should have left the car here and walked to work. I could have been there hours ago. I could have explained it all to Mr. Sanders, and even that old wart would have understood how terrible this is and would have forgiven me for being late. It would have been quite a walk, but I could have done it, even bad as my feet are.

In fact, if I had any sense at all, she t ought, I'd just leave this car right here and walk out of this hideous place and take a bus home or something.

But if I left it here, I'd have to come back for it tomorrow, and I'd *never* come back here for anything.

If I didn't have this car, I could just walk out of here and be free, she thought. But I'm tied down to this car. I don't own it; it owns me. It always has, she thought. With the payments and the repairs and the licenses and all that expense I can hardly afford, this dumb car has always owned *me!* And now I'm stuck in it here, and if somebody doesn't come and move their dumb cars, it's going to be my coffin! I'm going to *perish* in it if somebody doesn't come along pretty soon and move one of these dumb cars and make room for me to get my dumb car out of here. Dumb cars. Dumb cars! My gosh, cars practically rule the whole world!

Where are the people who parked these cars here, she wondered. Surely they're not still in there waiting for that stupid race to start again! If they are, the race cars own them. They do!

Olive Canfield, in her hunger and thirst and exhaustion, was having a moment of clarity. With her eyes closed to rest them, she was seeing automobiles as the masters of the earth. She saw the whole world covered with highways and parking lots and traffic signs and racetracks and drive-in restaurants and drive-in car washes and drive-in theaters and drive-in banks and garages. And she saw the people of the earth spending their lives getting out of the way of cars and earning money to support the cars and sending all their tax money to build roads for the cars to run on. Then for a glorious instant she saw a world in which there were no cars. She saw a great sloping meadow full of flowers with people walking in it and a blue sky overhead and soft heavenly music playing. . . .

She opened her eyes with a start and looked around. Here she still sat, in a car surrounded by four other cars in the middle of a field surrounded by a racetrack surrounded by streets in a city surrounded by interstate highways.

Well, Olive Canfield thought.

She straightened up in the seat. She turned on the ignition key and stepped on the gas pedal. When the engine was running, she set her jaw firmly, put the car in reverse, gave it gas, and released the brake. With a lurch the Falcon banged against the car parked behind her. She kept shoving the gas pedal down. I'll move you, you dumb car, she thought. The motor whined, and the tires lost their traction. She stamped on the brake and shifted into forward and drove against the rear of the car ahead with a crunching sound, and she kept accelerating. It wouldn't move, either. Reversing again, she smashed again into the front of the car behind her. She was starting to laugh and feel exhilarated. "I'll move you, you dumb—" *Bang.* "Move, you—" *Crash.* Fore and aft, pieces of headlights and taillights fell to the ground. Bumpers bent. Chrome chipped. Grilles caved in. License plates twisted and screeched against each other. The motor of the Falcon whined and its gears whirred and Olive Canfield laughed. It didn't even matter now that the car in front and the car in back weren't really being moved out of her way. The important thing was that she was feeling better.

When her tires finally were slithering in the muddy ruts she had made, and the Falcon could no longer go forward or backward to batter the two other cars, Olive just turned it off, jerked her house key off the ring, climbed out, slammed the door with all her might, and walked away, feeling free, feeling like a person again.

*   *   *

The Coles had done everything they could think of doing to find Kevin. They had done everything at least twice. They had waited in a long queue to gain access to a telephone, then had commandeered it for half an hour and called every hospital in the city. Cliff Cole almost had to fight some of the other people who wanted to use the phone.

Now the family was at the police control post. They had given a description of Kevin to a harried-looking policewoman and had been huddling together in a corner of the room for more than two hours waiting for some kind of report, which had never come in. The time had dragged. Marjorie wanted to do something else to find Kevin, but they couldn't think of anything they hadn't done already. Marjorie's eyes were inflamed, and she had to rest with them shut every few minutes. She ached all over. They all ached all over.

Finally, Pam said, "You know, if I was Kevvie and I couldn't find us, you know what I'd do?"

"No, hon. What would you do?"

"I'd go to the car."

"The car?"

"Sure. Except for our seats, that's the only place he knows around here. Where the car is."

Cliff and Marjorie looked at each other. "What do you think?" Cliff asked.

"Let's all go," Marjorie said. "Let's stop at the grandstand and get Keith and all go to the car. I swear we're going to stick together from here on."

"But what if he isn't there?" Cliff said. "God forbid," he added.

"Then we'll just have to come back here and keep trying," said Marjorie. "At least we'll be together."

In the field north of Twenty-fifth Street there was still a large encampment of tents and recreational vehicles and cars. From the encampment came whoops and the noise of radios. The field and both sides of the street were strewn with soggy trash. A few cars and pedestrians were still moving along the street away from the Speedway.

As the Cole family drew closer to the house where they had left their car, their pace picked up. Keith started to run ahead to the car, but Marjorie called him back. "Stay with us," she said. Her jaw was firm.

"Why can't I go see?"

"We're all going to see."

"He's not in it," Keith said as they came close enough to see the car.

"It's locked," said Cliff Cole.

The car sat there in the grass. The other cars that had been parked in the yard were gone. There were deep tire tracks, and a stone bench was lying broken on the ground.

"Oh, dear God," Marjorie said in an exhausted voice. "Where can he be?"

They straggled up to the car, not yet able to think of what they would do next. Cliff rested his hands on the car roof and let his head droop forward.

"Sir," a woman's voice called from the house.

Cliff looked up. The dark-haired woman was standing in the doorway, smiling.

"You son's in here," she said. "The little guy's a mechanical genius. He fixed our car!"

Nobody felt like scolding Kevin.

The Coles—Cliff and Marjorie in the front with Kevin sitting snugly between them, and Keith and Pam in the back seat—were on Highway 31 heading north in the dusk for Kokomo. Kevin told them about the start of the race as he had seen it, and about how he got his black eye in the crowd. He told them about his conversation with the boy in the house, and about fixing the carburetor of the Volvo, but was careful to leave out the lie he had told about his dad being a race driver.

They told Kevin about their day: about seeing the race car come crashing along the wall, about the flood of fuel and heat, about the hurt people, about wandering around trying to find him. He listened, blinking sleepily, smiling when they told him about the woman calling him a mechanical genius. He was quiet for a minute, thinking about what they had seen, trying to visualize the race car crashing.

"Wow," he said. "I wish I coulda seen that."

Cliff and Marjorie glanced at each other over his head, and said nothing.

The car rolled toward Kokomo in the gathering darkness. Pam and Keith were asleep in the back seat, their heads leaning together. The motor thrummed. Marjorie kept her eyes closed and tried not to remember the moment of the big wreck. I'm sure there's a bottle of Murine in the upstairs bathroom, she thought. Kevin seemed to be asleep; he was still. But as Cliff slowed down for the Kokomo cutoff, Kevin said, "I'm sure glad we've got our tickets. I can't wait to go back and see the race tomorrow."

Marjorie moved abruptly. "Forget it," she said.

"Huh?"

"We're not going back there," she said. "Never, never, never again."

"Whaaaat?" he whined.

"We're not going back to the race," said Cliff. "That's absolutely final. And if I hear one bit of crying about it— if you so much as mention it—you're grounded for a week."

Kevin strained and struggled with a rising fury. He knotted his fists between his legs and gritted his teeth, and his lips drew up tight and white and distorted. It was all he could do to keep from exploding into a tantrum of self-righteous protest. That race was the greatest thing in the world, and he wanted to tell them they would be crazy not to see it if they had tickets.

But he didn't say anything. In the scarlet defiance in his mind, an idea was forming.

Nick Alef patrolled through the motel's lounge and lobby, corridors and restaurant, and decided Diana hadn't arrived yet. Should call home, he thought. But there were lines of people around every phone, some with their luggage, and there were people thronging the motel desk. Conversations were going on everywhere about reservations and plane schedules. It'll be bedlam around here with this postponed race, Nick thought. The city had about half again its population on Race Day, and by now on any ordinary Race Day they were all on their way out of town. But they're race fans, Nick thought. They'll stay by the thousands rather than miss the "500."

I'll try to call home later if I get a chance, he thought. Right now I'd better try to find a table. He edged through the door into the lounge, trying not to bump people with his bulky equipment bags. " 'Scuse me. 'Scuse me, please." Oh, to be just a writer again, he thought. Encumbered with only a notebook and pencil. He peered around in the dim, warm light within the crowded lounge.

The room was cozy, full of people at closely set tables; their laughing faces were lit from below by candles flickering in red glass holders. There was a bar along one wall, peopled mainly by men in racing jackets. The walls were lined with large Leroy Nieman oil paintings of the 500-Mile Race. Opposite the entrance was a piano bar, presided over by a large, smiling woman with glittering eyeglasses on a neck chain. Her facile improvisations on an organ were filling the room with lively sound. "Hello, deah," she called across the room to Nick as he entered. She chuckled low in her throat as he started into the room. "Dis must be da place," she said, and went back to her playing.

Nick had some luck. In a deep corner, a couple gave up their small table just as he came by, and he dropped quickly into one of the chairs, swinging his bags into the other. From this table, Nick could watch the entrance. At the adjacent table there were four flushed, laughing, middle-aged people, two of them very fat.

"Hi. How'd you like the race?" the fat woman asked him.

"Ha-ha-ha. What race?"

"Yeah!" they chorused. "What race!"

"You can share our waitress when she comes back," a white-haired man at the table said to Nick, shouting over the din. We've already done the hard part. Got her attention."

"Good! Thanks!"

> *"Sure as God made little green apples;*
> *It don't rain in Indianapolis in the summertime."*

Laughter and jeers went up around the room. "That's

the third time she's played that," the white-haired man laughed. His eyes were sparkling, his face florid. Nick estimated he was on cocktail number four or five. "I'm Gene," the man yelled, extending his hand. "My wife, Ruthie, and Gerald and Ella, our friends!"

"I'm Nick. Glad to meet you." God, he thought. What a nice private place I picked for a delicate conference with Diana. Oh, well. "Gerald and Ella, eh?" Nick said. "I presume Ella Fitzgerald, and Gerald Fitzella?"

The fat couple shook with laughter. "Oh, Lord," groaned Gerald. "I never thought of that!"

"Join us?" the man named Gene asked.

"Uhm. Well, we're all in this together, huh? But I am expecting someone."

"Well, have a drink on us, anyway."

"No argument from me."

"We're really starved," the fat woman said. "If anybody else is ready to order, what say?"

The waitress brought drinks. Nick sipped a straight rye and gazed at one of the Nieman paintings as the waitress took the foursome's food orders. Thousands of little speckles and blobs and smears of bright-colored paints, massed together to make a vague panorama suggesting crowds and speeding machines. A lazy man's pointillism, Nick thought. Where would Nieman be if it hadn't been for *Playboy*, he thought. Maybe *Playboy*'ll set me up that well.

The din went on and on. Nick worried about not having called home, and watched the door impatiently for Diana. The man named Gene was talking about some children named Allan and Janet. "Both brought down straight A's all last semester. We're really proud."

"Hey," the fat woman cried. "Why don't you and Ruthie come stay with us tonight, and come back for the restart tomorrow, long as you're in town?"

"I'm tempted, but can't," said Gene. "Now, listen, you guys. You lost your tickets, so I insist you take ours. I know you like your Tower Terrace, but try this fourth turn tomorrow." He fished in his shirt pocket with two fingers.

"We'll do it," Ella said. "But you've got to let us pay you for them, Gene."

"The hell you say! They're already paid for, and we can't use 'em! Absolutely won't hear of it."

Nick noticed that the fat man didn't seem really interested in the tickets, but Ella's face shone.

Gerald looked wistfully around and caught Nick's eye. He leaned toward him. "We didn't really lose ours," he said. "We threw them away."

"No kidding," Nick said, feigning astonishment. "Why?"

"Aw," said Gerald, "we had a day. I had enough Speedway for a while. Our car's still sitting in there in the infield—and I got upset by the big crash. You know—"

The fat woman cut off her husband's statement. "Oh, Jerry," she said. "Tell them about the woman in the next car."

"Yeah! Do," Gene exclaimed. "Funny!"

"Only that this poor lady got caught in the traffic this morning and was trapped in the Speedway all day. Ha-ha! Can you imagine that?"

"I can't imagine anything worse," Nick said.

"Oh, was she ever steamed," Gerald exclaimed.

"Hey, haven't I seen you in the paper or on TV or something?" Ella yelled to Nick.

"Could have," Nick said. "I used to be a newsman. Columnist. On talk shows and stuff."

"Oh! You're a celebrity!"

"No. Just used to do a lot on the media hereabouts. *Used* to. Actually, I'm the world's youngest has-been."

"Oh, come now."

"Ha-ha-ha."

"You look like a star!" Ella cried.

Nick gave a small, sour smile and wished the woman would shut up. But she was gazing at him so expectantly, as if she were dying for him to be someone famous. So he said to Ella, "I still do special films and programs. Produce them, I mean, independently. Mostly on—ah—safety."

"Oh, wonderful! I think safety's so important. Jerry and I have never had an accident, have we, Jerry?"

"That's right. No, you just have to be awfully careful to be safe. I mean, you have to drive for the other guy as well as yourself."

Great conversation, Nick thought. We're already quoting old traffic safety slogans. "Safety pays," he said. "Careless driving can be a *grave* situation. The life you save may be your own."

"Ab-so-lute-ly!" exclaimed Gerald, who was taking it all very much to heart.

Nick felt he should somehow turn them off. He didn't like being drawn into their group like this, with Diana coming. "You take racing," he said. "That has a direct bearing on the safety problem."

Ella leaned forward across the table, an intent look on her face. "That's right," she said. "Cars are so much safer because of things they learn on the racetrack."

"If you say so," Nick said. "As you know, they've been reinventing the rearview mirror for forty years right here at this very Speedway. Right?"

"Wh—"

"What I'm talking about," Nick said, "is the effect racing has on the whole 'speed-and-power' mentality about cars. I mean, what do they advertise in cars? Getaway, zoom, sexiness, prestige, and all that crap, right? Never efficiency or a safe way of getting from one place to another. Impalas. Cougars. Chargers. Mustangs. Dusters. Grand Prix. And the fuels. 'Get up and go.' 'Tiger in the tank!' 'The Racer's Edge.' 'A. J. Foyt uses Valvoline!' 'National driving champ So-and-So drives a Monte Carlo!' 'Cadillac paced the "500"!' That kind of irresponsible B.S. that comes out of Detroit and the goddamn racetracks." Nick was surprised to be getting so wound up about this. "I'm talking about the kind of turn-on that puts a kid in a muscle car covered with racing stripes and makes him think he's Richard Petty or Bobby Unser or somebody, so he goes peeling rubber down a residential street and hits some poor inno—" Then he stopped himself. That was it. He was seeing Timmy lying broken on Twenty-fifth Street. He sat there, breathing fast, his fists clenched, his jaw set. Don't take it out on these people, he thought.

"Well, hey, just a minute," Ella said. "Do I get the idea that you think racing is *bad* for safety instead of—"

"Was I being too subtle? Then let me state it this

way—No. Never mind. If you like it, that's your business. As for me, I'm tired of seeing people die for speed. I think the American public has been brainwashed for half a century by checkered flags and chrome and tail fins and young studs in racing helmets. But that's my opinion."

Gerald and Ella were trading troubled glances. Gerald sipped his drink and put his fat chin on the heel of his hand and looked thoughtful.

Then the fat couple started talking between themselves and seemed to be having some sort of a disagreement about racing, or perhaps about what he had said about racing; Nick couldn't hear much of it because the music was growing louder. The entertainer was getting lots of requests and lots of applause. She was extemporizing lines for the songs and interrupting herself with comical lines. She's good, Nick thought. Doesn't take herself seriously. Nick was getting into a strange mood. He was anxious because he thought he should be at home, and, at the same time, because Diana hadn't shown up.

"Hey!" the entertainer was shouting. "What're we celebrating? Anything?"

"ANYTHING!" several people called back.

"I'll drink to that!" she laughed, picking up a glass from the organ top and sipping. "I'll drink to anything! Hey! *Oooh*—

> *"There's a shanty in old Shantytown. . . ."*

Nick was getting submerged in the place now; the drink was making everything fuzzy and rhythmic and silly. It was as if the lounge were becoming an extension of his own senses, an organic part of him. All so silly, so dumb, he thought. All bullshit. That's my trouble—I can see that everything's bullshit. What the fuck am I doing here?

He found himself gazing at the Nieman painting on the wall again, and it seemed much more interesting now. All those little dots and masses of color. That's what life's really like, he thought; you don't really see life, just shapes and impressions made out of little dots on a flat surface of time, seeming to make a picture every day or hour or minute or second, all flowing together, flux, fluidity. And speaking of fluidity . . .

"Would you watch my stuff, folks?" he said. "I got to go powder my bladder."

As he left the room, the profound, dim, living, pulsating room, he passed by a long table where several wealthy-looking men and women sat, very expensively dressed, the women tanned and wearing low-cut gowns, the men mostly in white sport suits with white shoes, all talking and laughing very loudly. One of the women, a striking blonde whose face looked slightly familiar, watched him go by and smiled surreptitiously at him. He returned what he thought must have been a very dopey-looking smile and went on, having trouble steering past the men on the bar stools.

Ought to drop this silly *Playboy* thing and go home, he thought while standing at the urinal. Last thing I need to do is stay out for all hours when things are the way they are at home. Last thing I need to do is get involved with this Princess. And unless I misread the signs, we're getting involved. It was a scintillating possibility—just the thought of photographing her in the nude shook him to his very center—but what a crazy thing for me of all people to be involved in, he thought. Jesus.

But goddamn it, he thought, you've got to make *some* kind of a move before you get trapped in the treadmill forever and turn into one of these goddamn married Midwest zombies.

Well, wait for her, anyway. You've got a date with her and shouldn't stand her up. What the hell, it's a natural! Ask her, anyway. She'll probably say yes, and you'd be a fool not to, he told himself, zipping his fly and pushing the flushing lever. He washed his hands, looking at himself in the mirror. Lean. Strong-looking. The short, dark, glossy beard, the wise gray eyes in slightly wrinkling sockets, the big forehead with its thoughtful lines and faint freckles.

This noble creature, he thought, using its miraculous brain and the precious hours of its lifetime to write safety slogans and other B.S. Man, oh man. Whooey. Alef, he thought, you better grab any brass ring you can get.

When he stepped out of the rest room, he heard a woman's voice. "Nick?" It wasn't Diana's voice.

He looked around. In a carpeted corridor leading off the lobby there was a row of tables and chairs next to big windows overlooking the Speedway golf course. In one of those chairs there was a beautiful woman sitting alone at a table: the blond woman who had been with the rich people in the lounge. "Is that you, Nick Alef?" she said.

"Yes. And—wait a minute," he said, approaching the table. "I know you—"

"I know, the nose job's throwing you off," she laughed. "And the bleach job. Remember our French licks at French Lick?"

"Katherine! No kidding! My God, did you feel me thinking about you all day? What are you doing? What are you doing here?" Their four hands were a knot between them.

"I'm married to a tycoon who's interested in the Speedway. I'm an actress now, Nick." Her laughter had just a tinge of drinker's hoarseness in it. "You haven't seen any of my, uhm, movies?"

"No, I—"

"It's just as well. Can you sit down for a minute?"

"Uh, sure. I'm waiting for somebody, but I—"

"A female somebody?"

"Yeah. But, uhm, just business—you know."

"Sure. Oh, gee, Nicky. I almost called your home today."

"Whew. Thanks for the 'almost'!"

"Oh, I wouldn't have. I don't want to give you trouble. But I think of you every time I'm near Indianapolis."

Nick sighed and blew, remembering his own remembering. "But what's this about you, an actress with a rich husband? You've come a long way, baby."

"Very rich, yes. A girl's got to provide for herself in this world, you know. Face-lifts and fanny-lifts notwithstanding, a sex object gets obsolete in a hurry if she can't act."

"You don't think you can act, hm?"

"Oh, of course not. You know me. I never could pretend."

"Well, I don't know," he chuckled. "You mean you didn't fake it a time or two there in French Lick?"

She gave a low laugh. "I didn't have to with you—and you only, you darned satyr."

"Hm, hm. Thanks, I needed that. I was just looking at myself in the mirror in there—"

"Oh, but you look finer than ever. You really look like a writer."

"That's the important thing—to look like one—I guess."

"You were starting a book when we—"

"Yeah. I finished it. Didn't sell, though. Done another book since then, too."

"My gosh! How prolific! What's it about?"

"It's about a pound. Eight ounces of sex, seven ounces of violence, and one ounce of socially redeeming value."

She laughed. Not the girl-laugh he remembered, but one that was more husky, more exciting in a different way.

"It didn't sell, either, though," he said. "So I'm just flacking along. As much photographer as writing these days. I could tell you I'm doing fine, but you and I don't pretend. To each other, I mean. Right?"

"Nick, honey, I wouldn't have believed you, anyway. Don't worry. You'll do something great someday. But we're all selling our asses these days. Don't feel badly about it, you old— That beard is fabulous on you, Nick. When did you—"

"About three years ago."

"I wish you'd had it at French Lick. It looks—interesting. Very tactile, I imagine."

"I haven't heard any complaints. Jesus, Katherine—"

"I'm called Kitty now."

"Kitty. That's good. I remember you stretch like one. Listen, I've never forgotten that profound and hilarious time—"

"Did we laugh, Nick?"

"Did we laugh! Remember that one thing you said— It may be indelicate of me to reminisce this way with a rich married lady, but I was, you know, kissing you down there, and you said— Do you remember what you said?"

"Remind me."

"You said, 'Come on, honey, put your fucker—' "

" '—where your pucker is!' Oh, God, yes." She laughed, a hand over her mouth. "And all your puns— I remember 'Ladies and genitalmen' and— Oh, Nick. Today, you know, I heard a song on the radio—'Is That All There Is?'—and I thought, I guess so. But no, there's Nick. But those were just thoughts. I wouldn't have dared to call you. I didn't expect—"

He sighed and disentangled their hands, which were warm and moist. "Is, uhm, is your rich man good to you?"

"Yes. My Werner poo-pie is very generous."

Nick sighed. "He's going to come looking for you, though. Well, I don't know what we do now that we've had this—this serendipity, do you? Maybe we ought to go in with some innocent-sounding tale of where we know each other from, and make introductions all around."

"If you don't mind, why don't we *not* do that?"

"Not?"

"Maybe we could keep each other a secret. I'll be in town another day or two because of the rain-out. Do you have a pencil?" She wrote something inside a matchbook and gave it to him. He looked at it as he clipped his pen into his pocket.

"Dold. Oh, you're right here, you mean? Those new VIP suites?"

"Mhm. Nick, please, I really would like to see you tomorrow. I have my own suite; it'll be all right. You don't need to call. Just come up. If you can. You know." She looked down the corridor and through the lobby as they rose, then stood on her toes and kissed him quickly on the mouth. An exciting musky scent came up at him from her cleavage.

He waited in the corridor a minute after she had gone back to the lounge. He had a sudden powerful desire to call home, to go home. But there were still no phones available. He looked around for Diana, then went into the lounge. Katherine—Kitty—didn't look up at him as he passed. He scanned the men at her table to guess which one might be her Werner poo-pie. Next to her was a stout, tanned, totally bald man of about sixty, listening with his eyes half-closed while another of the men strained forward and talked vehemently in his ear. That one's got to be Werner poo-pie, Nick decided. He's obviously the moneybag of the crowd.

"Hey, we thought you'd fallen in!" Gene Roepke said when Nick returned to his table.

"I did! But all I could grab was the flush handle, and that just made things worse."

They all laughed. Nick saw Kitty glance toward the burst of laughter and smile, and somehow it made him glad that she saw him in the center of laughter.

"We were just talking about this fuel shortage they're all talking about these days," Gerald said warmly. Apparently they hadn't remained upset with him over his remarks about racing. "What do you think about it?"

"Ah, I'm glad you asked," Nick said, feeling good again. "It just so happens that I've been working on a solution to it. See what you think of this. . . ."

When Diana appeared in the doorway of the lounge, limned by light from the lobby and peering in the gloom, Nick rose and waved. She made her way toward him, radiant and golden, and Nick noticed that Kitty was among the many who turned to watch her and see him kiss her hand and clear the chair for her. Diana surprised him by stepping close and hugging him, putting her cheek beside his. The foursome he had been talking to were big-eyed at the sight of her. As he slid the chair back for Diana, he glanced and saw that Kitty had turned her back to her group and was lighting a cigarette with jerky motions. Careful, he warned himself. This could get to be an ego trip.

He introduced Diana to the two couples. "Well, now, she's worth waiting for!" Gene said loudly. Then, with a display of that surprising kind of propriety that even drunks seem to show on certain occasions, the four politely turned back within their own group, wordlessly relinquishing their claim on Nick, and left the handsome couple to themselves. Nick was very grateful.

"I just couldn't get away from Harry Kuntz," she apologized when she was settled with a cocktail. "He kept showing me off. I met all kinds of famous people."

"Exciting, uhm?"

"Gee, not really. Kind of depressing. I mean, I've met so many famous people all month, and it seems like what they're all scared of is that they'll be forgotten."

"Heavy stuff for such a pretty young head."

"Well, even I think about it, you know. I mean, look, here I am in the papers and on TV all this month, and you know, I don't mean I'm famous or anything, but after the '500' Festival, nobody'll remember me."

"I will."

She laughed a melodious girl's laugh that made him forget all his misgivings about going through with their project. "I appreciate that," she said. "I mean the public, though. I mean, I'll just be another ordinary coed. Just anonymous, you know."

I won't even have to lead up to it, Nick thought, she is. "Are you saying the fame bug has bitten you?"

"Oh, gosh. I don't like the sound of that. Applied to me, I mean. But I guess it has, in a little way."

"Well, if you don't want to be forgotten, you just stay in the public eye. The way you look, why, it's a cinch for you."

"How do you mean?"

What the hell, he thought. No point in stopping now. Full speed ahead. "Well, I mean, for example, I could help you. And you could help me at the same time. Uhm, you see, I'm a pretty fair photographer—well, better than fair—and I know beauty when I see it, and I sort of like to think I've discovered you. Well, what I'm saying is, with my ability and your beauty, I think we could get you started on your way to a lot of, well, exposure. This Festival Princess thing is a terrific break, timewise, if we exploit it pretty quick. Hope you don't mind the word 'exploit.' I mean it in a good sense."

"Sounds groovy to me! What do we do?"

"Just talking, okay?"

"Sure."

"Okay. You remember I said I used to see you lifeguarding. Well, it looked to me like you're, you know, pretty flawless all over as well as your face, okay?" He saw by the change in her eyes that she knew exactly what he was getting at, so he decided to get right to it. "What would you think of posing nude?" They had come to the point so fast he felt dizzy.

She toyed with her glass, not looking at him. She tilted her head and watched the liquid move in the glass. "Well, it's about the third time I've been asked that this month."

That alarmed him. "What?" he said. "By whom?"

"Other photographers."

"Well, what, did you, uhm—" He was feeling a strange anger.

"I said no."

"Well, good. I mean, fine. Uhm, then you—then you wouldn't—you wouldn't do it, then?"

"Not for them."

"What about for me?"

She looked at his eyes now, a level gaze. "I'd think about it. You're different." Then she looked down shyly.

He took a deep breath and sighed it out. He straightened up and sipped his drink. He felt good. "How different?"

"Well, I like you. I mean, they were—like, when they asked me, it was like gross, like they were dirty little people who just wanted to see me, you know. I mean, to them I would just be a dirty picture. But you, you seem to like me—I mean, *me*. You know?"

"I do. I really do. Hey, let's drink to that!" He grinned, leaning back in his chair and waving for the waitress. He liked the way this was going. She *liked* him! She *trusted* him—that's what it was. This was a pretty heady moment. He felt a powerful, tingling sweep of desire and readiness in his loins. Watch yourself, he thought. Nick always had mixed feelings about new desires of this sort. They hurt his conscience and complicated an already complex life.

When the new drinks came, he explained to her that he was talking about the big one. "*Playboy*," he said. "No grubby little stuff. They pay big. I could pay you a thousand out of it. Have you ever had a thousand dollars of your own?"

"That's a lot of allowance."

"And listen, with *Playboy* there isn't that lowbrow connotation, you understand. I mean, you're a sort of a celebrity. And this festival thing is a natural, you realize that?

Why, you're a natural for Playmate of the Year. And then we're *in*."

A part of him listened to himself, incredulous, as he made his play. But she was obviously swallowing it. She apparently wanted to believe whatever he said. She looked flushed, a little hesitant but excited about the idea. He could tell that. Of course she would be. In this month, seeing her done up as a wholesome Princess for a Midwestern corn-fed apple-pie glamour festival, he tended to forget sometimes how she had enjoyed flaunting herself around at the swim club. Inside that virginal gown, he reminded himself, there's an exhibitionist. I believe there is something inside her that's going to like posing naked. It's going to turn her on. I think so.

"But," she said, "I have to think about it. My family, you know. And the festival people would be against it—"

"What can they do?" he asked with a happy shrug. "The festival's over by then. What can they do, sue? Don't worry about them. Harry Kuntz? What can he do?"

"My dad works for him, you know. Maybe he would make things rough on Daddy."

"Well— Listen, you may not know men very well, but I'm willing to bet Harry Kuntz would really—I mean down inside, of course—really flip over it. Don't you see how it would reflect on him? People would look at you in that centerfold and they'd remember that he was your sponsor, and that'd made him feel like even more of a big shot than he already thinks he is."

Diana was remembering how Harry had paraded her around among the celebrities at the festival activities and at the race today, and she realized that in some ways Nick was right about that. Harry likes to think people are wondering whether he's ever made it with me, she thought. They'd really wonder it if they saw me in *Playboy*. She shivered at the thought of her whole body, that whole naked body she enjoyed so much, being seen and appreciated by millions of men. She had a thought of Harry Kuntz sitting in his bathroom looking at her in the centerfold and playing with himself. It was very funny. But—

She shook her head and gazed at the candlelight and squeezed her hands between her knees.

Nick Alef could see the complex doubts flickering

through her face and was afraid that if he didn't get her to come out and promise, he would lose her. She would very likely think her way out of it. In a way, he hoped she would. Rationally, that would be the best thing.

But by now he really didn't want her to back out.

"It's mainly my family," she said in a small voice. "Daddy's job, and Mom— You don't know how proper, how un-hip they are, Nick." She remembered the weeks of absolute hysteria and self-recrimination they had gone through when she thought she had missed a period last summer and they had found out their dear, darling, peaches-and-cream princess daughter wasn't a virgin. She had let them think it was one of the boy lifeguards from a family they looked up to, even though she wasn't really sure it was he or one of three other guys she had made it with that month. God, they had just about died. And then it had proved to be a false alarm, but by then the harm had been done, and she would still be living with it, except that, thank God, they had deliberately buried it in their memories and, by the process of wishful thinking, had finally restored her virginity. All that had been a ghastly secret that never even got outside the walls of their home; even Harry Kuntz had never gotten wind of it, so they had been able to cover up the shame in their own minds. But if she suddenly were printed naked in five million or whatever it was magazines, the whole world would know about it, and, even worse, all Indianapolis would know about it.

"Nick, I want to, but please understand, I've got to think about it before I say yes. You don't *know*. I've just got to think about it."

"There isn't much time. We should shoot it in.the next day or two while the race is still in the air around here."

"I know. I—I'll let you know tomorrow. I—" She reached across the table and put her golden hand on the back of his big sun-darkened hand with the dark hair on the fingers. "I've just got to think about it."

"Don't let anybody talk you out of it," he said intensely. "You've got to do what *you* want to do. Please," he said, putting his other hand on top of hers and pressing hers between both of his, "don't discuss it with anybody because I know—I'm scared of this—they'd sure as hell talk you right out of something that could be great for *us*. You just have to do what *you* want to do!" He couldn't believe himself, still pursuing this so avidly when he should have thanked God for her hesitation.

"Of course I'd never talk it over with anybody. Don't be silly, Nick. It's *our* business, right?"

"It's our business. Right." He sighed and seemed to shrink. Her eyes searched his face, appealing for something more.

He put his hands on the corners of the table and inhaled and exhaled vigorously and looked around the lounge. He was suddenly aware of the people and the music again; it was like reentering the world. They had been an island of intensity all by themselves. "Well, what do you say, Diana? Do you have to go now?"

"Are you trying to get rid of me?"

"God, no!"

"What do you want to do?"

"Well, I don't know." He glanced at his watch. It was eight o'clock. "What do you want to do?"

"Why don't we just continue what we're doing and see what comes to mind."

Aye, he thought. "Sure! How about maybe one more drink now that we're through talking business"—he paused, and she laughed—free, relieved laughter—"and then maybe we could go someplace. Okay?"

"Okay. Fine."

"Oops. Don't look now—" Diana followed his gaze out the door into the lobby. There was Harry Kuntz, with his usual perplexed, pouty look, glancing about.

"God, maybe he won't see us," Diana said. But he did. He came toward the lounge and in through the door.

"Hello, deah," the singer shouted across the room at him. Harry looked at the singer in surprise, half-smile of ruffled dignity flickered on his face; then he came to their table.

"Well, I've been looking high and low for *you*," he said to Diana, not glancing at Nick.

"Hiii, Ha-rrrry," she said. "What is it you want?"

"What are you doing here?" he said.

"Well, what does it look like?"

"Now, don't you be flip with me, Diana. God knows, I might never have found you."

"What a tragedy that would have been," Nick said.

Harry looked down his nose at Nick and then turned to Diana again. "Do you really think you should be here? Drinking?"

"Don't you drink, Ha-rry?"

"That's beside the point. I'm a bit over twenty-one."

"Yes. A bit."

"Now, Diana, you're in my charge. And this doesn't look very good for a Princess—"

"Harry, I am in your charge, and I appreciate your concern, but I'm not in your custody."

"Excuse me, Mr. Kuntz," Nick said. "She's in good hands with me. Why don't you just, uhm, leave her here and go your way? Maybe your wife wants you." Maybe mine wants me, he reminded himself.

"Come on, Di," Harry said. "I think I should drive you home, don't you? Your parents—"

"Harry, look. There was no Victory Banquet tonight because there was no victory. Now, since there aren't any festival functions going on, why shouldn't I just have an evening on my own?" She knew the answer to that, of course. Harry simply didn't want anybody who knew him to see *his* Princess out with another man. *His* Princess, she thought; the pompous ass thinks he owns me for the month of May. Suddenly she thought again of Harry sitting in his bathroom with the door locked and his pants down around his ankles and her nude magazine photograph opened up before him. I may have to do it just for Harry's sake, she thought.

"Diana," Harry said severely, "I think you should come with me, I really do. After all, there is the race tomorrow, and—"

"Why don't you let her do what she wants, Mr. Kuntz? What do you want to do, Diana?" Nick was aware of Gene and Ruthie, Gerald and Ella at the next table, all pretending to be minding their own business. And though Harry was blocking his view to the Dold table, he presumed Kitty would be watching this, too, with interest. In a way he felt Harry had come just in time, but in another way he felt embarrassed, felt his ego trip dissolving.

Diana looked from one to the other of them, her elbow on the table, her chin resting on the palm of her hand.

Then something settled in her face. She wanted to stay with Nick, but she knew everything would be easier, much simpler—especially whatever she decided about Nick's proposal—if she let Harry take her home now. Harry had a lot of leverage in her life because of her parents, if not because he was her festival sponsor. And she really did need to get away from Nick and think about his idea away from the influence of his presence and without cocktails steaming up her mind. "Nick," she said, "you understand, don't you? There are lots of reasons. I'll see you tomorrow, and—you know." She winked at him, tilting her head and smiling to project reassurance. "You did tell me to make up my own mind."

"Yeah. I did." Though disappointed, Nick was also relieved. He thought immediately of Becky and Davey, and about film he needed to develop. Things would be better on the home front if he got home tonight. He didn't want Becky doing frantic things in the background when and if he started the *Playboy* project with Diana. "Sure," he said. "I understand. Whatever you want, Diana."

"You really *do* care, don't you?" she said, taking his hand and squeezing it.

"You bet I do."

"Harry, go get the car, then. I have to powder my nose before we go."

Harry looked at her uncertainly. "How do I know you'll come?"

Eyes flashing, she turned suddenly to face him. "Don't insult me, Harry," she hissed, "or I'll change my mind!"

Harry left, and Nick stood up and dealt some five-dollar bills onto the table, then draped her pink knit shawl over her shoulders. He picked up his camera bags and said good night all around the next table, and they walked out into the lobby. He saw Kitty watching, expressionless. "The ladies' room—" he said.

"I don't really need it," Diana said. "I just wanted Harry to go away for a minute. Nick—"

"Yes?"

"I appreciate this. I was right. You really are a prince. You won't be sorry." The headlights of Harry's car were moving in the parking lot outside. Diana put the strap of her white purse in the crook of her arm, placed her hands on both sides of Nick's face, and licked her lips. Then she quickly put her open mouth on his lips and kissed him hard, and their tongues touched for an instant. They went outside, and he ushered her into Harry's official "500" Festival Cadillac pace car.

Nick was happy about several things. One thing he was most happy about was that Kitty had seen Diana leave the room with him instead of with Kuntz.

Isn't that strange, he thought. That I care about that.

He started the long hike home. The great stands of the Speedway towered beside him as he walked.

God, he thought. I've got to go through all this again tomorrow.

Lloyd Skirvin brought his car to a stop on a stretch of country road off Highway 136 west of Indianapolis. He turned off the lights, put the gear level in neutral, and set the handbrake, but left the engine running. It was totally dark except for the glow of the city under the clouds in the east, the lights of an airliner descending toward the distant airport, and a few cold blue farmyard lights a mile or two down the road. Crickets chirped in the cool, damp air. "Okay, y'all. Le's all git nekkid now."

Renee gave a little, uncertain laugh in the darkness and said, "You're not kiddin', are you?"

"Honey, I don't kid."

"He really don't kid." Worms laughed in the back. He was already out of his shirt and was unfastening his trousers, giggling drunkenly. "C'mon, now, baby," he said to Puggles. She began slowly unbuttoning her shirt.

"Are you sure this is such a good idea?" said Renee.

"Honey, ol' Lloyd Skirvin don't have nothin' *but* good ideas. Now, you better hurry up there."

The girls were a little afraid of doing this, but they were more afraid of not doing it. They had had enough beer and Four Roses that they didn't care a whole lot about anything. And the pornographic movie they had just seen at the art theater had made them laugh a lot, and they had become pretty stirred up in their different ways. It was just that now something was starting to happen to them instead of up on a movie screen, and the sudden reality was a little scary. But they slipped all their clothes off and then sat there with the night air on their skins and wondered what was going to happen next. Renee found herself being excited by the feeling of the air on her body and the texture of a car seat under her naked buttocks and thighs.

"Now," Lloyd said, chuckling low, "if you two little jaybirds will jes' git out and walk up there in front of th' car a little way—"

"What?" Puggles exclaimed loudly in back.

"Come on, honey, nobody's gonna get hurt or anything if you do what we say." There was both reassurance and menace in his voice. So the girls got out on the asphalt road and stood beside the car, their forms pale and vague in the darkness. The hard pavement was cool and damp under their feet.

"What if a car comes?" Renee said.

"Won't no car come," Lloyd said. "Now y'all walk up there 'bout fifteen feet and then turn around, y'hear?"

"This is crazy," Puggles said. But they walked forward and then stopped and turned to face the car. Puggles kept reaching out and touching Renee's arm and grasping her wrist, as if to know she was not alone in this crazy thing they were doing.

Suddenly they cringed together, blinded by white light. Lloyd had turned on the headlights.

"Yowee!" Worms yelled inside the car, leaning forward over the seat back and staring at the sudden, white, absolute nudity of the two very young girls in stark contrast to the darkness of the roadway. "Man, don't they look good!"

"Hey, what's the big idea? Hey, whaddya doing? Hey, you aren't gonna run over us, are ya?" The girls were yelping, squirming, and crouching in the blaze of light. To the two men watching through the windshield, it was not unlike seeing the girls on a screen. They laughed together. Worms in the darkness of the back seat looked at their dark, bushy little crotches, hooked his thumb over his hardened member, and pushed it down, feeling sensations flash through his lower abdomen. The girls had stopped squirming now and stood in the light, giggling with their hands over their mouths. Renee reached over and cupped her right hand under Puggles's firm young breast and shook it up and down twice; Puggles reacted by turning with a screech and throwing a mock slap at Renee's backside.

"Hey, you two jaybirds," Lloyd yelled. "Get in. They's a car comin'!" Headlights were shining in the rearview mirror, far down the road.

The naked girls ran bouncing to the car and swarmed in, slamming the doors shut. The headlights in the rearview mirror were growing rapidly. "Damnation," Lloyd laughed, releasing the handbrake and shifting into low gear, "that fuckin' car come along too soon. Ol' Stud Boar there didn't even have no time to finish jerkin' off!" Worms yowled in denial. Lloyd stepped on the gas and let the clutch out fast, and his tires squealed in the still night. Soon he was doing more than eighty down the country road, shrieking around curves and sailing over rises in the road with a soaring and bouncing that made their stomachs turn over. "Give them two jaybirds another belt of that 'ere whiskey," he yelled. "They mighta got cold out there on the road." Worms poured the whiskey, and the girls tossed it back without tasting it, as Worms had taught them to do, and once again were able to keep it down. They shot past a road sign, and Lloyd suddenly stood on the brake, bringing the car to a fishtailing halt, then slammed it into reverse gear and the car whined backward to the intersection. It was a gravel road, and Lloyd turned into it and raced into high gear. "Hey, Stud Boar," he yelled, "reckon these jaybirds ever been in a drift?"

"Doubt it!"

"What's a drift?" Renee called above the roar of the motor.

"Find a curve here and I'll show you." Lloyd yelled. Soon they saw the white road curve ahead to the left. Lloyd bore down on the curve, making no effort to brake or decelerate. Renee felt her heart rise up with the feeling that they were going too fast to make the curve, but she was too petrified to cry out. Lloyd eased up on the gas just a tiny bit as he went into the curve, then stood on it again. The rear end of the car began to slip sideways toward the outside of the curve. Lloyd waited until the car seemed almost in an uncontrolled skid, then turned the steering wheel to the right, clutched it in both hard hands, emitted a terrible rebel yell, and gave the car more gas. Gravel rattled and the car vibrated violently and the engine wailed and the girls squealed in exhilaration, pressed to the right by centrifugal force. Coming out of the curve, Lloyd straightened the wheel gradually and stood harder on the pedal, and then they were barreling along straight ahead.

"That there, jaybirds, is what a drift is," Lloyd yelled to the quaking girls. "Now, they ain't no sane man would do that 'cept on a racetrack he knowed real good!" Worms was laughing hilariously. The girls were speechless.

At length Renee got her tongue off the dry roof of her mouth and said, "You ain't gonna do that again, are you?"

"Not 'less I come to another turn in th' road!"

After a while the car came onto another asphalt road, and pretty soon a little town loomed up in the headlights. Lloyd tore through it at about ninety, laying on the horn. "Wake up, you dumb muthafuckas!" he yelled out the window. And suddenly Renee saw something move onto the edge of the road; a pair of eyes burned yellow in the headlights. She screamed. There was a quick impact under the car, and then nothing. "Muthafuckin' hound! Coulda killed us," Lloyd snarled. Renee felt sick.

"Stop," she said. "Where are my clothes? I don't feel good. I think I'm gonna upchuck."

Lloyd glanced into the rearview mirror and gave the car more gas. The motor wound up still higher. "Fergit that," he yelled. "We done picked us up a goddamn county mountie or somethin'."

Oh, Jesus, Renee thought. She looked back and saw red flashers perhaps half a mile behind. If they catch us like this, they'll put us ten feet under the jail. As the car sailed through the night she groped for her clothes, wanting to get dressed but afraid to take her eyes off the road at such speed.

"Jus' leave them clothes be," Lloyd yelled. "Ain't nobody gonna catch us!"

He's crazy, she thought. She had felt all along that

Lloyd and Worms were a real wild pair of dudes, and that had been just fine. But now she decided that he was really crazy. She remembered the wild yell he had given as they watched the race cars pile up in the flames, and she thought of his scornful anger after running over the dog. I've gotta get dressed, she thought. If he ever stops this car, I'm gonna get out and run. She found her panties on the floor and started to step into them. But suddenly Lloyd reached over and smacked her on the side of the head. The car wobbled frighteningly with his move, and he quickly got his right hand back onto the steering wheel.

"I said, leave them clothes be!"

Worms was turning to look out the back window, and Puggles was doubled up like a fetus, too scared even to think of getting her clothes. She had a strange notion that if she moved so much as a finger, it would throw the car over that thin line between controlled speed and uncontrolled speed. She knew it wasn't so, but she had that notion and couldn't move.

"I think you losin' 'im, Lloyd," Worms yelled.

"Yeah, them goddamn cops ain't got no nerve. Hold on, jaybirds!" There was a dirt-road junction ahead. Lloyd let up on the gas, downshifted and, without braking, swung left onto the dirt road, snapping off the headlights at once. As they thundered along the rough road in the terrifying blackness, Worms watched out the back window. The flashing red lights of the police car didn't follow; they shot past on the paved road and disappeared. "Y'shook 'im, Lloyd!" Only then did Lloyd brake the car; the brakelights glowed red along the roadside for a moment. He turned the car around in two or three grinding lurches, then roared back up the dirt road toward the paved highway, his headlights still off, turned right, and sped off in the direction from which they had come.

"They goin' be cop cars 'round here thick as stink on shit," he said. "Hold on again, jaybirds." Now, still without lights, he went on two wheels into a faint light patch that he had correctly presumed to be a gravel road. It was easier to see without headlights than the blacktop or the dirt road, and they tore along it in rising spirits. Going over a rise between what appeared to be two pastures, they looked back and saw the flashing red beacons of two police vehicles in the distance, one far to the west, one to the southeast, but none, apparently on this road. But Renee had run from authorities too much in her young life to feel they were in the clear yet. *You can't outrun the radio.* That was the axiom. You could think you were scot-free, and suddenly in front of you there would be a car sitting across the road or street with a star on its door facing you, and cops all around with big, bright flashlights.

Lloyd took three more turns up back roads before deciding to turn on the headlights again. Renee was thankful they were no longer flying blind but feared they could still be encircled. She had, in fact, an awful sense that police cars from coast to coast were prowling through the night just waiting for this Mercury to appear. They're just everywhere, she thought. They're just everywhere waiting to stop you and put you in locked, bright rooms and bore you out of your skull with questions and lectures. She was feeling terribly let down and exhausted now and just wanted to stop all this crazy racing around and crawl in somewhere and go to sleep. But Lloyd and Worms were obviously getting higher than ever because of their escape, and were bantering back and forth with remarks and laughter, and Lloyd's foot was getting heavier on the gas again. The city glowed off to their right, and the road went on and on, fence posts and telephone poles and darkened houses whipping back past the car in a blur.

And then Lloyd's right hand came over in the dark and thrust between her thighs and moved up to her crotch, and his strong fingers probed around, touching places that hurt and then flashed with pleasant sensations her stupefied mind was not ready for yet. She grasped his wrist and tried to push the hand away, but it was too strong. Gradually she relaxed her thighs and felt his finger go deeper, and she squirmed down on it, angry and afraid though she was. Suddenly the hand pulled out and cupped around the back of her neck and pulled her down toward him. Oh, God, she thought. I know. She thought about resisting but was terrified that any struggle would make them end up wrapped around a tree. She yielded and her face went down toward his sour-smelling lap next to the steering wheel. She was disgusted and afraid, but at the same time the rigidity of him stood there unseen in the drumming darkness, a magnetic presence. It had been a long time since she had done this to anybody, and she did not dislike doing it, but she wondered what it would do to his driving, which, she felt, had had them on the very verge of being killed for half an hour now.

She had expected his to be uncommonly hard, and it was; and she had expected him to be uncommonly rough and demanding, and he was, pressing down on the back of her head so forcefully with his hand that she felt like gagging. Only by scraping with her teeth was she able to warn him, and he eased the pressure off the back of her head and let her do it her way.

Her way was good enough, and when the spurting started he was sucking air through his bared teeth and holding her head so she wouldn't try to get away from it, and he stiffened his legs and mashed farther down on the accelerator pedal, and the speedometer needle was on 115 when they burst into the lighted outskirts of the town of Lebanon. They crossed three streets during the time of his ejaculation, and the car did not swerve an inch. Lloyd yodeled in appreciation of his own incredible control. And from the back seat came Worms's hysterical laughter.

There were police cars in the town of Lebanon, but Lloyd Skirvin's white Mercury had whisked through the outskirts and back into the country darkness so fast that if they had seen it, they would have thought it was an apparition.

Gene Roepke had intended to be back in Chicago by this hour, but it had been hard to get away from the Rumples. Gene had heartburn from all the butter he had eaten on his rolls and baked potato and all the drinks and coffee. He wished he had a seltzer or Rolaids or something. It was very late, and there was not much traffic on Interstate 65. Next town, I'd better gas up, and maybe they'll have antacid of some kind, he thought. Ruthie had fallen asleep as soon as they got out of Indianapolis. I've never seen her drink so many cocktails, Gene thought. And that Nick character. Absolutely zany. That invention idea of his to take care of the heating fuel problem: a fart suit! I thought I'd die laughing.

Gene was having some trouble seeing the signs. They looked blurry unless he squinted. Good thing I had plenty of coffee after all that drinking, he thought. Main thing is not to get sleepy.

LEBANON NEXT THREE EXITS

That's where I'll fuel up, he thought.

It's no wonder there's a fuel shortage. I imagine I've seen half a million cars today, and that's just in one little part of the world on one day, and they're all burning gas and oil. Never stops. *The sun never sets on the internal combustion engine*—that's what that Nick had said.

Fart suit. Ha-ha-ha-ha.

Alef had told them over their after-dinner drinks that the reason so much gas and oil is wasted on heating is that people heat and air-condition whole houses full of rooms instead of just the air next to their skin where it counts. He had said the solution would be to have heat and cooling not in the houses but just in insulated suits like the ones astronauts wear on the moon. It would require maybe one-thousandth as much fuel to heat a suit as a room; your body heat would do most of it. But if you needed more heat, you could just use a tiny heating element on the suit. From electric batteries, or burning gas from tiny propane cylinders on the suits. That made sense. Those ideas were wild, but there was good thinking behind them.

He had gone on to say you wouldn't even have to get fuel from the big oil and gas companies. Cars have been run on methane gas from chicken manure. It wouldn't take much poo to heat a moon suit, he had said. As a matter of fact, he had added, you could probably heat it all day just by eating beans and radishes and burning a little blue pilot light off your farts. Gene started laughing voicelessly, remembering that. God, what a thought! Gene visualized the blue flame of the pilot light and shook with laughter. He couldn't stop. Tears came to his eyes. Well, they had really enjoyed meeting that Nick. And that gorgeous gal he was with. Wow! And Gerald and Ella really seemed to enjoy themselves, too. Amazing how they never get tired of being together, he thought. They're really good company.

LEBANON KEEP RIGHT

Gene went up the ramp, turned onto a street, and drove toward a service station glowing in the night.

Just a shame Gerald and Ella don't have kids, though, he thought. They'd be great parents. Give another dimension to their lives. What would Ruthie and I have to talk about after all these years if it weren't for those wonderful kids of ours? Wondered that sometimes. Strange to think about it. But without them we'd be almost strangers. She's in her world, and I'm in mine.

He glanced at her, feeling a very unusual sadness and compassion. She slept, her head pillowed on a folded sweater against the car door. When he looked back to the road, there was a white car shooting straight across his path at terrific speed. Gene reflexively jerked the wheel. His right front wheel went off the edge of the road, and the steering wheel spun out of his grasp. His car went under the bed of a parked semi at forty-two miles an hour. Ruthie was decapitated in her sleep, and Gene bled to death from his carotid artery before the police arrived. In the middle of the night they became traffic statistics.

PART II

May 29, 1973

NICK Alef had a bad time trying to wake up. The alarm pulsated next to his head, and he knew it was 6:30 A.M. and that the race was scheduled to start at 9:00.

Nick calculated in his stupor and realized that he had had only three hours' sleep. It had been after 9:00 when he arrived at home last night. It had been too late for them to take Davey out to a theater to see *The Poseidon Adventure* or *The Legend of Boggy Creek,* and after a futile and awkward attempt to salve the boy's disappointment and get him to bed, including a promise to take him to the movie tonight, Nick and Becky had had a long discussion that had covered everything from his diminishing credibility as a father, and the humiliating news that a small boy had fixed their long-dormant Volvo, to Nick's poor performance as a husband. That discussion had continued until 1:00 A.M. and had ended with their undressing, going to bed, and making an insincere effort at reconciliation. He had worked pleasurelessly upon her for another half hour, his mind occupied with the knowledge that he still had to get up and develop film. He had resented the time they were spending in this hypocritical embrace; he had resented the castigations she had heaped on him; he had resented this challenge to him to perform. Panting and sweating, he had finally managed to arouse himself enough for the performance only by fantasizing about a nude Diana Scheckley, or a nude Kitty Dold, or some entity that metamorphosed back and forth between the two. Nick despised himself when he did that, but he despised Becky even more for creating circumstances in which

213

that was necessary. This bullshit about everything having to be psychologically just right for a woman to have
happy intercourse, he had thought angrily. What about
the poor guy who has to get it up and do the performing?
What about his psychological requirements? It was so
rare anymore for both of them to be in the right state of
mind or the right time frame simultaneously.

After that, he had had to lie in the dark waiting until
he thought Becky had gone to sleep before he dared to
get up and go down to the darkroom. She didn't like it
when he made love to her and then went away to do
something else; she was always quoting some feminist
who had written that for once a woman might want to do
it not before something else or after something else but
instead of something else.

Then he had worked until almost 3:00 in the darkroom, and finally had dragged himself back upstairs to
bed, to find that Becky wasn't asleep at all; she had
stayed awake reading all that time just so she could have
the triumph of giving him a dirty look. At last they had
turned the light off, and he had fallen asleep to a series
of bad dreams sometime about 3:00 A.M. And now here
it was 6:30 with another day of that damned race still
ahead, and many arrangements yet to be made for the
shooting of his *Playboy* spread with Diana—*if* she had
slept on it and decided yes.

And Kitty was expecting him, too. In spite of everything, he had been yearning for her. She made him feel
like a winner, and he needed to feel like a winner. He
realized, of course, that she might consider him differently today after having seen him with Diana last night;
she might be jealous and not welcome him at all, or she
might tease him about it and ask questions. Either would
be interesting and good for his ego.

But, he thought, brushing his teeth, the way today's
shaping up, when in hell will there be time to see Kitty?

He reached for his running suit, which was hanging in
its usual place on the bathroom door. It was stiffer and
heavier and smellier this morning, and he wondered why
Becky would never simply take it down and throw it in
with the other washing. She washed everything else in
the house regularly, but would never wash his running

suit unless he personally carried it down to the laundry room; it was as if it had become some kind of symbol of her general discontent.

Shit, he told himself. You don't have the strength to go out and run two miles this morning, anyway. Or the time.

Reluctantly, he hung the suit back on its hook. He listened to the steady rumble of Speedway-bound traffic outside and felt depressed. Those rare times he gave up and skipped his running, he really felt like a flop.

Something else had been bothering Nick since his discussion with Diana the night before.

She had said other photographers had asked her to pose nude for them. Even if she wouldn't do it for them, it might mean that somebody else had had the idea of a "500" Festival Princess Playmate feature. There are plenty of princesses, and there are hundreds of photographers here who might have had the same idea, he thought.

Since he had first had the idea, Nick had been secure in the notion that it was his exclusively, and that no one else would come up with it. Of course, it was likely that some other photographer might be doing a nude spread related to the "500" using some other models; one of the recent fixtures at the Speedway was a busty blond former Playmate from Indianapolis, June Cochran. Surely photographers had approached her with the idea. But Nick had presumed that only he had the boldness and the manner to approach a real "500" Princess about it. After Diana's remark last night, though, he had felt that awful sense of urgency about it.

Don't want still another of my great ideas to go down the drain, he thought. I've been too little and too late with just too goddamn many original ideas. That's why I'm scrambling the way I am now.

Sarah, the Rumples' once-a-week housekeeper, arrived just as they were loading their spare picnic basket into the car. Her brown face revealed how surprised she was that they weren't dressed up to go to work. They were in sweaters and sport clothes.

"I left you a whole lot of dishes," Ella said. "I've been cooking chicken again this morning. Now, please remember not to use a steel scratch pad on the skillet."

"I'll remember, Mrs. Rumple." Five years before, Sarah had ruined some Teflon and had never been quite forgiven. "When'll you be back?"

"If the race is over before one, we're going on down to the office and work this afternoon. You can call us there if you need us this afternoon. Mr. Ralph's there this morning. If anybody calls here about business, they can call and give him the message."

"Okay, you all have a good time!" Sarah cried as Gerald backed the car out of the driveway. Gerald looked up at the ominous gray sky and turned south on Crittenden Avenue. Behind Sarah, the phone began ringing.

"The Rumples' residence."

"Uh, hello, I'm calling long distance for Mr. or Mrs. Rumple."

"Oh, my. They just left, ma'am."

"Do you know where they can be reached?"

"Well, they was goin' to the Speedway, but after noon they be in they shop."

"Well, listen, can you get a message to them? I'm Claudia Snyder, Ruthie and Gene Roepke's next-door neighbor. Have them call me as soon as you hear from them, at this number. You have a pencil?"

Sarah wrote down the number. "Allan and Janet wanted me to call," the woman said, "because the Rumples were such good friends of their parents—"

"Yes, ma'am, yes," Sarah said, all these unfamiliar names milling around in her head while the dishes and pots and pans and skillet lay there needing to be done.

"Did they know about the accident, do you think?" said the woman on the other end of the line.

"I surely don't know," said Sarah. "What accident that be?"

"Well, the poor dears were killed in an accident down near there last night. The visiting hours at the funeral home will be tomorrow—"

"Oh, pity sakes," cooed Sarah. "Well, I will sure have them call this number soon as they can."

"My heavens, my heavens," she said over and over to herself as she dialed the number of the E & G Carpet Care Company. "Mr. Ralph?" she said. "I got a message here for. . . ."

Olive Canfield slid a tray of fresh, warm yeast doughnuts into the rear of the showcase and straightened up. She was exceedingly tired. She had spent an almost sleepless night, wrestling with dread and conscience. She had finally gone to sleep at about three, and had had bad dreams about Mr. Sanders, who kept coming toward her shaking his fist and wearing a Speedway hat, and kept locking her out of the bakery. The alarm had awakened her at four; she had set it very early to allow herself time to get a bus downtown and then transfer to another bus that would take her within three blocks of the bakery. She had kept expecting the telephone to ring or a policeman to come to the door and arrest her for banging up two cars and leaving her own car in the infield of the Speedway. But the phone hadn't rung. She had left the house before six, caught the bus, and reached the bakery in time to open it and get everything started. Mr. Sanders would be coming in any minute now. She could only pray that, finding everything so nicely under way, he would forgive her for yesterday. If the police or the insurance people come after me, she thought, I'm going to need this job in the worst way. God, let him understand what happened. He's been an awful old grouch since Mrs. Sanders passed on, but there's got to be some good down deep in everybody. Ooops. Here he comes now. He's early.

"Well," he said, hanging up his straw hat and donning his white baker's cap, "look who decided to come in." He wore a white shirt with elbow-length sleeves. There was fine yellow hair all over his sunburned forearms. The first thing he did every morning upon arrival was scrub his hands vigorously with Lava soap. The rapid, rasping sound usually irritated Olive's morning nerves, but this morning she was so grateful that he hadn't— yet, anyway—told her she was fired, that it was almost like music to her.

Mr. Sanders wandered through the kitchen, peering at everything over his spectacles. Now and then he would stoop to sniff the aroma coming off this tray or that. Then he got his brown-glazed ceramic mug out of the cupboard, the lopsided one he always drank from, the one his dear departed wife had made in one of her ceramics classes. In red she had painted *Max* on one side. He filled it with some coffee that Olive had made in the thirty-cup urn. He sipped at its edge, his round, ruddy face thoughtful above his name on the cup, his spectacles misting with the steam from the coffee.

Well, she thought, hurry up and give me the verdict.

"Okay, Mrs. Canfield," he said at last. "Sit down a minute, please." He sat on a chair at one side of the table in the center of the kitchen and motioned toward a chair on the other side. "Now," he said. "Tell me again all this cock-and-bull about why you never came in all day yesterday. It better be good."

If you think it's a cock-and-bull story now, she thought, wait till you hear it. She laced her fingers tightly together in her lap out of sight beneath the table, cleared her throat, and, looking as straight at his skeptical, blond-lashed blue eyes as she could bear to, she recounted the tale from the beginning, up to, but not including, the destructive tantrum in which she had banged up the other two cars. Throughout the story he said nothing, just puckered his lips, frowned, and sipped at his coffee. "So that's your story, hmmmm?" he said. "Pretty wild."

"Except for the day my Raymond passed away, Mr. Sanders, it was the worst day of my life." She congratulated herself on having said that. It was a built-in reminder to Mr. Sanders that she really did need the job. He nodded at that, his gaze going distant. Olive slumped, relaxing a little. That was it. He'd have to believe it or not now; there was nothing more she could do.

"Listen," he said, leaning over the table and clutching his coffee mug firmly between both short-fingered hands. "Did I ever tell you what I think of all that race hoo-ha? It's a damn plague on this city, that's what. Four times in the last fifteen years, my help gets sucked into that damn place in the traffic, and my store opens late. Every New Year I start telling myself, Max, don't be a fool. Sell out and go to a town where they don't have no car races."

Olive couldn't believe her ears. Here was Max Sanders, on a day she had expected him to fire her, telling her for the first time ever what he felt about something.

"Your car isn't here, I notice," he said.

"I was blocked in by parked cars. I finally had to leave my car there and walk to the bus. What's a body to do? I still don't know how I'm ever going to get my car out of that place. I don't ever want to go back there. It was too awful. You just don't know."

He got up and refilled his cup with coffee. "You know," he said, his back to her, his finger holding down the urn's spout handle, "those people who go to that race are insane. I got a friend who works at the Holiday Inn across the street from there, and do you know what he said those race nuts did last night? A bunch of them dirty bums from the infield, they came into the restaurant last night after there was a banquet, and stole the leftovers before the busboys could carry them out. Stealing garbage! What do you think about that? Okay, Mrs. Canfield, now what we got to do is, we got to get your car out of there after work. Otherwise it won't have any tires or battery or hubcaps or anything left. People who steal garbage will steal anything. Look, we'll talk about it in a minute. Here's a customer."

She looked at him, surprised beyond words. She waited on the customer, who bought apple turnovers, glazed doughnuts and cinnamon rolls, and left.

"You mean," she said to Mr. Sanders then, "that I've still got my job?"

"Well," he said, with a grudging little smile, "maybe I haven't ever said it, but you're the best help I ever had in this place. Since my Helen helped me. Rest her soul."

"It's now a quarter till nine, WIBC Indianapolis, time to join Sid Collins and the Indianapolis Speedway Network."

THE FIVE HUNDRED,
THE FIVE HUNDRED,
THE GREATEST RACE IN THE WORLD,
FROM THE OP'NING BOMB
TILL THE RACE IS DONE
IT'S THRILL AFTER THRILL AFTER THRILL!
THE FIVE HUNDRED,
THE FIVE HUNDRED,
THE BIGGEST AND BEST OF THEM ALL!
AND UNTIL THAT CHECKERED FLAG'S UN-
*   FURLED,*
IT'S THE GREATEST RACE IN THE WORLD!

"Direct from the Indianapolis Motor Speedway, the 1973 Indianapolis Five Hundred-Mile Race! Brought to you by Cadillac Motor Division of General Motors Corporation and your authorized Cadillac dealer. And by STP: the Racer's Edge!"

For the second day in a row, Gerald and Ella Rumple were sitting in a traffic jam on their way to the Indianapolis "500." Their early start had done them no good.

"Shoot," Gerald said. "I wouldn't've expected so many people to be coming today, because of work. But unless this starts moving right now, we're going to miss the start of the race. And I can't see much point in all this if we miss the start."

"Oh, come on, now. Where's your old racing spirit? I swear I've never seen you like this. I couldn't believe my eyes when you threw away our tickets yesterday."

"I thought— Well, it seemed to me that it was all right with you, too."

"Well, it wasn't. All I can say is, I'm sure glad Gene gave us his."

"Well, I'm glad of that, too, now. But—" He sighed. "I personally think we should be going to the office instead, this morning. Especially if we're going to miss the start."

Gerald's enthusiasm for the race had not fully revived after yesterday's grim and unsettling impressions. He thought of the things that photographer, Nick Alef, had said, and also of the things the man in the nearby seat had said about Roman circuses. Once or twice in the fifteen years he and Ella had been race fans, they had heard people say unkind things about the "500." But yesterday, because of the remarks of both those men, and the long wait in the rain, and the sight of the big crash so close by, Gerald had been strangely upset.

"Let's don't even talk about it," Ella said. "I get mad at you every time I think of you throwing those tickets away. Turn the darn radio up. I think they're starting to announce."

"STAY TUNED NOW, FOR THE GREATEST SPECTACLE IN RACING!

"This is Race Day, May twenty-ninth, 1973. The Place: the Indianapolis Motor Speedway, scene of the running of the fifty-seventh annual Five Hundred-Mile Race! If those words sound familiar to you, perhaps it's because you heard them before—in fact, just about twenty-four hours ago, when we took the air yesterday. It was ten-fifteen A.M., Eastern Standard Time, when we greeted you from this same Master Control Tower to begin what was to end as a complete day of utter frustration. More than three hundred thousand fans filled the stands and infield on the Westside of the city, preparing for the annual motor classic here at the Speedway. The skies darkened, the black clouds hovered above, as eleven A.M. nudged nearer. Then the rains began, and set us back more than one hour. We stayed on the air with you for the first sixty minutes, then retreated, along with the rest of the drenched humanity, into a state of wait-and-see. This continued until Chief Steward Harlan Fengler gave the contestants the green light to move their powerful machines trackside. At two-fifty-eight, Eastern Standard Time, the call was given for the engines to be started, and the parade lap began. At three-oh-two, when the green flag was waved after the pace lap, a grinding crash took place as the rear of the pack neared the first turn and left in its wake the upside-down race car of David 'Salt' Walther, as well as—"

* * *

"Jesus Christ, Cliff," exclaimed one of the four men standing around Clifford Cole beside his desk. "If that had been me, I mighta shit my pants!"

"Yeah," said Cliff, smiling weakly, then hurrying on, "it was terrible. Just terrible. I didn't really want to talk about it, but you asked me how I liked my first 'Five Hundred,' and all I'll say is, my first was my last. 'Scuse me. My phone— Hello?"

"Cliff?"

"Hi, honey. How you feelin'?"

"Cliff, when you left this morning, was Kevin's bike in the garage?"

"You mean his bicycle or—"

"His trail bike."

"Uhm, well, I don't remember; I didn't really look. Why?"

"Oh, dear."

"What? What's goin' on, Marj?"

"I don't know. When I went in to wake him up for school, he was gone—"

"Gone?"

"There was a note on his bed. It said he wasn't going to wait for the school bus but was going to walk."

"Kevin never walks."

"I know it. He never writes notes, either. His bike's not in the garage."

Cliff compressed his lips and exhaled through his nose, frowning. The other men had drifted away to their desks. "Darn that kid," he said. "He's been told ten times not to ride that bike to school. On the streets at all. I'll skin him alive—"

"Cliff," Marjorie interrupted, her voice very anxious, "I called the school, and he's not there. They checked."

"Oh, for cryin' out loud— Well, listen, hon—uhm, don't get upset, okay? Could be the race yesterday just got him so het up about speed that he played hooky and, uh, and went out to run some trails or something, or that little track the kids have over by, you know, there by the junkyard."

"Cliff, you've got to do something about him. You can't just keep making excuses for—"

"I'm not excusing him! I didn't say hooky is all right. I'm just saying he's probably okay—just like yesterday when we went out of our minds worrying about him at—" He paused. "Uhm, Marjorie," he said slowly.

"Are you thinking what I'm thinking?"

"No, no. No, honey. Cancel that. He's got a lot of brass, but he'd never try that. Would he?"

"Clifford, just hold the phone. I'm going to see if his Speedway raincheck is in his room. In the clothes— If it's gone, Clifford, I swear to Heaven I'm going to call the state police. Because sure as God made little green apples, he's halfway to Indianapolis by now!"

Just as Nick Alef started out of the house to walk to the Speedway, Becky came up with a suggestion that almost stopped his heart. "Why," she said, "don't I go along with you as your assistant? Like in the old days?"

Oh, Jesus, he thought. Diana and Kitty both flashed into his mind. He wasn't sure what the day would hold as far as either of them was concerned, but whatever it was, Becky's presence would ruin it all. "Are you kidding?" he exclaimed. "It's too complicated. We haven't made arrangements. We—" He saw her face hardening. She's suspicious, he thought. Mustn't protest too much. So he looked thoughtfully at her, as if he might be considering it. "But what about Davey?" he said. "And—and I thought you were going to call about that job at the ad agency—"

"Yes," she said. "You're right. Never mind. It was just a thought."

He kissed her good-bye and joined the river of race-bound people, relieved but strangely let down. If she had come along, her very presence would have kept him from doing something that he was contemplating with such anxiety. In a way, it might have made his day easier. He really did not want to give in to the temptations offered by either Diana or Kitty. They were offering him choices at a time when he was unusually susceptible. He thought back to the first time he had been unfaithful to Becky. It had been about ten years before, when, as a newspaper reporter, he had covered the annual meeting of the Indiana Chamber of Commerce at the French Lick resort in southern Indiana. Kitty had been there—Katherine, then. She had been visiting the resort with a high school chum of hers who worked conventions at the stately old spa as a semiprofessional hooker. Katherine had been considering that line of work herself, at her friend's urging, and had been sitting in the lobby one morning weighing the pros and cons when Nick appeared in a nearby chair and struck up a conversation. They had soon found their way to his room, and then had spent most of two days in bed conducting a marathon of erotic stamina and exuberance beyond anything either of them had ever experienced before. In interludes of satiation they had played and laughed like naked children—precociously hip and witty children, to be sure—and Nick's whole self had expanded; his mind had made clever universal music, using her candid and shameless personality as the sounding board. He had written something—he remembered it now:

Cupid took his little bow and shot me full of Eros.

He had not gone to any of the Chamber of Commerce meetings. He had simply emerged from his room for an hour each afternoon and collected press releases, then had edited them and read them over the long-distance telephone to the rewrite man at the paper in Indianapolis while Katherine squirmed naked on his knee, trying to distract him into laughing or stammering.

While they were disporting themselves, she had decided not to go into the call-girl business. "Just the constant usage alone would tend to wear out the equipment, wouldn't it?" she had said. He had agreed, urging her not to start that kind of life. "You're too smart," he had said. "And you're too good for it. What you've got to give is too priceless to sell. You're life itself."

She's been selling it all these years, of course, Nick thought now as he showed his credentials at the Speedway gate. But to a more select clientele. One can only imagine the parade of agents and producers and porn-film studs that has passed between her legs since I did.

That thought almost made him give up the whole thing. Having a love affair with someone really special might be grounds for adultery, he thought, but to step outside the bounds of matrimony and risk all the guilt and self-recrimination just to follow a procession of ghosts across her well-trodden *mons pubis*— What the hell was I thinking of?

Nick hadn't played around as much over the years as Becky apparently thought he had. He was, in fact, proud that he had turned down as many chances as he had. It's not all that easy to stay faithful to a woman who uses her tongue only to lash you with, he thought. (Good line— ought to write it down.) Well, I can always look at it this way: I've already cheated on Becky with this woman once, so it's not really like being unfaithful again—is it?

"Lou Palmer is in the south pits. Lou, do you have some information for us?"

"Yes. We are not going to get our nine-o'clock start, Sid Uhm, we have a track inspection underway at the moment. There is, as you can see from the Tower, some dampness along the main straightaway, but it is not that that they are concerned about. That is drying rapidly enough that if we get two—a pace and a parade lap—in, it should be pretty well blown off, lifted up, and dried out. But between turns one—to my south—and two, there is some dampness, and it is up against the outside retaining wall on that short straightaway between turns one and two, and that is the groove, and the tires just aren't built to adhere to a wet track. So it's going to be too slippery to run on for a bit. They have the blower out there; they'll be working on it, attempting to dry it, with skies threatening, so we have a delayed start. Can't give you an estimate of how long."

The Purdue University Marching Band played the National Anthem, and the drivers stood at attention near their race cars. The brassy echoes hung in the air, then faded into the rush of voices. Nick Alef looked quickly around in the area in front of the Tower but did not see Diana anywhere. The crowd was almost as dense as it had been the day before. Here and there were scattered empty seats, but the fans kept streaming in, harried from the ordeal of extraordinary traffic jams both outside and within

the oval. Many of the Speedway's part-time traffic hand-
lers had had to go back to their regular jobs, and there
were only about half as many to direct cars to the
parking areas as the day before. Even now there was a
background dissonance of honking horns. Now and then,
a small, steady engine noise could be heard above as the
Goodyear blimp swam slowly through the air like a giant
silver sausage.

All the race cars sat in rows on the track, except that of
"Salt" Walther. Crews had worked through the night in
the garages, replacing bent and broken parts, aided by an
entrepreneur who had a complete machine shop set up in
a bus parked in the Speedway parking lot.

The length of fence and two steel posts torn out
by Walther's car the previous day had received temporary repairs, and many fans in the grandstand area wandered down to see these tame vestiges of yesterday's
holocaust, as if to confirm to themselves that they had actually witnessed such a spectacle. A Cadillac convertible
made slow inspection trips of the track, now and
then stopping so that its occupants could get out and look
at the wet places and talk to each other about them. Men
with brooms were sweeping the wet track surface over
and over in the south end of the main straightaway, as
the fans watched through the fence and made comments
and gave advice. Farther around, on the south leg of the
oval, a crew was using a mobile heat blower on the damp
surfaces high on the slope near the wall; its high-speed
motor droned without inflection.

The fans waited, growing more restless. The steady
rush of their voices grew louder and higher, increasing as
the wind increased. Now and then there would be a ripple
of clapping for no apparent reason, whistles, a raucous
voice yelling, "Let's go!"

The sky was overcast again. A lingering sunbeam
glowed far in the north and then faded. The wind
smelled damp and grew stronger; the colored flags along
the back of the Tower Terrace rippled, streaming almost
horizontally from their staffs. Gary Bettenhausen, deep in
the cockpit of his race car, drowsed with a driving glove
laid across his face.

As the weather became more somber, the crowd became more agitated. Now and then a rhythmic clapping would begin in some section of the grandstands and spread until all along the straightaway the air pulsated with the beat of thousands of handclaps, and a chant of "Let's get go-ing, let's get go-ing, let's get go-ing, let's get go-ing" would swell in time with it. Then it would diminish and a few moments later would start somewhere else in the crowd and build up again.

A reporter came into the Speedway pressroom. He laid out his notebook and called his paper. "At the driver's meeting, Fengler fined Foyt, Revson, and Krisiloff for improving their position in the pace lap yesterday. A hundred dollars apiece. Huh? Yeah, a hundred bucks is no skin off their ass. Foyt said as much. Yeah, he did; he said he'd accept the fine, that it was worth it, if he did pass, to keep him out of the accident. Revson said he was just following Krisiloff and didn't realize he'd passed anyone. Krisiloff said he was just busy getting his car going and was behind Savage and ahead of Revson where he was supposed to be. Got that? Yeah. That's about it. Uhm, King, of USAC, recommended that stiffer penalties might be in order. Huh? No, nobody's openly blamed anybody for causing it. Yeah, I've heard that, too, but you know these guys. They never say anything 'cause they know they might be the one to fuck up next time. Sure, there's always someone in there tries to sneak up. What they oughta do, if you ask me, is black-flag anybody they see sneaking up. That'd cost him a lap or two, and by God, that would mean something. Yeah. Okay. Let you know if I do. See ya later."

Still looking for Diana Scheckley, Nick Alef stood and listened as an announcer interviewed a world-famous mechanic. It was George Bignotti, a big, happy-looking man with a high forehead. Bignotti over the years had had had five wins at the Indianapolis Speedway: two with Al Unser, two with A. J. Foyt, and one with Graham Hill.

"George, you've been around here many years, long

enough to know about how these drivers— You know, they talk about the pole car coming across the start-finish line first, and yesterday I think Bobby Unser was grabbing a lead going into the number one turn, but you were remarking what your feelings were as far as the green flag."

"Yes, actually, when the cars are all lined up properly, whenever they turn on the green, and wave that green flag, the race should be on. They can't wait to get to the starting line, because if they back off hitting the starting line because somebody in front of them isn't going quite so fast, well, twenty guys in the back might run over 'em. So the best thing to do is race, and try to get out of the way as quick as possible."

Nick listened and grinned.

Well, well, he thought, some original thinking. The true concept behind automobile racing isn't that you're going *toward* something; you're running to save your ass.

Sitting in a big armchair in his suite, Werner Dold had held forty-five minutes of long-distance telephone conversation with his secretary in Cleveland, with a lawyer in Boston and a lawyer in Nevada. It had been difficult getting the calls through because of the unusually heavy telephone traffic in Indianapolis. Not anticipating that a quarter of a million race fans would still be in the city on Tuesday, the phone company had not assigned enough extra operators. Werner understood all that, but it made him impatient and scornful. He always thought of everything; why couldn't Indiana Bell, he wondered.

Now he went out onto the balcony and looked over the crowd. A moderate wind, not too damp, was blowing. On the backstretch, just out of the second turn, there was a Cadillac pace car near the outside wall. There were several men in the car. The car was going forward, stopping, backing up, stopping, and going forward again. Werner watched this curious activity for a while before he realized what was going on. There were some wet spots on the racetrack there, and they were trying to dry them out with the movement of the car.

The track-drying machine in the south straightaway was surrounded by track maintenance workers and was still droning away. The crowd was subdued, but now and then they would start chanting for action.

Without Doc Upton here talking to him and forcing cocktails upon him, Werner could think better and appraise the situation more clearly. It was a surprisingly big crowd for a workday. Apparently, these fans would do almost anything to keep from missing the race. For those here in Indianapolis and central Indiana, it would mean merely sneaking or begging a day off from employers who, for the most part, would condone it or at least be resigned to it, as it was a big part of the city's culture. Many of the employers are probably here themselves, anyway, he thought. As for the fans from out of state, they would have had to change travel plans, extend their room reservations or try to get new ones for another night, and iron out all sorts of difficulties. Werner Dold considered all this and knew that Tony Hulman must also be considering all of it. On the one hand, he thought, it must reaffirm for Tony the incredible pulling power of the place. A magic, almost. That's great for Tony, but not too good for my purposes, Werner thought.

On the other hand, those people out there are not terribly happy to have delays again this morning. A thing like this could disenchant a lot of people. And if Tony knew they were very disenchanted, he just might listen to my proposal. Werner was banking on the possibility that even Tony Hulman could get fed up with this.

Werner turned and cast a glance at the window of Kitty's suite. Its curtains were still closed. She had been staying alone a lot this trip, and seemed unusually quiet. She had seemed preoccupied last night in the lounge and this morning when they had breakfast together. He liked her to be cheerful. It reflected well on Werner, who gave her everything a woman could conceivably desire.

He had never been under any illusion that Kitty loved him in a romantic sense. One of the sad things about having a fortune, he had learned, is that you should not delude yourself with the notion that anyone loves you for yourself. You can, at least, let yourself be taken by someone whose acumen you respect. And Werner did respect Kitty's acumen. He did, in fact, admire her very much. I made mine the best way I knew how, and did anything necessary to get it, he thought, and now she does the same. "Would you have wanted to marry me if you hadn't known of my wealth?" he had asked her once. And she had replied, "Would you have wanted to marry me if you hadn't seen my ass on the silver screen?" He felt a flush of deep appreciation for her. By God, he thought. Why don't I—He went into his suite and closed the window. He stopped at his mirror and adjusted his ascot, and the waistband of his white slacks, which neatly hugged his girth. He sprayed a puff of Zizanie de Fragonard under his chin, then went out the door of his suite and rapped on the door of hers.

"Who is it?" came her voice from within.

"Werner."

The bolt clicked, and the door chain rattled. She let him in. She was wearing a full-length nightgown. That seemed strange to him; she had already been dressed today, for breakfast. She smiled at him, but with her mouth only. Her eyes showed no pleasure; she was pretending to be pleased. "Well. This is unusual."

"Yes." He glanced around the room. It was perfectly made up. "After a while," he said, "I'm going to go down and mingle with the crowd. Thought I'd stop in first, though, and tell you how lovely you looked at breakfast. I've been thinking of you this morning, my dear, and hoped we might unwind a little together. If I wouldn't be intruding—"

She knew what he was after. It didn't happen often. "I've been thinking of you, too," she said. He knew that was a lie, but he appreciated her ability to say it so easily. She gave a saucy little wag of her head and untied his ascot. "Mm," she said, "how sexy you smell."

In a moment she had him undressed, and he lay on his back on the bed, a mound of white flesh. She performed her disrobing routine, which succeeded in arousing him. She straddled him, because his weight was too great for her to bear. She did it all quickly but without apparent haste, and smiled and made all the motions and noises of extreme pleasure, and kept her eyes closed. Obviously, she intended to have him satiated and on his way within fifteen minutes, and that was all right with Werner because he considered his time most valuable. He smiled as she squirmed and rode upon him. What a woman, he thought. If she were as good an actress in the theater as she is here . . .

Eyes squinting against the wind, his head encased in the familiar snug weight of his crash helmet, Kevin Cole held the throttle of his bike open and rode southward along Highway 31 toward Indianapolis, the cool wind whipping his clothes against his lean little torso and shins. He stayed to the right edge of the road. His luck seemed to be holding awfully well. He had come a long way without being spotted by a police car of any kind. Now and then a fast auto would overtake him, whispering by on his left. The bike engine purred faintly warm under him, and the springs and suspension soaked up the regular slight jolts of the tarred road seams. In his Levi's pocket was his precious Speedway raincheck ticket, printed in four colors, with its winged wheel and signal flags.

There were many bad things in the back of Kevin's mind that would have to be dealt with when their times came. It might be hard to get into and out of Indianapolis through all the state police and sheriffs and traffic cops, illegally riding this off-the-road bike and having no license because he was too young. And there was the possibility that the school principal at Kokomo might call his home about his absence, in which case he might have to do some very convincing lying when he got home. What he would tell them would be that he had just gone out and run trails all day. That would be an offense, but no worse than he had done many times before. Anyway, he was thinking, if they're too stupid to go to the Speedway 500-Mile Race when they've got tickets, the heck with them. Golly! I can't believe such dopes!

A car edged up on his left. It stayed abreast of him instead of going on around, its tires rushing on the pavement beside him. Kevin kept his face straight ahead. At this speed he knew better than to take his eyes off the road, particularly when there was a car alongside, so close. Go around, he thought angrily. You're spookin' me.

Then the car's horn honked lightly, twice, and the vehicle began to draw slightly ahead. Kevin glanced over, and a wave of dismay went through him. There were the roof lights and the familiar painted stripes of a state police cruiser; there was the trooper inside pointing to the right side of the road. *Oh, shit, shit, shit.*

As Kevin slowed down and the police car dropped back to follow him off the road, the realization fully dawned on him: he was really in trouble! Not only would he miss the race, he would catch it at home as he had never caught it before. His dad probably would ground him and lock up the bike for months. To be brought home from this ride by the state police would mean absolute doom. So, in desperation, Kevin began looking for an escape.

He knew he couldn't outrun the cruiser. Here on the highway he didn't have a chance.

But out there in those fields and woods—they can't drive a car out there. . . .

The trooper pulled his car off the highway onto the grassy berm and followed at a distance as Kevin slowed his cycle. Kevin kept moving slowly along the roadside. He was looking for a place where there was no fence between him and the field. The trooper honked again, but Kevin kept rolling, not quite stopping. And there it was: at the edge of a cornfield the wire fence suddenly turned at a right angle away from the road course. There was a meadow beyond it, mostly knee-high grass and a few dark weeds, and about two hundred yards across the meadow there was a thick copse of trees. Just as the trooper honked for the third time, more insistently now, Kevin suddenly twisted the throttle, angled away from the road, dipped into and out of a water-filled drainage ditch he knew the police car couldn't cross, and gunned away into the meadow toward the trees, standing up off the jouncing seat, the trooper's car horn like a bleat of astonishment sounding faint in the wake of the bike's noise.

Sure hope they don't shoot kids, he thought.

It was a longer walk to the fourth-turn seats than to their customary Tower Terrace seats, and the Rumples had to stop every few minutes, puffing, and set down their picnic basket and rest. It was a heavy load, but they were glad to have it, because from the looks of the weather, it was going to be another long day at the track.

"Not too much farther," Gerald said, panting. They looked up through the towering grandstands and the long, curving lines of bleachers.

Gerald and Ella were wearing brilliant red rain suits, which made them look even bigger than they were. They looked like a pair of round plastic walking toys as they made their way along. They had no intention of getting as wet as they had the day before, and even though it was not raining this morning, they had donned the suits before leaving their car.

At last, checking the tickets the Roepkes had given them, they found the seats. This time, they didn't have a ticket for a third seat. But for the moment, they had plenty of room; several seats on both sides of them were still vacant. They put their provisions on a seat next to them, sat down panting, and surveyed the raceway from this unfamiliar viewpoint.

"Actually, these are great seats," Gerald said.

"They are," Ella agreed. "I didn't realize how much better you can see from here." They were sitting a few yards above the head of the main straightaway, a few rows back from the low concrete retaining wall. Atop the wall was the high fence of wire, cables, and posts, and just on the other side of it, the velvet-smooth pavement of the track. Just to their left was the banked curve of the fourth turn sweeping away into the north short straightaway, and stretching away to their right almost a mile was the long main straightaway, which bent away out of sight into the distant first turn. They could see the platform upon which starter Pat Vidan stood to wave his flags, far down by the starting line. Gerald got out his binoculars and adjusted them to determine how well he could see the pits. He could see all of them, though they were diminished in size. In their Tower Terrace seats they had been able to see only the pits that were directly down front.

"Hey, this is really nice," Ella exclaimed. "Why don't we try to order tickets for these seats for next year's race? Maybe just a little way up there so maybe we could see the third turn, too. Imagine being able to see what happens in three turns! And we should buy another pair of binoculars."

Gerald only grunted in answer. There was still a nagging doubt in the back of his mind as to whether he would be coming to the race next year at all. He probably would, of course, but now and then he would think about the man who had called it a Roman circus.

A tall, big-boned woman with a rough-looking face and a tooth conspicuously missing came hulking along the row, her plastic raincoat rustling; she stopped and told Gerald to move his picnic basket out of her seat. Then, apparently not as hostile as she had seemed, she leaned forward, looked the Rumples over, grinned, and said, "Well, here we go again, hey?"

"Yep," Gerald said.

"Hey," the woman said, "what happened to the Chicago people had them seats yesterday?"

"They had to go home last night. Today's a workday for ol' Gene."

"Ah. Tough."

"Actually, we should be at work, I guess," Gerald said. "But they gave us their tickets."

"Well, what the hell. You folks like racing?"

"We sure do! Don't we, Gerald?"

"Yes."

"Lucky you both do. I used to have to drag my old man here. Finally he just quit comin' with me."

"He didn't like racing, huh?"

"Oh, he liked it okay. But he said he couldn't stand to be around me. I get too excited." She grinned, and Gerald tried politely not to look at the gap of her missing tooth. "Once I got t' rootin' for Parnelli Jones—remember the year he drove the turbine car?—and I got so carried away I socked Hank's ear—Hank's my husband. That was the last time he came to the race."

"Well, you must be a real fan," Gerald said, making a mental note to be ready to duck if this big woman showed signs of becoming excited.

"You bet," she said. "Hey, I'm Ivy Yarbrough."

"Gerald Rumple. And this is Ella."

"Haya do."

"I think they're going to be able to run it today, don't

you?" Ella said. "We were here yesterday, and we didn't want to waste another trip."

"Well, I'll tell ya, honey," Ivy Yarbrough said, "I'm gettin' mighty tired of gettin' up at five in the morning. But if it takes 'em till the Fourtha July to have this race, I guess I'll be gettin' up at five in the morning till the Fourtha July. I couldn't ever stand to be at home while it was on, could you?"

"That's the way we are," Ella said. "Isn't it, Gerald?"

Gerald nodded and leaned back so the two women could talk back and forth across him. He was beginning to wonder *why* women like these two were so desperate about being here. He listened to them, and even though he himself had been almost that religious about attending the "500" for many years now, he didn't like the echoes he was hearing now of his own zeal. He thought back to the beginning. He had started coming to the races with Ella as a part of their courtship—not exactly against his will, but to please her. Then he had found out a couple of years after their marriage that she had started coming to the race in her high school days because she had had a crush on a boy who worked on Mauri Rose's pit crew. That had hurt Gerald and made him a bit jealous, but she had talked it down and minimized it time and again until Gerald had, on the surface of his mind, anyway, forgotten about it and become a race fan in his own right.

Still, he thought now, it was Ella who got me started on all this, and I've never been as religious about it —religious, that really did seem to be the word—as she is.

Here he was, leaning back out of the way of these two religious race fans, thinking his own thoughts, while they talked about A. J. Foyt and Mario Andretti and Offenhauser engines, and Gerald sensed that Ella was now talking with this woman in this animated manner because he himself had become less responsive. Ella really might not even be aware yet that this was happening, but it was. Ella had to jabber excitedly about all the details of the race, and Gerald understood now that if he didn't respond enthusiastically, Ella would just aim it at some more responsive ear.

"Excuse me," he said suddenly to them. "Ella, why

don't you change seats with me, and then you can talk to each other easier?"

She looked at him blankly for a moment, as if annoyed by the interruption; then it dawned on her what he had said, and a hurt look came over her face. "But honey, I wouldn't leave you out."

"Don't worry about leaving me out. Here. I'll trade seats." He got up, and she did move over closer to the big woman, but she kept looking at him with a slightly suffering look.

"Don'cha worry 'bout him," boomed Ivy Yarbrough. "If he gets tired of comin' to the races with you like my Hank did to me, why, you'n me can come together!"

"Hahahahahahahaha! Oh, that's nice. But Jerry wouldn't ever stop coming to the 'Five Hundred' 'cause he loves it too much, and we always do everything together, don't we, Jerry?"

"Yes, dear."

The race cars had been sitting on the grid in front of the grandstands for an hour. The drivers were out of the cars, wandering about or talking with their crews. Crewmen went out to some of the cars carrying heating units that were attached to the cars to keep the engine oil from cooling during the delay.

Down between the first and second turns, the monotonous drone of the track-drying machine suddenly went off. The fans, thinking that meant the track was dry enough for the race to start, began applauding and craning their necks to see the action begin up by the starting line.

Then a wave of disappointed moaning filled the stands as the drying machine started again.

It had just run out of gas.

As he prowled in the crowd on the walkways behind the Terrace for good photographic possibilities, Nick Alef found himself continually juggling images of three women, and their places in the present circumstances of his life. All three, he realized, were of great importance to him, but in very different ways. Becky's life was interwoven through every thread of his own life, and though he yearned to be away from her, away from the responsibility of her and toward the freedom of an uncluttered life in which he could interact naturally with any other human being or take direct action upon any opportunity, he understood that to break away from her would be like pulling a yarn end in a sweater: everything would disintegrate, the secure and rooted part along with the shabby and resentful. Diana Scheckley's life was not bound in any substantial way with his; there were no commitments, yet because of the golden, dreamlike opportunities she symbolized, she was at the moment of more immediate importance to Nick than anyone, Becky included. She was like —like—he hated to define things in his mind with clichés, but she was like a light at the end of a gloomy tunnel of frustrations, through which he believed he could return to the sunny realms to which his unusual talents seemed to entitle him.

And Katherine—Kitty. She had been a brightness in his memory for so many years. To elaborate upon the metaphor, he thought, she's like the light left back at the start of the tunnel. He remembered his sunny room at the resort hotel at French Lick, her undergarments hanging on a chair arm and her voice singing above the rushing shower in the bathroom. He could remember that so well.

The wind, damp and misty now, blew cool against his face. This is a juncture, he thought. It's one of those rare days when you have free choices to make. If you do what's right, you'll never get any credit for it; if you do what's wrong, probably nobody'll ever know it. And what's right with respect to Becky herself might be wrong with respect to our lives as a whole. There's nobody at your shoulder to give you any advice on what to do. So what do you do?

Well, he thought, long ago—so long ago you can scarcely remember it—you were brought up to do the right thing.

Yeah, he thought. If you can figure out what *is* the right thing.

You noble ass, he thought. Why can't you, as most do,

just take opportunities as they come, instead of por-
ing over moralistic equations?

I can, Goddamnit, he thought. I've been learning how
to do it just like everybody else.

He came to sidewalks where throngs of people, many of
them muddy and bizarrely dressed, flowed slowly along
with vacuous eyes. There was a vendor surrounded by
people. He was selling little toy replicas of race cars. The
cars all had the same number painted on them: 77. People
were buying the little souvenir cars almost as fast as the
vendor could handle the money. Why would so many people want those silly things, Nick wondered. Why number
77? Then he remembered, and understood: 77 was
Walther's car. The wrecked one.

There. See? he thought. There's a man who knows how
to take an opportunity.

In a line of traffic three cars wide, Lloyd Skirvin drove
his car at a crawl along Sixteenth Street. The Mercury trembled. Its high-powered engine was not adjusted
for creeping in traffic jams. Whenever he brought it to a
complete stop, as he had to do every few seconds,
he would step on the clutch and rev the motor several times. *FRRRRRD-n, FRRRRUD-n, FRRRRUD-n.*
Even that noise, and the traffic noise all around, failed to
awaken his three passengers. Renee lay across the front
seat, her head on his thigh. Her straw-colored hair
lay tangled, uncombed, slightly greasy-looking. There
was dried mud on the knees and seat and ragged cuffs of
her denim bell-bottoms. Her eyesockets looked hollow and
shadowy as she slept. She sure was good, Lloyd thought.
He looked at the bone of her hip and thin forearm
lying across it. Not skinny, but nothing extra. He remembered the flat belly and how tight she had been on him.
The closer to the bone, the sweeter the meat, his pa had
used to tell him.

But that one there, he thought, glancing over the seat
back. Puggles slept sitting up, with her head back, her
mouth hanging open. Her face looked sallow, and her eyes
had puffiness under them. There was a red pimple on her
chin. That's the one really likes to fuck, Lloyd thought.

He remembered her incessant cries last night in the back of the car the two times ol' Worms had put it to her. And Lloyd remembered, too, how round and firm her hips and thighs had looked in the headlights last night. He liked some meat on his gals, no matter what his pa had said. Lloyd was halfway sold on making Worms trade with him. Just ain't no waya knowin' which one you'll like best till you done put it in 'em a few times, he thought.

He took a pull of warm beer and then snuggled the bottle down by his hip behind Renee's head ,and draped his shirttail over it because they were almost to the Speedway gates, where cops were standing all around trying to direct traffic.

Lloyd grinned at a trooper as he turned past. Got away from you chickenshits last night, didn't we, he thought.

And he remembered, with the satisfaction of great accomplishment, getting his wad off at 115 miles an hour without losing a hair of control over the car. That, he sensed, was a quality that would make him the greatest. He didn't know that he especially wanted to get out of the stocks into championship cars and someday race in a fancy place like this. But he felt that if he ever did, he could run away with it. He remembered the ball of flame and the upside-down car he had seen yesterday. Now, a real driver, he thought, wouldn't panic and skid in that stuff like they done. I coulda drove around that and went right on.

Only chickenshits lose control, he thought.

Nick hurried on through the crowd. There was a mist, not quite a drizzle, cool on his face. He couldn't tell whether it was enough to wet the track and stall the race again. This place was so big that sometimes there would be rain in one corner and not a trace in another.

Another day of photographing rain-soaked spectators? Could do worse. He had unloaded a lot of yesterday's wet-spectator pictures to the papers and race magazine editors, not to mention the excellent batch of crash photos. And they were anxious to see some of the color work and movie film he had told them about. Soon as it was back from the labs he'd know how much money there'd be from that.

When he had first looked out this morning, he had thought it was going to be a clear, bright day. But this racetrack this year—this whole month—had been like that Joe Btfsplk in the comic strip, he thought. Always a rain cloud overhead.

He was eager to find Diana. If she's decided yes, he thought, I can make all the arrangements this morning and we can do the posing this evening.

Then he remembered something: that grease monkey who'd said he'd get the race car set up only if he could watch. Damn.

I'll just have to arrange a car through somebody else somehow, he decided. It's for damn sure she'd never do it with some filthy stooge standing around with his tongue hanging out.

"Now to Luke Walton!"

"Again the cars have been rolled into position, thirty-two of the magnificent thirty-three! And again we're in the pace car, stationed at the pylon, ahead of the field! The pace car is a busy operation during the parade lap and the pace lap. . . . Jim Rathmann, 1960 winner, does the driving; he sets the speed according to instructions from Chief Steward Harlan Fengler, who is reached by two-way radio operated by Astronaut Al Worden! There are two guest riders, Dollie Cole and Chris Schenkel. And while he is marshaling the field, Tony Hulman operates a movie camera! Drivers and pit crewmen are poised now for the four words that set the 'Five Hundred' in motion! Now all ears are glued to them! And now here is the man who inscribed them so deeply in racing tradition, the president of the Indianpolis Motor Speedway, TONY HULMAN!"

"GENTLEMEN, START . . ."

Nick was returning to the Tower to look for Diana in the crowd of officials and celebrities when he suddenly became aware that the crews were getting ready to start the race cars. It had come upon him unexpectedly. There was a misting in the air, even an occasional raindrop, which he had presumed would extend the delay. But now the track announcer was introducing Hulman.

Hey, what the hell, Nicky thought. He turned around and began hurrying southward.

Reason told him that there couldn't be two starting-lap crashes on consecutive days, but intuition urged him to go to the place where he had shot the many spectacular crash photos yesterday. Maybe this morning's delay will have the drivers as spooked as yesterday, he thought. He had hoped to talk to Diana for a few minutes before going down there and stationing himself. But first things first, he thought. You can find her after the race starts and settles down to routine. He made his way southward. During the parade and pace laps there would be time to get down toward the pylon. But it was a long walk.

The crowd was still. Then came Tony Hulman's voice: *"GENTLEMEN, START YOREN-JUNS!"*

The fans were on their feet, suddenly yelling, applauding the words they had been waiting an hour to hear. The engines began whooping to life, their great, hollow, deep bellowing shaking the ground. The fans were whistling, yelling, and clapping in thunderous response. *FRO-OOB-m! FROOOOB-m! FROOB-m!* Crews were moving with purpose and haste among the rows of race cars, and the hot exhaust rose off the track. The revving of engines continued for about a minute as Nick hurried along. Then the roar of the crowd swelled still higher, and he heard the track announcer cry, *"AND THE PACE CAR IS MOVING AWAY!"*

Nick watched the Cadillac accelerate into the southwest turn, pennant fluttering, its privileged passengers smiling at the crowd, Dollie Cole's face radiating the benign elegance of a beautiful woman secure in almost Olympian social status.

And a few yards behind, once again, came the gleaming fleet of whooping, snarling race cars, looking as much like squat, hard-shelled insects as machines, preceded and followed by a roar of massed human voices. Nick looked up the straightaway and saw through the haze of exhaust that no cars remained at the starting post; all, apparently, had ignited this morning and moved off. In the tumult, individual voices of unusual power and shrillness could be heard yelling, "GO, MARIO!" or "GET-TEM, A.J.!" or "YEE-HA! GO, ROGER, GO ROGER, GO!"

Shimmering in their own heat, the vehicles thundered out of sight through the first turn.

Nick situated himself in the same place where he had been at the start the day before, prepared his cameras, and waited.

At the north end of the oval, the deep thrumming of the motors was building up, and now the pace car came out of the north short straightaway and dodged through the distant fourth turn, followed by the fleet of racers. The crowd roared and whistled.

"Go get 'em, Mario!" a woman shrilled somewhere nearby.

Nick, for some reason—perhaps because of yesterday's crash, or maybe because of the jumble of personal uncertainties inside him—was being unusually stirred today by the parade of big cars. His recurrent fear of their awful potential now was alloyed strangely and unexpectedly by a flush of excitement that went prickling from his scalp down through his back and thighs. He was astonished at himself; he found himself seeing the procession of strange, gleaming, flat powerhouses with an almost painful clarity of detail; he realized that his heart had sped up its beat and that the growing thunder of their engines was making his insides feel like jelly. He experienced a new kind of fear, the fear of an unknown awful something. Once while a child he had heard a radio adventure story—it was "Jack Armstrong," if he remembered correctly—about a column of ants grinding its irresistible way through a jungle, bringing down plants, animals, and men in its path, an incomprehensible and uncomprehending progression of hard-shelled appetites. It had evoked a terror in him that had provided nightmares for the rest of his childhood, yet he had always wished he could hear it again, and again experience that awful imaginative dread. Now this column of powerful thrumming shells went past, somehow reminding him of that, and evoking the same delicious disgust.

Remember that, he thought as the cars grew larger and crossed the starting line to begin the pace lap. This is something you need to figure out.

Nick's face felt damp. A cool mist seemed to cling to his skin, and now and then he would feel the minute cold kiss of a sprinkle of water. He should have worn a hat, he thought, but he disliked hats.

That track's got to be damp, he thought. I can't believe they're starting.

"Victory Lane is where each of these thirty-three— thirty-two now that 'Salt' Walther's in the hospital after the accident yesterday—want to be in little over three hours! It's been their burning wish all of their lives! The entrance to that hallowed strip of ground is narrow, and filled with many obstacles to overcome. From drawing boards around the world to build these cars, engine shops, and mechanical genius, they've gotten this far, and all that's left is the performance of the car for five hundred grueling miles, plus the skill and determination of the best drivers in the land—two from out of the U.S., in David Hobbs of England and Graham McRae of New Zealand. It takes much preparation, indomitable perse- verence, and an ideal to succeed, and perhaps in a more down-to-earth racing connotation, to stand on it, for eight hundred turns that lie ahead! And if your RPMs are revving along with ours right now, we're united by that same thread of love for auto racing. This is the siren song; this is Indianapolis, Indiana, on Race Day! Over two million dollars' worth of brilliantly colored and finely tuned equipment is straining at the leash, anxious to start their trip."

Though turned up to full volume, the portable radio of one of the photographers next to Nick was almost drowned out as the cars followed the Cadillac by once again.

"Now coming into the number one turn, PICK IT UP, Mike Ahern!"

"Thank you, Sid. It's the morning after in turn one,

and in the midst of the soggy litter of yesterday's wild party we wait now, and here they come—the Cadillac pace car on the high bank—into full view! Johnny Rutherford in the bright orange McLaren, Bobby Unser in his snow-white car alongside, hoping to take the lead like he did yesterday before the accident—outside, the blue-and-gold colors of Mark Donohue, and the field is in GOOD SHAPE, through turn one, into turn two, and Howdy Bell!"

"Sid, it's beautiful over here! We turn the page, and it's chapter two in our book here of the 'Five Hundred' for this year; the colors are brighter and more brilliant today —as we see the second row—the bright red of Swede Savage—Gary Bettenhausen, Mario Andretti—Krisiloff, Unser, and Caruthers, Revson, Johncock, and Bobby Allison in the blue car. They're up to Doug Zink!"

"Thank you, Howdy, and we have up here on the back-stretch the field in a little better shape than it was yes-terday at this point! A few stragglers toward the end of the pack—Jim McElreath and Sam Sessions hurrying now to catch up. They're up to turn number three, and here's Ron Carrell!"

"Doug, thank you!" The field is here, and along with it that same intensity of excitement that we felt—not so many hours ago! There's A.J., the Aztec orange number fourteen, and Mel Kenyon's bright red Atlanta Falcons' number nineteen—Bill Vukovich in the yellow Sugar-ripe number two! They're at four; here to report the ac-tion, Jim Shelton!"

"Right, Ron! Well, the pace car leading the fine group of gentlemen and cars—we could use the old saying 'Wish you were here'—regardless of a few problems, it's still one of the most thrilling racing events in the world! Now let's check: see if they go—"

"Oh, God. Oh, God." Ella Rumple, standing between her husband and Ivy Yarbrough in the fourth turn, was rapidly squeezing her fleshy legs together like someone desperately needing to urinate. Beside her, Gerald held their radio next to his ear, hearing a description of the suspenseful moment that was occurring right under his own eyes.

"—see if the pace car goes into the pits—and it looks

*—as if—IT WILL NOT GO INTO THE PITS—so
they'll go another time around! Sid, pick 'em up!"*

"Pat Vidan is waving a *RED FLAG! The pace car
is going around—the red flag is out! The red flag is being
waved!"*

Gerald was stunned. He was stunned to realize that,
like the Pavlovian dog of which he had learned in high
school psychology class, he reacted with his glands to
the words "red flag." He had not seen anything happening, but he believed something awful must have happened.

Nick Alef heard the moaning chorus of engines grow
louder, and then the cars came in rows and swung out of
the far northwest turn, coming for the starting line. He
was confused by his feelings, by his strange recall of that
ant army.

Something's going to happen, he thought. There can't
be this much tension, this much power wound up like
this without something awful happening to relieve it.
Please don't let anything happen, but something has to
happen. . . .

And then nothing happened. The crescendo of motors
wound down, and the moment deflated like a balloon
with a leak. A great moan came from the throats of the
hundreds of acres of people and then sank into an angry
babble as the pace car rolled on down the straightway
and the race cars slowed down.

"Oh, no!"

"Goddamn it! What now?"

"Red flag! Where did it happen?"

"Nothing happened. They just stopped the fucking
start!"

"You sons of bitches. YOU SONS OF BITCHES!"

"Fengler, you lily-livered, senile old horse's ass!" Someone screamed in a voice that hurt his ear. A few at a
time, the fans wilted and sat down. Most looked exhausted, morose; some even looked pouty, as if they were
about to cry. A few were laughing. But Nick Alef
suddenly felt better, felt his old, amused cynicism coming back. That's it, he thought. Coitus interruptus. Ha-
ha! One of these days every fucking machine in the world

is going to fizzle out like this all at once. But what the hell stopped it? He walked forward, feeling the clean, cool drizzle on his forehead and cheeks, and hitched up his belt. For the first time in several oppressive years, he felt he had understood something very basic, very clear, of extreme importance, one of those vivid insights that used to come to him when he was so much younger, when he was naive. . . .

He felt very free and very wise, superior in his wisdom to the thousands of people here around him, compressed within their dim skulls behind their glum faces. He was inexpressibly relieved that something, whatever it had been, had stopped the race, had eased off that foreboding tension.

There are a quarter of a million unhappy people here, and one happy one, he thought. Nice feeling.

The pace car came by slowly. Nick saw the tiny red flag swooping and twirling far up the pit wall. The first rows of cars went by him at less than racing speed, and cars in the back of the pack simply stopped along the straightaway.

Nick was sweating under the arms; his knees were unsteady. He still did not know why the red flag was out, but he was profoundly grateful.

"Lou Palmer has some information for us, in the south pits."

"From the observers' stand, there is indication of some rain now, on the racecourse itself. That explains the red flag. We've got to hold the race. We can't run in the wet here. John Martin, meanwhile, had to dart into the pits in an already heat-blistered automobile. They're looking over the front end of it right now. And this may be to his advantage. It certainly is not to the fans' advantage; it is the fact that the track is again picking up some moisture. So, the field comes to a halt; the pace car will be replaced; probably additional fuel will be allowed because of the critical situation, the limited amount of fuel available. Back to you now in the Tower."

"All right. And Luke Walton, you let us know again

when Tony will say 'RE-RE-START your engines,' if
he says that."

"Now, see?" said Gerald Rumple, slapping his palms
down on his fat thigh. "Have we wasted another trip, or
have we?" He sighed in annoyance. He was just about
fed up with this frustrating occasion.

"It's just awful! It's not fair. Somebody ought to do
some— I mean, I wish there was some way they could
do something about this—this rain." Ella threw her hands
up, not knowing at whom or what to direct her anger.

"Well, okay. Now, look. Let's get out of here and go
on down to the shop. It'll be forever before they get
started again. They might not even be able to today.
Come on, hon—"

"No, wait! They might—"

"Come on, Ella! We've got work to do! We can't just
wait our lives out at this Speedway of yours."

Ella looked at him, stunned. "Of *mine?*"

"It's yours from now on," he said, with more finality
than she had ever heard in his voice. "I feel silly being
here. Let's go."

She stared at him in anguish, while big Ivy Yarbrough
looked at them knowingly.

"Just another hour," Ella pleaded when she was
able to speak. "Then we'll go to the shop if they don't
start it by then."

Gerald sat down slowly. He was trembling. It had
scared him, hurting Ella's feelings like that.

"Well, listen, dearie," Ivy Yarbrough said, putting her
arm over Ella's shoulders. "You'n me'll watch this goddamn race till they get it started, if it takes a week. If
he won't watch it with you, you can depend on me." She
shot a scornful glance at Gerald that made him turn his
face away and silently mouth a retort. But he stayed.
He'd give another hour to Ella's folly. He'd go that far.

"You know, Sid, if they weren't concerned about the
public listening in and or that have paid to come in here
and watch this event, they could certainly start this thing
on the yellow flag, and let the cars run, and if there is

*a little moisture on the track, they'd be running under
the Electro-Pacer, and the cars would, draftwise, absorb
some of the moisture. But Mr. Tony Hulman likes to give
his people their hundred percent worth of their ticket
dollar."*

*"Well, they're sure getting two hundred percent so far.
We've had two days of activity out here; we've had the
world's biggest drenched picnic, and the race hasn't even
started yet, so I'd say they're more than getting their
money's worth."*

Diana Scheckley stood holding a plastic rain cover
over her head, looking around. Harry Kuntz stood beside her, looking impatient and bored. "Come on," he
said, "let's go inside."'

She shook her head. "Go on in," she said. "You don't
have to stand out here with me. Go in where your important people are."

"Whom are you looking for, as if I didn't know?"

"Harry, don't you understand? It's just none of your
business." She set her chin and kept looking for Nick.
In front of the Tower some of the crews were now pushing their race cars off the track and into the pits.

Diana had decided she would pose for Nick. She had
thought about it for hours last night, visualizing how it
would be to have one's nakedness shown in a magazine that millions of men would look at, and the idea had
frightened and aroused her by turns. It had been one of
the strangest nights of her life, just Diana and her imagination. She had changed her mind several times. At last
she had decided, yes, she would do it. Having decided,
she had become so wide awake and stimulated that she
had masturbated finally to release herself for sleep. It
really had been an odd night.

After a while, Diana sensed that Harry was no longer
hovering near her. She turned, and he was gone.

*"Sid, I thought a while ago—and I did not call it in
to you, perhaps I should have—I have a black notebook,
and on it I spotted a drop. And I said, 'Perhaps it came*

*off the roof,' and then I said, 'No, after yesterday, it's
only my imagination.' After the race actually started, the
pace lap and parade lap, I still felt little drops, and I
think perhaps I still feel them now, and perhaps that's
why we have gone back in. It's not—it's not really rain.
It's just—about every minute or two I feel a little drop
on my hand. Perhaps that's it, Sid. I don't know. Back
to you."*

*"Well, if it's not rain and it's wet, they still don't start
the race. Ron. Ha-ha-ha. Let's try—let's keep an eye on
the pace car down here. Some people are getting in. Jim
Rathmann's alongside—without the wheel—so until he
gets in, I'm not going to be too concerned."*

When it became evident that the start of the race really
was delayed again, Nick Alef left his post and wandered
back toward the Tower, hoping to find Diana. He cut
through the Terrace seating section and went up the
walkway behind it. The rain was still fine, but was now
sifting down faster. He turned and went along a walkway.
The same endless processions of people were plodding
along the damp promenade, some of them draped with
blankets. Concession stands along the way emitted the
smells of hot food, and queues of thirty and forty people
waited at each one. A man a few feet ahead of Nick
was lugging a pressed-plastic foam cooler that was obviously quite heavy. Suddenly the cooler broke under
the strain, and its load of beer bottles—apparently an
entire case of them—cascaded to the concrete and broke.
Nick stopped and raised his camera. The man stood there
for a minute, his face a mask of dismay. He cursed
viciously. Then he shrugged, got a straw out of a sack,
got down on all fours, and began drinking the beer off
the sidewalk, while other people walked through or around
the beer puddle or stopped to watch him and laugh. He
was still sucking muddy beer up from the ground when
Nick reached the end of the roll of film and walked on.

Kevin Cole considered himself a very good trail-bike
rider, far better than anybody his age he knew. The

trouble was that in here there wasn't any trail. There were tree roots on the ground, and wild grapevines hanging down, and little swamps full of little trees so close together he couldn't get between them. He would run the bike ten or fifteen feet and then would have to dismount and lift the heavy front end and push it several yards in another direction. A long stem with stickers on it caught his arm and pulled him off balance, and his bike fell and he fell on top of it. He got up and with great effort picked the bike up again. Then a bush got tangled between the front wheel and the motor mount, and he couldn't go any farther forward. He stopped and struggled with it, panting and whimpering. One of his shoes was full of water. Bugs were biting his face. He freed the bike and started pushing it in another direction. A stick got caught between the spokes of the back wheel and stopped it dead, and Kevin almost fell. Trying to hold the bike upright while reaching back to extricate the stick, he lost his footing and toppled over, and the bike fell on his arm. He yelled in pain. He pulled his arm free. It was skinned. He was furious. The Indianapolis 500-Mile Race seemed to be getting farther and farther away. He kicked the bike and hurt his foot. "You damn shit!" he yelled.

"Now, is that any way for a little boy to talk?" said a voice nearby.

It was the state trooper.

Becky Alef, fortified with a cup of coffee, a lighted cigarette, and a great deal of nervous throat-clearing, sat down at Nick's desk and dialed the telephone number of the advertising agency. She was nervous for two reasons. One was that she had resigned from her job as a copywriter for the agency several years ago when Nick went into business for himself, and she wasn't sure how friendly they would be. The other was that she had been a housewife for so long now that she wasn't very certain about how well she could bring off a businesslike telephone conversation.

The phone receptionist's voice was not one she recog-

nized. Of course not, she thought. Not after all this time.
"Is Mr., uhm, Blivins there, please?" she asked.

"Mr. Blivins is no longer with us," said the receptionist.

"Then, uhm—" Becky was flustered by that surprise
and had to search her mind quickly for other old names.
"Mr. Ross, then," she said. "He's still president, isn't he?"

"Yes, but he's not in today. Can anyone else help you?"

"Well, maybe Mr., uhm, Becker could—"

"I'm sorry, he's out of the office today, too."

"Well, how about Mr. Lawrence?" The names of the
account executives were beginning to come back to her
now; having remembered Mr. Ross, she seemed to be
remembering the other names by association.

"Mr. Lawrence isn't here, either," said the voice on
the telephone. "To tell you the truth, ma'am, none of
the gentlemen of the firm are in today." Having said
that much, the receptionist apparently decided to let down
her official manner and unburden herself. "The fact is,
all those characters are out at the Speedway. It's a mess.
I'm ashamed to say it. I mean we're—the girls, y'know
—just sitting around here."

"Heavens. I didn't know there were that many race
fans there. I used to work there, you see—"

"No kiddin'! What's your name?"

"Uhm, Rebecca Alef."

"Gosh, you musta been before my time. No, I don't
think they're all race fans, but those who aren't, they're
out there because of clients involved in the festival, or
in the race, and like that. I tell you, hon, things are
just at a standstill. Every place I've talked to, half the
people stayed off work. And the airport, I guess, is just
a mess."

Becky sighed and waited for the receptionist's disser-
tation to run down. "Well," she said when it did, "would
you tell Mr. Ross that I called, and that I'll call back
tomorrow?"

"Sure will, hon. But don't tell him what I said about
all the guys being out, will you? And your name again
was, uh—"

After she hung up, Becky leaned back in Nick's old
chair. It smelled slightly of mildew. The basement was

damp; there was a place on the east wall where water was beginning to seep through the cement block. She looked at the gloomy floor joists overhead. What an awful place for him to have to work in, she thought. No wonder he gets depressed. She leaned forward and persued a stack of papers on the typewriter table. It was material he'd been working from to write the speech on no-fault auto insurance that he'd been complaining about. The one he'd said she couldn't have understood. She looked at headings. "Benefit levels," they said. "Retention of right to subrogate." "Threshold versus formula." "Tort liability." "First-party coverage." Maybe he's right, she thought. God, how can he stand to write this crap? Knowing the kind of thing he likes to write . . .

Becky was a little bit disturbed; she was coming close to understanding his standpoint in their perennial arguments, and that was uncomfortable. She thought about getting some of his old book and story manuscripts out and rereading them. She really did like them. She used to read them with excitement and admiration back in the days when he was writing them and trying to sell them. Then when he had given up on them and resigned himself to what he called his flack world, she had stopped reading the old manuscripts because they made her feel dismal and guilty, somehow.

Suddenly Becky wanted to see him and be with him. I bet if I could reach him now and tell him I was coming over to help him work, he'd really be happy about it. He just said no about it this morning because we're in the habit of saying no to each other's ideas. I bet I could—I could have Davey stay with the Plew kids next door, and he'd be all right. It would be fun to be at the track with Nick again.

But how'll I ever find him?

If I could get a call through to him, we could meet someplace over there. Let's see. I know!

She called the newspaper and got through to the pressroom at the Speedway. Most of the town's newspaper and television reporters had worked with Nick when he was a real journalist.

"Pressroom."

"Is Nick Alef there, or has anybody seen him?" she asked.

"Hey," the voice yelled away from the phone. "Anybody here know a Nick Alef?" Then the voice came back on. "Nobody here knows a Nick Alef."

She hung up. That surprised her. But then, she thought, he's been out of it for a long time, just free-lancing. She didn't like to admit it to herself, but yes, probably only the older reporters would remember him. He's always referring to himself as the world's youngest has-been. Suddenly she felt sorry for him. She had seldom felt sorry for Nick. That was the way he was. He'd make you mad at him before he'd let you feel sorry for him. Or let you help him.

Well, she thought, so much for going to the Speedway. Unless he just happens to call home. And he never just calls home.

"WIBC—Ten-Seven-Oh in Indianapolis."

"This is Sid Collins in the Master Control Tower at Indianapolis, Indiana. The time is now ten-thirty-one and forty seconds, Eastern Standard Time. We came on the air for an hour and forty-five minutes—yesterday over three and a half hours—trying to get the fifty-seventh annual running of the 'Five Hundred' under way, and, uhm—we're about one step further back from where we started. Ha. When we came out this morning, we had the cars on the track. Now they're back in the pits. I think we're receding. We'll go back to the drawing boards and mail everybody a copy."

Nick Alef sidled up to a pair of pit-crew mechanics who were pitching pennies in the drizzle, killing time. The older one, who was chewing tobacco, nodded to Nick, whom he recognized as one of the regular lensmen. Nick returned the nod and stood watching for a while.

After the older man had beaten the younger one in the game, the younger one moved away. "Was you wantin' to talk to me, son?" the older mechanic asked.

"As a matter of fact, I was," Nick said. He was nervous

about asking this because he was beginning to realize
how remote his chances were. He squinted into the rain
and gazed off into the bleachers, then looked at the
mechanic. "My name's Nick Alef. I've, uhm, got a
special kind of photo assignment from a magazine, and,
uhm, I need to get some good color shots of a race car."

"Looks like y'come to th' right place. Mess of 'em
here."

"Well, you see, my problem is this: I need to photograph one with some special lighting—uhm, actually in
the privacy of a garage. I mean, with nobody around.
Just me and the car."

The mechanic looked at him suspiciously, rolling his
quid in his jaw. "Nobody around?"

"That's right."

"Not even the owner or mechanics?"

"That's right."

"Well, now, son, I don't think that's very likely t' happen, d'you?"

"Mmm, why not?"

"Well, son, I sure won't let nobody go near my car
without me bein' there t' make sure he don't do nothin'
to it."

"Oh hell," Nick laughed. "I wouldn't *do* anything to
it, other than take some pictures."

"Yeah, sure. But how do I know that? I mean, that's
'bout eighty thousand dollars' worth of race car there. And
this here's a million-dollar race. Now ya gotta admit,
somebody might be wantin' t' get in and find out something' somebody's doin' or maybe do some little thing t'
one of these cars to get it out of the race."

"Oh, maybe. But I'm not a racing man or gambler
or anything. You've seen me here. You know I'm just
a photographer."

The mechanic leaned away and spat. "Where'd you
say you're plannin' t' do this picture-takin'?"

"Well, I know it'd have to be here at the Speedway.
In your garage."

"How long would it take?"

"Maybe an hour or two." Come on, Nick thought.
This was the third crew he'd asked. If he had to keep
asking all afternoon, some of these guys might mention

it to each other and it would become even harder than it already was to arrange it. Besides, he thought, that grease monkey who wants to watch might hear that I'm trying to arrange it with somebody else's car, and get mad and start talking.

"Well, son, I hate t' turn you down, but, couple of things. One, I'd be fired flat out if I let some feller shut himself in alone with my car. Two, sometimes we work most all night long on those cars if they need it, an' I just don't see how y'd ever find a good time t' do it."

"Okay. Thanks. 'Preciate you listening."

"Don't mind doin' that. Got nothing' else t' do right now."

Nick walked away, realizing how inadequately he had planned this part of the project. All he had really worked on was how to get Diana to agree to it. And he wasn't sure he'd accomplished even that yet. Of course the Speedway would be the best place to do it, and now would be the best time, to get authenticity into the picture story. But these garages were such busy, secretive, guarded places. And women weren't supposed to be there. Probably the best thing would be to wait until after the race and make arrangements with one of the special shops in town that built or modified race cars, and do the photography there. More room, better light, privacy— all that. Or have a car outdoors in some secluded parklike setting for shooting in early-morning light. Actually, that would be far more aesthetic than any garage possibly could be, he thought.

But that just wouldn't be at the Speedway. Got to be able to say it was really shot here!

It appeared there was only one thing to do. Get that cruddy little mechanic who had said he could arrange it, and have him go ahead and do it. Maybe for a hundred or a hundred and fifty bucks he would agree to set it up and not stay around to watch.

Maybe. But the watching seemed to be what he was most interested in. Well, we'll see, he thought.

Nick found the unsavory little man sitting on the pavement under the rear wing of his race car with two other members of its crew, resting out of the drizzle with their backs against the rear of the car, over which a tarp had been drawn. The mechanic greeted him with a wave, and Nick summoned him away from the others with a jerk of the head. The mechanic came swaggering over like a happy troll. "Hi Mr. Alef."

"How's it going?"

"You can see—not too good for racin'."

"How about our project? Still think you can get the car for me?"

"Think so. But this rain's sure messin' up the schedules. Lotta guys wonderin' if they'll be able to make the Milwaukee race this weekend."

"So I've heard. What about this evening? Could you set it up for this evening?"

"Maybe. If they ever decide whether they're going to race or not."

"Before dark? I want to use available light if possible."

"Well, like I said, it depends. I'll try. Check back with me when Fengler makes up his mind about runnin' the race, why don'tcha?"

"Okay. Now, look. There's one other problem that's come up. Uhm, she won't pose if anybody else is there."

"What?"

"She doesn't want anybody else to see."

"Y'mean not even me?'"

"I told you she's class. She's reluctant to do it at all, let alone with somebody looking over my shoulder."

"Well, piss on that, buddy. What's in it for me?"

Nick sighed. "I guess we never did discuss a price, did we?"

"Listen, man, it better be good. I could get my ass in a sling."

The little jerk all of a sudden isn't very friendly, Nick thought. "What would you ask?" he said.

"Well. Two hundred bucks."

"That's steep."

"Find somebody else if you think you can."

"Two hundred. Okay. After I sell the pictures, okay?"

"Hell, no, man. In front."

Nick wondered how he could scrape up two hundred. There were checks forthcoming from yesterday's shots, but they'd be sent in the mail several days from now.

He grimaced. "Well, now, look. How about three hundred after I sell them? It's a sure thing, you know."

"Uh-uh."

Nick blew out a breath between tight lips. "How about this, then: a hundred now, two hundred when they're sold, and a set of the pictures?"

"Fuck that. I can see the cunt pictures in the magazine."

"I guess your main thing is, you want to watch."

"That, or two hundred cash right off."

"Okay. One of the two. I'll let you know. See you later. And you're keeping it to yourself, remember."

"I told you I was."

All right, Nick thought, heading north. I'll just have to talk her into letting him be there. As a guard, I'll say. God! It's harder to make out with a damn car than with a model!

What you ought to do, he told himself once more, is just drop the whole idea. And go drown your regrets in Kitty.

"I have to apologize, as now, as you know, Lieutenant Governor Orr made me an ambassador of goodwill for the State of Indiana yesterday. Did you hear about that, Fred? I mentioned it here—"

"Yeah, I did hear. And he's got good taste—"

"Now two of us; Chris Schenkel was made one a couple of years ago for his talking about Bippus and Huntington, and his hometown—and now Orr has commended us for our efforts on behalf of Indianapolis, the State of Indiana. We're very happy to talk about it. I can, then, as an ambassador, apologize for the situation, for the folks who have come to the five-hundred-mile race for the first time, and repeat once again that this is the first time in fifty-seven years this has ever happened. Now, we hope it will happen only once every fifty-seven years, so do come back and see us again. I imagine there are a lot of transistor radios around the track listening to us right now, as a matter of fact, trying to determine what they should be thinking about doing. Johnny?"

"It was my feeling, Sid, that ambassadors were sup-

*posed to do something more than merely apologize. I
thought ambassadors were supposed to accomplish something to rectify the situation. Ha-ha-ha."*

*"Well, I'm sure there'll be unlimited powers to stop
rain and things of that nature, but we always assign that
to Mr. Hulman, and he's working on that, and I still think
before this day is over, we will have a race. Just like
you said yesterday, Fred."*

*"Ambassador Sid Collins, I thought you could walk
on water."*

*"Ha-ha. Well, this is the day to test it, anyway, isn't
it?"*

The fleet of fire trucks and tow trucks was again running around and around the Speedway oval. Nick Alef
took a few photos of them as they sped by. Now and then
the people in the grandstands and Paddock and Tower
Terrace seats would applaud one truck or another as it
sped by, though not as much as they had before. It looked
like a prolonged exercise in futility. Rooster tails of water
sprayed up in the wake of each truck. And all the trucks
had their windshield wipers on. The rain was falling
steadily.

The long straightaway was dark, gray, wet. Suddenly,
through the drizzle, something whizzed past Nick's head.
It was a bright pink Frisbee. Laughter and applause went
up from the fans huddled in the stands. Gary Bettenhausen, hatless, his hair hanging in damp strands, bent and
caught the spinning saucer at knee level.

Nick changed the setting on his Minolta and started taking pictures. Bettenhausen, Billy Vukovich, and some
other drivers and mechanics soon had the pink Frisbee
sailing all over the pit area. Nick got one especially good
shot of Bettenhausen standing on one foot upon his own
inverted reflection on the rain-slick pavement, the pink
disk just leaving his extended right hand. In the background were race cars under shrouds, and beyond them,
race fans grinning from under umbrellas, rain hats, plastic tarps, and limp newspapers.

Then other Frisbees began sailing out of the spectator
areas. And for a few minutes Nick was kept busy photo-

graphing a sky full of wet Frisbees. It looked like an invasion of little flying saucers.

Nick jotted in his notebook: *R. 4, 5/29. 12:50 Drvrs unlax, rain frsbs &c.*

Bob Collins, sports columnist for the *Indianapolis Star,* was working on his special humor column for the back page of Wednesday's morning paper. His tan, round Irish face was serious, as it always was when he was writing funny material.

"After two days of watching nature's remedy help rhubarb grow at the Indianapolis Motor Speedway, experts have released some interesting statistics," he wrote.

"It has contributed directly to 198,413 damaged livers and probably, indirectly, to 3,750 divorce cases. We'll have to wait awhile for the paternity suits."

"Wonder what kind of nasty stuff Murray's writing by now," one of the sportswriters said to another.

Jim Murray, the *Los Angeles Times*'s syndicated sportswriter who traditionally came to Indianapolis to pan the "500," was getting near the end of his column and was concentrating on how to put it. He lifted his left hand from the typewriter keys and with the end of a straight finger adjusted his spectacles on the bridge of his nose. Then he typed: "God must be trying to tell them something. Every time they try to start this race, it starts to rain. Or burn."

"They predict at two o'clock this afternoon, light rain showers with winds about ten miles an hour out of the southwest. They say that the ceiling will be intermittently up and down, coming as low as seven hundred feet, with two and a half miles' visibility; light rain showers and fog will continue until it will start to break up at four o'clock this afternoon. By that time, the ceiling's supposed to be at twenty-five hundred feet with an eight-thousand-foot overcast, seven miles' visibility, and NO RAIN at four o'clock, Lou. How about that?" . .

"Yeah, how 'bout that? But there are no headlights on any of the equipment down here, and I don't know that it's going to do us a lot of good. It's remaining very damp at the Indianapolis Motor Speedway; moss has now appeared on the innersoles of my shoes—and I suspect others'; it is not a good forecast."

Nick saw people gathering in the garage area, and heard them shouting and laughing. He pressed forward.

In the center of the semicircle of watchers, some drivers and mechanics were having a desultory game of soccer. Al Unser made a few heavy tries at sending the ball around with his feet, but little Mario Andretti, in his white driver's suit, his damp curls drooping damply over his forehead, was running circles around everybody, booting the ball this way and that. Andretti was from Italy. He was at home with a soccer ball. Nick took a few photos of the action.

He looked at his watch and shook his head. The only things moving around here today, he thought, are pink Frisbees and orange soccer balls.

Lloyd Skirvin had sent Worms to get some hot dogs and had told Renee to go with him. Lloyd had stayed in the car, in the driver's seat, and Puggles was sitting in the back seat. "Don't hurry back," Lloyd had told them as they walked away. They had disappeared among the parked vehicles, Worms bareheaded, Renee holding her jacket over her head. She was beginning to wish she had dressed more warmly before running away from school yesterday.

Puggles sat back in the car, waiting to see what Lloyd would do or say. She was a little frightened. Lloyd had been sullen all morning, evidently unhappy about something. He had been drinking one beer after another for two hours, and his remarks toward Worms and Renee had become steadily more brutal. He seemed to be all bottled up with anger. He glowered at Puggles over the seat back now, and puffed hard on the short stub of a cigarette. He drained the last beer out of a can, rolled down the car window, and threw out the can and the cigarette butt. The can clanked among the many other empties that lay outside his window.

Now he grinned. "Hey, honey," he said. "C'mere and give me a hand with somethin', will ya?"

"What?"

"C'mon." He opened his door and got out, then tipped the seat forward and reached in toward her. "C'mon, I said."

She climbed out and stood in the drizzle with him, looking at him, her round face sallow and blank in the gray daylight. She had had several beers, too, and swayed a little. Lloyd smirked and reached down to open his trousers. "We goin' to have us a li'l target practice, y'heah?" Puggles looked astonished, then giggled drunkenly as he exposed himself. "Now, y'all jus' take aholt there, y'heah? Take aholt, damnit, girl. Y'deaf or somethin'? Good. Ahhh. Real good, honey. Now y'all see that cigarette butt lyin' there? Now y'all aim at that sumbitch an' we goin' piss it all apart, okay? Okay, heah we go now. No, wait, now. Yeah. Heah we go."

Puggles was giggling so hard her aim was off.

"Don' squeeze, damnit, an' look where you aimin'. Ah, now y'gittin' it. Right on the mark. Hee-hee-hee!"

People passing by stopped to watch the lean, hard-faced man and the soft-faced young girl standing among scattered beer cans between the automobiles, laughing and aiming the arc of urine. It seemed as if it would never stop.

"Okay, now, baby," he was saying. "Lessee can we shake off them last two drops. Ooooh," he began reciting, "you can shake it, you can milk it, you can slap it up 'side the wall, but they ain't a damn thing you can do to make them two drops fall!" Puggles was about to collapse with laughter. Several of the people who had stopped to watch began laughing, too, and, becoming aware of them, Lloyd leered and shook his penis at them. Then he shoved Puggles into the back seat of the car, climbed in after her, and shut the door.

"Okay, now, honey. Think maybe you got a place t' put this ol' thing?" She shook her head and scooted away from him. "Whaddya mean, honey?" he said. "Now, c'mon, I know you like it. I heard y'back heah squealin' like a stuck sow."

"I'm sore," she said.

"Aw, don't shit ol' Lloyd, now," he said, grabbing the waist of her jeans and jerking the snap open. "You tryin' t' say that li'l ol' peewee of his hurt you?" She struggled to get his hand off the zipper, but his fingers were too strong. In a moment he peeled the garments off her lower body and dragged her, wriggling, down to a supine position in the back seat. He put his hand on her neck, with his thumb at the base of her throat. When she whimpered, he pressed bruisingly hard with his thumb until the air was shut off. She submitted, her eyes wide, watching the flush of effort darken his forehead. Scalding pain shot through her abdomen, and returned and returned in waves as he flexed his hard body repeatedly upon her.

After a while the pain became compounded with an intense itch and then an ascending progression of thrills that began running the length of her body. He had reached a crazy place she hadn't known she had, one that Worms had not reached, one that nobody had ever reached. She hung onto him and bit into his hard shoulder to keep from slipping away somewhere, because she felt she wouldn't be able to come back. But she couldn't keep from going away, and the last thing she saw, opening her eyes one moment before going away, was a group of laughing faces looking in the car window.

Diana's reaction was, unfortunately, just what Nick had expected.

"Nick, I wanted to do it, but I can't do it with somebody else watching!" Diana's face was drawn in a grimace, against the rain and because she was upset. Nick squinted and looked off into the stands because he didn't like to see the displeasure in her face. He couldn't blame her.

The stands were emptying now, but there were still tens of thousands of fans waiting, waiting. . . .

"Diana, listen," he said, putting an arm over her shoulders and walking her toward the Tower. "It's very hard to arrange a thing like this. The mechanic has to be there for security reasons. You won't even know he's there—"

"Like heck I won't!"

"He'll be at the door. He'll keep his back turned. And— You know, when you're posing, it's like, well, it's all business, sort of, you know? We'll be doing a very professional job of it. Feelings aren't involved in it that much. You'll just be like a pro, that's all."

"I don't think I like that. My feelings *are* involved. Involved with you. I'd be very conscious of you seeing me that way!"

"Okay. I know. Me, too. But it'll work. And then when the shooting is done, we can get away together and relax. And get to know each other the way we've been trying to." You're just talking, he warned himself. Tonight you take Becky and Davey to the movie.

"I told Harry Kuntz to leave us alone," she said. "but I've got to spend a couple of hours this afternoon with his festival people."

"Good. Good, good. My dear girl. My beauty. Hey, listen. I've got a terrific idea! We can get started on some of the shots right now! The setting, the clothed shots. The Tower here, the track, you under a checkered umbrella, talking to a driver, or—yeah, like Revson, maybe Tony Hulman, if we can catch him for a minute— Or, like, a minute ago I saw Mike Hiss wearing some gag glasses with little windshield wipers on them. Hey, how about this: you sitting under a bright orange or red tarp or something with—maybe Andretti or somebody. Terrific, huh? Some thigh, maybe—"

It was working, thank God. She was beginning to smile, responding to his enthusiasm. Sure, he thought. The way to get somebody over reluctance is just to start!

The Rumples sat in their car on a road inside the Speedway, stopped in traffic. In the next lane there were cars headed in the other direction, also stopped. There were knots of stopped automobiles everywhere. Some of the drivers were trying to get in, and some were trying to get out. Gerald drummed his fingers rapidly on the steering wheel and let out frequent sighs. Ella gazed out the window, glum, not speaking to him.

"Well, here we are again," he said. "Sitting in another Speedway traffic jam."

"Oh, so what?"

"So I'm getting tired of it. I think this'll be my last. I'm not kidding you, Ella, I've had enough. There are other things to do in life besides sitting here reading the same bumper sticker for an hour at a time."

"I don't know what's got into you. I guess Ivy Yarbrough must think you're just awful!"

"Well, that's mutual."

"Think of me! I was embarrassed. After I told her how we love the race and all— But you, I just don't know what's come over you, Gerald."

"Rain clouds, for one thing. Ivy Yarbrough for another. Of all the loud-mouthed, bl—" He stopped himself. He had started to say "bloodthirsty," remembering how the big woman had screamed in the pace lap for Mario Andretti to "run them bastards into the wall."

"Ivy's all right. She just gets carried away."

"Yeah," he mumbled. "At least she doesn't faint, I'll bet."

"Gerald!" Tears welled up in Ella's eyes, and she quickly turned her face to the window and stared out, her chubby fist pressed against her mouth. The windshield wipers clicked monotonously.

Gerald was sorry he had mentioned that. But he'd be damned before he would admit he was sorry. "There, thank God!" he muttered. "I do believe we're beginning to move. A few feet, anyway."

Nick left Diana at the Tower and walked back through the sifting rain to find the mechanic. He found him once again hiding under the tarp over his crew's race car.

"It's okay with her," Nick said. Diana had never actually agreed to pose with the mechanic present, but Nick was confident that she would not protest any more about it once they actually got into the garage. She had seemed pleased and excited about the outdoor shots they had just taken. She'll be all right now, he thought.

The mechanic was happy again. Nick was to bring Diana to the garage area later in the afternoon, when the cars were put away, and they would smuggle her in when—and if—the rest of the crew left. "Just get a blanket or tarp over her, and we'll walk 'er in that way. Like that, see? You can't tell whether it's a man or woman." Nick looked. A figure slogged by, obscured like a monk under a blanket, the edge pulled forward like a cowl against the rain. "Listen," the mechanic said, giving Nick a gleeful punch on the shoulder, "I'm really glad it's workin' out, huh?"

"Yeah. Me, too." He was. But he was scared.

He looked at his watch. There wasn't much to do now. The race still had not been officially called off for the day, but Nick was certain it would be. Everyone and everything was draped against the rain. The pavements were covered with a sheen of water. Nick's hair was hanging wet, and he was becoming chilled. He thought of going to the pressroom and hanging around there to warm up. But there was another thought insinuating itself, a much more appealing notion.

This is the opportunity to go see Katherine—Kitty, he thought. Maybe just to have a drink. Get warm. He didn't really want to try to get to bed with her. That would be too involved a thing, he thought. I'm taking enough chances with this Diana thing. But it would be nice to pass an hour with Kitty. Who knows? She might not want to go to bed, either.

On the other hand, maybe she would.

Wow, he thought as he set off through the infield toward the Sixteenth Street Tunnel. Scary day. Scare-ee. Brrr.

He walked through an enormous field of cars. Cars parked, cars lined up, their engines and windshield wipers running. Horns were honking everywhere, and the car roofs were shining wet from the fine rain. Nick grinned at a thought: This is what hell must be like—an eternity of trying to drive into or out of the Indianapolis Motor Speedway but never quite getting in or getting out. It'd make Tantalus and Sisyphus thankful for what they've got. Among the cars, people slopped through the mud, draped in the blankets and plastic sheets that had virtually become the official Speedway uniform in the last couple of days. Others went by with their coats pulled up over their heads; still others moved bareheaded, squinting, their hair hanging limp, water dripping from their noses.

The tunnel was thronged with cars and people trying to go both ways, and its walkways underfoot were covered with litter, trampled into a black muck. Outside the tunnel, Nick turned left and walked around the end of the motel toward the gate that opened onto the new VIP building. As he went through the gate he saw a stocky man with a white raincoat and cap coming the other way. The man's jowly, deeply tanned face was familiar. Then Nick remembered: last night in the lounge. Why, it's her Werner poo-pie. Dold. For a moment the sight of her husband unnerved him. But evidently he was going away from the VIP suites, toward the Speedway. And she had said, after all, *Just come up.*

So here we go, he thought. After all, we're only going to have a little drink together. If she's not worried about him, why should I be?

Taking the matchbook out of his pocket, Nick looked inside and verified Kitty's suite number one final time. Then he went up and along the balcony onto which the suites' doors opened. The suites' spectator balconies were on the other side of the building, so there was hardly anyone here to see him go to her door. He stopped before the door and raised his hand to knock. A powerful reluctance took hold of him, and he lowered his hand. A radio was playing within. It was the race broadcast.

Last night when he had seen Kitty, it had seemed that they knew each other so well that they were intimates reuniting. But now he wondered whether they really knew each other at all: I don't think there's much left of the delightful, wanton girl I knew ten years ago. He started to turn away from her door.

But again he hesitated.

You have to see what's in this, he thought. He always tried to believe that moments meant something. He had felt since his encounter with her last night that this rare coincidence was being given to him and that it was meant to prove or teach something. About himself, perhaps. He rapped lightly on the door.

A few seconds passed, then the radio went silent. The doorknob turned, the door opened a crack, and he saw her eye glittering. Then the door shut and a chain rattled, and she opened the door to admit him. She watched him as he stepped in, her eyes wide and intent.

The drapes were drawn, and the only light on was in the bathroom. The bedspread lay in a wad on the floor; the sheets were rumpled and damp-looking; the pillows and blankets lay in a heap on the carpet beside the bed. There was a dense, musky odor in the room. It was the way their room had looked and smelled during that long, orgiastic weekend they had had in French Lick so long ago. Obviously, someone had just been in here with her.

"God, I'm glad you decided to come," she breathed. "I've been afraid you changed your mind." She was wearing a negligee, and there was around her head the smell of aerosol hair shellac, that thick, choking chemical smell he hated so, the smell Becky used to bring back from the beauty salon one day every week until it had begun to strain their budget. He thought he would gag on it as Kitty pressed a passionate, slippery kiss all over his mouth. Within the slight garment her flesh felt soft under his hands, not youthfully firm as it had been before, but soft without tone. "Glad you didn't get here sooner, though," she laughed. "Werner poo-pie dropped in. He just never does that."

"He doesn't but he did."

She shrugged. "Collecting his rare conjugal dues. And I do mean rare. He won't be back for a month at least."

"I just saw him."

"Saw Werner?"

"The man you were with at dinner last night. The, uhm, bald one. He was going over that way."

There was a momentary darkness in her eyes when he mentioned the previous evening. She's remembering me with Diana, Nick thought. Then she said, "Yes. He was going to the track."

Nick looked at her intently, examining her. The wonderful serendipitous magic, the intense friendliness he had felt upon seeing her last night, was no longer there. She evidently had just crawled out from under her husband —that fat old man—had done her hair, and was now receiving her lover, and could be candid and flippant about it.

She took his jacket. "You're quiet," she said. "You're tense, aren't you? Don't worry. Nobody'll bother us."

"I'm not worried."

"What's the matter?"

"Nothing's the matter."

"Something is. I can tell."

Bad start, he thought. We're like strangers. "Keep talking and you'll convince me something is wrong," he said, "but everything's fine as far as I'm concerned." He looked around the room restively.

"Maybe you need a drink. Right there on the cart is anything you need. Help yourself while I visit the little girls' room and finish making myself nice for you. I'll have a little Seven-and-Seven. Here's a towel. Your hair's soaking."

Alone, he toweled the rainwater out of his hair and looked around the room. The bed that fat old man had just left. Damp, wadded Kleenexes lying on the carpet around the wastebasket at which, apparently, they had been thrown, probably from the bed. And on the nightstand, lid off, was a square jar of Vaseline. He stared at it. PETROLEUM JELLY.

Jesus, yes. Petroleum. The petroleum people in our boudoirs, even. Lubricating our fucking machinery.

Soon cleansed with Massengill powder, sprayed with FDS, her armpits sticky with fresh deodorant, Kitty daubed her throat with cologne and flushed the toilet. She had made up her mind not to mention that young blonde she had seen with Nick. Jealousy's for kids. That was another of her mottoes. She opened the bathroom door. "Now, Nicholas, my darling—"

But that was all she said.

He was gone. There was a Seven-and-Seven sitting on the dresser, and an empty shot glass.

Just don't let me catch you feeling proud or pious, Nick warned himself as he went out of the gate and plodded along behind the high bleachers back toward the Sixteenth Street Tunnel, the rain, heavier now, wetting his hair again. You know damn well that if she'd been at all like the old Katherine, you sure as hell wouldn't have walked out like this. He took deep breaths, and his heartbeat was slowing. Her whiskey was still warm inside him and was buzzing in his head a little; he had bolted down four successive shots of straight Scotch while mixing her Seven-and-Seven. Preventive medicine, he thought as he joined the troops of people entering the walkway of the tunnel. You could get pneumonia out here this year.

Suddenly he had a hard time swallowing, and his eyes smarted. Katherine, he thought. He remembered something she had said last night: *We're all selling our asses these days.* Katherine. I'm sorry about this.

Come on, you noble ass, he thought. Who're you feeling sorry for, her or yourself?

Werner Dold was experiencing a rare state of mind. It had dawned on him as he made his way along the pedestrian walkway of the Sixteenth Street Tunnel into the Speedway that he was surrounded by people he didn't know, by people who didn't know who he was. It had been years since he had been in such a situation. Here were people, ordinary people, poor people, middle-class people, people who had no idea of the wealth and power he represented; they were pressing against him, hurrying around him, getting in his way, coming past him without even seeing him. No one knew or cared who he was. No one was coming up to him with that scared smile that always signified a desire to snuggle up to his wealth. Werner Dold was anonymous in a mob.

When he was a boy, Werner Dold had walked unknown like this in crowds on the downtown streets of Cleveland and Cincinnati, hungry, unknown, driven by a desperate desire to get, somehow, a slice of the American pie, to own the big buildings that rose all around him, to be in a vast office by himself on a top floor, with people permitted into his sanctuary by appointment only. And nobody on the streets of Cleveland or Cincinnati, of course, had known of his dream or cared about it, just as none of these milling race fans in a tunnel at the Indianapolis Motor Speedway now knew that he had realized that dream. What an odd, exhilarating experience this was: a dreamlike experience. He wondered why it had never occurred to him to do this before. He had wandered anonymous in the "500" Festival social events, but that had been a different world. Everybody at those functions expected every stranger to be somebody important. Here, nobody had such expectations.

Werner stood at the end of the tunnel. The rain had increased suddenly, and people were pausing at the mouth of the tunnel before dashing out. The air in the tunnel had been full of exhaust fumes and the damp smells of people, blankets, sweaters; the air at the end of the tunnel was fresh, cool, and wet. It smelled very good. Werner paused here, backing up close to the concrete wall out of the way of the pedestrians, and looked at them as they went by. He had never, even in his youth, really looked at passing faces on the streets; always he had been too driven, too full of hungers and schemes, to care about seeing people's faces. And in later years, at cocktail parties and board meetings, he had looked into their faces only to try to determine how weak or strong or venal they might be, how much they might be willing to do to gain his favor, to make deals with him. Now he looked at faces—in this noisy, damp tunnel's mouth—for the first time. The faces were so incredibly various, so different. No two were quite identical. Like fingerprints, he thought. The young people were so tall, so well-formed, with good features, with good teeth of the kind it had cost him six thousand dollars to have reconstructed in his head. They take their looks for granted, he thought. They don't try to dress to look nice. Do any of them wander down the streets of cities now with private dreams of owning the big buildings, of having suites of offices and being approached by appointment only? From what Werner had read, the young didn't have those dreams anymore.

Nobody knows who I am, he repeated to himself several times. I am just an old man in a raincoat and a cap. They don't know I've just come from a twenty-thousand-dollar suite, from the bed of a starlet they have seen on the screens of drive-in movie theaters. How many of these men walking by me have looked at Kitty's nakedness on movie screens and in magazines and had fantasies about her, he wondered. Not one of you knows—you, who just glanced at me and hurried on, you with the skinny woman on your arm—not one of you knows that Kitty is mine. Not one of you knows I can buy this Speedway you love so much. Werner took off his blue ascot and stuffed it into his pocket. Now, he thought, I look still more like a nobody. I could do anything now. I could— I could do something undignified, unproud, like I used to have to do.

He remembered a time in Cincinnati, when he was about fifteen years old, when he had stood sheltered from the rain under the marquee of a downtown movie theater and asked passersby for a cigarette. The moment came to him whole from his memory: the rainy sidewalk, the streetcars ringing by on their steel rails, the smell of tobacco smoke in the cool air, air like this.

On the advice of his doctor, Werner had stopped smoking cigarettes many years ago, and now indulged only in an after-dinner cigar with his brandy. Wouldn't it be wonderful right now, he thought, to bum a cigarette from a total stranger, as if a cigarette were the most desirable and necessary thing in the world, as it was then. How good a cigarette could be then!

Now Werner Dold was terribly taken with his thought. How good everything was when you couldn't afford it! A bag of hot chestnuts, their charred, split hulls breaking away, the steaming sweet meat inside; a cool beer in a schooner on a dark wood bartop; and of course a two-dollar piece of ass on a squeaky downtown hotel bed was paradise. But even a mere cigarette . . .

For a long time Werner stood there in the tunnel with the people streaming by, remembering these things, and he began to desire a cigarette with all his soul. A tall man had stopped nearby, standing by the rail that separated the pedestrian walkway from the car traffic in the tunnel, a lean man in a rain-darkened corduroy sport coat, his shirt collar open, cameras and bags hanging by straps from his shoulders and around his neck. The man was pausing in the tunnel's end, evidently hesitating as Werner had before going out into the rain. He had a short, thick beard and a good face. He was shaking a Pall Mall cigarette out of a red package. He took the cigarette out with his fingers, glancing toward Werner and then quickly away. He reached into the side pocket of his jacket and took out a book of matches, struck one, sucked in the smoke, and then blew it out in a stream. Let's do, Werner thought.

He waited for some young people to dart by into the rain, holding newspapers over their heads, then approached the lean man. "Say, excuse me," he said. The lean man's eyes widened a moment in surprise. "I was wondering if I might bum a smoke from you," Werner said. How funny it was to hear himself saying this. It was, strangely, one of the most enjoyable moments he had ever experienced.

"Uhm, sure," the man said, again extracting the red package from his pocket and shaking a cigarette out.

Werner put the cigarette between his lips, faintly smelling the tobacco. If I became as recognizable as Tony Hulman, he thought, I wouldn't dare do something like this. "Do you have a light?"

"Sure," said Nick Alef. And, nervous and astonished though he was, he thought of the old recitation: Shall I also kick you in the ass to get the wind started? He reached into his coat pocket for the matchbook, then remembered just in time that it had Kitty's handwriting in it, her suite number. "Here," he said, holding the coal of his own cigarette to the end of Werner's. He studied the thick, tan jowls, the powerful but delicately manicured hand that he knew had been so recently upon Kitty's body. He fancied that he could even smell her scent again upon this man. Nick held his own hand as steady as he could, but it was shaky. All sorts of probabilities raced through his mind. Maybe Dold had noticed him last night, even seen him talking to Kitty. Maybe, recognizing him just a few minutes ago, he had turned and followed him back to the VIP building and watched him go to her suite. Why else would Kitty's rich husband be waiting here in the tunnel and stopping him on the pretext—the *ridiculous* pretext—of bumming a cigarette?

"Thanks," Dold said. "A cigarette *can* be good, can't it?"

"Sure can."

"I was out of them and didn't want to walk through this rain looking for a vending machine."

"Don't blame you," Nick said. What now? He thought.

"Race fan, are you?" Dold said.

"Uhm, yep," Nick said.

Werner inhaled the cigarette smoke and looked at the lean man. He had forgotten how powerful cigarette smoke could be to someone who hadn't inhaled it in a long while; his fingers and cheeks felt as if there were a silent buzzing going on in them. A race fan, Werner thought. He realized that he had never talked to a real, ordinary race fan before. Only to Doc Upton and other local society people who watched it all from above, so to speak. "Tell me, then," he said, "what is it you people come to see that's so wonderful you put up with all this mess?"

The lean man appeared to be very uneasy. He looked at Werner and then over his shoulder and then back at his face.

"What is it?" Werner repeated.

The lean man shrugged. "Well, the cars, I guess. The excitement—"

Werner leaned on the rail and pointed his cigarette at the lean man's face. "Ah, yes," he said. "But the excitement of what? The crowds? The danger? The blood? Fire?"

What's he up to? Nick wondered. What's he leading up to? But hell, I'll talk to him. I'll play race fan for him. "Well," he said, "it's not very smart to talk to a race fan about blood and fire. You don't think we come here to see those, do you?"

"I've often wondered."

"Hell, no," Nick said, remembering all the standard disclaimers he had heard race fans use as they rationalized their passion. "We don't want to see anybody hurt. It happens sometimes, sure. But we hate it when it does happen." Nick found it exceedingly droll to hear himself parroting these statements. But all this time he was expecting Werner to drop the topic and bring up the question of his relationship to Kitty Dold.

"Well, tell me this," Dold went on. "Do you think people—now, this is purely hypothetical, of course—do you think you would keep coming to this race if it could be made absolutely safe? I mean, if they could drive around the track at two hundred miles an hour with absolutely no danger of crashing and burning, would you people come out here just to see the cars run that fast?"

"Of course not."

"It would be boring, perhaps?"

"Terribly boring. Except maybe to a few technically minded people. Record keepers and such. Sure, it gets boring."

"Then you're admitting that it *is* the danger you come to watch!"

"I didn't say it wasn't. Of course it's the danger."

"But didn't you just say you hate the accidents?"

"We don't hate the accidents," Nick said, trying to put together an unfamiliar viewpoint, finding it terribly ironic that he should be playing devil's advocate on this subject —particularly in an absurd encounter with this strange man. But as he tried to express it, he began to understand something about it. "You see, we, uhm, we love to see a spinout. Or smoke suddenly pouring out of a car. I mean, it makes us hop up off our chairs. Gets some adrenaline pumping in our bored old selves. I mean, life's so bland for most people, they love anything that'll make them jump up and scream. What's really a trip is when a car actually hits the wall and a few tires and things go rolling down the track. But here's the point: then we see the driver get out alive. He's, uhm, he's triumphed, see, over that machine that just tried to kill him. That's what we like to see."

Dold stood smoking his cigarette down to a short butt, apparently thinking about that. "So you think that's it, do you?"

"Yeah," Nick said. Maybe there's some truth to that, he thought. For some fans, maybe that's it.

But he had seen many things here at the Speedway that had convinced him that, down deep, some people liked it better when the driver didn't get out.

Intelligent, Werner thought. This fellow has given it some thought. Naive, perhaps, or else trying to ennoble the motives of himself and his fellow fans. But he articulates things—complex things—quite well. Like to have a man like this working for me. As a communicator, perhaps, maybe in public relations when I buy the Speedway. "What's your name?" he asked.

Aha, Nick thought. Now we get to the crux of it. All this to find out who I am. "Uhm, my name's Richard," he said.

"Richard? Richard what?"

"Richard, uhm, Bixley," he extemporized hastily. Hope he doesn't already know my real name and know I'm lying, he thought.

"Bixley. Well, Mr. Bixley. I'd enjoy talking more to you about this, about many things, really. But, uhm, am I keeping you from anything?"

Nick thought he detected sarcasm in that question. "No, nothing," he said.

"Why don't you jot down your address and phone for me? Uhm, do you ever do any writing?"

"He does know me, Nick thought. "Why do you ask?"

"Oh, you look like a writer. And all those cameras. I just guessed—"

"That's the important thing,"—Nick repeated his standard line—"to look like one."

"Here," said Dold, handing him a pen and a fine leather pocket-size appointment book, opened to a blank address page. Nick wrote quickly: *Richard Bixby. 3912 N. Oxford.* Let's see, he thought. *546-5209.* He gave the pen and book to Dold. Dold looked at it.

"Oh. Bixby?" he said. "I'm sorry. I understood you to say 'Bixley.' "

"Uhm, no. It's Bixby. By the way, I didn't get *your* name."

"Well," said Dold, "would you mind my not telling you that just yet? I have my reasons."

"Well, I just gave you mine freely enough." Yeah, he thought. Didn't I, though? Ha.

"Yes, and you were kind enough to give me a cigarette, and a lot of your time. Aaaaand, some insights. I thank you indeed, Mr. Bixby. You'll know who I am when I get in touch with you. Sincerely, I would like to talk to you. About, uhm, business. I may have a position opening up, and if I do, I believe I could use a man like you. You are an Indianapolis man?"

"Yes."

"How much do you make?"

Jesus Christ, Nick thought. Who's playing whose game here? "Well, how much do *you* make?"

"I'm sorry. I didn't mean to pry. Whatever it is, I'd double it—within reason, of course—if you turned out to be the right man. Heh-heh. Now, listen, Mr. Bixby—uhm, may I call you Richard?"

"Sure," said Nick, smiling crookedly. "Call me Richard. Call me Dick if you like." He laughed inside at the absurdity of this strange game. Tricky Dick Bixby, he thought.

Now here's a man, Werner Dold thought, who doesn't know me from Adam. But he's spending time standing here with me, telling me his true feelings about something that's important down deep to him. This, then, is the way total strangers can be to each other, when there's not an awareness of money between them. I didn't realize how much I had insulated myself from the world in that office of mine. That mansion. That private plane. Well.

He took a deep breath. He was really enjoying this. Just a simple, honest, guileless, man-to-man encounter. To most people an everyday occurrence; to him a rare adventure. Suddenly he felt warmth for this laconic, bearded fellow, this intelligent race fan. "Tell you what, Dick," he said. "You're an honest fellow, and a thinking man, I believe. There's something I'd like to discuss with you. Unless you're in a hurry, why don't you let me buy you a drink?" Detecting reluctance, suspicion, in the fellow's eyes, he suddenly took hold of his upper arm and turned him back toward Sixteenth Street. "No excuses, now. We'll just trot over to the motel. They've got a nice lounge there. Say, doesn't this Hulman have a gold mine here?"

Nick was still convinced that Werner Dold knew, or suspected, rather, that he was Kitty's lover. Yet the man seemed so genuinely friendly, so eager for his company, that he no longer felt any fear of him, and allowed himself to be hurried along toward the cocktail lounge. Evidently Dold really hadn't learned Nick's real name, and accepted that it was Dick Bixby. But still, what a strange way to treat someone he suspected was his wife's lover!

Then a curious notion dawned on him, an explanation,

perhaps: Suppose Dold is one of those guys who get their jollies out of their wives' love affairs? Jesus! Kink-y!

But it was a weird situation, a most amusing one. Sure as hell a lot more interesting than standing in the rain looking at a wet racetrack. And another nice drink or three wouldn't be hard to take at all.

Kitty Dold had paced her room, confused, crushed, for several minutes. She had drained the Seven-and-Seven Nick had poured for her, drained it in one long swallow, then with shaking hands she had sloshed out two more shots of the whiskey and bolted them down.

It had happened so fast she could hardly believe it had actually occurred. The one man in the world who had ever really meant anything to her, really meant anything to her down deep, the only man who had ever taken her out of her own control, had knocked on her door this afternoon like an answer to her prayers, ten years of prayers, then had spoken a few meaningless and uneasy words to her and vanished.

It's because of that blonde, of course, Kitty had told herself, at last grasping a conceivable explanation. He's in love with that blonde. She's no older than I was when Nick and I—

And then, feeling suddenly that all the elasticity had left her flesh and her soul, trembling and angry and heartsick, Kitty had stripped off her lingerie and, afraid to look in the mirror, had dressed in white slacks, a flowered blouse, and a raincoat and had left her suite, afraid to be alone in it with herself. Thinking, appalled by the prospect of a meaningless lifetime as the property of a rich, fat old man, her one bright fantasy extinguished, she had trotted across the wet pavements to the motel. She had gone into the lounge but had been depressed by the sight of the roomful of dark, stupid-looking drinkers there, and, remembering with a pain in her breast the sight of Nick Alef in that very room with that young blond girl, she had turned away with a groan and walked like a ghost through the lobby to the tables at the other side where she and Nick had met and talked alone last night. With a Kleenex over her mouth and the meaningless green grass of the golf course beyond the picture window swimming before her eyes, she had sat down at a table, blowing her nose repeatedly and fumbling through her handbag for she knew not what, as people passed up and down the carpeted corridor.

After a while she had slumped into a tearless, vacant calm, gazing out at the empty wet grass of the golf course and the dark-green trees and white, barnlike buildings and the gray sky and misty rain.

Then slowly she had become aware of someone alone at the next table, someone as silent and abstracted and apparently lost as she was herself. He was a slim, blond-haired young man in a military uniform—Air Force, it was—who was gazing over the green also, but who had begun turning to gaze at her for minutes at a time. His face was narrow, fine-featured, sensitive, as Nick's face had been when she met him, before the beard. His eyes were sad and haunting.

Kitty Dold, out of her own sadness, smiled at him.

"Ellll-la," Gerald called softly from his office, rising from his chair with his eyes on the newspaper he was holding. There was a smile on his lips but malevolence in his eyes. He walked into the cubicle outside the office, where she was working on the bookkeeping. She had started right to work on it when they arrived from the Speedway. She was running her fingers over an adding machine and moving her lips. She came to the end of a sum and looked up. Gerald put the paper down on her desk and tapped an item on the sports page with his knuckle. As she started to read it, he strolled back into the office, humming. He sat down at his desk and picked up a pen and pretended to be looking through invoices. They were alone in the building. Ralph had locked up the office and gone on a service call before they arrived.

In a minute Ella appeared at the door of the office and stood there, holding the newspaper. She leaned against the doorjamb, tilted her head, and looked at him. "So?" she said.

He looked up as if surprised to see her there.

"So?" she repeated, holding up the newspaper.

"Oh, that. Just thought you'd be interested."

" 'Oh, that.' And your point was?"

"Uhm, nothing. Just that, well, they did fine some drivers for sneaking up in the pace lap. Just wondering whether that might have caused the crash yesterday."

"It doesn't say 'sneaking up,' Gerald."

"Well. 'Improving positions.' Same thing."

"But you chose to say 'sneaking up,' Gerald. Why?"

"Just a simpler way of say—"

"I'll tell you why. Because A.J. was fined. Right?"

"Well, he was."

"Gerald, how can you be so petty?"

"Me? Petty? What's petty? I just show you a newspaper—"

"And give all these insinnuendos that A.J.'s done something terrible!"

"*I* did that? I don't even know what an 'insinnuendo' is."

"You insin— You know what I mean. Don't be funny!"

"Ella, you're the one who's protecting him. I didn't say or even insinuate anything."

"Oh, the hell you didn't!"

"Ella!"

"I don't care! I know what would make you happy: for someone to—for 'Salt' Walther or the USAC or somebody to come out and accuse A.J. of causing the crash! You're that silly jealous of him!"

"Ella! What a thing to say!"

"Here! Take your damn newspaper, you smug— you—" She threw the paper on the floor and slammed the door.

Gerald sat in his chair for a few minutes, letting his pulse rate slow down. He had had to say practically nothing; she had reacted far more violently even than he had expected her to. He was thus able to say to himself: How unreasonable she is about anything concerning that race!

And that made it possible for him to feel even more righteous about it. How unreasonable she is— He ran that over in his mind as if imagining how it would sound to a marriage counselor.

For Gerald had been thinking this afternoon about marriage counselors.

But now his conscience was beginning to bother him. And he didn't like having a door between him and Ella, a door that had been slammed in anger. That had hardly ever happened in all their years together. That race has brought us to this, he thought.

So Gerald sat and waited for a seemly amount of time to pass. Then he got up and opened the door. She wasn't at the bookkeeper's desk. He turned and went down the hallway to the back of the building. A sofa and an old refrigerator and a table stood by the door to the truck garage. Two of the three trucks were parked in the garage.

Ella was sitting at the table, gloomily eating a bowl of ice cream. She didn't look up when he came in. Gerald was afraid he had gone too far. "I've got an idea," he said, keeping his voice as casual as he could. She didn't reply. "They've postponed the race again till tomorrow morning," he said. She pulled the spoon out of her mouth and sat looking up at him. He said, "You would, uhm, you would go with me to the race tomorrow if I said I was sorry, wouldn't you?"

Ella put the spoon down in her ice cream dish and swallowed. Her eyes grew misty. Then she held her arms up to him. In a moment they had their faces on each other's left shoulders and were patting each other gently on the back.

They were like that when the garage door rumbled open and Ralph drove his service truck in. He clambered out quickly and hurried to them, his mouth opening and closing as it did when he was excited. Under his gray-billed cap his eyes bulged, and his Adam's apple rose and fell in his turkey neck. "Hey," he said, "listen, Mr. Rumple, I'm really glad you're here! Your housekeeper called down here on the phone this mornin', and she gave me this number for you t' call." He drew a slip of paper out of his jacket pocket and gave it to Gerald. "I couldn't make out what she was sayin'. But that there's a number you're s'posed to call. She said it was important."

Gerald and Ella hovered over the paper and looked at the telephone number. "That's the Chicago area code, isn't it?" Gerald said. "Well, let me get into the office and see what we've got here."

Gerald settled his bulk into the chair, which creaked loudly. He dialed the number, and while the phone rang, he bent, wheezing, to pick up the afternoon paper that Ella had thrown on the floor.

The phone was still ringing when he saw the small headline on an inside page about the crash that had killed Gene and Ruth Roepke.

The first thought he had was of all the drinks he had ordered for Gene.

"Now, just suppose, Dick," Werner Dold said to Nick Alef, "just suppose there were a financier who wanted to buy this Speedway from Tony Hulman. Hulman's getting old, you know. Do you suppose that man would have a chance?"

"I doubt it," Nick said. He and Dold had found a table in the lounge; they were on their second martini now, and Nick was feeling very much at ease. Every once in a while he would pause in his thinking and wonder why Dold was talking about everything under the sun but Kitty, but that question meant less and less the more he drank. The lounge was jammed with people, many of whom were standing with their drinks because there was no place to sit. Out in the lobby the registration desk was crowded with agitated and angry people, some of whom were trying to extend their stay another night because of the delayed race, and others who were arriving and unsure whether they could obtain vacant rooms. Nick's thoughts turned occasionally to Becky; he was thinking mellower thoughts about her since—and perhaps because —he had been virtuous enough to walk out of Kitty's room. He had thought about calling home, but the phones were all in use again.

"But he's getting along in years," Dold was saying. "And his Speedway must be a lot of headaches. Maybe he's getting tired and would like to retire."

"Oh, I don't think Tony has too many headaches with it. He's got a staff of really capable, loyal old-timers who take care of things. Clarence Cagle keeps the place up and does all the modernizing, Bloemker in P.R., Jo Quinn about everything else— Listen. Anybody has his price, they say, and unfortunately I guess that's true. But this place"—he paused, waving an arm in the direction of the Speedway—"this place is an institution. A legend. Tony bought it from Eddie Rickenbacker, who was a legend himself, and Tony got part of that intangible along with the place. But hell, Rickenbacker *wanted* to unload it. It had been closed down for the duration of the war and was just falling apart. People thought Tony was insane to put good money in a weed field. But Tony had watched races here in his youth. Maybe he understood what it means to people to have a place where you can come and, well, watch heroes. Who knows?"

Werner Dold knew all this history. He was remembering his own trips out here after the war, remembering how it had looked then, remembering why he had decided against buying it. He felt a disturbing awareness of time, of long-ago choices that had changed everything.

"—anyway," the lean, bearded man was saying, "this thing now is a gold mine, as you put it, wrapped in an aura of intangible stuff that you can't set a price on."

Werner Dold sighed and ate the olive out of his martini. "But let me ask you this, then," he said. "Do you suppose that that 'aura' might be affected by what's happening this year? I mean all this rain, the—the death of Pollard, the accident yesterday that hurt Walther and all those spectators? I mean, do you suppose that might hurt the aura enough to make Tony consider selling it? Couldn't, perhaps, somebody—that hypothetical financier I mentioned—make an opportunity out of this mess?"

Suddenly something dovetailed in Nick's mind. I'll be damned, he thought, I believe *he's* the hypothetical financier he's talking about. I believe he's thinking about buying it! Nick had been out of journalism for a long time, but he still felt he had the facility to sniff a story when it wafted through the air. "Well," he said, fully attentive now, "if *you* were that financier you're talking about, what would you do? Would you wait until the off-season, or would you try to approach Hulman now?"

"Well, ordinarily, I'd— Well, in the first place, I would have done a lot of research in advance, of course. Income, attendance, and as much as I could learn about the aura you spoke of—I'd try to understand that fully, you know. I'd also investigate the current condition of the rest of Tony's fortune—the Clabber Girl business, gas company, Coca-Cola plant, and all that—because that could have a bearing, of course. Ordinarily, I'd go to him off-season, but I think this year, after the way things have been going, I'd wait until the letdown right after the race—after it's finished, or better yet, rained out—and, well, I might give the bad publicity of this year's troubles a chance to soak in. You know, that bunch of fans getting burned could be the best thing that ever happened— What was it Shakespeare, I think, said: 'Strike while the iron is hot' or—"

Nick turned his face away and swallowed a laugh. "Or while the time and tide are hot, or something—yes. Go on."

"Well, that's what I'd do."

He's already researched it all, Nick thought. He knows Hulman's empire inside and out. He's really into this. Holy Christ. Nick thought. This could be quite a story I've happened onto! What I couldn't do with that story in this town. "Bartender," he said, "another for my friend here." Loosen his tongue, he thought. "Well, uhm, how much would you offer Tony for the place?" he asked, turning back to Dold.

But Werner's face, his demeanor, had changed. Suddenly he was sitting up straight; his fingers were curled tightly; his face was stolid. Oh-oh, Nick thought. He knows he's said too much.

"Look, Mr. Bixby," Dold said. "It's been nice talking with you. I'm sure you must be on your way, as I must. Bartender, cancel that last one. How much do I owe you?"

Wow, Nick thought, finding himself standing in the crowded lobby, blinking in the light and noise. He couldn't remember ever having been so quickly and effectively dismissed. Those tycoons really know how to shut you off. Jesus. Weirdest goddamn thing. Maybe those martinis made him forget I was with his wife, and that's why he talked so much. Then I got too close.

Nick went to the front door of the lobby and stood watching the rain fall. Wonder how much Kitty knows about this, if anything, he thought. Wonder if I dare go back and try to find out, after that disappearing act I pulled. Could make up an excuse for her: tell her I remembered a call I had to make. Something. Maybe I could sneak a photo of Dold while I'm here. That would lend credence if any editor doubted my story—and they sure would.

It was hard to think straight because of the martinis. But he felt he had to find out as much about this as he could because he was sure he was the only person onto it. And he could sell a story like that. Just the speculation about it would make a story. Have to work fast, though. Bet he's going to approach Tony today. Or maybe tomorrow or something. How would I do this? Touchy stuff. Jesus. If I were the first to ask Tony for comments — Then, even if he made a public statement that he was considering an offer, it'd be awhile probably before he'd say who made it, and I'd be the only one to know. Good story. Goddamn. Good story! Nick Alef would be re-remembered again. Return from obscurity, he thought. He chuckled, seeing it as a headline: NEWSMAN UNCOVERS SPEEDWAY SALE—RETURNS FROM OBSCURITY. Ha-ha. Silly ass! Nick pulled his camera off his shoulder and went back into the lobby. He made a meter reading and set the lens. He stood back behind a knot of people and watched for Werner Dold to emerge from the lounge. It was like an ambush, and he felt ridiculous. God, would I feel silly if he saw me shooting his picture after our long talk, he thought.

Silly, hell, he thought. This is a good opportunity. A weird day, but a lucky one. While he waited, he wondered whether—and how—he could get back in with Kitty and pick her brains. May have to screw her for this, he thought. Screw and then talk in the languid afterglow. I can think of worse things. Be ready, he thought; she may require some winning back.

Must be more careful, Werner Dold thought as he signed the bar tab. Getting carried away like that by a little unfamiliar camaraderie. All right, though. Didn't really tell him anything. But his ears were beginning to perk up.

Thoughtfully, Werner made his way out of the lounge. Probably shouldn't have rushed him off so abruptly, he thought. All in all, what a pleasant diversion it was just to talk to an intelligent man. Excellent fellow. Friendly, just sarcastic enough to indicate he knows something about the world. Will get in touch with him, I think, if I make the Speedway deal. Bixby. Uhm. Fellow like that might make one a good biographer.

Werner paused before the cigarette machine in the lobby. He remembered the cigarette he had bummed in the tunnel. That was good, he thought. Terrible how I've shut myself off from the ordinary world. He looked at the various labels displayed in the cigarette machine. There were many new brands he had never tried. Ought to buy a package of each, he thought, and see how they taste. Winston. That's new since I quit. Vantage—Kent—Lark. Camels. They were good, I remember. But with filters?

Werner could not operate the vending machine. It required money, and he never carried money with him anymore. The first few years as a wealthy man, he had carried thick rolls of currency with him—two or three thousand dollars—just for the pleasure of knowing he had it. Then he had become used to the idea of being self-sufficient, finally growing secure in the notion, and it had become more and more convenient for him to use credit in all its ingenious new forms. Now he carried neither bills nor coins; now his driver always paid the highway tolls out of the garage allotment; if Werner wanted cigars or any sundries while away from home, he charged them to his hotel account or sent somebody out to get them.

While gazing at the cigarette machine and wondering about the new brands of cigarettes, he heard his wife's voice coming from nearby in the lobby. He turned and saw her just as she saw him. She was passing nearby, going toward an exit, her hand in the crook of a man's arm—an Air Force officer, a handsome man with wavy blond hair and sunken eyes. They were both looking very thoughtful, very close. She glanced up, and her step faltered just an instant; then she came on toward him, grandly holding one hand out to him and leading the officer with the other. "Werner, my darrrrr-ling!" she trilled. "I want you to meet this wonderful man, Captain George. Carl is one of the released Vietnam War prisoners. Carl, this is my husband, Werner Dold."

"Hu—hi." The man had a troubling, lusterless look in his eyes.

"Uhm. Yes." Werner shook his hand, barely looking at him.

"Werner poo-pie, what on earth are you doing, wandering around down here among all the common people?"

"Just being democratic, my dear, like you. Quite a nice change for me, I must say. I had a few drinks with a most pleasant fellow who didn't know who I am. Very interesting, that was. A writer. Bixby. Ever read anything by a Bixby? Have you, Captain? Well neither have I, but I think it would be good, judging by his conversation— well, my dear. Where are you two going, if I may ask?"

"I—I wanted Carl to meet you. I was bringing him—"

"Ah, but you knew I was going to the track, remember?"

"Oh—oh, of course. I'd forgotten."

"Well, that's where I'm going." He leaned to kiss her on the cheek, and growled low, "Be very careful of yourself, my dear. You wouldn't want to make me unhappy in any way, I assure you. Right? You really wouldn't want to make me unhappy." He turned and walked away, stiff-backed, without looking at Captain George.

Nick Alef, unobserved, had just snapped three photos of Werner Dold gazing at a cigarette vending machine when Dold suddenly turned to look at someone. Nick followed the glance, and his heart surged when he saw that it was Kitty. Astonished, Nick recognized the Air Force officer she was with, the same man Nick had watched yesterday at the track, that handsome, slight captain with his air of delicate vulnerability.

Nick hung back behind a knot of talking people and watched Kitty and Werner and the captain having their brief encounter. He wondered what the captain's relationship to Kitty was, and what it could mean to Werner Dold.

Perplexed, Nick watched Werner kiss her cheek and walk away abruptly.

Kitty and the captain then stood and talked quietly to one another as Werner marched out the front door. They seemed to be hanging there in uncertainty, as Nick himself was. Then they went to the front door; Kitty peered out, then led the officer outdoors, as if he were a placid child, by the hand. In a state of wonderment, and with a kind of unpleasant, dreadful comprehension beginning to insinuate itself into his thoughts, Nick crossed the lobby quickly and followed them outdoors. He saw them go through the covered driveway between two buildings of the motel and vanish around the end of the structure. He went to the driveway and from there saw them making their way among the cars in the parking lot, going evidently toward the VIP building where her suite was, their legs reflected in the film of rainwater on the asphalt. For a moment a bizarre notion entered Nick's drink-befogged head: he imagined that Kitty was taking this handsome young man to her room, and that Werner had gone to meet them there for some strange, aberrant game à trois, as he had suspected earlier when Werner had led him by the arm toward the motel.

Nick followed them as far as the gate, disturbed by a strange sort of regret. He watched them go up the stairs to the second-floor walkway, then along it to the door of her room. Then he saw that he was mistaken: Werner obviously was not meeting them up there after all; instead, he emerged from behind someone's luxury traveling van that was parked beside the VIP building, and peered around the corner of the van to watch Kitty and the young officer up on the walkway, his hands deep in the pockets of his raincoat. Obviously he had been hiding in wait there to see if she would take the young man to her room. Nick couldn't see Werner Dold's face, just the back of his head. Did he watch me go up there just like that? Jesus, he thought. The poor guy.

Nick looked up to Kitty's door again. The young man had gone inside. But Kitty had paused for a moment— perhaps to watch out for her husband—and she had seen

Nick standing there by the gate gazing up at her. Her eyes were upon him, and although she was some distance away —a hundred feet or so, it seemed—he thought he saw in her face and posture both defiance and anguish. Or, he was to think later, maybe that's only what I would have expected to see.

It was over in a moment. She went through the door into her room and shut it. Nick remembered the sound of the chain she had slid back to admit him through that very door, what—less than an hour ago? Nick stood in the rain, blinking, trying to assimilate all that he had seen and heard in the last few minutes, these few very personal minutes in the midst of two long rainy days, on the fringes of a mob of hundreds of thousands of people.

After a few moments of reflection, he dropped his eyes from the blank, firm panel of the closed door and saw Werner Dold still standing at the van. What will he do now, Nick wondered. Surely not something common and impulsive like going up there and banging on the door and making a scene.

At that moment, Werner Dold slowly turned away from gazing at the door. He came walking with slow steps toward the gate, his head down, his eyes hidden under his cap bill, his hands clasped behind his back. Nick turned away. Dold went past him without seeing him, paused in the parking lot as if deciding whether to go toward the track or the motel, then turned left and trudged toward the motel. To the bar, I suppose, Nick thought. Could you blame him?

Worms and Renee had wandered over most of the infield looking for hot dogs. But every hot-dog stand was sold out. People stood waiting around the concession stands, their cuffs and ankles muddy, their hair hanging damp and limp, their arms hugged across their chests, as if hoping hot dogs would suddenly appear from Heaven.

Worms looked at Renee. She had said hardly a word; her eyes seemed to be gazing through him, gazing through everything. It made him uncomfortable. He put his hands on his belt and craned his neck, surveying the sodden, littered field. "Well, fuck it," he said. "I don't think they's a goddamn wienie in a hunnerd miles. Watcha wanta do, honey? You wanta go back t' the car?"

"No. I don't wanna go back to the car."

"Then whatcha wanta do? Let's go someplace. I got rain runnin' down th' crack a my ass." He stooped, took off his right shoe, poured water out of it while hopping on the left foot, put the shoe back on, then did the same with his left. He saw something on the ground that looked like a ticket. He picked it up. It seemed to be a couple of tickets, torn off at one end, wet and stuck together. He put them unthinkingly in his shirt pocket.

Renee sighed and looked around, then started walking. He followed her. She had removed her jacket from over her head and now was just wearing it, her fists stuffed into her pockets. Her yellow hair was now in strings, with water dripping off the ends.

She led him back to a place they had passed half an hour earlier, near the Snake Pit. She stopped and stood looking at a bright red van with psychedelic designs airbrushed on its sides. There were two bewhiskered young men with shovel hats sitting in the van. Now and then someone would approach the van and one of the youths would roll down his window and talk for a minute. Then something would be passed through the window, which would be rolled up again, and the visitor would go away.

"You got any money?" Renee asked.

Worms shrugged. "Some."

"Gimme ten bucks."

"Huh?"

"Just ten dollars. C'mon."

He pulled out a thick, split-seamed wallet, stripped a dirty rubber band from it, and peered inside, holding it close to his face so she couldn't see whether it had much money in it. Dealing with whores had taught him to open his billfold that way. He withdrew a ten-dollar bill and, very slowly, gave it to her. "Thanks," she said, folding it and refolding it until it was a tight green pellet in her hand. Then she walked over to the van, talked with one of the young men for a while, touched hands with him, and came back glancing all around. "Come on," she said. "Let's go find a place to sit." And she walked away toward the Snake Pit.

Under the few trees there, the ground was a solid carpet of people, covered with tarps and wet blankets, sitting up, lying down in each other's arms, or standing with blankets draped over them, looking like morose, soaked monks, gazing out over the trash-strewn area. Here and there were walls and pyramids of empty beer cans, some as tall as a man, being built one can at a time by young men who were getting their beer from seemingly bottomless coolers.

Worms and Renee stepped among the dormant bodies until they found a small space near the base of a tree, just enough space for them to cover with Worms's jacket and lie down. Renee took off her jacket, and they covered their heads and upper bodies with it as well as they could. Fortunately there was little rain reaching them here because of the foliage above. The roots of the tree caused a slight elevation of the ground here, so, though the earth was damp, they were at least not in a puddle or on soft mud. Renee opened a plain box and took out a crude cigarette wrapped in tan paper. "D'you know about smokin' joints?"

"Sure," Worms said. He lit it with his Zippo, and they sat with their heads together under her jacket, sipping at the end of it, holding the smoke in, passing it back and forth. It became a strange and cozy world under the jacket. Soon Renee stopped being aware of the sour stink of Worms's dirty clothes and just enjoyed the lightness of her limbs, the silent hum of her nerves, the feeling of slack flesh. "Whooeee," Worms said. "What d'you think?"

"Not the best," she said. "But good." She really didn't know, but he had asked.

They lay down when the cigarette was gone. She rested her head on Worms's arm, and they adjusted her jacket until it covered their upper bodies up to their noses. They lay there looking up the dark tree trunk to the dark-green, almost black, canopy of leaves. Now the sky appeared to be closer than the leaves; to Renee the foliage looked like dark gaps in the gray-pearl canopy of sky. They talked quietly to each other under the jacket.

"Is Lloyd your boss?"

"Hell, no. We're partners. I don't work for nobody. He drives and I keep things runnin'."

"Who's more important, you or him?"

"Well, like I said, we're partners."

"One of you has to be more important."

"Well, I don't think so."

"Who owns the car?"

"Well, he does. But he couldn't run that car very good without me. I'd say if one of us is more important, it's me."

"He couldn't fix his own car?"

"Not and drive it, too."

"Can he fix a car as good as you?"

"I don't know. Maybe almost. But not and race it, too."

"Can you drive as good as him?"

"I can drive fine. I've raced."

"But not as good as him, huh?"

"Knock it off," Worms said. "I can drive as good as anybody."

"But if he can fix a car as good as you, and you can drive a car as good as him, how come he does the drivin' and you do the work?"

"Well, like I said, he owns the car."

"Well, then, he's more important than you."

"No, he ain't!" Worms didn't like this talk. He wanted Renee to recognize his importance, but on the other hand he couldn't say anything to put down Lloyd, who was his true friend and hero. "He jus' does th' drivin' because he's, well, you seen it. He's just a movin' mutha."

"Are you a movin' mutha?"

"Not the same kind. I'm a hell of a driver, but he's a movin' mutha."

"You know what I think?"

"Uh-uh," Worms said.

"Movin' mutha means he's crazy."

"Listen. You don' know Lloyd. He's a good ol' boy."

"Crazy good ol' boy."

"You jus' don' know 'im like I do," Worms said, frowning.

"*You* don't know him like *I* do, either."

"What d'ya mean?"

"Unless he's fucked you."

"Oh."

"What do I know? Maybe he has."

"Hey, knock that off. Lloyd an' I ain't like—like what you're sayin'."

"Well, how do I know?"

"Listen, kid—"

"Whaddaya wanna do? Hit me for saying things? Like he does?"

"Well, jus' watch your mouth, that's all."

"I think he fucks you all the time," she said. She didn't care if Worms got mad enough to hit her. She didn't think she'd feel it if he did. "People can fuck you in different ways, y'know."

"Lloyd don' fuck me no way. He's my friend."

"Friend, huh? Would your friend fuck your girl?"

"What girl?"

"Puggles."

"He ain't—"

Renee broke into a giggle. "You're dumb. You're really dumb. He told you to go get hot dogs and take me with you. 'Don't hurry back,' he said. And 'course you always do what he says, so you leave him there with your girl. And if you don't think he's in her pants right now, you *are* dumb."

"Sheee-it."

"You're dumb. If he's fuckin' your girl, he's fuckin' you."

"Shut up about that now, y'heah? You just pissed off 'cause he put you outa th' car to fuck her."

"See? You admit he is."

"Who th' fuck knows? Who cares? She ain't my girl, anyhow."

"She was your girl all yesterday and last night. And I was his girl."

"Yeah? That's what's got y'bowels in a uproar, ain't it?"

"I couldn't care less. I just feel sorry for you."

"Sorry for me? Ha! Piss on that. I don't need no sympathy. You feel sorry for me? Ha! That do beat all!"

"I do, man. I been fucked all my life by crazy sons of bitches, and I feel sorry for anybody who gets fucked by crazy sons of bitches. Lloyd's a crazy son of a bitch if there ever was one, and you let him fuck you all the time, so I feel sorry for you, that's all. Other'n that, I don't give a shit."

Worms looked at her eyes above the edge of the jacket. Then he sat up and got a cigarette and lit it. He settled back, leaning on his elbow, smoking. "How olda you?"

"Fifteen."

"Fifteen. Fifteen punk-ass years old, and you complainin' crazy sonsa bitches been fuckin' you all y'r life? That's a laugh."

"Yeah. Ha-ha. That's a scream, huh?"

Worms laughed. He stopped and took another draw on his cigarette and then began laughing again. She lay beside him, looking up at the leaves and smiling a nasty smile. "Fifteen years old," he laughed. "How many sonsa bitches was it fucked you in all that time?"

"Every single one of 'em," she said. Then she laughed. But Worms didn't get it. "Listen," she said. "You know when the first crazy son of a bitch did it to me?"

"When?"

"When I was eight."

"Eight?"

"Yeah. You know who that first crazy son of a bitch was?"

"Who?"

"My pa."

Worms looked at her for a moment with his mouth open. "Jee-sus," he said.

She gazed up into the dark leaves. Her flesh felt as if it were sagging off her bones, as if nothing connected her flesh to her bones. "Let me tell you," she said. "It hurt like hell. He was a crazy son of a bitch, though, like Lloyd, and he didn't care if it did hurt me. It did, though. It almost killed me. The other crazy sons of bitches who did it to me since then didn't hurt so much, anyway. Not even Lloyd, and he hurt. D'you know fuckin' doesn't have to hurt? But Lloyd makes it hurt 'cause he's one of those crazy sons of bitches, who likes to hurt. I didn't liked being fucked by Lloyd as much as you like being fucked by Lloyd." This time, Worms didn't protest against what she was saying. Renee looked up at him, at his heavy, dull face, the thick lips, the dimpled, unshaven chin. "You and Puggles sounded pretty good back there."

He grinned smugly, gazing across the racetrack. Trucks

were still speeding through the turn with water misting up behind them. "Yeah, we done okay," he said.

"Puggles is really horny," Renee said. "She'll fuck anybody who looks at her." Renee watched his face, and with satisfaction watched the smug smile fade out. "That's all she ever talked about at the Girls' School. She'd lie there all night talking about cock. This guy's cock, that guy's cock. This guy was great, she'd say. That guy sent me up the wall, she'd say. Did she tell you you were great?"

"Uhm, yeah."

"I knew it. She says that to everybody. That's smart, I guess." Now Worms really looked somber. "Me, I can't say that unless it's true," Rene went on. "It isn't true very much of the time. Do you think you're pretty good?"

"I ain't heard no complaints," Worms said.

"Prob'ly not. Girls hardly ever complain. I mean, what good would it do? Hey, do you think I'd like it with you?" He looked at her, at the strange, cold girl with the thin face and blue eyesockets, this girl who said things that bothered him. "I mean," she said, "do you think maybe that's *one* thing you can do better than Lloyd Skirvin? Or would you have the balls to do it to me without his permission?"

"What is this shit?" he asked in an indignant voice.

"Would you?"

"Well— Hell, yes."

"Then why don't you?"

"Well, by God, maybe I just will!"

"Whoopee. When?"

"Well, I dunno. Maybe, uhm—maybe tonight sometime—"

"Why not now?"

"You kidding? Here with all these—"

"Just what I thought. No balls. Give me a cigarette."

"Wait a cotton-pickin' minute! I'd do it right now if they wasn't all these people—"

"Lloyd would right now, people or not."

"Goddamn you. You the one that's crazy."

"Well," she said. "If you won't, I can find somebody who will." She got up quickly, staggered for a moment with dizziness, then picked up her jacket and turned to make her way out of the mass of people. Worms lumbered to his feet, his face perplexed, and grabbed her arm. She stared at him, scorn in her eyes, a hard little smile on her mouth. They stood there for a moment, staring at each other. Somebody on the ground nearby laughed. Worms looked. There were five or six people, mostly young men, looking up at him and grinning. Worms realized that some of these people must have heard what they were saying. His mind was slow and cloudy, confused by the vast amount of beer he had drunk and then the marijuana and Renee's disturbing talk. But her challenge had aroused him. He was up to the challenge. It wasn't for nothing that he was known as Ol' Everready.

"Hey, buddy," said a strong young male voice nearby, "you better do it or I will!" Laughter went up all around.

Renee looked toward the voice and smiled, her eyes half-closed. "Yeah?" she taunted. "Are you all talk, too?"

There was more laughter all around. Worms's anger flared. He could not stand being laughed at by strangers. While hating Renee for causing people to laugh at him, he was remembering her slim, pale body as it had looked in the headlights last night. It had been Renee he had really wanted, not the common-looking brown-haired Puggles. Goddamnit, he thought. He wanted to throw this crazy girl to the ground and shove it home to her, something she wouldn't forget, something to make her stop thinking she should feel sorry for him, something to show her he was not a second-rate anything—

The young men were standing up all around now, getting ready to watch what they were sure was going to happen. Renee was yielding now, leaning toward him, looking at him with crazy eyes and laughing in a silly kind of way he had never heard before. Once in a Delaware whorehouse Worms had screwed a crazy-in-the-head half-breed girl in front of Lloyd and two other race-car drivers and four mechanics, all laughing and yelling, "Put it to that nigger, Stud Boar!" And shit, it didn't really bother him if somebody watched; when he was ready he could do it hanging from a tree if there wasn't any better way available.

"Come on, you goddamn smart-ass little Yankee cunt," he said, swinging her to the ground.

She was laughing hysterically as he pulled her pants off. The circle of watchers grew as the coupling began. Some laughed as they watched, but most of the faces became very serious. Drunken girls watched and tittered; the young men mostly became still and breathed hard. Renee looked up at some of the faces; as she had expected, the men were watching her face more than they were watching the action below. She had stopped laughing as Worms worked violently upon her.

Near the first-turn fence there was a round-bellied young race fan wearing a shirt imprinted:

RACING IS FUN

He was bored. Two days now he had come out here and scrambled for a place on the first turn. Aside from that crash on yesterday's start lap, he hadn't seen any racing for two days, and he was bored.

Now he heard laughter and whooping over by the trees and saw people ganging up there. He crawled out from under the tarp that he and his wife had strung up like a lean-to. "Be right back," he told her. He went over to the gathering and forced his way in and was rewarded by the sight he had hoped for. There was a young couple doing it right there on the ground.

The man was really pumping away.

The girl was smiling and looking up at people's faces. She was watching the watchers.

Actually, Nick Alef thought as he cut through the infield, who cares if some tycoon does want to come to Indianapolis and buy this glorified bean field from Tony Hulman? What does it matter? Why should I care about being the first man with a story that means nothing? He was rationalizing, of course, because it was beginning to seem he really wouldn't be able to get anything definitive for a story on Dold's attempt to buy the Speedway. Nick had always thought the whole "500" and its festival were blown far out of proportion in Indianapolis, and now he told himself that a story on it was not really so important. Still, he thought, it's as important as people make it. And it would be a real scoop if you knew just how to break it.

That, and his recent impressions of Werner and Kitty Dold, created a jumble in his mind as he made his way, confused and inebriated, through the mud and the crowd. He gazed around as he went. It's a happening, he thought. It's so gross, on such a scale, that even its grossness is tremendous, he thought.

Traffic was still creeping out of the parking field. And there were thousands of people still in the infield and the stands. Rock music and yells wafted through the rain. Everywhere was the blended hushing and humming of automobile engines. The infield was like a city dump with people and cars in it. Scarcely a foot of ground could be seen anywhere that was not covered by muddy paper, glass, metal, or food waste. Broken chairs and smashed coolers had been abandoned all about. And the infield fans were finding what amusements they could in this wallow. Nick looked in on a circle of laughing spectators under a tree and was astonished to see a man and a very young blond girl copulating in the mud under all those eyes: a ridiculous sight, the man's flabby buttocks rising and falling, flexing and relaxing, pasty-white flesh with sparse black hair and small red blemishes; the girl's legs and feet spraddling and wobbling in the air as if she were swimming upside down. On the other side of the circle, also watching, stood the race fan who, years ago on Twenty-fifth Street, had run over Nick's son Timmy. Nick did not see him, and he did not see Nick.

Nick looked for just a minute at the ludicrous coupling. He thought of aiming his camera at it, but instead, just shook his head.

As the man's plunging became more desperate, Nick saw the girl wink up at the spectators.

"Oh, Lloyd," she said. And when she said the name, the man suddenly stopped moving and opened his eyes. He pushed himself up on stiffened arms and stared at the girl beneath him, his face red from exertion.

"Lloyd?" he exclaimed.

Nick wandered away, bemused.

Kitty and I would have been doing that by now if I had handled things a little differently, he thought. Surely we wouldn't have looked that ridiculous at it. Well, maybe we would have. Maybe everybody does. But at least we wouldn't have had a crowd watching.

A few yards farther on, Nick saw a soiled youth with a dirty red bandanna tied on his head, holding a big, clear plastic bag of potato salad. The youth's eyes were glazed; he had a beatific expression on his face and was obviously half-stoned on something or other. He was holding the bag open in front of him and offering its contents to passersby. Despite the fact that the potato salad was streaked with mud, many were accepting his offer, scooping into the mess and eating it out of their muddy palms as if they were starved.

Nick felt water in his shoes now. He was walking through a low area of ground where rainwater had collected and the earth had been churned into a viscous brown stew of mud, torn sod, and litter. Several automobiles sat in this area, some apparently abandoned in hub-deep ruts. Nick heard a roaring car engine and whoops of laughter. Looking to his right, he saw a curious activity going on. A car, mud-brown all over, was slithering about on the muddy ground, its spinning wheels throwing up water and gouts of mud. Two young men, muddy from head to toe, lay on the car roof, whooping drunkenly, trying to maintain a grip on the vehicle as its driver strove to throw them off with his starting, swerving, and braking. As Nick watched, one of the young men slid off the roof and fell sprawling in the mud, mere inches from the wheels. Immediately, one of the other young men ran to the car and scrambled up on it to try his luck. The car roared; the mud-smeared youths laughed, cursed, and whooped, leaped aboard, fell off, and threw empty beer cans at the car.

Nick took photos of this activity for a few minutes, then slogged on, shaking his head. All these bizarre sights seemed to be unfolding before him as if to underscore the awful sense of unreality that had begun to pervade the day—indeed, the whole duration of this arrested spectacle. To his left, a human form rose about ten feet into the air and fell, rose again and fell; it was a girl, screaming each time she was flung up. A gang of young men gripped the sides and corners of a blanket. Each time the girl landed in the blanket, they jerked it taut and lifted it to toss her aloft. As Nick went by, he was startled to note that apparently the girl was clad in mud and nothing else. That sight, not surprisingly, had also attracted a large crowd of spectators. Again, almost like an automaton, Nick raised his camera and photographed the sight. The girl's screams, Nick noticed with curiosity, did not seem to be the screams of exhilaration, as one would have expected them to be; rather, they had a sobbing edge of panic to them. This only added to the ambience of disoriented time and reality that had been bothering Nick since this morning when he had had his strange recollection about the army ants.

It's just crazy time, he thought. Crazy time.

And he remembered then that the phrase—*"crazy time"*—had been one of Kitty's terms, something she had said often during their orgiastic weekend a decade earlier. *Crazy time.*

"There it is," Olive Canfield said.

Mr. Sanders drove his Econoline van with the SANDERS' BAKERY sign very carefully through the mud and stopped it near the back of her car, on as firm a piece of ground as he could find. "Looks like somebody's run into it," he said. "One of these lousy Speedway drunks." Olive smiled weakly.

Actually, her car didn't look too badly damaged. In her mind during the insomniac night, the car had been reduced to a misshapen mass of crumpled metal. She hadn't had the nerve to tell Mr. Sanders about her tantrum, about bashing her car deliberately against the vehicles that were blocking it in. Mr. Sanders was so sensible, despite his temper, and she didn't think he'd condone that kind of destructive outburst.

"Now, you just stay here out of the mud," he said. "Give me the key and I'll see if I can drive it out. If I can't, I'll hook a chain to my truck and we'll pull it out."

"The, uhm—the key's still in it," she said, fingering her broken key ring.

"My God, you shouldn't have done that! It's a wonder the car's still here!"

"It was dumb of me. But I was so upset—"

"Aaaah, that's okay—Olive." He smiled at her and patted her understandingly on the wrist. It was the first time he had ever called her Olive and the first time he had ever touched her. And here he was, going out of his way like this to help her get her car out of this terrible place. And she had always thought he was just simply an ogre. She felt stirred down deep by her new appreciation of him.

Mr. Sanders got down from the driver's seat and bent down, the bald, sunburned crown of his head showing, and studied the rear bumper of her car. It was bent awry; chrome was chipped off, and one of the bumper guards was lying on the ground. He picked it up. He got into the car. Then he got back out and took a piece of paper out from under the windshield wiper and brought it to her. It was waterstained and limp with dampness, and was barely legible: *I think I bumped your car. I'm very sorry. If I had any insurance I'd leave the phone no. But I don't. Sorry.*

Olive felt like laughing, but it would have been hard to explain to Mr. Sanders if she had. It really must have been a drunk, she thought, if he thought *he* hit *me.*

"Don't worry about it," Mr. Sanders said. "I got a cousin who has a body shop. He can fix that up for practically nothing."

He got back in the car and started the motor. It took a little bit of rocking, but Mr. Sanders seemed to know how to handle the gears without spinning the wheels, and in a minute he had rolled the car out of the muck and turned it to face the exit. The grille was missing a few pieces, the front bumper was crooked, and the glass of one headlight was out, but the front didn't look as bad as she had expected, either. Mr. Sanders came back and got in the truck, grinning. "Easy as pie," he said. It was one of his favorite expressions, and suddenly, for the first time, Olive realized it was a funny thing for a baker to say. She smiled.

"Mr. Sanders, you're a real cupcake," she said. She hoped he would laugh at that, and he did.

Then he looked at her car again. "This is nutty," he said. "How could a car hit you in the front and back, both?"

"Oh, uhm—" She searched her mind quickly. "That didn't happen here. I, uhm, ran over a grocery cart the other day in a parking lot." She didn't know why there wasn't also a note from the driver of the car that had been parked in front. Maybe he had just driven off without even looking at the back of his car. Whatever the reason, Olive was happy. Her car had been rescued from the Speedway by this fine man, and she still had her job, and apparently she wasn't going to be arrested for wrecking two cars. She was beaming. "How can I ever thank you?"

"Well. Well, if you're hungry, you might come over to my house and help me eat a roast I put in this morning. It's too big for me alone."

Olive got in her car and followed the bakery van into the line of traffic that was still trickling out of the Speedway. She wasn't afraid of any old Speedway traffic jam anymore, not with Mr. Sanders up there with his van to lead her out. Whenever they stopped in the traffic, he would wave out the window at her. She could see his face in the van's outside mirror. She would smile and return the wave. There was a little sign pasted on the back of the van that she thought was very funny. It said:

HIT ME EASY.
I'M FULL OF PIE.

They came back to the car together, but not really together. Worms walked slightly ahead, keeping Renee in the corner of his eye but never really looking at her, and she ambled very slowly, humming a monotonous rock music theme, that was hardly a tune at all, not meant to be sung, and it irritated Worms, as she had meant it to. She looked to the left and right as they went along, and when he did look at her he would find her glancing off into the distance or, if toward him, in a vacant sort of way that made him feel he did not exist.

He was sure she had done that on purpose—calling Lloyd's name instead of his while he was screwing her. But Worms was not quite bright enough to understand what she was doing. All he knew was that she had tried to make him feel that Lloyd was not really his friend, and then she had made him feel like a fool himself.

It had all been so much nicer with Puggles. Puggles was just simply a good piece of ass who was happy to get fucked and laugh at your jokes and then not bother your head. Puggles had made him feel like a man.

This Renee was something else. She was smart; first she made him crazy hot for her, then she made him feel he was weak or dumb somehow. When she had cried Lloyd's name, it had made Worms lose his power, it had made him lose his hard-on, and he had become aware of the people watching and suddenly hadn't been able to finish.

And now she was walking along and humming and making him feel he wasn't really there. And he just didn't have any idea what she would do next; that was what was bothering him now. Maybe she was planning to tell Lloyd that Worms had fucked her. She had been right about one thing: Worms was a little bit afraid Lloyd wouldn't like it that he had done it to his girl.

Jesus, Worms thought. What if Lloyd didn't really even try to make it with Puggles, and what if we go back now and Renee tells him what I done to her? I didn't really think Lloyd was going to try to make it with Puggles; it was this Renee kid who made me think he might.

Shit, he thought. He just couldn't get all this sorted out. He didn't like girls who screwed up his thinking this way. Lloyd had been his best friend for a long time, and this goddamn smart-ass Yankee cunt didn't have any right to come along like this and mess up everything.

There was the Mercury ahead in the muddy field. Worms had a mind to tell Lloyd they ought to get rid of these two crazy Yankee jailbait cunts and get everything back to the way it used to be. *Shit,* he thought again. *Shit.* He turned and glowered at Renee. "Come on," he snarled at her. "Stop draggin' your ass." She just gave him a sick little smile and kept humming the song.

There wasn't anybody in the Mercury. Worms opened

the door and looked in. Another six-pack of the beer was gone, and Puggles's clothes were in the back seat. That really confused Worms, who was already about as confused as he had ever been. Those clothes would have to mean that Puggles was somewhere around this Speedway naked. Great fuckin' blue groundhogs, Worms thought. This is the craziest bunch of—this is the goddamnedest thing I ever seen. You jus' don' know what the fuck'll be next.

"I know where they are," Renee said after scornfully watching his bewildered face for a while.

"Yeah, I guess you would, you're so goddamn smart. How do you know where they are?"

"I see 'em." She pointed. All he saw was a bunch of young guys nearby, tossing a girl up in a blanket. Then he looked closer. The girl looked like Puggles. She was screaming, and it did sound like Puggles. And there was Lloyd standing alongside the bunch, watching, looking drunk as a hoot owl with that hard, mean half-smile of his.

"Goddamn," Worms yelped in sudden glee, slapping his knee. "If that Lloyd don't beat all! Look what he's thunk up now!" By God, things ain't no different at all, he thought, and he headed toward the group. "Boy, they's no two ways about it," he exclaimed, "that Lloyd's a good ol' boy!"

After the gang of young men stopped throwing Puggles in the blanket, it looked for a while as if they had their minds set on a gang bang. They gathered around the naked, mud-smeared girl and started grabbing at her, feeling her breasts and buttocks, whooping and laughing and passing her from one to another. Puggles was out of her head. She was moaning and gasping and staggering, either extremely drunk or completely dizzied by the tossing, and hysterical. Probably she would have succumbed to a gang assault at that moment without really knowing what was going on, but Lloyd stepped into the group, put his strong, hard left hand on the back of her neck, and started dragging her out of the circle. Two of the young men snatched at her arms to try to keep her there, but Lloyd grabbed and twisted their thumbs with such force that they dropped back, looking astonished and shaking their arms in pain. "Git back, goddamnit," Lloyd said to the group in a flat, menacing voice, emphasized by a wolf's grin. "I jus' loant 'er t' you boys t' play with, not t' keep. Git yer cotton pickin' paws off there, heah?" In spite of their high-spirited drunkenness, the young men took heed, sensing perhaps that he was dangerous. To support Lloyd's withdrawal, Worms shouldered his way among the young men and took Puggles's arm and helped Lloyd drag her away. "Where th' fuck you been, man?" Lloyd demanded.

"They jus' wasn't no food noplace," Worms said. "I looked all t' hell an' gone." Renee was walking along with them now as they hauled Puggles toward the car, looking curiously at her friend's agonized face, her slack mouth, her mud-darkened body. Puggles was not really walking; she was semiconsciously placing one wobbly knee in front of the other and sagging between Lloyd and Worms. Some of the young men sauntered behind, still looking lustingly at her full, young nakedness.

When they got to the car, Lloyd hauled the uncomprehending Puggles into the back, laying her down on the seat, where she rolled her head back and forth and made little crying sounds in her throat. Tears were running down the side of her face, making white trails in the dirt. Then she drew her legs up and curled into a fetal position and lay there moaning. "Git back there and git them clothes on 'er," Lloyd told Renee. Then he waved Worms into the front passenger seat, started the car, and roared out of the muddy field with the tires flinging defiant mud at the young men.

Near the Tower, Nick Alef saw someone he had hoped he might see. It was Al Bloemker, the Speedway's director of publicity. White-haired, with the mild, shrewd face of some well-fed Anglican cleric, Bloemker stood listening to a foursome of men in checkered blazers, his hands thrust deep in his pockets, chin tucked down. Nick stayed nearby, not close enough to intrude but ready to claim Bloemker's attention if he left the group. He did, shortly, and Nick fell in step with him. Squinting at the dark sky, he said, "I was just wondering whether you Speedway folk are about to throw in the towel."

"Towel?" Bloemker said, peering at Nick from under his hat brim with a trace of a smile.

"I mean, such a mess you guys have had out here this month— What if somebody were to come up to Tony right now and offer him a big fat price to take this place off his hands?"

Still with that slight smile, Bloemker said, "How much you offering?"

Nick threw his head back and laughed. Then he said, "Seriously, though, Tony's what? Seventy-two now? Does he ever think of getting out of it?" Nick tried to sound as if he were only speculating idly.

Bloemker answered just as casually, not even turning his head to look at Nick. "Nah. He's having too much fun."

Gerald Rumple sat staring in amazement at Ella. He couldn't believe what she had said.

"Surely," he said, "That's some kind of a bad joke."

"No," she replied. She was standing before him, her face set firmly and defiantly, but her glittering and wavering eyes showed him that she was not altogether unashamed of her pronouncement.

"You," he said very slowly, "would stay here and go to that race tomorrow instead of going to Chicago for your friends' *funeral?*"

She blinked rapidly but kept her chin resolute.

Gerald crossed his thick arms over his chest and leaned back in his chair to scowl at her, his mouth hanging open. "Do you—do you—I mean—we're Allan and Janet's *godparents,* Ella! Good God Almighty, do you mean to tell me that that—that race out there is more important to you than seeing those poor kids through tomorrow— through, I swear, the worst day of their *lives?*"

Ella swallowed. She knew how bad it looked. But she couldn't admit even that much, because if she started trying to explain all this to Gerald, who seemed to have lost his understanding of it, she would surely go to pieces. So she stood firm. "Ivy'll pick me up tomorrow morning and take me to the Speedway, so you won't have to worry about how I'll—"

"Worry?" He slammed his palm on the top of his desk. "Oh, never mind *that!* As of now, I couldn't care less what you do or how you do it! Ella, I thought I knew you—I thought we were as close as any two people could be. But, oh, man!" He shook his round head from side to side. "I swear you're some kind of a stranger to me. Ella, you—and—I—are—in—trouble."

She stared at him, aware that the gap opening between them was indeed deeper and more dangerous than anything they had ever experienced in all their years together. If Gerald, of all people, couldn't comprehend how important it was to see this race through— "I—I'll drive up just as soon as the race is over—I'll bring the Olds, and I'll be there early in the evening to see the kids—"

Gerald spun his chair around to his desk and with abrupt movements began putting things away.

"Lady," he said without looking at her, "as far as I'm concerned, you needn't bother. I wouldn't want you to put yourself out!"

Diana Scheckley had never been so scared. She felt like a criminal—and worse, like a criminal who is sure to be caught. She pulled off the hooded poncho Nick had found to disguise her. She and Nick and the ugly little mechanic had entered the garage practically like burglars. It was a miracle no one had seen them. There were other people still working in nearby garages, and occasionally their voices and movements could be heard. The mechanic was staying by the door, which he had locked, and Nick was being as quiet as he could while hurrying to set up his tripod camera before the little daylight filtering in could fade. The daylight itself worried her. There was daylight coming in, which meant that people could see in if they happened to look. She could hear people outside the building. If they did look in, they would see what was going on and probably would start a big gathering or even get the officials to come in, and then there would really be trouble. She didn't know what the garage rules were, but she had heard that women were traditionally barred from the garage area entirely. If women weren't supposed to be here, she knew for certain that a naked woman would really be against the rules. Her heart was pounding, and Nick, the only person who could conceivably reassure her, seemed so nervous and short-tempered right now that his demeanor only added to her own apprehension.

The only pleasant surprise was that the garage was a clean place instead of dark and cluttered and dirty. It was, in fact, almost spotless, and so orderly it seemed more like the gynecologist's office where she had gone with her pregnancy alarm than like a place where they worked on cars. The race car itself sat gleaming in the middle of the room like some enormous piece of medical equipment.

Now Nick was leaning toward her and moving a light meter up and down near her body, first from this angle, then from that. He looked thoughtful for a moment, then looked at her and grinned. "You're biting your finger-nails, honey," he said. She hadn't noticed she was doing it. It was a habit she had only recently overcome. "Take it easy," he said. He squeezed her forearm. "Everything's going to be all right." He turned away and went back to the camera on the tripod and made some settings. "God, I wish the sun were shining out there," he said. "I could sure use more light."

Diana jumped at the remark. "Maybe there just isn't enough light, huh? Maybe we shouldn't try it?"

"Relax, Diana. We're this far. And this'll be our only opportunity. I'll make it work."

"Shhh!"

They looked to the mechanic, who was keeping the vigil at the door. Diana felt prickles of fear descend the length of her body.

"What?" Nick whispered.

"Nothing, just don't talk so much," the mechanic said. "And hurry up, for Christ's sake."

Nick came close to her. His face was shining with sweat, and his hair was damp and wild-looking, and he did not seem nearly as self-possessed as he always had. She had usually seen him smiling, and now with this intense, worried expression, he didn't look warm or attractive at all. It's just that I'm scared and upset, she thought.

"Okay, now, honey," he said barely above a whisper. "I want you to start getting undressed. But I'll stop you now and then for partially dressed poses. This is the kind of session we should have a whole day for, or more, but we'll have to do what we can in a few minutes. Now, after we get the totally nude shots, I've got a few special kinds of underthings here for you."

Her heart was racing now. "Tell him to turn around," she said, glancing toward the mechanic.

"Don't worry about him. He's not looking. See?"

"But I know he will when I take my clothes off."

"I said don't worry about him. Okay, now, look. We don't have a bed, so we can't do much of that usual spread-eagle stuff, but I think that'll be good, really, because lying down in a garage wouldn't make that much sense, anyway, would it? Now, just one thing I want you to remember: be as natural and open as you would be in your own bedroom at home. I mean, don't try to hide pubic hair by posing a leg over it or holding a piece of clothing over it. They want that in these pictures, you see?"

"Oh, Jeez—"

"It's okay. Now start undressing, and just act natural. Act like you're real interested in the race car. Act like you're undressing for it—"

"That doesn't seem very natural—"

"Shhhh!" said the mechanic, and they froze again. "Nothing," he hissed. "Just keep it down!"

She began undressing, and Nick began moving around. "I'll have to touch you to help you," he whispered. "Is that okay?"

"If you have to, you have to, huh?"

Just as she had expected, the mechanic was watching. Oh, well, she thought. So what?

"That's great," Nick said. "Okay, I want the bra off and the blouse clear open, okay? And lean over and look into the cockpit— Don't look at me— Don't look at the camera— Good! Get out of those panty hose. Are your panties bikinis? Good! Pull the skirt up around your waist— No, that looks too bunchy. Better take it off— Good. Oh, damn. You've got panty-hose marks on your waist. Hope your skin fades fast. God, your breasts are perfect! Beautiful! Put your left arm close to your side there and squeeze that breast up there a little— Good. Wet your nipples with spit. They like them erect. Hey, great! Let me get a few close-ups— Oh, terrific! That gooseflesh is terrific. Got it in the crosslight for texture. Oh, God, Diana, you look better than I'd dreamed! Okay, now, let me get back here— Now stand on your tiptoes and bend forward like you're looking at the engine. No, straighten your back and bend from the hips. Good! No, wait. Once more, with your mouth open and looking very intent— Oh, great! Terrific profile— Now try the same thing with the panties off—"

She was totally naked now, and Nick and the mechanic were both looking very intently at her pubis. The mechanic had deserted his vigil and was standing so close that Nick had to shoulder him aside. Their eyes on her made her feel a thousand times more naked than naked, and she realized that it was very pleasant, better even than skinny-dipping or sunbathing nude under the open sky. Her nipples were puckered, and her skin felt as if it were being licked and fondled by the cool air.

"Now sit back against the car—"

"Careful," the mechanic said in a thick voice. Diana felt the cold, smooth skin of the vehicle on her buttocks and the backs of her thighs and shivered with excitement.

"Great!" Nick breathed. "Now open your legs. Farther, come on—farther. Come on, they love this— Oh, fantastic. Now turn your head to the right— That's it— your chin clear on your right shoulder— Fantastic! Open your mouth, shut your eyes— Act like the car's caressing you. Great! Oh, Jesus God, fantastic!"

She could hear him breathing close now, and glanced down, and he was holding a camera by hand, kneeling almost between her knees and aiming up along her body. She arched her back and imagined how it would feel to have his stiffened flesh entering her just now; she writhed and a little moan escaped her lips. She heard the camera flick and the rewinder whirr time after time now. "Touch your nipple," he said. "Good! Now touch yourself down there— No, just with one finger, like you were trying to arouse yourself down there— Could you? Come on, just rub a little—"

She glanced under her eyelids, looking up into the filtered pale light of the room. Nick was still kneeling close in front of her, clicking the shutter. The mechanic was standing slightly behind and beside him, with a hand in his coveralls pocket, and it looked as if he were playing with himself; his mouth hung open, and his eyes were glassy, staring at her openness. And the room was not a cold place like a clinic now, it was a place full of a strange electrical excitement and warmth; she felt the tickling of her own juices within her now, and she stroked the silky hair. She shut her eyes again, and there were moving clouds of color behind her eyelids and her face felt hot. Waves of desire were rolling through her as she moved her hips. She didn't care about anything now; she reached in and her middle finger touched the place inside.

"Good! Go on, go on," Nick was coaxing, and his voice thrilled her and she pressed and rubbed a few more strokes and then the feeling was coming and she couldn't have stopped it if she had wanted to and she could hear herself gasping. But as the flashes of pleasure subsided, she felt and heard movements around her and heard Nick's voice saying something angrily, and something hard hit her foot. She suddenly came back to her senses sagging with weakness, and opened her eyes and saw Nick struggling with the mechanic. "—crummy little son of a bitch, don't you touch her!" Nick shoved the little man toward the door, where he stood, panting, glowering.

Oh, my God, she thought, suddenly crushed with shame, feeling utterly filthy, grossly ugly. Oh, my God, my God, what did I do? I didn't know I was like that.

Nick's head was swimming; his heart was thudding rapidly. He couldn't believe it had happened quite this way. She actually brought herself off, I think, while the camera was on her. Jesus Christ, what have I done here?

I was right about her, though, he thought. What an exhibitionist! Nick was disturbed by the fact that he had had her do this while the mechanic was watching; it was a sordid aspect that robbed the moment of its strange,

erotic beauty, and Nick gladly would have thrown the
mechanic out through the window when he made that
lunge at her.

But I do have her on film, he thought. I didn't think it
was really going to be possible, but it was.

"Please, I want to get dressed now, Nick. Please." Her
face was white; she looked sick. No wonder, he thought.
Almost sick myself.

"Sure, hon. That's it. We're finished, and you were
great—" Her eyes glistened and she put her fingers over
her mouth when he said that. God, what's the right thing
to say, he wondered. "Diana, I'm so proud of you, you're
a real pro, a real model. Honey, what an *actress!"*

She blinked, pulling on her panty hose, and then even
managed a wan smile. That, apparently, had been the
right thing to say.

"Come on, hurry up," the mechanic hissed. He was
now looking more surly than ever.

Crazy time, Nick thought. I can't believe this. *Crazy
time!*

It was almost dark when Puggles finally got herself
together and was able to sit up. She had her legs drawn
up in front of her and her chin resting on the heel of her
hand, and she was staring with unblinking hatred at the
back of Lloyd's head as he drove, apparently nowhere in
particular, from time to time swigging on a can of beer
laced with whiskey. Lloyd wasn't talking.

Renee wasn't talking yet, although she had a lot of
things ready to say when the right time came. Worms
wasn't saying much, either, because he was afraid Renee
was going to tell Lloyd about what they had done in the
Snake Pit. Worms was as baffled as he was scared, because even though he felt that what they had done would
make Lloyd mad at him, Renee had been the one who
had made it h ppen. But Lloyd might not believe that.
And he probably wouldn't like it even if he did believe
it.

Lloyd was driving through the Westside of Indianapolis; occasionally Renee would see a theater or drugstore
she recognized. He wasn't doing the same kind of crazy

hell-driving he had done the night before in the country, but he was getting drunker and drunker and driving erratically and aggressively in the evening traffic and exceeding all the speed limits. He went through several red lights, and the ones he did stop for, he would race away from with tires squealing. At one point he cut into the right lane too sharply and forced a station wagon off the road; it slithered to a halt on the muddy berm behind them, its horn blaring. Lloyd didn't even bother to give his customary finger sign or yell his customary obscenity; he seemed intent only on getting drunk and working something out in his mind. Worms had never seen him like this, not quite like this, and he was a little alarmed. He thought it was bad judgment, that it might get them stopped by the police with the girls and the booze and the marijuana in the car. And besides that, it wasn't even any fun. But he didn't want to criticize Lloyd, or even make any suggestions, while Lloyd was in the kind of mood he seemed to be in.

Puggles leaned close to Renee and spoke into her ear. "Listen," she said. "I want out of here. Will you come with me?"

"What's up?"

"He's crazy, Renee. He raped me—it hurt like anything—and there were guys watching us through the window. And when he got done, he drug me out of the car with my clothes off and got those guys chasing me around in the mud. He said it was like a greased-pig contest, and laughed all the time. Then they started throwing me in a blanket, and I got so scared and sick I just went out of my skull. Renee, I'd kill him if I could. But I just wanna get away. Oh, goddamn, I'm gonna cry if I keep thinking about it. I wanna get out if we ever stop. I wanna call my mom."

"What's all the secrets back there, babies?" Lloyd called over his shoulder.

"Up your ass," Renee snapped.

"Worms, smack that little shit in th' mouth."

Worms started to turn around in the front seat, raising his hand.

Renee glared at him. "You don't have the balls to hit me, you fat fink."

He knew what she meant, and held his hand in the air, uncertain.

"Jesus-fucking-Christ," Lloyd exclaimed, "you gonna let a little kindygarden cunt talk t' you like that? Hit 'er up side th' goddamn head."

"Come on, you fat fink. I dare you."

"Aw, hell," Worms said weakly, lowering his arm. "Ain't worth th' energy."

"Shit, it ain't!" Lloyd exclaimed. "Want me t' do it fer ya?" He raised his right arm and lashed into the back, but Renee ducked out of the way.

"Big tough dudes," Renee said bitterly. "Big buddies. Betcha bugger each other."

"Shut yer goddamn mouth or you've had it, I swear t' God," Lloyd snarled.

"You know what your big fat fink buddy did?" Renee cried. "Tell Lloyd what we did under that tree, fat fink!"

"By God, I'll beat your ass blue!" Worms yelled, turning, rising on his knees, and lunging back for her with both arms. His right hand raked her right eye as she ducked, one dirty fingernail going under the eyelid and scratching the eyeball.

"Ow, damn you!" she screamed, cringing back in the seat and slapping one palm over the painful eye. "You fat fink son of a bitch, you screwed me under that tree, didn't you? Tell him! Tell your buddy we smoked pot and fucked under a tree. You fucked your buddy's girl, didn't you, you fat fink son of a bitch!"

Lloyd suddenly brought the car to a skidding, grinding halt at the side of the road. Worms, who was trying to get his hands on the kicking, slapping Renee, was thrown off balance by the sudden stop, and his back hit the dashboard and the back of his head hit the ceiling. Lloyd lashed out with a backhand blow then that caught Worms hard on the nose. "What's this shit?" he snarled.

Worms was stunned, hurt; suddenly his whole world was flying apart too fast for him to understand it. "No, Lloyd! She made me do it— She—" And then he realized how dumb that sounded and started blubbering, and he opened the car door and scrambled out and started to run into the darkness where he could hide from all the craziness and from Lloyd's anger and Lloyd's hard hands.

Lloyd thrust his door open and started after him, yelling, "Hey, wait—wait a goddamn minute—"

And as they vanished out of the headlamps' white light, Renee and Puggles squirmed out of the car. They hesitated. "Pug! Can you drive?"

"No!"

"Oh, hell! I can't, either!"

"Run, then!"

And they sprinted off into the darkness in the other direction, Renee holding her hand over one eye and with the other trying to see where they were going.

They ran until they were out of breath, not looking back. They turned down dark alleys and went along the sides of long, dark factory buildings and crossed railroad tracks. They didn't know where they were.

After a while they saw a Dairy Queen drive-in. "I wanta call my mom," Puggles panted. "Just let me call Mom."

They went in. There were five or six people in the place. No one paid any attention to them, dirty and wild-eyed as they were. Puggles put a dime in the pay phone and dialed her mother's number. The line was busy. She tried again in a minute; it was still busy. Another minute passed, and she tried once more; it was still busy.

She didn't want to call her mother anymore. Instead, with the change from Worms's ten-dollar bill, Renee bought them each a large charcoal burger and an order of fries and a chocolate shake. They ate the sandwiches and fries and drank the shakes. Then they each got a banana split and went outside and sat down in the dark next to a fence behind a bush and ate their banana splits and had marijuana cigarettes for dessert.

Becky Alef was trying to keep herself busy with housework. But there were clocks in every room, and she kept looking at the clocks. Davey was in the family room watching television.

If Nick doesn't get here in about five more minutes, Becky thought, it's going to be too late to go to the movie. Damnit, there wasn't anything happening at the racetrack today. It can't be his work that's keeping him. I know what's keeping him. I'm afraid I know what's keeping him.

Don't think about that, she told herself. Just leave it alone.

She peered into the family room. Davey was sitting slouched far down on the sofa, his hands in his pockets.

He knows his dad's going to fail him again, she thought. He's learned he can count on that.

Nick, you son of a bitch, she thought, this boy would be better off without you. He and I would both be better off without you. What's the point of having a husband and father who does nothing but break your heart and break promises?

If I get that job at the agency, she thought, I can take care of Davey myself.

She stopped in the middle of the kitchen, under the lamp, and laced her fingers tightly across her waist. She shut her eyes and braced herself. She thought of the dismal travesty their marriage had been for the last few years, and she made a decision.

If he doesn't come home tonight, she thought, I call a lawyer.

Gerald Rumple pulled off the interstate highway at Lafayette, had the car's tank filled at a Shell station, and went into a Howard Johnson's next door where he had two scoops of maple walnut ice cream and a cookie and a cup of coffee. Then he got into the car, drove up the ramp to get back on the interstate toward Chicago, and headed north into the night. He drove down a long grade into the Wabash Valley, across the bridge, and then up a long grade out of it, and the lights of the Lafayette interchanges were finally behind him. About two hundred miles to go, he thought. He was lonely. He had never made the trip to Chicago without Ella sitting beside him in the front seat, warm and soft in the dark.

The car whispered along. There was very little traffic. The road was level and wide. Now and then he would think of Ella standing there before him in the office refusing to leave the race to go to Chicago with him. He would shake his head and draw hissing breaths between his clenched teeth.

That race, he thought. He detested it now, and tried to

remember whether he had ever really liked it, or whether it had been just a part of his togetherness with Ella. He didn't think he had ever really liked it. Oh, sure, like everyone, he'd get gooseflesh at the start, and it could be interesting if you concentrated on details. But as Ruthie Roepke had said once, "After the start, you might as well just wander off and have a drink."

Cars and speed, he thought. Cars and speed. He remembered the man's remark about the Roman circus. It's the danger, he thought. Just to watch the danger.

Danger.

Gerald pressed his foot a little harder on the accelerator, and the speedometer needle rose to 75 under its glowing glass on the dashboard. They're heroes because they drive fast, he thought. A.J. makes a fortune just by driving fast.

The road unreeled in the headlights of the car and flowed back under, the dashed divider lines coming constantly into the headlights' beam toward him like a visible, monotonous Morse code. Gerald pushed the gas pedal down harder, and the air rushing past the windows began to whine and whistle ominously. His heart sped up a little as he saw the needle climb past 90. He had never driven faster than 80 before. He held the steering wheel with both hands now and breathed faster. Somewhere in his mind a warning was whispering about state police and about blowouts. But the road was so open and so wide and there were no headlights or taillights in sight now, and Gerald felt a rare kind of excitement, enhanced a little perhaps by the knowledge that he was breaking the speed laws. He never would have done this with Ella in the car, of course.

It would be a kind of a private, secret delight to know you'd gotten that little needle above 100, he thought, even just for a few seconds. . . .

The pedal still wasn't quite to the floor, and now Gerald forced it the rest of the way down. His heart was pounding very fast now, and his mouth was dry. The lines in the road were coming so fast now they were almost blurred to a solid line, and the roadside reflectors were flashing by through the right corner of his eye like tracer bullets. The motor thrummed with a frantic power, and the car felt as if it were scarcely touching the road. Daring to take only the quickest glance at the dashboard, Gerald saw that the speedometer needle was now between 100 and 105. His body, usually a great, slack, uncomfortable weight, now felt light, strong and taut as a drawn bow, a living, thinking connection between the squashed accelerator and the vibrating steering wheel. The wind wailed around the car, and Gerald grinned and forced himself to keep all his weight on that right foot. He wondered whether the speedometer actually could be made to reach the 120 of its highest register, but the pedal was absolutely solid on the floor now, and 108 seemed to be as far as that shining needle was going to climb.

When he raised his glance from the speedometer, he saw red taillights gleaming far ahead, at what would ordinarily have seemed like a very safe distance. But they were closing so astonishingly fast on him, it seemed they must be coming backward. Gerald's heart leaped into his throat, and he had an instantaneous fear that to brake or even to veer into the other lane would throw the car out of control. Seeming to rise off the car seat with tension, watching the red taillights looming before him with a deadly swiftness, Gerald took his foot off the gas pedal and touched the brake; he made himself inch the wheel to the left, and shot past the slower car as if it were backing up; he held onto the wheel in panic as his car began to wobble and fishtail.

Then he recovered it. His hands were slick on the wheel, and he had to force himself to swallow as he drove placidly along now at 75 miles an hour, seemingly at a crawl. His heartbeat was almost painful, and he couldn't seem to get enough breath into his heaving chest.

But after a while he was physically back to normal, though exhausted. The road disappeared backward under the car at a safe, exasperating crawl, and he thought of the long, long miles ahead.

But wow. A hundred and eight miles an hour. Twenty-eight miles an hour faster than I've ever driven before. A hundred and eight miles an hour!

Imagine, he thought. They go twice that fast for three hours at that race. With turns and lots of other cars.

Never knowing what's around the next turn—oil on the track, or a car spinning, or. . . .

It seemed so deadly boring to be creeping along this highway at a safe 75 miles an hour now.

Golly, Gerald thought. I can understand a race driver, I think.

But I sure can't understand a race spectator.

Davey had moped off to bed at ten, and now Becky was in her bed, alone, with the light off. The house was still.

Nicky had not even called, and Becky lay in the darkness, deciding things she was going to do tomorrow. Becky had heard on the news that the race had been postponed for still another day. Tomorrow she was going to go to the Speedway and see if she could see Nicky with that Festival Princess. Just to see it with her own eyes would be enough to remove the last trace of doubt from her mind, and then she would feel justified in calling a lawyer and filing for divorce.

I should have done it years ago, she thought, and I could have spared myself all this miserable crap.

She just hadn't realized how easy a thing looks once you've actually made the decision to do it. Making the decision is the hard thing, she thought. Once you've done that, you aren't afraid anymore, and you know you can go ahead and manage to do whatever it is you have to do.

She wasn't sure she would be able to find and watch Nicky in the Speedway crowd, but she thought it would be possible. She knew what his basic pattern was when he worked the race, having gone with him as his assistant a few years. He usually tried to be somewhere between the starting line and first turn for the start; then he would gravitate toward the north end of the pits and the fourth turn as the race settled down. That way he could be close if anything happened in that tricky fourth turn, as it so often did; he could also keep an eye on the cars that went into the pits and have a pretty good idea when he saw them go in whether they had serious troubles or not.

No, Nicky wouldn't be too hard to watch. She would

take her binoculars and stay near the head of the straight-away and just watch him like a hawk.

He likes to know women are looking at him from the crowd, the conceited son of a bitch, she thought. Well, here's one woman who'll be watching him tomorrow. Then we'll see how much he can deny when I tell him in detail what I watched him do. Then I'll say, "Nicky, you goddamned rutting Casanova, from now on you can talk to my lawyer." Maybe I'll take a camera, too, she thought.

She made those plans with grim satisfaction. But she cried for a long time before finally going to sleep. She cried because of their son and because of the dreams they had had back in the old days, dreams about being a family like that Quaker family in their favorite movie.

Worms stopped running. He was on a weedy slope; the river was a few feet below, dark, foul-smelling, reflecting distant streetlights. He sat down on the riverbank, wheezing like a winded horse. On the other side of the river, about a mile away, he could see the tall buildings of downtown Indianapolis. The ground was wet and cold under his seat.

He lit a cigarette with his Zippo. It was harsh in his throat and lungs after all the running and panting.

Worms wondered now why he had run from Lloyd. Surely Lloyd wouldn't have beat him up over a nasty little piece of jailbait like that Renee. They had been good friends for too long. They had tried each other's girls out before. With Lloyd's permission, of course. But this time Lloyd hadn't given permission, of course. Worms remembered what Renee had said: *Would you have the balls to to do it to me without his permission?* Well, he had, and there had been hell to pay. And she had also said, *Lloyd's a crazy son of a bitch if there ever was one, and you let him fuck you all the time.*

Worms had been thinking about that all evening. He kept telling himself, No, Lloyd's my friend. He's a hard case, but he's my friend, and we been through a lot to-gether. Lloyd and I done more fun things than I ever done before we got to be friends. And hell, Lloyd don't really care enough about no girl t' dump on a friend because of one. Lloyd always said far as women was concerned, he was a 4F. Find 'em, feel 'em, fuck 'em, and fergit 'em. Now this Renee. Lloyd wasn't all that shot on her. He wouldn'a really cared 'bout me bangin' her.

If I'd of asked.

Well, she sure's hell screwed us up. Smart little Yankee cunt. Goddamn! She never even give me back the change from my ten bucks! Jee-sus! Man, I been took good.

Tell y' one thing. If I ever see Lloyd again, I'll see whether he's fuckin' me or not. Maybe I just thought too high of 'im to notice. Sure, he likes a joke on me. An' he always takes first dibs on ever'thing. But shit, he's th' driver. He's the one that wins th' prize money!

Still an' all, he couldn't do it without me. I'm as important as he is, like I told her. If I ever see him again, we goin' be equal. He ain't all that much better'n me, drivin'. Jus' a little crazier. Way he was drivin' around town tonight, Jee-sus, that was dumb. I woulda knowed better.

Down the river a way, he heard a voice shouting. He listened. He heard it again. Yep. It was Lloyd's voice. And it was calling for him.

Let 'im yell, Worms thought.

Then he heard the car horn. Long, insistent honks. Then the voice again, closer this time, yelling, "Hey! Hey, Billy Joe!"

Oh, it's Billy Joe now. He mus' really want me bad. Been Worms ever since that time he pissed in my fishin' bait. It's Billy Joe or Stud Boar when he wants t' git me t' do somethin'. Yeah, by God, like she said, people can fuck you more ways than one. An' maybe by God he *has* been a-doin' it to me right along.

The car horn was louder now, and Worms could hear the Merc's engine. He'd recognize it anywhere or anytime. Maybe it was Lloyd's car, but that engine was his. He'd sweated in that son of a bitch more hours than he could count, tuning it, fixing it when it broke, modifying it. By God, that motor got a friend, he thought. I been good to it as I been to Lloyd. Guess ol' Lloyd knows he's up Shit Crick without a paddle without me. Listen to im up there.

"Billy Joe, where you at?"

Worms didn't answer. He just flipped his cigarette butt toward the river. It made an orange line through the night and broke apart in sparks down on the bank. Then Worms heard a car door shut just up the bank from where he sat. "Billy Joe," Lloyd's voice called. "Come up here. I ain't gonna hit ya."

He musta saw my cigarette, Worms thought. "You come down here if you wanna see me," he said. Goddamn! He'd never dared talk like that to Lloyd.

"Come on up here or I'll leave your ass t' rot," Lloyd's voice said.

"Then go th' fuck on!"

There was silence for a minute, and Worms expected to hear the Merc start up and roar away. His heart began to pound in anticipation of that sound. He'd heard that ol' Merc engine of his fade down the straightaway at a hundred county racetracks, but it always came back. God, it would be sad to hear it fade away for good!

And then Worms heard footsteps in the weeds behind him. Lloyd had come down. He had made Lloyd come down! Worms didn't know whether to expect a kick in the kidneys or what, and his scalp crawled in anticipation, but at least Lloyd hadn't driven the Merc away. He had come down!

There was a metallic clink and a faint circle of warm light. Lloyd squatted down beside Worms, lighting a cigarette. He shut his lighter and hunkered there, gazing over the river, the coal of his cigarette glowing.

"Them girls run," he said.

"Good. Glad t' be shed of 'em."

"Me, too." Lloyd's cigarette glowed. Worms got one out and reached into his pocket for his Zippo, but Lloyd's lighter flashed first and Worms put the end of his cigarette in it and drew. Lloyd had never held a light for him before. "Yep," Lloyd said. "Them two was gittin' under my skin. Hey, how 'bout we go git drunk ag'in an' celebrate?"

"Now, that don' sound too bad," Worms said.

Nick Alef drove Diana's Camaro downtown. She sat in the passenger seat, her head back against the headrest, wrapped in introspections he did not want to disturb. Her state of mind seemed so delicate right now, he was afraid that she might change her mind and not let him use the photographs they had taken in the garage. The only thing she said was, "I'm tired. I've never been so tired."

"We'll get you some good rest," he said.

He drove the car into the garage of the Hilton Hotel, up the spiraling ramps, until he found an empty parking space. "Do you want to stay here while I check in?" he said. "I mean, if they have a room?"

She nodded, let the seat back a notch, and lay back with her eyes closed. Not wanting to register without luggage, Nick got his camera bag out of the back of the car, locked the door, and then took an elevator down to the lobby. Boy, this is going to be a riotous night, he thought. I should just take her home. Or rather, let her take me home.

To his surprise, someone had vacated a room with windows overlooking Monument Circle. That was important to Nick, and he was delighted.

Let's see, he thought. Dare not write a check for this; Becky would see it. He fingered through his billfold and was relieved to see that he had enough cash for the room. But just barely. He wouldn't have had the gall to borrow any from Diana under these circumstances.

As he returned to the parking lot elevator, Nick saw a row of pay telephones. He had a powerful impulse to call home. With some excuse. Some lie. But he couldn't think of one that would be convincing enough. And he wasn't up to talking with Becky now.

Tomorrow the consequences, he thought. He swallowed hard, thinking of Davey and the movie he had promised him.

This is for Davey, he said to himself as he got in the elevator. We need the money. We desperately need the money.

When he got back to the car, he had to awaken Diana. She followed him like a dopey child as he carried his equipment and her purse and they boarded the elevator to go to their room.

The room had two large beds. It looked warm and luxurious and restful in the glow of table lamps. Nick went to the window and looked down on the Circle. The limestone shaft and statuary of the Soldiers' and Sailors' Monument, white as bone, glowed in the pale light of floodlamps. Nick pulled the drapes. "Perfect for what we want," he said. He turned around. Diana had taken off her shoes and lay, otherwise totally dressed, prone upon one of the beds, sound asleep. Or maybe pretending to be, he thought; surely nobody can fall asleep that fast.

Well. This is going to be an interesting night.

Blowing a loud sigh, Nick took off his jacket and hung it in the closet. It was damp and did not smell good. He turned on the bathroom light, checked the room for cleanliness, and wondered what they were going to do about brushing their teeth in the morning. Then he grinned at his own mundane thoughts. Nothing's ever perfect, is it, he thought. Not even Paradise, probably. He came back into the room and sat down on the other bed, hands on his knees, and stared at this golden-haired child who lay face-down on the other bed. He looked at her shapely calves and delicate feet, and at the backs of her knees. He had an impulse to kiss her there, a strange, stirring desire to kiss the backs of those knees. No, not now, he thought. If she's not really asleep, she might be annoyed by that, tired and mixed up as she is right now. He sat there gazing at her, thinking of the almost incomprehensible fact that a few short hours ago this sleepy girl had been writhing in naked abandon under his camera's eye.

The heavy stillness of the room pressed upon him, and he yawned. Maybe I'm as tired as she is, he thought. Ought to be. Holy Christ, what a day. His mind scanned back over the aborted start of the race, his negotiations for a garage and car, his strange encounters with Kitty Dold and her husband; he thought of Kitty and the Air Force officer and wondered what might be going on now in her room; he thought of Dold's plan to buy the Speedway, and about the couple fornicating in the mud in the Snake Pit, and the naked girl being tossed in a blanket. He remembered again the surreptitious and somehow grotesque photo session in the garage. And now he sat here, his whole soul feeling leached out, nasty inside from all the drinks he had had earlier in the day and whose effects had worn off. He gave another great yawn and wished he had stopped to get a bottle. Wonder if I could get room service for a couple of drinks right now, he thought. No; if I did that, I might not be able to pay the bill in the morning.

He got up and went to his coat, got his cigarette pack out, and lit a Pall Mall. He remembered that curious ruse of Dold's—or whatever it was—of the cadged cigarette. He stood near the foot of Diana's bed and smoked and yawned.

Standing there watching the sleeping girl, he thought of Picasso's oft-repainted theme, the sleeper and the watcher. An image like a dream within a dream, he thought.

He found himself swaying and blinking. He stubbed out the cigarette in an ashtray, and with a great sigh extended himself upon the empty bed.

He awoke with a start to find the lamps still burning. Diana was sleeping on her back now; he realized that he had been awakened by her snoring, a nasal purring now and then punctuated by a snort. He looked at his watch; it was ten minutes past midnight. Sometimes Becky's snoring would awaken him just like that. He quickly put that thought out of his mind, but was left with a heavy, almost frightening, sense of guilt. With a groan, he swung his legs off the bed, went into the bathroom, shut the door, raked his throat, and spat into the toilet. He ran water in the sink until it was cold, then filled a glass and rinsed his mouth. He urinated and washed his hands. When he opened the door and stepped into the room, Diana was sitting cross-legged on the bed, blinking. "Hi," she said. "Sorry I zonked out on you."

"It's okay. I did, too. How're you feeling now?"

"Better. Dirty, though. Can I have a cigarette?"

He lit two as she stood up and took off her coat. She hung the coat beside his, then reached under her skirt and stripped off her panty hose. She sat down on the bed beside him, smiled a drowsy smile, and sipped the cigarette. "Ugh, strong. You should smoke filters."

"I shouldn't smoke at all."

"That's true."

"Well," he said. "Here we are all by ourselves in the middle of the night. What do you think about that?" His hands were shaking.

She shook her head and blew smoke out through elaborately pursed lips, obviously a neophyte smoked. "I never thought we'd make it," she said.

"Nice here, though, huh?"

"Yes. I need a bath."

"Fine. I personally inspected the bathroom, and if any bathroom's good enough for this Princess, it's that one right in there."

She put her cigarette in the ashtray, stood up, and without hesitation slipped her dress off. His heart leaped at the sight of her glorious golden body. This was an entirely different moment, far better than that furtive undressing in the garage. She planted a tobacco-scented kiss on his mouth and then, in bikini panties and brassiere, went into the bathroom and shut the door. Soon he heard the rush of bathwater behind the door, and the flushing of the toilet. The sound rushed out louder as the door opened; getting the nice fragrance of soapy humidity, he turned. She was standing in the doorway naked.

She had tied her hair up off her neck with a kerchief, in Grecian style, and looked like a goddess out of a mythology book. "Save water," she said. "Bathe with a friend?"

He got up as if in a trance, his heart seeming to do acrobatics in his breast. By the time he was undressed and stepping into the hot water with her, he was exhibiting a tremendous throbbing erection, which she looked at with a smile but did not mention.

"I love your physique," she said.

"As you know, that's reciprocal."

He was in almost unbearable excitement as they bathed. Her skin gleamed wetly; her flesh was firm, as if pneumatic, under his hands as he soaped and rinsed her. He had been wondering all month whether she was of as sensuous a nature as her ablutions by the swimming pool so many years ago had made him suspect she was. Obviously she was; he found that she lost her ability to speak when her nipples were being kissed. In midsentence she would go silent, her mouth still moving, then her lips would form silent O's.

He wanted to please her. If he could ever do anything right with an opportunity, he thought, it would be to please her. He was almost twice her age; he was confident that he knew how to bring her pleasure as much as anyone ever might have before; no one, he thought, could ever have appreciated this perfection of hers as he could.

"Leave the lights on," she said. He had intended to. She obviously was aware that he not only desired but worshiped her body.

Nothing mattered to him now but pleasing her. She talked nonsensically and rolled her head to and fro as his mouth kissed her all over and burrowed into her moist and fragrant genitalia. Her torso began to surge and he looked, incredulous, up over the flawless smooth belly and the lolling white breasts, the turgid nipples, the closed eyes and ecstatic mouth. Every exhalation of her breath was a low, unconscious cry. He knew when she needed him inside her. Kitty's long-remembered quip rose in his thoughts: *Put your fucker where your pucker is.* And if it is physically possible to smile in such a situation, he smiled. Diana yelped as the long, slow, electric insertion began, then her regular cries resumed, growing louder and louder. His own readiness was such that he knew it would require his total concentration to control himself, and he swore that he would do that. He remembered when with Kitty ten years ago he had learned how to restrain his sensations by sheer willpower, and thus had, she had said, driven her clear out of her head by containing himself and pursuing her from one orgasm to another and still another. So now, as then, he put his whole mind into concentration upon technique, never letting his mental presence spill over the voluptuous brink upon which it hovered; he thought of all sorts of things to keep from falling out of control; he thought of the ludicrous and gross sight of the two people he had seen fornicating on the ground at the Speedway; he thought of the man drinking beer off the ground through a straw; and at one point, being frightfully close to release, he withdrew until he was scarcely inside her, and forced himself to see the awful image of Davey sitting at home waiting in vain for his father to come home and take him to a movie. Diana clutched frantically at him during that hiatus, trying to draw him back in, and when he had control again, with a great shudder and his heart full of bittersweet anguish, he thrust himself suddenly all the way in again. She screamed and went into spasms; he gritted his teeth and poured sweat and focused his entire being upon the task of holding back his pleasure. Thus they worked on and on in the night, she going from one peak to another, he concentrating on the mechanics of what he was doing, red behind his eyes, his thoughts mumbling against membrane.

Sometimes he had wondered about this supraliminal lovemaking of his, whether some might think it a joyless thing, with performance the criterion. But no, he had decided; the joy was in the giving, in the observance of his partner's pleasure; a thing of this intense intimacy has to be a conscious thing, a thing of the mind before it is a thing of the body, because, he thought, it is like death; if it is to mean anything, one must try to understand it intellectually before giving in to it. One would want, for example, to have cogent last words to be remembered by, he thought now; and he was intrigued by that thought having formed at this moment.

And then, hearing and feeling and sensing that Diana was almost spent, he knew that his mental effort was done; now was to be his moment of beauty, which he seemed to have earned. Opening his eyes to devour the flushed, perfect image of her, the trembling eyelashes, the closed eyelids, the small white teeth within the rounded lips, the flawless artistry of this body that contained her young life, he put his mind aside and let his heart go, and, transported by the tragic awareness that everything is fleeting, he released himself into the miraculous blending of their selves, groaning, calling, and spilling. And with him, feeling this, she went into a final spasm.

They awoke sometime before daylight and smoked cigarettes. "Did you ever hear of Phryne?" she murmured.

"Of Athens?"

"Yes."

"Yes." He remembered: the legendary courtesan of bedazzling physical beauty who had posed naked for Praxiteles's statues of Venus. "I didn't know you knew about such things," he said. "I'm glad. What about Phryne?"

"I feel that I was her once. Before. You know."

"Who else have you been?" He was afraid she would say Cleopatra; once Becky in a moment like this had expressed her secret belief that in some long-ago life she had been Cleopatra. It would be such an awful mockery now, like life imitating art, if Diana said Cleopatra.

"Phryne is the only one I can remember," Diana said.

They made love again the same way, and then, toward daylight, they slept. Fortunately, he was exhausted enough to go to sleep without thinking of Becky and Davey.

PART III

May 30, 1973

"IT'S *a quarter till nine. This is WIBC Indianapolis, your favorite station, with some cloudiness, rain, and fifty-five degrees; time for Sid Collins at the Speedway!"*

"Direct from the Indianapolis Motor Speedway, the 1973 Indianapolis Five Hundred-Mile Race, brought to you by Cadillac Motor Division of General Motors Corporation and your authorized Cadillac dealer. And by STP, the Racer's Edge.

"Well, two days ago, on Monday, we greeted you at ten-fifteen A.M., *Eastern Standard Time, for the annual speed classic. And after talking for almost four hours, we signed off, to return yesterday morning at this same time. Yesterday, we added to the record-breaking postponement for the second day, as the weather failed to cooperate, and the nearly three hundred thousand fans returned to sit huddled under umbrellas and brave chilly wind. Then they all went home, as the second vigil was unrewarded with a run. There was a start, though; we made it through a parade lap and a pace lap, but scattered drops of water on the north turn brought out the red flag in place of the green flag. This is Sid Collins this morning, in the Master Control Tower once again, clutching a four-leaf clover, a rabbit's foot, a horseshoe, in hopes that today might have differed from the past two. It has not. It is still raining in Indianapolis. There are just a couple of thousand fans in the area of the starting line and the environs of the racetrack itself, and it doesn't look right now as if we'll have a race for quite a great number of hours."*

331

*   *   *

Nick Alef drifted toward the surface of sleep, aware that his hand was stroking a cleft in warm flesh; then he awoke knowing that it was not Becky's flesh.

Diana, he thought, with a poignant and fearful rush of remembering.

Beside him, she moaned incoherently from the margins of sleep and shifted positions, and he felt the firm contours change and turn sliding under his hand, and her breathing grew rhythmic and shallow again. His loins tingled with their memory.

Nick didn't open his eyes, but lay with his palm upon her haunch and let himself be washed slowly by the returning recollections of yesterday and the night. It was like lolling in a tropical surf, full of lazy sensation and an awareness of rare good luck. But there were regrets, dangers, and guilts swimming deep, like sharks unseen under the blinding surface of it.

This is a great fortune, he thought, but a risky one. Somehow his success or failure was being determined by things happening in these three days. His luck so far had been good, and his prospects were promising. There was his photography of the race itself, which so far had been made of spectacular opportunities well taken; there was this photo project with Diana, which was all done now, except for the unhurried morning shots he would take here today with Indianapolis's landmark, Monument Circle, as their backdrop—that, too, had been an opportunity both made and exploited. And then there remained in the back of his mind still another opportunity that might help lift him out of the rut his life had become: his discovery that Werner Dold was planning to buy the Speedway. That, according to his old reportorial instincts, was a good break, which he could develop to his advantage as the day wore on and a way became apparent. He was rested now and felt capable of anything.

He opened his eyes then and looked at Diana's mussed golden hair and tawny shoulder. A swelling, ruddy-nippled breast moved toward him; she was awakening and coming to him with a smile.

Nick refused to let himself think of home.

*   *   *

Becky Alef woke up when Davey turned the knob of her bedroom door. He stood there in cotton pajamas, his hair mussed by sleep. He looked at the pillow beside his mother and then said, "Where's Dad?"

"Uhm, well, he had to leave early to go to the track again, 'cause they're going to try to run the race again today."

"Oh," Davey said, and went away. She didn't know whether Davey believed her or not. Probably not. Maybe I should just tell him Nick stayed out all night, she thought. I'm going to have to tell him a lot of things today, she thought, remembering the awful promises she had made to herself. Maybe if I told him his dad stayed all night with another woman (the thought caused a terrible sinking heaviness in her breast), it would make it easier for him to stay on my side through this.

On my side, she thought. What an awful phrase. They had tried never to divide Davey, no matter how bad things had been. They had always done their fighting out of his presence, and Becky had always made excuses for Nick, for Davey's sake. Losing Timmy had been enough for any boy to go through, and so they had always been careful to insulate him from their troubles.

But he's going to have to learn now, she thought, getting up. Now. Or this evening when I get back from the Speedway.

An unfamiliar sound in his ear woke Gerald Rumple. It was a buzzing sound like a ship's klaxon he had heard one night across the foggy water of San Francisco Bay when he and Ella had gone there on a vacation. He opened his eyes and was in an unfamiliar room, alone in a small bed.

Then he knew. It was the guest bedroom of the Roepke's home. The sound was the electronic alarm of a clock-radio beside the bed. He pushed a button on the top, and the alarm stopped and soft music began.

Gerald had seldom awakened without Ella beside him in the last ten years, and he missed her terribly for a moment. Then he remembered her refusal to come up to

Chicago with him, and he became very angry with her and was glad she wasn't there.

Gerald had arrived late in the night and had spent a terribly emotional time with Allan and Janet, and finally they had all gone to bed well after midnight. He had made an excuse for Ella's absence, saying that she had caught an awful cold at the Speedway on Monday and was too sick to travel.

Now Gerald lay heavy with dread. He was unfamiliar with death and funerals and couldn't understand why they would have people come to the funeral home all day today to look at two caskets that were closed because Gene and Ruthie had been mangled too badly for anyone to see. And Gerald was hungry. Usually if he awoke without Ella beside him, there would be the smell of bacon in the house. She got up early only to cook.

Now Gerald got up and put on his bathrobe, then went to the bathroom. You'll have to be the chief cook and bottle washer and everything else today, he told himself while he was brushing his teeth. The Roepkes had had no close relatives, and except for the help of neighbors like the Snyders, the children would have to rely on Gerald alone.

It would be so tough facing these two beloved orphans this morning. Blinking, Gerald opened the bedroom door and went into the hallway of the big, quiet house. He went first to Allan's room. Allan, a slight, good-looking boy with Gene's wavy hair, was lying there already awake, gazing at the ceiling. Gerald went to his bedside, and the boy looked up at him.

"How are you this mornin', old buddy?" Gerald said.

"Okay."

Gerald held out his hand; the boy reached up and took it, and they squeezed. "You ready for today?"

"M-hm."

"Listen, you kind of help your sister along today, will you? Be real good to her. Big-brother stuff, you know?"

"Sure." Allan said it bravely, but tears suddenly started filling his eyes, and he got up swiftly and silently and went blinking to the bathroom in his pajamas. Gerald felt wrenched inside. He went out and down the hall and tapped on Janet's door.

"Come in."

Her room was bright with big celluloid flowers and stuffed animals and flowery curtains. There was a highway STOP sign on the wall and a poster that said:

LO
VE

She was looking at him when he came in, the pretty face in a mass of long brown hair, and smiling a wan smile. He bent over and kissed her on the cheek, and she put her arms around his neck and pulled him to make him sit down.

"How about it?" Gerald said. "You ready for today?"

"If you be with me, I am."

"I be with you."

She smiled. God, he thought. She's so loving. What's she going to do in a few years without her mother, out in a world full of young marijuana-smoking boys who don't know how clean and delicate she is in her soul? "Listen," he said. "I know for a fact, but don't you tell Allan I said this, that womenfolks are really a lot more grown-up than menfolks, so I want you to kind of help your brother today, okay? Be real sweet to him."

"Okay."

Gerald went down to the kitchen and got bacon and eggs and butter out of the refrigerator. The house seemed so huge, so empty.

He went through the unfamiliar motions of starting the breakfast. Now and then he would hear water running in pipes in the walls, and he knew the kids were getting ready for this awful day.

But they're facing it all right, he thought. They're great kids. The kind of kids I've always wished we could have had.

He stopped in the act of tapping an egg on the edge of the skillet.

We're their godparents, he thought. Technically we're responsible for them now. I mean, we could be.

He turned the egg in his hand and thought. It was a big thing growing in his mind all at once. It was bigger than anything he had ever thought of, even bigger than going into the carpet business on their own.

He wanted to tell Ella about this thought, and he was angry that instead of being here where he could turn to her and say it, she was 240 miles away, probably at that idiotic racing arena with that awful, loudmouthed Yarbrough woman, talking like a couple of chatterboxes about A. J. Foyt and Mario Andretti and Roger Mc-Cluskey.

Ella, he thought. Wait till you hear what I'm thinking. You don't know what you're missing.

And as the kitchen grew warm and fragrant with the activity of cooking, Gerald began to hum.

Ella Rumple and her newfound racing companion, Ivy Yarbrough, sat in their seats near the fourth turn and gazed out from under their umbrellas at the long, long, curving lines of uncovered bleachers, upon which the rain was falling with a steady hushing sound. Ella had never, in all her years as a race spectator, seen the vast Speedway so empty. Here and there among the sweeping horizontal gray lines of seats, tiny figures of race fans huddled under tiny umbrellas.

Ella kept thinking about Gerald, sad and angry about his absence, by turns. And now and then she would have a feeling of shame because she hadn't gone with him. Ivy made desultory efforts to cheer Ella, but with little success.

There was nobody within forty feet of them. The rain pattered on their umbrellas.

For the third day, the trucks were running over the track below them, trying to take off the surface water.

Ella tried, as she had been trying, to fathom the strange mood that had caused Gerald to throw away their Tower Terrace tickets Monday after the "Salt" Walther crash.

Finally she gave that up. "Hold my umbrella a minute, will you, Ivy?" she asked. Ivy held it in her left hand and her own in her right as Ella unfolded the *Indianapolis Star*, which she hadn't had a chance to read this morning because she was too busy cooking. Its front-page banner headline was:

JUST FOR TODAY, RAIN GO AWAY

Under that was a two-column headline:

TWICE-POSTPONED RACE
READY FOR 9 a.m. TRY
IF WEATHERMAN AGREES

There was a big, three-column photo, on the front page, of the infield by the first turn. It was titled:

BAD DREAM IN SMELL-O-VISION
INFIELD CROWD NOT COOL,
JUST SOGGY; TRASH PILES UP

Under the banner headline was another headline:

FEDERAL GASOLINE TAX HIKE
UNDER STUDY
PUMP COST
COULD RISE
BY 6 CENTS

There were two Speedway stories farther down on the front page. One was a traffic story:

SPEEDWAY CAR EXODUS
WORST IN MANY YEARS

The other was:

DELAY OF "500"
MAY MOVE BACK
MILWAUKEE RACE

There were more race stories and photographs on pages 6, 11, and 13, and in the sports section; there was an editorial titled "The Race Fans," and a cartoon about the weather at the Speedway on page 30. On page 16 there was the Race Scorecard; on page 17 there was a column about Speedway fans, and half of the back page of the paper was full of photographs showing race drivers and mechanics waiting in the rain, tossing Frisbees and playing soccer. Also on the back page was a humor column by Bob Collins, headed:

INFIELD FANS IN HIGH
SPIRITS (& VICE VERSA)

While Ivy's left arm ached from holding Ella's umbrella, Ella read every word of all the race stories and all the cutlines under the pictures.

"Ooooh, that Jim Murray," she muttered through clenched teeth, her fat, pretty face as hard and furious as she could make it. "If that awful, snotty man doesn't like the race, why does he come here?"

"What's the old killjoy say? I didn't read him this morning."

"Just listen to this: 'These are ballistic missiles. . . . You can't time 'em, you have to track 'em. . . . By the time you hear one, it's been there. It's a blip. They should have their own STATE to run in—or a remote part of one, like the proving grounds for the atomic bomb. They shouldn't be set down in the middle of a country fairground on a cow pasture track in the middle of two hundred and fifty thousand people throwing hot-dog wrappers, beer cans, balloons, Frisbees, footballs, and fried chicken in the air. It's like sailing an aircraft carrier up the Wabash. . . . God must be trying to tell them something. Every time they try to start this race, it starts to rain. Or burn.' Ooooh, that sarcastic s.o.b.! Who does he think he is? And listen to this: 'They haven't run a lap yet and already there's one dead and several burned at Indy this May. Like I say, it's a nice place to have a picnic, but I wouldn't want to drive my car—' Ooooh, I hate that man! JIM MURRAY," she yelled to the empty bleachers, "GO HOME!"

"Yeah," Ivy said. "What an asshole." Jim Murray for years, in one way or another, had ridiculed the "500," and Gerald and Ella, like most race fans, had enjoyed hating him with fervid indignation, reading his every word.

"Nnnng," Ivy groaned. "Can you take your umbrella now, Ella? My arm's killing me." She took it, and Ivy twisted her arm to and fro, getting the ache out of her shoulder. The rain still hushed softly on their umbrellas and spattered on the acres of seats and flowed down the banked surface of the racetrack. In the distance, fans were straggling into the stands.

Then Ella's eye fell on a small story about the auto crash at Lebanon that had killed Gene and Ruthie Roepke. She sighed, shook her head, and clucked her tongue. "And to think," she said. "We're sitting in their seats."

Ivy read the article and wiped her nose on the back of her hand. "Well, one thing, anyway," she said after a while. "They'd probably be glad to know their tickets aren't being wasted."

"We hope he'll be back if we have a run tomorrow or the next day, or whenever; Freddy Agabashian was heading for Alamo, California, he thought—but as you heard, he is here. Several of our broadcasters have late-night news and sports programs, but are ready for the escorted police convoy early each morning. Many of our runners and statisticians have other jobs, but they've stayed with us, too; and Jack Morrow, producer, leaves here and goes home to redo his format for the next day. It's become almost a way of life. And yesterday, Fred, when we started on the color of the race cars' paint jobs, I knew we were getting down to the bitter end of a long trail, didn't you?"

Kevin was in solitary confinement in his bedroom in the Cole family home in Kokomo listening to the Speedway Network on his radio. He had not even been allowed to leave home to go to school that morning. His parents had been ordered to bring him to the juvenile division of the police department in the afternoon.

"We should at least send him to school," Kevin's dad had said at breakfast that morning. "He did miss all yesterday because of his escapade."

"Not on your life," his mother had replied, looking hard at Kevin. "I don't trust him. He'd probably run away from school."

"Aw, Mom, you can trust me!"

"I could trust you if I were an absolute fool, but I'm not, not anymore," she had said. "After breakfast you're going right back to your room, and you're going to stay there until lunch. And then after lunch, you're going to return to your room, and you're going to stay there until your father comes home from work this afternoon and takes you to the police station."

That had made him mad—his mother saying she didn't trust him. But what had really stunned him, what had really made him hate them and think they were terrible tyrants, was that yesterday, after the police had brought him home, his dad had chained and padlocked the trail bike and called the want-ad department of the Kokomo paper and put in a motorcycle-for-sale-cheap advertisement. Kevin had thought his dad was kidding, but this morning there had been a telephone call about the ad, and Mr. Cole had asked the people to come over. They had come over—a boy from Kevin's school and his father —and Mr. Cole had sold them the cycle, still muddy from Kevin's escape effort through the woods. Kevin had looked out the window, a high whine of pain and fury in his throat, while the man wrote a check. They had loaded it in the back of the man's pickup truck, and Kevin had watched it disappear down the wet street among the houses, gone forever. Kevin had gone into a screaming fit when his dad came in, and had had to be put bodily into his room while Keith and Pam watched, not daring to smile. Then Mr. Cole had gone to work and they had gone to the school bus, and now Kevin was in solitary confinement in his room, guarded by his mother, who told him to shut up every time he opened his bedroom door and whined for her. He was madder than he had ever been in his whole tantrum-filled lifetime, but now the tears and the fury were cooling down into a cold, calculating bitterness fraught with plans for revenge or, at least, escape.

But there was noplace to escape to and no way to escape to anyplace and—for the moment, anyway—no obvious way to get revenge. So he lay on his stomach on the bed, leafed through the latest issue of *Rodder and Super Stock* magazine looking at the ads for superlifters, cams, rocker arms, blower drive kits, manifolds, dynos, and super jacker air shocks, and listened to the radio.

"I know that Tony Hulman's main interest is the fan. He naturally is concerned about the race, too, but he was really very concerned last night when we spoke with him, about the fan getting a chance to enjoy the event, and use his ticket, and stay here, and he's probably more anxious than anyone to have this race run off as close to schedule as possible. So I would anticipate we'll go on day by day, wouldn't you, Fred?"

"I can't see any other way of doing it, Sid. Today looks rather dismal. I think the only Five Hundred-Mile Race we're going to have today, Sid, at the rate it's going—the trucks have logged around three hundred and twenty-seven miles already, and I think they will have completed their five hundred miles on this race track today, because they are, in anticipation, trying to keep the track dry, as dry as is humanly possible. At least they are getting the excess water off of it, running around here."

"You know, Tony tells the story that when he bought this track, back in 1945, and the first race under his aegis in 1946, he says, I think a little more than tongue-in-cheek, 'I really wondered if anybody'd show up.' That may be his feeling again, right now, today, if they have a race, because the people, if it did clear up, are downtown, and they're in business, and some are fifty and a hundred miles away, and if they had enough time, they might come back. But the stands are virtually vacant. It looks like a deserted ghost town, doesn't it?"

"Sid, I'm quite positive, if suddenly the sun came out, and all of the radio stations informed the public that the race was gettin' ready to run, I think there'd be some absenteeism around here that'd be fantastic. And they'd be here. Believe me. These are race fans. They make it!"

Mmm-hm, Werner Dold thought. Imagine Tony *is* concerned about those fans right now, with millions of dollars worth of rainchecks out and the fans finally deciding it's not worth the bother to come back.

Werner turned off the radio and paced back and forth in his suite, puffing on his after-breakfast cigar. He was becoming awfully impatient. He hated to be away from his office three days in a row like this, although his long-distance calls and conference calls this morning had allowed him to dispatch all the urgent decisions there. He was getting restive, too, because he thought that perhaps right now might be the time to go find Tony Hulman and broach his offer, now while Tony must be discouraged; he felt that this might be the best time to do it, but was, strangely, finding himself a little afraid of actually doing it. He didn't know why he felt this apprehension about confronting Tony; he was never afraid of anybody, especially people whom, like Tony Hulman, he could afford to buy several times over. Maybe "afraid" isn't the word for it, he thought as he shed his dressing gown and pulled on a Givenchy blazer to go out on his balcony. Maybe "reluctant" is a better word. Werner had a vague, troubling sense that Tony Hulman had something, some intangible something, perhaps something accreted through his years as Mr. Speedway, that was, if not actually power, at least something powerlike that Werner really wasn't sure he could obtain. He slid the plate-glass door open and went out into the chilly air, rolling the olive-green cigar gently back and forth between his thumb and forefinger. He was remembering two faces now as he looked out at the swamp of mud and wet trash across the track and the rain veiling the distant, dark background of trees, golf fairways, and dark, distant grandstands. There were cars coming in, quite a few of them, it seemed, but the great curving canyons of benches were dotted with very few spectators. The faces Werner Dold was seeing were Tony Hulman's— with that vacant, brooding expression he had shown at the ball earlier in the month and his sudden shy smile upon becoming aware that he was being watched—and Dick Bixby's, as that lean and bearded man had sat beside him at the motel bar yesterday asking him when one would approach Tony and how much one would offer. Werner had worried about that ever since. Bixby had become too keenly interested too quickly, and Werner was afraid he might have hinted his secret to somebody who might leak it to Tony or to the papers before the offer was made.

Werner just didn't want Tony to hear about it and have time to reflect before he could approach him personally and make the offer. Even if Hulman did want to sell, the price would go up as he and his staff thought about it.

Werner had gone to the Athletic Club last night for dinner with Doc and Mrs. Upton, and had asked him, "Do you know anything about a Richard Bixby here in town who might be a writer or publicist or something?"

"Bixby? Bixby? No, the only Bixby I know is a stock-broker. What does he look like?"

Kitty had not gone with him to dinner. When Werner had phoned her room to invite her, she had professed a headache and cramps due to her time of the month. Frankly, Werner had doubted that. He was quite sure she was giving her evening to the Air Force captain. He suspected that the two of them were in her room now. She hadn't come out for breakfast.

But Werner Dold had not tried to get in touch with her. He wasn't ready to know or do anything about that yet. He had enough on his mind with this dilemma about the Speedway. Whatever Kitty might be up to was a different kind of thing, and it would be a mess to deal with. It would be too distracting right now.

"Good and wet?" Nick called.

"Yes," Diana's voice replied from the shower.

"Good. Now, come in here quick."

She emerged naked from the bathroom, water standing on her golden skin in droplets or running down in rivulets. Although he had made love to her three times during the night and morning, this new sight of her caused him once again to tumesce. But he had work to do, and quickly. "Now, stand right here. I want your body facing me, but your face looking out the window. Out that way. Good. You might brace yourself with your hand on the back of the chair. Give a little twist to your torso. Good!"

Wow. Perfect, he thought. She was crosslighted by morning daylight, and every water droplet had its highlight. Her nipples were puckered, and the windowlight glinted in a droplet upon her left nipple. The nipple itself almost seemed to be glowing, a translucent tissue that the costly lens was recording with absolute fidelity. And outside the window, a few hundred feet away and several stories below, was Monument Circle, its fountains flowing, the formal beds of red flowers: the one other Indianapolis landmark that was almost as well-known as the Motor Speedway. Nick felt they had been very lucky to get this room at the Hilton, because even in these bedroom scenes he wanted to show evidence of Indianapolis and the "500" Festival as constant reminders that this was not just a nude girl but a genuine Festival Princess. The Monument Circle outside the window, the festival decorations on the lampposts, would serve that purpose perfectly.

"One great thing," he said as he moved her and the camera about, "is that I've already got so many good shots of you in the parade, and the Queen-judging and all that. Those are naturals for the clothed shots of the feature. You know. Now, my beauty, I want you to lie down on the bed."

"Oh, do you? Why, what do you have in mind?"

"Well, as they call them in the trade, the beaver shots. I want you to lie and wiggle around as if you were trying to seduce me."

"Do you suppose it might work?"

"It'll work. When I get done with my camera, I will undoubtedly have to go to work upon you with another instrument."

She did as she was told. She writhed and wriggled and fingered her nipples and her thighs and her genitalia. Nick had loved her totally and well; they were now full intimates, and she was no longer self-conscious at all. But she did not let herself become as aroused as she had on the race car. She hated to remember that. Too, the incredible novelty of posing in the nude had worn off. She would never have believed one could get used to such a thing so quickly, if ever, but she had. Last evening, the big part of this nude posing for her had been the erotic adventure with Nick; the business part of it, the publication of her pictures in *Playboy* and the money, had been secondary. This morning, the business aspect of it was growing in importance.

She was beginning to feel professional.

*   *   *

Billy Joe Marshall (that's who he was, he remembered first thing, not ."Worms" anymore) awakened to the sound of light rain on the car roof, feeling bad at one end and good at the other: he had a pounding headache and a rigid, tingling piss hard-on. It was day; outside the car window the sky was gray and the window glass was moving with flowing water. He could hear Lloyd Skirvin snoring in the front seat. Wonder where we're at, he thought.

Vaguely he could remember last night's succession of liquor stores and hamburger joints, then a bar where a girl danced topless on a stage to jukebox music, wearing black-and-white-checkered bikini panties, and finally an adult movie theater on the Westside where they had sat drunkenly snickering at the sight of people fuckin' and suckin' and cornholin' each other on the screen. They had had a good ol' time, without them two crazy-ass jailbait Yankee cunts around; they had been able to hoot an' yell and say anything they wanted to. But now Billy Joe Marshall, formerly "Worms" Marshall, was all alone here in the back seat of the Merc with a big stiff-on and nobody to put it in, and for a moment he lay there fingering it, proud of its thickness and length and hardness, and remembered how good it had felt Monday night all snug in that young Puggles, and he wished she were here right now to help him get it off.

Then he remembered that crazy bit with Renee with all the people watching in the Snake Pit, and he was glad they had run off. They was nothin' but trouble, and you could always find some nice simple cunts that weren't no trouble. Well, not always; he and Lloyd hadn't done very well last night.

Billy Joe Marshall sat up and looked out the window to see if he recognized where they were. It was the parking lot of a shopping center. The car was parked alongside a big square receptacle marked GOODWILL INDUSTRIES. Beyond it there was a row of storefronts: a drugstore, a loan company, a pet shop, a florist's shop, an auto supply store. Billy Joe looked at the auto supply store and tried to remember if there was anything they needed for the Merc. He had thought about getting a pair of those woven plastic seat cushions that were supposed to let air circulate under your seat, because summer was almost here and there'd be a lotta hot days on the road. He had thought about buying them to please and surprise Lloyd. But now he thought, Well, fuck that. If he wants one a them things, he can git it hisself.

Goddamn rain. Man cain't even git out an' take a piss in this goddamn town, without he gits rained on. He pulled his jacket up over his head and reached forward to open the door. He had to disturb Lloyd in order to squirm out of the back seat, and Lloyd mumbled angrily. But that's jus' tough shit, Billy Joe thought. He stood in the rain and relieved himself against the Goodwill box, his erection relaxing as he did so. He reached in his shirt pocket for his cigarette pack. But the smokes were gone. He felt something in the pocket and pulled it out. It was the Speedway tickets he had picked up off the ground in the infield yesterday while he and Renee had been going around looking for hot dogs. He had forgotten about the tickets. They had dried in his pocket and were stuck together, but he got them apart and looked at them. There were three of them, and they were all for seats in the Tower Terrace. Well, now, that sounds pretty high on th' hawg, he thought.

Lloyd got out of the car, lowered his pants, and squatted down between the car and the Goodwill box. His straight blond hair was standing out all over one side of his head and mashed flat by sleeping on the other side. As the rain wet it, it all began to droop. "What time is it, Worms?"

"Jus' call me Billy Joe."

"Billy Joe. What th' fuck time is it?"

" 'Bout ten. Got a smoke?"

"Here. Smoke this. Hee-hee."

"Up yours. Gimme a cigarette, you ol' Movin' Mutha."

"Here. Ahhh. There ain't nothin' as overrated as a piece of ass, an' there ain't nothin' as underrated as a good shit."

"Yeah?" said Billy Joe, completing the litany which they had learned from a restroom wall. "Well, either you don' know how t' fuck, or else I don' know how t' shit. Hey, ol' buddy, I don' know if they ever gonna have a race here or not, but if they was to have it, how'd you like t' watch it in style?" He showed the tickets to Lloyd, who was up now, closing his belt buckle.

"Hooo-eee. Where'd y'git them muthas?"

"Found 'em on th' ground."

" 'Tower Terrace.' Hey, bet they be some good, clean high-class cunt up there!"

"Wouldn't doubt it a-tall," Billy Joe Marshall said proudly.

For the fourth time, the captain was crying. He had cried once at midnight and again when they woke up at four; then as daylight was starting to leach out the corners of the room, they had awakened again and he had cried himself back to sleep. Now it was—Kitty stealthily reached to the bedside table and picked up her watch—eleven o'clock. Half an hour ago they had awakened again and held each other and fondled, and again the captain had been overcome with weeping. Kitty lay beside him now, running her fingers lightly up and down along his hairless, smooth white chest, and tried to figure some of this out. Kitty had had impotent characters in her bed plenty of times, so that wasn't new to her. Sometimes she had been able to help them. A few times she had even made some impotent who hadn't been impotent—but only very crummy pricks who really needed to be shot down. This guy, this captain with all his hero ribbons, was a weeping impotent instead of a sulking impotent or a raging impotent. He wasn't her first weeping impotent. In her experience there were about three weeping impotents for every sulking impotent, and probably only about one out of five impotents was a raging impotent. So she was fairly used to weeping impotents. But this was a different weeping impotent, somehow. He didn't cry because he couldn't perform; he couldn't perform because he cried. This one didn't start bawling and sniffling because he had failed; he would cry before and during his failure. He was an unusual case, and whatever his problem was, it was deep and wide and far more than just a bedroom problem.

The thing Kitty couldn't figure out was why she wasn't getting fed up with him. Usually she could allow an impotent a couple of tries, and then she'd want to terminate the business and get rid of him. There are limits to patience. But now here was this poor crybaby of a hero, all blond and smooth-skinned and a regular bottomless fountain of tears, evidently, and with scarcely an erection to his name, and yet she didn't feel impatient at all. On the contrary, she felt as if she could lie here for a month waiting for him to run out of tears and get it up, if it took that long.

She raised herself on an elbow and looked at his face. He didn't blubber or bawl or toss and turn. He just lay on his back with his eyes toward the ceiling, swallowing hard, tears flowing down into his ears. And he didn't try to turn his back on her like someone ashamed of his impotence; instead, he seemed to appreciate the attention she gave him. She had stroked his forehead and smoothed back his hair several times, and while she did it he looked up at her wordlessly and adoringly, the tears silently flowing.

She had asked him twice if he just wanted to talk, but so far he hadn't been able to get anything out, although he had seemed ready to talk once, after a long, thoughtful time. But when he had tried to talk, he had only swallowed hard a few times and then had given up.

Now Kitty felt a sudden unusual urge. She leaned over his face and very gently put her lips closer and closer to his eye until he closed it, then pressed a gentle kiss upon his closed eyelid. Then upon the other, and then she kissed the wetness away from his temples. And as she did this she was suddenly surprised by a great, rising, sweet sadness, a rich, happy kind of sadness such as she had felt only once before in her life: an abandonment to caring. She recognized it and was frightened by it because it was something that took the control of a situation out of her hands and made her vulnerable. She cradled the captain's head in her arms and rocked a little, her eyes shut, and remembered the other time in her life she had felt this.

It had been ten years ago, when Nick Alef had cried in her arms the last of their nights together in the resort hotel at French Lick. Nick had not cried as an impotent—on the contrary, she had lost count of the times they had made love that weekend—no, Nick had cried, he explained, "out of sheer appreciation." Because of things like that, Nick Alef had been the only man before who ever, as she expressed it, "fucked her head."

And now—she could hardly believe what was happening to her—this dear, pathetic, suffering Air Force captain, this fountain of unexplained tears, somehow was managing to fuck her head *without even fucking her body.*

When he went to sleep he had bad dreams, and he was terrified of waking up. When he slept he would dream of the brilliant green land sweeping by underneath him and the little clusters of huts and then the slight jolt as he released the napalm bombs, and then he would be climbing and would look back and see that little pool of orange fire and black smoke he had left in the village. Then he would wake up with the fear that they were going to take him into that little room to make him watch them destroy Brighton's skin.

This was the first time Captain George had slept with anyone since he was brought back from the Cong prison camp, and because there was someone beside him he could not get deep enough into sleep to get below the level of the bad dreams. Then he would have to come through the ordeal of waking up, and instead of the little room where they destroyed Brighton's flesh, here was this luxurious room with the beautiful naked lady beside him. He would feel ashamed because he was back here in this luxurious room and Brighton had not lived long enough to come back. Brighton was dead because Captain George had not said the things the Cong had wanted him to say. So when Captain George would wake up terrified from his bad dreams of the firebombs, here would be the smooth skin of this beautiful lady, and all Captain George could think of was the smooth skin of Brighton being destroyed with pliers and slivers, a new area of skin each day, while he was forced to watch. Or he would see the burned skin of the Vietnamese village boy whom the Cong would bring in and make him look at every week or so.

Captain George understood that he was lucky to be here in this luxurious room with the beautiful naked lady who was trying to be nice to him, but for those reasons he could not do what he should have been able to do with her, even though it would be something he had dreamed of for a long, long time. And he felt guilty because he could not do what she wanted him to do, and he couldn't explain to her how it was about the skin because she couldn't possibly understand it and she would probably be angry with him and go away, and he would be alone again. He had been all alone in the prison camp, except for seeing Brighton every day, and he had been alone since he got back in the States because his finacée, Patti, thinking he was dead, had married somebody else. He couldn't remember very much about Patti, except that she had an appendectomy scar on her belly.

Now he lay here looking at the ceiling and thinking these things and trying not to cry, but the tears would just pour out, and he felt as if there were a thumb pressed on his throat.

At one time the beautiful naked lady had kissed him on the eyelids, and he had been able to go back to sleep. He wished she would kiss him on the eyelids again.

In Kokomo, Marjorie Cole was cleaning her oven. She paused and looked at the wall clock. Cliff would be home soon to take Kevin to the police station. Marjorie was in dread of that, but she knew it had to be done, and she was doing the hard and unpleasant jobs in the house to keep from thinking too much about it.

Music was playing on the radio. A short time ago an announcer had said during a news break that weather conditions at the Indianapolis Motor Speedway were improving and the race would probably be started in the early afternoon. Marjorie had shaken her head and compressed her lips and thought unpleasant things about that Speedway, about all the horror and the trouble it had caused her family.

Above the radio music she heard a car door shut. She thought Cliff must be home a little early. She went to the front window and looked out, being careful not to touch anything with her rubber gloves, which were brown with the evil-smelling, caustic oven-cleaning sludge. Cliff's car wasn't there.

She went back to the kitchen. She thought she heard a car start. She shrugged. Must be a neighbor.

Another half hour passed. She had finished the oven and was defrosting the refrigerator. Got to get one that defrosts itself, she thought. If Cliff gets that raise. Or maybe we could apply the money he got for Kevin's cycle against it. Hm. Better see that Kevin's clean and get him dressed. Cliff'll be here any time now.

She went down the hallway and tapped on Kevin's door. His radio was on, loud. There was no answer, and she knocked again. "Kevin?" she called. Still no answer. She tried the knob. The door was locked. Aha, she thought. Sulking and defiance, is it? "Kevin, you'd better unlock this door. You're in enough trouble the way it is!"

There was still no response. "KEVIN!" she yelled. Nothing. "All right, you!" she yelled with her face at the doorjamb. "Your dad will be here in a minute, and if you don't open up, you've had it! Do you hear me?"

She heard the front door open, and then Cliff's voice called, "Marjorie?"

"Cliff, come here! This boy—"

"Hi. Wasn't sure you were here. Where's your car?"

"It's in the garage. Cliff, see if you can get this door—"

"No, it isn't."

"What?"

"Your car's not in the garage."

"Oh, dear."

They hurried outside.

The garage was open, empty.

Kevin's bedroom window was open.

THE FIVE HUNDRED,
THE FIVE HUNDRED,
THE GREATEST RACE IN THE WORLD,
FROM THE OP'NING BOMB
'TIL THE RACE IS DONE
IT'S THRILL AFTER THRILL AFTER THRILL!
THE FIVE HUNDRED,

THE FIVE HUNDRED,
THE BIGGEST AND BEST OF THEM ALL!
AND UNTIL THAT CHECKERED FLAG'S UN-
  FURLED,
IT'S THE GREATEST RACE IN THE WORLD!

"Direct from the Indianapolis Motor Speedway, the
1973 Indianapolis Five Hundred-Mile Race. Brought to
you by Cadillac Motor Division of General Motors Cor-
poration and your authorized Cadillac dealer. And by
STP: the Racer's Edge! Stay tuned, now, for the Great-
est Spectacle in Racing!"

"Olive, may I ask a favor of you?" Mr. Sanders said
in a very pleasant voice.

"Of course." She smiled at him, and he returned the
smile. She had never seen him so happy as he was here
in the bakery today. Their work had seemed effortless;
their movements in the kitchen had been synchronized
and harmonious all day; it was afternoon already, but it
seemed as if they had been here only minutes.

"We're out of almond extract, and I didn't order any.
We'll need it this afternoon, and I wonder if you could
drive over to the supply house on Twenty-first Street and
get us some."

"Of course."

The sky was clearing up. It's about time for some blue
sky, she thought as she drove out of the bakery parking
lot and headed east on Tenth Street. She turned north on
Tibbs Avenue, heading toward Twenty-first. Don't want
to get too near that Speedway, she thought. Nothing to
worry about this time of day, though, I'm sure. It said
on the radio they were going to start the race at nine,
so the traffic jams have to be all over.

She drove happily up Tibbs, remembering with pleasure the nice roast she and Mr. Sanders had had last
evening at his home. Such a nice home! He had a housekeeper who came in twice a week, Olive had learned, to
keep it as spick-and-span and bright as it had been when
Mrs. Sanders was alive. He had changed nothing about
the house after she passed away, he had told Olive. But

after dinner he had asked her what she thought might be done to make the living room look a little more modern, and he had listened attentively as she cautiously, then more freely, gave suggestions. To Olive, it had been significant that he had asked her that and had listened to her advice. He's beginning to think of you as more than just an employee, she had thought to herself on the way home later. And then this morning at the bakery he had greeted her by her first name, with smiles, and as they worked together he had hummed, and—

Wooops!

Suddenly in the middle of the Sixteenth Street intersection there was a policeman standing in front of her, motioning for her to turn. She didn't want to turn. She was going to Twenty-first Street. She looked at him and pointed north, but he shook his head emphatically and waved for her to turn onto Sixteenth. And suddenly there was a lane of cars clear across the intersection blocking her way across Sixteenth. The policeman was growing angry because of her hesitation; she was stopped in the intersection and blocking a lane of traffic. Horns began to sound, and she looked and saw that there were several lanes of cars backed up on Sixteenth Street and she was being ordered into one of those lanes. This didn't make any sense! There wouldn't be Speedway traffic at this hour! She felt an old horror coming back. She rolled down her window and yelled at the policeman that she wanted to go on north. But now he was waving with more violent arm movements and growing red in the face, and the shrilling of his whistle was joined in a terrible uproar with the blaring of car horns. "Oh, no," she said out loud to herself. "Not this time." Clenching her teeth and squinting in determination, she continued to inch her car straight forward until the policeman suddenly realized he was in danger of being caught between the front of her car and the side of one of the cars athwart her path. Perhaps the sight of the Falcon's battered front end made him fear she was somebody to be reckoned with. He came around to her window and yelled at her above the honking horns, "Lady, this is a tough enough job without people like you. Get that goddamn car going— THAT way—or I'll arrest you right here and now!"

"All right," she hissed at him. "But you'll be sorry!"

He stepped aside. Olive turned the wheel, gave the car some gas, and went into the lane he had indicated. The traffic began roaring forward all around her. She drove about eighty feet, suddenly began blowing her horn loudly and insistently to give everybody warning, and then, not caring whether anybody hit her or not—almost wishing someone would, in fact, because she had had a little taste Monday of the grim satisfaction of making metal crumple and glass smash—she jerked the steering wheel hard to the right, swinging in behind the bumper of an accelerating car in the right lane. There was a tremendous screeching of tires behind her and a smashing jolt that threw the rear end of her car a foot to the left, but not enough to stop her, and she steered on across the right lane, bouncing over the curb as three or four other cars banged bumpers in domino succession behind her. She prayed no one was hurt—surely no one was at this slow speed—made a sweeping U-turn through a front yard, accelerated along the sidewalk, went around the end of a guardrail onto the pavement of a corner filling station, honked her way through a lane of traffic on Tibbs, and in a moment was on her way north again. In her rear-view mirror for a moment she saw the policeman standing in the intersection staring after her, apparently too astounded to move.

When she reached the supply house, smiling grimly, she went straight to a telephone and dialed the bakery.

"I'm here," she said tersely. "But I may take awhile coming back. The Speedway traffic is running again, and I just may drive clear outside the county to avoid getting anywhere near it."

Mr. Sanders chuckled on the other end of the line. "That's fine, Olive. No hurry. I'll see you when you get here. Don't take any shortcuts."

"Don't worry," she said. "I'm a very careful driver."

"Right now, the Cadillac Eldorado pace car convertible has the top down. In it, Speedway owner Tony Hulman; Dollie Cole, wife of the president of General Motors; and awaiting Jim Rathmann, winner in 1960

here, who once again will try to drive the pace car and get this race under way! This is Sid Collins, the voice of the 'Five Hundred' here in the Master Control Tower. To my right, once again, let's say hello, and hope this is the last time before we—three and—plus hours from now— say good-bye. Here is, courtesy of the Champion Spark Plug Company, Freddy Agabashian."

"Hello, Sid, nice to be back with you. It's sunny now, and I think we'll have a start, and we'll have a race."

"Further down to my right is John DeCamp, who'll be our chief statistician. John took care of cars out of the race; perhaps this afternoon, John, we can keep track of those still in the race."

"Let's hope we can, Sid, because this is the most excited I've been since the—that first time on Monday!"

"Yes, I think even though we've been talking and sitting around various suites and various offices and saying, 'Isn't this dismal, isn't it dank, isn't it terrible,' once they get those cars out there, and the Indiana sunshine does come out, we're feeling racy, and set—to—go!"

When Lloyd Skirvin and Billy Joe Marshall came staggering up the aisle carrying a laden cooler between them and made their way snickering and whooping to the three seats designated by their tickets, some of the well-dressed fans already sitting nearby looked at them in astonishment and loathing, and those over whom the two had to climb to reach the seats wrinkled their noses and turned their heads away. The two were damp, unshaven, begrimed, their clothing wrinkled and so stained by mud, food, oil, sweat, urine, spilled liquor, and dried semen that it was hard to tell what color it was. And they gave off a rank, sour effluvium of odors that could have awakened someone out of a dead faint.

"Oh, no," a dignified-looking man right behind them whispered to his wife as the filthy pair of pals hoisted the cooler onto the middle seat and gawked around. When they started to sit down, some clapping sounded nearby as fans applauded the emerging sunshine; Lloyd turned in all directions and gave exaggerated bows with a mock expression of coy gratitude on his face. Immediately Billy

Joe yanked the top off the cooler, pulled out two still-warm cans of beer, and gave one to Lloyd. They snapped the tabs off with a flourish, spraying beer over several people in front of them. A young man and his girl friend hunched their shoulders under the sudden rain of beer, and the young man turned around with a grimace on his face. When he saw the cold eyes of Lloyd Skirvin looking straight at him out of that hard, cruel face, he dropped his eyes and turned around to face the front. Lloyd then leaned forward and down and stared intently, with his mouth hanging open, at the girl's breast, which was round and firm under a soft yellow sweater. Her face went pink and angry, and she turned away and drew her coat across her chest. Billy Joe had watched all this, and he went into braying laughter.

Suddenly, just down in front of the Terrace, a racing engine coughed to life and began whooping powerfully, followed by others, for a brief warm-up in the pits. A cheer went up throughout the crowd, and Lloyd and Billy Joe yodeled their approval, then watered their tonsils with long chug-a-lug pulls on their beer cans.

The cars thundered for about seven minutes and then were shut down. Soon, while the track announcer described the activity over the public-address system, the crews began pushing the race cars out onto the track and lining them up in rows of three. Lloyd Skirvin stood and looked down studiously at the brilliant, strangely conformed vehicles, and with his whole being—mind, hands, arms, shoulders, neck—tried to comprehend what would have to be the totally different feeling of operating such strange machines. It would be so different to sit so low—almost lying down, mere inches from the road surface—and in the center of the broad, flat body instead of at the left side. To be able to see the rubber of all four tires might be helpful; to have no roof overhead would be strange. Lloyd was accustomed to speeding with his head outdoors in motorcycle races, but to sit in a car with his head outdoors—well, he would have to get used to something like that.

He looked at the wide, low shape of the car body, scarcely more than knee-height, and considered the idea of having that huge, exposed engine right behind instead of in front of him. He thought how it would be, as the driver, to be fitted into that fragile front end like a foot in a shoe, just barely able to see over the tops of the tires. He looked then at the smooth-paved track with its very slight banking in the corners, and he saw the black path of tire rubber that showed the route these "500" drivers always took through the turn.

And then he and his body understood it all. He was sure that he knew exactly how it would all work and exactly how it would all feel, and if someone put him in one of those contraptions right this minute, he could win this race with no trouble at all. It'd be as tame as a fat coon hound.

The race cars were lined up on the track and the drivers were getting in as Nick Alef and Diana Scheckley made their way along the Terrace section toward the Tower. The sun was shining through dissolving clouds, casting an intense, pearly light through the skies. The air once again seemed to vibrate with suspense. Thousands of fans were flowing through the aisles and walkways.

Diana walked slowly through the throng, squinting against the glare, hanging onto Nick's arm. The thousands of voices filled the air with shrill babbling and a murmuring undercurrent. Diana felt a strange, frothy excitement, a giddiness almost. Passing faces, faces she knew, looked at her and Nick, smiled, hurried on. Diana knew how she looked in sunlight, her hair shining golden, her face tanned and young, and she felt the admiration of the people as she moved among them. She looked at Nick, and he was looking at her; they smiled and winked at each other. In her loins there was the moistness, the sensitivity, the languid, almost-itching aftereffect of their four couplings. As she walked she could feel the small pad of folded toilet tissue she had placed in the crotch of her panties to absorb seepage. She was having strange, thrilling thoughts. This many people, she thought. They don't know, or maybe they do know about us. They look at us and know.

This many people. And this is just a few compared to the millions that will see me in *Playboy* magazine.

God, she thought. That's incredible. Her heart seemed to skip; there was a strange, unsettling disequilibrium in her stomach at the thought of it. She tried to imagine which of the hundreds of poses would be the one that would be printed on the big, folded page, but there were so many to remember; they seemed to flow together in her memory, and her body could not really recall the attitudes of any of them. The only one she could separate out from the whole drift of memory was the one on the race car. With the smooth enamel of the car's body cool under the skin of her thighs. And the climax. She had made Nick promise not to use that one. But she had a fascinated, impatient desire to see it when it was developed.

She realized suddenly that she didn't even know which of these race cars it was. She hadn't asked last night. She hadn't even noticed the number on it in the terrible excitement of the photographing. She began looking at the cars as she and Nick walked by, but they all looked alike, except for the colors. Now she couldn't even remember what color that car had been. Imagine that, she thought. Was it red? Do I remember it was red? That one, maybe? Close by, next to the inside wall, sat a bright red race car with the number 40 on its nose and its rear wing. No. Somehow it didn't seem in her memory to have been a red car like that.

The driver was getting into it. Oh. It was that big young blond one she liked, the one who reminded her of a lifeguard. Swede Savage. She watched him while Nick stopped nearby and took pictures. In his shimmering driving coveralls with vertical racing stripes down the left breast, Savage stepped into the narrow cockpit and lowered himself down into it like someone getting into a bathtub. Or— Suddenly, feeling a slight chill of fright, she thought: Wrapped in those garments, with his cloth hood over his head and covering his mouth, then his helmet donned over the hood, lying down in his driving cockpit, he reminds me of the mummy lying down in its sarcophagus in that horror movie I saw a few weeks ago.

"Honey, listen," Nick was saying to her. "I'm going to

be all over the place this afternoon, and I've got all this paraphernalia. Would you mind carrying this one film bag so I won't have to? It's, uh—" He winked at her. "It's our *Playboy* film."

"I'll guard it with my life," she laughed, thankful to Nick for interrupting her macabre thoughts.

"You'd better!" He draped the small, purselike leather bag on her shoulder. "Our future's in there, gorgeous."

"Our future's in the bag," she said. He grinned and kissed her on the nose.

Becky Alef finally saw Nick and the blond Princess. Through her binoculars she saw them arriving together and walking near Victory Lane. Becky was both satisfied and painfully crushed inside; she was seeing the ugly truth she had come to see but had hoped, underneath her sense of purpose, not to see. Nick's arm was around the girl's waist, and he was walking jauntily, smiling a big smile, obviously enjoying being seen in her company and on such familiar terms. You son of a bitch, she thought. You vain, pompous, horny, conceited, cruel, irresponsible, son-of-a-bitching Casanova, I wish you were dead. Oh, God, I mean it. I wish the son of a bitch was dead and rotting in his grave!

Becky had come to the track this morning, she thought, so well prepared emotionally to see this, but now she was seeing it and it was shaking her a thousand times as badly as she had expected it to. She had even brought her own Minolta with a telephoto lens, intending to take pictures of Nick and the blond girl together if she saw them, pictures she could give to her lawyer. Now she fumbled with the camera and tried to make the settings to photograph them over there on the other side of the track, but her hands were shaking violently and the little knobs and numbers were blurred by her tears. It was the first time she had ever actually seen him with another woman; always before in his affairs there had only been evidence: enough evidence, ill-concealed evidence, both actual physical evidence and the evidence in his demeanor, but only evidence. She sobbed and made little whining sounds of frustration in her throat and prayed that he would die; her eyes spilled tears faster than she could blink them away and her nose ran as she tried to adjust the camera. She had to stop now and then and look through the binoculars to see if they were still over there, and she could barely see them through the curtain of tears. She was feeling more and more upset and empty inside, and her thoughts kept ranging back to their little house on Twenty-fifth Street, and their dear, timid, melancholy Davey, who would have to go through all the hell of the divorce, and now Becky was in a horrible dilemma, not at all certain that she could really face the terrible complex unknowns of a divorce suit but quite certain that she could not stand to be married to Nick another day. She felt as if she might disintegrate all of a sudden.

She was standing in the walkway behind the retaining wall and fence on the outside of the track, a little way down from the upper end of the straightaway.

Finally she had the camera ready. She took a deep breath and bit herself inside the lip until she had regained a bit of control over herself. She dabbed the wetness out of her eyes with a Kleenex and, mentally forcing herself to be as hard in her heart as she could be, aimed across the track at them and began taking pictures. Nick looked as if he were getting ready to leave the girl. He was looking up and down the track and talking to her, apparently deciding where to station himself for the start of the race. Then he kissed her on the mouth, and Becky got a picture of that. Nick moved southward, then stopped and turned around and took a picture of the girl waving at him.

Then he blew a kiss to her and moved on down the track, and Becky lowered the camera and suddenly broke down into uncontrollable sobbing. "Can I help you, miss?" somebody said to her, somebody passing through the walkway near her.

She just shook her head and leaned against the fence with her face in her hands and cried.

Nick was feeling grand. He had all the pictures he needed of Diana, and they were magnificent pictures; he felt in his bones that he had done a beautiful job, despite the many difficulties, of capturing her face and body in the most erotic and aesthetic manner: the long, soft, taffy-colored hair, the graceful hands and delicate features that bespoke her privileged upbringing, the flawless golden body. And that moment of sensuous frenzy upon the race car! That was far beyond his expectations. He was sure it would appeal to everything *Playboy* stood for.

And he had had her. He had spent the whole night with this indescribably desirable young woman. Never had he been intimate with anyone so physically perfect, so fantastically seductive. Except— Well, Katherine, perhaps. And, back in the beginning, Becky.

He turned his mind quickly away from Becky. But as if she had read his mind, Diana suddenly turned to him and said, "Nick, what about your wife? We've never talked about—"

"Honey, listen," he interrupted her. "They're moving the cars out on the track. Looks like they're hurrying to get this started. I've got to get down the track a way. I'll meet you like we said, okay?" He took her in his arms and kissed her. "We'll talk later." He hurried away. He heard her call his name. He turned and saw her waving at him, with the great grandstands and curved track of the Indianapolis Motor Speedway behind her, this perfect, joyous beauty—it was too good a shot to miss, a spontaneously perfect addition to the hundreds of posed photographs he had been taking of her.

He aimed, photographed her, blew her a kiss, and turned and went on down the track.

Everything's perfect, he thought. That's done, and I'm as good as *in* with *Playboy;* and now the sun's shining and they're going to race, and I have a feeling it's going to be a great day for race pictures.

I can't lose on a day that started this way.

The Purdue University Marching Band had not returned today. A recording of the National Anthem was played over the public-address system. The people in the stands stood up for it.

Even Lloyd Skirvin and Billy Joe Marshall stood up for it. They stood there with their beer cans in their hands and waited while the music echoed among the stands. Thousands of people had started for the Speedway this afternoon when they heard on their radios that the race was going to be run, and they had created incredible traffic jams on the grounds again because there were so few Speedway guards to direct traffic. Outside the Speedway there was a din of honking horns and police whistles. People who had parked their cars outside the Speedway were stampeding through the streets, trying to get into the raceway before the race started. They were darting through the lanes of moving traffic, dragging their coolers and food baskets, chairs, blankets, and children. The city and state police officers on the traffic detail were waving their arms, grabbing people out of the way of cars, blowing their whistles, and yelling at the top of their lungs to try to bring the stampede of fans under control.

That was what it was like everywhere in the approaches to the Speedway. In the stands inside the grounds, people were swarming like ants into the seating areas. Some of them stopped in the aisles and stood waiting for the end of the National Anthem. Others just squirmed among them and went on. Billy Joe Marshall stood for the National Anthem because he always had done it and because one of his three brothers had been killed in Vietnam. Lloyd Skirvin had gotten in the habit of standing up for it at races for the sake of Billy Joe's brother, whom he had never met.

When the National Anthem was finished, the people cheered and remained standing. They were looking down at the pace car and the rows of race cars lined up behind it. The crewmen with their starter equipment were standing around all the race cars, and the pace car, just a little way down from Lloyd and Billy Joe, was surrounded by people with microphones and cameras. Over the loudspeaker, an announcer was telling the crowd who the people in the pace car were. Then he paused, and his voice rose to an excited pitch. "LADIES AND GENTLEMEN," he cried, "MR. TONY HULMAN!"

The crowd erupted in whistles, whoops, and clapping.

"GENNAMUN, START YOREN-JUNS!"

"YeeeeeeeeeeeeeeeeHAAAAA!"

"Yoweeeee!"

"Go! Go!"

"Lets go! Let's go! Let's GO!"

FrooooOOOOOOB-M! FROOOOOOOOOB-M! FRO-OOOOOB-m! ROWWB-m! RRROWB-m!

Once again, Nick Alef stood near the south end of the straightaway with his cameras ready, and listened to the roar of engines ripping open the air. They snarled and whooped deafeningly for a whole minute or more while echoes of the track announcer's excited voice reverberated through the arena. The knot of lensmen and broadcast reporters separated and hurried away from the pace car, and then the Cadillac began to move. It came toward Nick and swept by, accelerating smoothly, setting up a wave of intensified cheering along both sides of the track as it went. Its passengers stared through sunglasses, smiling at the crowd. Then the great, whooping, droning parade of race cars came by, flashing sunlight and heating the air. The crowd was on its feet, yelling, waving fists in the air. Nick got some panoramic color shots as the brilliant stream of vehicles poured through the first turn. He turned and looked far up the straightaway. There was one race car still sitting above the starting line, not started, and little figures were milling around it. Then suddenly it started moving and, whining up through its gear changes, tore past at high speed to catch up with the pack. Nick got a shot of it. Number 12, it was. That would be, let's see: Bobby Allison. Nick always got a laugh out of these back-of-the-pack episodes. Although the driver was virtually invisible, only his visored helmet showing, like an attachment to the whole machine, Nick could envision Allison's face set in happy determination as he sped after the fleet. Nick imagined that Allison must be feeling the same kind of fierce, hopeful joy he was feeling right now.

Okay! Okay, he thought. This is gonna be my day!

"The question's been asked so many times: why men

race. With the danger involved, delays involved, frustrations involved, and the money involved— And it's been said that man has a universal need to test himself, to prove he is a man. Some people seem to want to tamper with their destinies; others come to watch. There's a bond the spectator feels with the man on the track, and these men who race today have a rare combination of sacrifice, hope, triumph, and despair. But the climax of their ambitions is this pilgrimage to the object of their dreams: Indianapolis! And they're here now to try to make this dream come true a few hours from now. Former winners starting today: Bobby Unser, and Mark Donohue on the front row. Mario Andretti on the outside of the second row. Al Unser's in the middle of the third row. A. J. Foyt back in the eighth row. National Driving Champion Joe Leonard in the tenth row.

"And now they come, heading for the number one turn. Pick them up, MIKE AHERN!"

"Thank you, Sid, and I have a feeling here of déjà vu, somehow, like we've all seen this before—but never in the bright Indiana sunlight, at least this year, and it's a beautiful sight to behold! Right now, the pace car swings into turn one, and here they come: the brilliant orange car of Johnny Rutherford, that snow-white machine of Bobby Unser, and outside, Mark Donohue in the gold-and-blue car. They are through here in pretty good shape —Car seventy-three, David Hobbs, is smoking badly— Into turn two. Howdy Bell!"

"Thank you, Mike. We have them. A great deal windier up here on top of this VIP suite. The pace car going by—there's your front row. Swede Savage in the bright red, Gary Bettenhausen in the blue, and Andretti in the red-and-white! They're not lined up particularly well, as Dave Hobbs continues to smoke, and he's up high, out of the groove, smoking more profusely as he goes down the backstretch toward Doug Zink."

"Yes. Thank you, Howdy, we have them here on the backstretch, and we also note David Hobbs—the field is spread out quite a bit, at one point nearly half a lap separating the front car from the rear car. A strong west-to-east wind, left-to-right for the drivers— They're up to turn three now, and Ron Carrell!"

"All right, Doug. I have them. Now the pace picks up, for this our THIRD pace lap of the fifty-seventh running of the Indianapolis 'Five Hundred.' The fans are here. They're back on their feet, some rushing to their seats! David Hobbs's car still smoking very badly, as they enter turn four, and here's Jim Shelton!"

"All right, Ron, they're just past me now, the front row here; they're still spread out a good ways. I don't know whether we'll get a start or not, but we'll find out in just a moment! Here is our chief announcer, SID COLLINS!"

Everybody was standing up and craning as the pace car and then the stream of racers swung below the fourth-turn seats. Ella Rumple stood beside Ivy Yarbrough, watching, and under her excitement was sadly aware that Gerald was not here to hold her hand as the race started. The leading rows of cars howled by.

"Will they? Will they?" Ivy cried.

"Look!" Ella yelled, swept by the old, awesome excitement and forgetting Gerald. "THE GREEN FLAG! Go gettem, A.J.!"

"MARIO!" shrieked Ivy Yarbrough beside her. "BLOW THEM SONSA BITCHES INTA THA WEEDS!"

"The pace car now is moving to the narrow pit entrance! It comes off into the pits— Here they come, down the mainstretch, the world's fastest flying start— The green flag is waved! AND THE 1973 INDIANAPOLIS FIVE HUNDRED-MILE RACE IS ON! MIKE AHERN!"

"Yeah, Sid, and it's a replay of Monday up front! Bobby Unser pinches 'em off in the head, then it's Mark Donohue, and then it's Mario Andretti! Johnny Rutherford has dropped to fourth! Howdy Bell in turn two!"

During the pace lap, Lloyd and Billy Joe had stopped their rude gawking and watched. And when the chorus

of engines swung to the north end of the straightaway
and rose in pitch, they could not ignore its music. They
could hear the resonant drone of superior machinery, a
kind of machinery they could only dream about. This
was big stuff. Lloyd knew it. He would never say anything was big stuff, but he knew big stuff when he saw it
and felt it and heard it, and this was big stuff for sure.

Drunk though he was, Lloyd was aware of the suspense in the crowd. When he drove in the starts of races,
Lloyd didn't think about the people in the crowd; he
thought only of how his motor was going and the way the
car and track felt, of the driving techniques of the others
in the race and what he would have to do to cope with
them. The fans were something you thought about before you got out on the track and when you finished driving the race. The fans paid admission and built up the
winner's purse. The fans were impressed, excited people
among whom you could usually find a willing piece of
pussy. The fans sometimes were assholes who threw
stuff on the track. But unless they did that, you didn't
have to give them much thought at all during the race.

It had been a long time since Lloyd had sat among
spectators and watched a race. When he saw races in
which he was not driving, he was usually busy at something in the pits or fueling area, and it was therefore a
strange feeling, this experience of being among the
watching eyes.

Now as the drivers got the signal and released the
pent-up power of their cars in a sudden rush down the
straightaway, Lloyd felt a kind of collective wish in the air,
and he knew he was a part of the wishing just like
the rest of them in the crowd, and he knew that whenever he raced from now on, he probably would think of
the crowd, because now that he was in the crowd watching this, he knew what most of them were wishing. They
were wishing, and he was wishing, for something to happen that would at least scare the living shit out of them.
Lloyd remembered Monday. He remembered standing
by the fence watching the burning car come spinning
across the track, and the people screaming and getting
sick. He remembered how he himself had felt, and that
wild, terrific yell that had come out of him.

He remembered Monday, and as the cars came yowling past the place where it had happened Monday, he knew this crowd was going to be expecting a lot.

"Our leader is Bobby Unser. He's followed by Mark Donohue! Mario Andretti—Johnny Rutherford—Swede Savage! And to Doug Zink!"

"And it's Bobby Unser by about fifteen car-lengths on the backstretch, as they go by our post! Up to turn number three— Here's Ron Carrell!"

"All right, Doug, I have them— Bobby Unser still out in the lead! Mark Donohue's taken second— Mario Andretti moves into third place as they go to four, and Jim Shelton!"

"All right! The great acceleration of Bobby Unser— It's paying off. He must be five lengths ahead of Donohue! They're in the homestretch, and here again is Sid Collins!"

"Bobby Unser, the Olsonite Eagle, is way out in front in car number eight, Mike Donohue is second, and Mario Andretti is third! Pick it up, Mike!"

"Yes, Sid! Seven, eight, maybe nine car-lengths now! Unser going by, then Donohue— Then it's Andretti, then it's Rutherford—Swede Savage—into turn two, Howdy Bell!"

"All right, your leader still Unser, as we said, by several car-lengths—Donohue—Andretti—Rutherford—Swede Savage—Gary Bettenhausen, in that order, past Doug!"

"Mark Donohue—then Al Unser— They're up to turn number three. Here's Ron Carrell!"

"Nineteen sixty-eight Five Hundred-Mile winner Bobby Unser by us right now, and Mark Donohue's second, Andretti third— Jim Shelton!"

"Hey, Ron, it's still the same! Maybe a little bit more! With Bobby Unser—he is really accelerating! Sid, how do they look to you?"

Well, they got through the start safely, Ella thought. Now the fans were all sitting down, opening soft drinks, unwrapping food. Ella reached into the basket for a piece of chicken. The race cars were sweeping through the turns in single file now, with monotonous regularity. Everything was going smoothly. Ella felt that the cars were going unusually fast. Unser seemed to be scarcely out of sight through the distant first turn before he reappeared in the north straight.

"GO, MARIO!" the big woman shrieked in her incredible voice, which pulsated in the air like a pea whistle.

"Come on, A.J.!" yelled Ella.

A man sitting three seats over in the row ahead yawned. The yawn infected Ella, and she yawned. She hadn't slept well without Gerald. The cars whipped by, one by one, flashing sunlight. Ella bit into the chicken drumstick.

She chewed. And whenever A. J. Foyt's orange Coyote zoomed past, she raised her fist.

By sitting on the forward edge of the car seat, Kevin could just reach the accelerator and brake pedals of his mother's Mustang. It was tiring not being able to lean back, but he held himself up and forward with both hands high on the steering wheel, and he could see the road by peering through the upper arc of the steering wheel. He could just see over the dashboard.

Kevin was in a desperate hurry. It probably wouldn't be long, he knew, before his mother or father saw that her car was gone, and he was sure they would call the state police. And the race might have started by now, he thought. He relinquished his right hand's tight hold on the steering wheel to reach for the radio knob, and soon found a station that was carrying the race broadcast. Darn! The race was already going on! The announcers kept saying that Bobby Unser was leading. It all sounded very fast and unbearably exciting. Kevin didn't know exactly how to get to the track, but he remembered that there were some signs along the streets in Indianapolis with arrows pointing to the Speedway. If he could find one of those, he could keep watching for them and eventually would get there. So far, he had seen no state police. Kevin listened to them talking about the speed of Bobby Unser, and was afraid that if he didn't hurry up and get to the Speedway the race would be over. He stepped harder and harder on the gas pedal, stretching his leg to do so. He was doing about eighty miles an hour when he came to the freeway that he remembered had taken his family around Indianapolis and close to the Speedway on Monday. He was delighted. Maybe you don't really have to know the way, he thought. All you have to do is remember things when you see them.

Wow, he thought. Think of this! Many, many miles from home, driving a car for the first time in his life without his dad in the seat beside him. And he was going very fast and finding his way. He didn't allow himself to think of the trouble he was in at home. There would be time to think of that when the race was over.

Maybe it wouldn't even be a good idea to go home. He didn't know what he could do if he didn't go home, but maybe it was something to think about later. All he knew right now was that it was better to be driving a car fast and all alone and going to the Speedway with a ticket in his pocket than to be going to the police station with his dad.

He hated his dad now. His dad had sold his cycle. Kevin didn't feel he owed his dad anything after that.

"Oh-oh," somebody said near Nick Alef, and a murmur went up among the photographers. One of three cars coming down the straightaway was pouring white smoke. The lensmen swung their cameras after it. It was a dark-blue McLaren-Offy with the white number 12 on its side. "I think Allison's blown an engine already," someone said.

"Allison has pulled to the inside, against the wall, about halfway down the backstretch—uhm, he should be almost in front of Doug Zink!"

"Yes, he is, Howdy, right in front of us, and he's getting out of the cockpit of his car right now— Car number twelve, Bobby Allison, appears at this point to be out of the race! Ron Carrell!"

"All right, Doug, and that bright Indiana sunshine—just beautiful right now! Bobby's still leading, and four, Jim Shelton!"

"Well, it's still the same, only seems as though Bobby Unser's picking up a little bit in each lap— Down to you, Sid!"

"Bobby Unser, almost all by himself—Mark Donohue's second, Andretti is third—Savage is fourth—Rutherford's dropped back to fifth—pick it up after five, can you, Mike?"

"Yes, all right. There goes Savage, Rutherford—and number five, Bettenhausen, followed by Al Unser, Lloyd Ruby, number twenty, Gordon Johncock—Howdy Bell!"

"All right, we'll try to pick 'em up there. As you've pointed out, there is Al Unser, and there goes number twenty, of course, which is Johncock—they're up to Doug by now, they're moving so fast!"

"And the field is starting to string out now, as the tow truck comes over here for car number twelve, Bobby Allison—up to turn number three, and here's Ron Carrell!"

"Doug, I took a look at David Hobbs, car number seventy three, and it's running very smoothly as they go to four—Jim Shelton!"

"All right. They're already past me here! This is a fast race! Down to you, Sid!"

Listen to that, Gerald Rumple thought as he drove with Allan and Janet toward the funeral home north of Chicago listening to the car radio. The announcers can't even talk fast enough to keep up with them!

"We have the run down after one lap, and two and a half miles—

"WE HAVE A CRASH, or— Something's happened on turn four! Can you see it, Jim Shelton?"

Oh, my God, Gerald thought. That's where Ella is! A wreck already— In his mind's eye there flashed a picture of a race car bouncing and shedding parts, the fans jumping up to stare. Turn four— Oh, dear God! Ella— Suddenly Gerald realized he had begun to hate this spectacle. He hated it because it had proved more important to Ella even than coming here to be with her godchildren at Gene and Ruthie's funeral. He hated that awful pause in the announcer's voice that had followed the crash: he hated whatever it was in people that made them want to see this; he hated to think of the race driver's sudden loss of control and his sudden jolt of hurt, and he remembered with a flush of embarrassment the stupid thing he had done last night, driving over a hundred miles an hour on the interstate because of the thrill of it.

"Yes, I can see it—it was away from me; he hit the outside wall and then went across the track—veered away from all the other cars—or all the other cars were veering away from him—and he slightly smacked the inside wall! I'll try to put the glasses on him—try to find out who it is— Back to you in a moment, Sid!"

At least they weren't stopping the race; it couldn't be too bad a wreck, Gerald thought. And suddenly it occurred to him that he shouldn't be listening to a broadcast about a car wreck while driving with these children whose parents had been killed in a car wreck while returning from this race; all at once he was horrified at the thought of the kids hearing this. "Enough of that," he said, reaching over and twisting the knob. "Sickening!"

He hated to turn it off without hearing the details.

And even more, he hated hating to turn it off.

Becky Alef just about had herself back under control. She was only sniffling now and then, blowing her nose in a damp tissue. Her hands were shaking. There was a white-haired lady beside her, dressed in black with a pearl necklace, who kept patting her gently on the back and telling her in a reassuring voice that nothing could be that bad, whatever it was. Becky would nod, blinking, and wipe her nose, and say thank you, and the woman would pull her close with her arm around her shoulder and say everything was going to be all right. "Come over here to my seat and take it easy a little bit," the woman said. "I'm right over here. I've got a vacancy today. My Ollie couldn't get away from the office." The race cars kept screaming past, pulverizing the air with noise, accelerating out of the nearby fourth turn and down the long front straightaway, and the fans were whistling, clapping, whooping in strident voices. A constant crush of them kept going by, pressing Becky and the helpful lady against the wall. It was not a very good place in which to try to regain one's tenuous self-control. But Becky was trying. Turning slowly, gingerly, as if afraid any abrupt movement might spill her soul, she nodded and allowed the nice woman to start leading her toward her seats. When you can talk without crying, she thought, you'll have to remember to tell this woman how unusually nice she is. Remember to tell her how much she reminds you of your mother. Do what she says. Sit down with her for a little while.

There was a bang. Tires screeched. The crowd rose up gasping and shrieking. Becky was terrified. She screamed and fell apart.

After the cars had gotten off to a safe first lap, Nick Alef had started walking back north to take up a post at the upper end of the straightaway. It was a long walk. So far there was nothing going on in the pits as he walked past them. He walked along with his camera ready, shifting his attention between the people along the fence and the race cars that came whipping past one at a time or in twos and threes. Here on the straightaway they shot by so fast that it was almost impossible to identify them. "They're in one eye and out the other before you can turn your head," Nick had once heard a race fan say. He had liked that expression.

He felt really good. The sun was shining down on the enormous place. The Goodyear blimp droned low in the sky. People were thronging along the walkways, a pressing influx of people who had not thought there was going to be a race today and were trying to get to their seats before they missed too much.

And suddenly Nick saw something happening in the north end of the straightaway. There was a race car going across the path of other race cars. It disappeared toward the inner side of the track and didn't reappear. Oh, Christ, Nick thought, feeling a quick surge of helplessness, knowing it was too far ahead for him to reach in time for good photos. The shriek of the crowd came to him, and he saw the people in the stands rising to their feet in a sort of tide of awareness. He had noticed that sometimes the fans would rise from their seats even before they knew where to look; they would rise up simply because the rest of the crowd was rising and they knew they might see something.

No smoke or fire came from the place where the car had disappeared, and the other race cars were still accelerating by him, still coming through that fourth turn, where it had happened. That meant to his practiced eye that it wasn't a bad wreck. No red flag yet; no, not even a yellow. Just a spinout, apparently. That was good. Nick didn't want any spectacular stuff happening up in that corner until he got there.

It was all so warm and soft and safe. Captain George was awake now and not trying to sleep, so the dreams were all far away out of his mind, and he was all right. His eyes were closed, and the woman's lips were now and then kissing his eyelids as he had been wanting them to. Everywhere, it seemed, her body was touching his body, and he wasn't alone. He knew—the main thing he knew was that he was at last not alone. And he was not crying now at the touch of her skin. He had almost cried a few minutes ago when he had heard the "Star-Spangled Banner" playing outside the building faintly in the distance. But he hadn't cried then, and he didn't feel he was going to cry now. She was the one who was crying now. She was crying silently; he felt the wetness of tears when she pressed her temple against his. He didn't know what she was crying about, but it seemed that it was right for her to be crying. She seemed to be happy enough, and very still, sometimes moving gently so that all the soft skin of the front of her body moved over his skin. But he did not have desire; there was no tingling of want in him yet, and he didn't know whether there would be. He just hoped she would not start trying to get him to do it because that might upset it all—all this calm and goodness that had happened to them after so long a night, after so long a time. She was kissing him so gently: his neck, his cheek, his forehead, his eyelids, his shoulders. They were enveloped in each other, hearing each other breathe, sometimes feeling each other's pulse. Outside now he could hear big motors roaring, coming close and then going farther away, but they were outside this luxurious togetherness and didn't matter. Captain George was hanging right on the edge of being okay, and he was closer to being happy than he had been for as long as he could remember.

And then suddenly the woman moved. She sat up. It scared him; his heart leaped. He opened his eyes to see what was happening.

The woman was sitting up in the bed. She had a look of total astonishment on her face. Her head was bent curiously to the side, and she was holding one hand up before her eyes and staring at it in disbelief. Then she pointed at it with the forefinger of her other hand and looked slowly around the room. As if addressing an audience, she said, "What th' hell's going on here? I was kissing my own hand!"

And then Captain George understood it, and she understood it, and understanding it together they both realized how absurd it was, how wonderfully, unbearably good; and they sat there naked like children, looking at each other, and they started laughing.

They caused each other's laughter to go on and on. One would sink weakly into the end of a spasm of laughter, and the other's gasping wheezes would make it funnier all over again. Carl George laughed as he had never laughed in his life. He laughed until the muscles of his stomach ached. Her laughter would come in small hiccups as she inhaled, and in raucous bursts as she laughed out.

It went on and on. They were red-faced, gasping,

flopping weakly about on the bed, slapping each other
on the shoulders, pressing each other's heads to their
quaking bosoms. And it just kept getting funnier. "I—I
was kissing my own goddamn hand!" she would wheeze.
"I was so—you know— Hell, I don't know!" And then
she would go helpless and speechless again with the
laughing. She got up out of the bed once and staggered
around the room with a dumbfounded look on her face,
imploring of her imaginary audience, "Can anybody
tell me what the fuck's going on here? I ask you, what
am I doing kissing my own hand?" And then she came
back to the bed and flung herself upon it, laughing.

Carl George was out of his head with hilarity. A great
crust of reserve and bitterness and fear was crumbling
away from his soul, and the delight of life was blowing
through the new openness of his spirit. All the terrible
things were falling away: the bad dreams, the painful
images in his mind—all were being flushed out by this
strenuous, blinding hysteria.

And eventually it subsided. They both had endured
more laughter than either ever had before. They were
spent. They now lay sprawled upon the bed, her cheek
resting upon his stomach, her eyes looking past his feet
toward the door. She dabbed at her running nose with a
Kleenex and once in a while squeezed her eyelids shut to
press out the tears. His abdomen now and then quaked
with feeble twitches of laughter. Unconsciously, she began stroking the reddish-brown hair at the root of his
penis, curling it around her index finger, looking at it
without really seeing it. And he felt the stirring of desire
now, the tumescence starting.

"You know what it was?" she said at last, in a small
voice, an awestruck voice. "It was just that I didn't know
where you ended and I began."

Werner Dold considered himself a realist. Being that,
he had been able to live with the possibility that his wife
might make him a cuckold. It was part of the price a rich
old man paid for a glamorous young wife. But she was
his. Her heart belonged to Daddy, she would say. Daddy
and his wealth and power and all the good things he

could provide. Anybody else would be good only for the physical release Werner himself was too busy and too old and too dignified to give her in the proportions she needed. He knew she adored him, and that part of him was his wealth and power, and that her soul was his. He and she knew things that no temporary lovers could know.

But now Werner stood near the wall that separated her suite from his and listened to the gale of hilarity that was going on in there, the man's laughter and Kitty's, and it was tormenting him. Now, he could tell, she was sharing something with that Air Force man, something beyond anything she had ever shared with him.

Werner vacillated. He wanted to go to her door and intrude, to stop it, to drive the Air Force officer out.

Then he didn't want to do it. It was beneath him. He was one of the richest men in the United States, and it would be sordid to intrude on a scene like that in there. Furthermore, an intrusion like that could erupt into violence, and violence could mean getting hurt, could mean arrests, could mean lawsuits, could mean scandal.

Werner resented having to think of all this. It took his mind away from his purpose in being here. It made it hard for him to decide what to do about Tony Hulman and this racetrack. He would have to decide what he might need to do about her in the future. If she really was deep with this Air Force hero, if she really cared about him more than she cared about Werner, there would be no advantage in having her as Mrs. Werner Dold.

But divorce could be a catastrophe. When someone is divorced from a billionaire, the press becomes very interested. It would become public knowledge that she had cuckolded him, and people in the press would recall those ridiculous movies in which she had gone around naked. Werner was beginning to feel that perhaps Kitty had not been a very wise acquisition. He had acquired her because he had let himself be persuaded by his desires instead of his head. For him, that had been a rare mistake.

And it looked as if it might have been a mistake that would prove to be very troublesome.

We'll see, he thought. We'll just have to wait and see. Just because they're laughing—that doesn't prove anything.

But the laughter filtering through from the other room was a kind of laughter he had never enjoyed. It was an unknown to him. And he was afraid of things he didn't know.

When Nick got to the place where he had seen the race car crash, an ambulance was just leaving. Peter Revson was sitting up in it with some attendants. The car was being slung onto the hoist of a wrecker. The wrecker's winch went into operation, lifting the whole bent race car off the ground to put it out of harm's way on the other side of the retaining wall. There were several photographers taking pictures of the operation. Suddenly something gave way and the car dropped with a grinding thump onto the wall, bending it up still more. Nick got a shot of that while the crewmen cursed. In the background, other race cars were wailing by, blurred by speed. That would be a good contrast, he thought. The dead car in the foreground, the whiz in the background. Power and junk.

He wrote in his notebook, then put it in his pocket. Wonder whether I ought to stay here now, he thought, or go see if I can find Diana. There wouldn't likely be anything else happening here. For a while, anyway. Lightning doesn't strike twice in the same place. Should go see her for a bit. He thought of her face and her body and their rolls and rolls of film. Accounts receivable, he thought, smiling to himself.

Then he remembered again Pollard's fatal crash, which he had missed by talking to a girl.

No, he decided. Stay here.

The air was feeling suddenly damp. Ella Rumple looked up. The blue sky was hazing over a little, and gray clouds were starting to creep overhead.

Suddenly Ella was jolted by a blow on her shoulder. Ivy Yarbrough had punched her with her fist. "Hey," Ivy yelled. "What's happening with Mario?" She was violently shaking a pointing finger toward the pits.

Gosh, how rude, Ella thought. But she raised the glasses and swept down the pits until she saw Andretti's red-and-white Parnelli-Offy parked in its pit with crewmen crawling all over it. She saw the driver hoist himself up and step out of the cockpit, his helmet still on.

"He's getting out," she said. "Looks like he's out of the race."

"SHIT!" the big woman yelled, hurling a half-empty Coke can to the ground. The brown liquid spewed from the can and spattered the clothing of people nearby. Ella was shocked. She would cry out in excitement or disappointment at a race. But she tried to be ladylike about it.

"Oh, well, what th' hell," the woman bawled, her big, gap-toothed grin suddenly showing. "Come on, A.J.!"

"YAY!" Ella cried, heaving up and down in glee. Ivy might be crude, but now she was a new ally, a new addition to Ella's cheering section. "Yay, A.J.!"

Gerald, she thought. Oh, you're missing a good race.

Harry Kuntz saw Diana sitting with two other Festival Princesses on a bench in front of the Tower. Harry didn't feel very good. He was hyperventilating and making continual clearing noises in his throat as he always did when matters were tense. Straightening his tie, adjusting his shirt collar with a couple of sideward juts of his chin, he went to where she sat.

"Diana."

The Princesses looked up. "Oh, hi!" "Hi, Mr. Kuntz," the two of them said.

Diana looked up, and annoyance flickered over her face. "Hi."

"I need to talk to you, Diana."

"Okay, what?"

"Uhm, would you excuse us, girls?"

"All right," Diana said when they had moved off. "What is it, Harry?"

"Where were you last night, Diana?"

"Harry, haven't I made it clear to you yet that where I go and what I do are my business and not yours? I know you're having a hard time comprehending it, but I don't *belong* to you—"

"I understand all that. You've made perfectly clear to me what you want and don't want, Diana. But this time I'm afraid it really *is* my business."

"What do you mean?"

Harry sighed. He looked around nervously, sitting far forward on the edge of the bench, leaning with his elbows on his knees, pulling the fingers of his left hand nervously with his right. "Uhm, well, something bad has happened, Diana. You've made something bad happen —happen to me—and you'll just have to straighten it out for me."

"What do you mean, 'something bad'?"

"I mean your parents think you were out all night with me."

"What?" She stared at him, looking indignant yet amused.

"That's what I said. They couldn't find you last night. You never called home. You stayed out all night, and they think you stayed with me."

"I don't believe this. This is ridiculous. All they had to do was call your house—"

"They did, Diana." He bit his lips tightly together and nodded his head up and down in short, quick nods. "They did. And I wasn't there. And so of course they jumped to a conclusion, and they caused my wife to jump to that same conclusion. And now I'm in quite a bit of a bind with your parents and my wife until you tell them where you were. I, uhm, I know where you were— with whom—but I didn't tell them. I'm counting on you to do the honorable thing and vindicate me, Diana."

She laughed. "Sure, Harry. I'd be more than happy to tell the world that I didn't stay all night with you!"

"All right, you don't have to—twist the knife. This is not a laughing matter, Diana!" Sullen, pouting, he watched, without seeing, a race car roll thrumming down the pit lane and stop. Its crew had swarmed all over it in an instant. "You were with that photographer all night."

"I won't discuss that with you, I told you." She held Nick's film bag close to her hip on the bench and ran her hand over it thinking about the rolls and rolls of undeveloped film inside with her image sensitized upon them. "But you can relax. I'll tell them we weren't together. Gladly."

"The problem is, I've already told them we weren't, and they didn't believe me, I'm sure. They probably wouldn't believe you, either—I mean, they'd just think we were both denying it—unless you told them where you really were. With that photographer—"

"Just a minute. Just a minute, Harry. If you weren't at home, where were you?" She gave him a sly, sidelong glance, grinning.

His face flamed. "That's—that's none of your business."

"Ahaaaaa! The old fox! Come on, Harry! Tell li'l Diana. Has ums been a baaad boy? Did ums go out aw night and do a dirty fing?"

"Now you stop that, Diana."

"Tum on, now, Harry, tell ol' Auntie Diana what ums did aw night! You tell me what you did, and I might—" He was squirming, and she loved it. Who knows where this pompous prig was all night, she thought. Probably out getting walked on by high heels or whipped— Wait till you see my pictures, she thought. Just wait till you—

The race car that had gone into the pits roared out again, winding up. Another car came in. And another. They rolled to abrupt stops in their respective pit spaces and were met by their agile crewmen. Other race cars, at intervals of three or four seconds, shot by like bright-colored bullets, sucking their shock waves of noise after them into the distance.

But suddenly Diana felt, as she looked at Harry's pathetic discomfiture, the weight of her parents' concern, the whole long interweaving of Harry's life with her family's life, her father's job; she remembered their awful, unreasoning anxiety when they thought she was pregnant. And she saw Mrs. Kuntz's ethereal, aristocratic face, her skin that was so thin, both figuratively and literally, her expression of perplexity that always looked like constipation, and she imagined her struggling with that same absurd, yet understandable, surmise—

"Harry, I'm sorry. I'll help you if I can. We can think of something that'll satisfy everybody. Tell me, and I won't tell anybody. Where were you last night?"

The little composure he still had seemed to dissolve under the unexpected kindness in her voice. He dropped his head far down and began intertwining his fingers rapidly. "Diana, I—" He shut his mouth and licked his lips. "You may never want to talk to me again."

"Come on, Harry. We're friends."

"Well— Last night I waited around—looking for you. Late. Finally I saw you and—and that photographer come out of the garage area. You looked all upset. I followed you to your car. I—I lost you then. But I heard him talking about the Hilton. I drove downtown and checked. I found the car in the Hilton's garage. So I knew you were there. I got your room number. But then I didn't—I didn't know what I could do— I started a million times to use the house phone, but what could I have said? I— Oh, Diana, forgive me! It was the worst night I ever spent— My imagination— My anger— Can you ever forgive—"

"Good grief," she muttered, looking at his dejected, slumping profile. She was angry, scared, touched, by turns. "You mean you were there—"

"I stayed almost all night in the lobby," he said. "It was terrible. Finally the house detective began looking at me, so I walked over to the Columbia Club and sat till dawn in their lobby. And I'm—I'm not even a Republican!"

She stared at this defeated man, this pompous ass sitting here with his whole soul suddenly hanging out, so pitiful with his tale of an all-night vigil—and "not even a Republican"! She couldn't believe she had heard that. She swallowed a laugh, then was flooded by a wave of pity. "Oh, Harry. You're incredible. You're absolutely weird! Why in the— Why would—"

Another race car zoomed into the pits, and one thundered out. The blimp prowled overhead. The track announcer's reverberating voice was swallowed again and again by the howl of passing race cars. The air rushed with the collective voice of the thousands of race fans in the stands. In the midst of all this sat Harry Kuntz—sleek, rich, proper Harry Kuntz—his jowly face sagging with his private agony.

"I don't know," he mumbled. I guess I—" His words were lost in the whine of another passing race car.

"You what?"

"I said I—" Again his voice was swept under a racing motor.

Diana glanced annoyed at the racetrack. "I still didn't hear you."

"I said I think I love you."

Captain Carl George surfaced from intense, delirious pleasure. An awareness of limbs, of humid perfume, of sweaty skin on sweaty skin, formed around him. Drone of engines. Her voice, making small *m*'s. The terrain of crumpled bed linen coalescing before his eyes like a photograph in developer. His loins flexing slowly; slick, hot membranes; a wonderful flood of ease throughout his nerves. Her temple pressed against his.

He raised himself on his elbows and looked at her face. She opened her eyes. She smiled.

"Hi," she said.

He smiled. "Hi. It's good to see you again."

"Mhm. Where've you been?"

"Same place you've been, I hope. Out of this world."

"Mhm. That's where I was, too."

He laughed. "What a coincidence."

Lloyd and Billy Joe were building a nice stack of empty beer cans on a vacant seat next to them. They were really putting the stuff away. The stack of cans swayed lightly in the wind. The sky was growing dark.

Lloyd had lost interest in the race. After the start it seemed to him that on that smooth track, all strung out like that, those guys were just driving around. The things didn't really even look much like cars. Once Lloyd had spent a few days with an uncle in Charlotte who had a slot-car racing track in his basement. The little toy slot cars had zipped around and around the track, and they had looked to Lloyd just like these. Lloyd's uncle would lean over the table, his body all tensed up, a silly expression on his face, operating the little hand-control box, looking down on the oval toy track, getting more and more excited, feeding the little toy car more and more zip, until it would finally fly out of a corner of the track and have to be picked up off the basement floor. Lloyd had lost interest in the slot-car track and any respect for his uncle after just a few minutes of that. Racing wasn't worth a damn to Lloyd unless you were in the seat, surrounded by the heat and the noise and vibrations, keeping the car right on the very outer edge of control. To sit up here in the benches with all these stuffy Yankee town folk wasn't much better than watching his idiot uncle play with his toys. What Lloyd was really interested in was that girl's tit in the yellow sweater. He just couldn't keep his eyes off of it. Whenever she turned to talk to her boyfriend, there in the corner of her eye she saw that crude, filthy, mean-looking man with his pale eyes popping out, licking his lips salaciously and staring at her.

To Billy Joe, it had been funny at first, Lloyd acting goofy about that tit. But it was getting old now. Billy Joe liked to look at these cars, and he especially liked to listen to them. When a car accelerated out of the pits a few yards down in front of him, Billy Joe could see all that beautiful machinery behind the cockpit, and already he was able to recognize the different engines by their tones as they went by. Billy Joe kept thinking how good it would be to work on those fine big V-8 engines, which he probably could do right off, or the Offys, which he could probably get doped out real quick if he ever had a chance to work on one. He was damn well interested in this race, and he wished Lloyd would stop acting a fool. Suddenly he got up.

"Where y'goin', Stud Boar?" Lloyd asked.

"T' piss," he said.

"Okay. You go 'head. I'll keep a eye on this tit heah," he said loudly. "Then you come back and watch it while I take a piss." The girl in the yellow sweater flashed a fierce glance at her boyfriend, who was pretending he hadn't heard it. The boyfriend nibbled inside his lips and twisted his hands together between his legs, and with feigned intentness and quick side-to-side head movements pretended to be watching the race cars shoot down the straightaway.

As Billy Joe got up to leave, he knocked over the stack of beer cans, which clattered and rolled in all directions under the seats. That got a braying laugh out of Lloyd.

"Jesus," a man's voice said within earshot behind him, "why don't some people stay in the Snake Pit where they belong?" Lloyd turned quickly, a killer's grin on his face, and searched for the source of the voice. All eyes were on the racetrack, except those of two or three women who, apparently feeling safe in their femininity, were looking straight at him with loathing. He stared and winked at them until they, too, turned their gazes back to the track. Lloyd turned to the front again. He watched Billy Joe go down the steps.

"Hunh," he muttered, just loud enough to be heard by the girl and her boyfriend. "Nobody wants t' git hurt. Jus' bad-mouth ahind your back. Goddamn gutless, yeller town Yankees. Yeah, tha's all, buncha damn yeller lilies. Y'know, only thing good 'bout yeller is it do look good on a tit. Hee-hee! Yeah, boy, I tell y'bout these Yankees. Sshyoooeee! See, trouble is they got no balls. *Bawls.* Fancy-ass town Yankees, they ain' got no *bawls.* 'Fraid they git hurt. Er git they hands dirty er some awful catasterfy like that, y'heah? But man, they sure grow some good tits up heah in Yankeeland, I ain't a-shittin' you one bit, nosireeebob, they 'shore do grow some good"— He paused, leaned almost down to the girl's shoulder to look at her breast, then glanced over at her boyfriend's flushed neck and profile—"tits! Up heah in Yankeeland, y'see, they grow these heah REAL FINE tits, but they don't grow no *bawls.* Now, folks, I'm here t' tell y' it takes some *bawls* t' drive a ol' stock car 'round a dirt course like us good ol' boys does down home, an' y'might git a little dust in y'r eyes jus' a-watchin' us do it, but up heah, well, I guess up heah where all th' money is, I guess it's jus' *tit* country up heah."

Suddenly the girl's boyfriend leaped to his feet and whirled around. He stood looking down at Lloyd, his eyes large with fear and anger. He was big. Lloyd sized him up with an insolent smile. He saw that this Yankee outweighed him maybe thirty pounds. And he had some kind of athlete insignia on the front of his coat. But that didn't worry Lloyd. Anybody who would have sat there that long eatin' shit like this Yankee had done didn't have guts. "Better turn 'round, college boy," Lloyd said. "Gonna miss y'r little race."

"I want—I want you to stop talking the way you are. I—"

"Why, boy, how's that that I'm a-talkin'? I mean, a man can talk, cain't he? I mean, we got free speech in this county, ain't we? Well, we do where I'm from. Don't know 'bout up here in Yankeeland." Lloyd looked all around. Everybody was watching; they all turned their eyes away quickly.

"Look," said the big youth. "Won't you just quit making remarks? We try to be civilized up here. We just came to watch a race and have fun—" The youth's voice fell away. It was obviously a strain for him to talk this much, afraid as he was, and with all these people watching him. People were shrinking in their seats, drawing inches away from this center of tension, but watching it with keen interest. A larger and larger circle of fans was becoming aware of an impending something here, and were turning away from the monotonous passage of race cars on the straightaway to look at this tense focal point where the clean-cut, nice-looking youth was trying his courage and his honor in the face of a lean, dirty, little yellow-haired man who wouldn't even bother to stand up for the confrontation. Some of them looked furtively at Lloyd's eyes, and they saw something very sinister, very dangerous there, something like the stare of a coiled viper.

"Well, now, boy," Lloyd said, stealthily gathering his legs under him and rising, "I reckon I'm 'bout as civilized as you are, ain't I? I mean, you wouldn't be tellin' me that, uh, that you civilized and I ain't? Oh, why, that would jus' hurt my ol' pa somethin' awful t' heah that, he tried so hard t' bring me up good. Y'wouldn' want t' hurt my ol' pa, would you?" His voice now was both an imploring whine and a final menace. It was obvious he meant for the youth to drop his eyes, turn around, sit down, and continue to suffer the remarks. The youth stood his ground, though his girl friend, now that he had made a stand for her, was beginning to fear for him. "Now I ask you nice Yankee folks," Lloyd said more loudly, turning to the people who were watching, "is this a free-speech country? Is this college boy heah more civilized than me?" He fastened his challenging gaze on the eyes of a fashionably dressed young sport fan sitting very close by. "You," he said. "Am I civilized?" He burped some beer. "I'm just as good as him, ain't I?" The flags along the top of the Terrace fluttered. A knot of race cars yowled down the straight. The track announcer's voice was reading numbers over the address system. The spectator dropped his eyes and muttered something. "What was it agin? Talk up," Lloyd said.

"I said yes."

"Yes what?"

"Yes, you're civilized."

"Yew fuckin'-aye-John I'm civilized, yew lily-livered, fancy-pants, ass-lickin', little Yankee suck-egg dawg." Lloyd turned sneering back to the big youth. "Yew heard that, din' yew, college boy? I'm as civilized as yew." Lloyd was burning with a fierce fighting pride now. He was sure now that he alone could outface everybody above the Mason-Dixon line. In his mind's eye he saw the souvenir license plate his pa had had on the front bumper of his Chevy. It was always encrusted with dead bugs, but there always showed through a proud Confederate flag and the legend:

HELL, NO! WE AIN'T FERGITTIN'!

But the Yankee college boy was still standing there, and there wasn't as much fear in his eyes as there had been. Lloyd realized that the boy was getting brave as the seconds went by, maybe getting the impression that Lloyd was a bluffer. Well, Lloyd thought. We'll see about that. Suddenly he jumped an inch off the concrete and stamped his feet and simultaneously yelled, "HYAW!" The big college boy flinched and almost fell backward. Somebody laughed. That was too much. Now looking ready to cry, his nostrils distended, tears in his eyes, his lower lip crumpled and downturned, and his even white teeth set on edge, he threw away his caution and lunged with upraised arms at Lloyd. Lloyd snapped his hard left fist out in a quick jab that broke some of the perfect teeth, split his lip, and stopped him cold. The girl and several spectators squealed and gasped. Stunned, blinking, the youth put his hand to his mouth, drew it away, and saw the blood; he moved his tongue and with it pushed bloodied pieces of enamel out and spat them into his palm; he seemed to have forgotten everything but this sudden unjust destruction of his good smile. His tanned face went white, and he stood staring in disbelief at the little pool of bloody spit and teeth in his palm. Lloyd waited with a mocking, quizzical look, his head cocked a little to the side, his left fist, laid open to the knuckles and oozing blood, held clenched and steady in front of his breastbone. He wouldn't let it quiver, even though it hurt like bejeezus. His right fist was cocked and ready, down by his right thigh. The girl tried to get around to look at her boyfriend's bloody face, then turned away wailing and covering her eyes when she saw it. In these motionless seconds, people were standing up, drawing back out of arm's reach but staying close enough to stare at the dirty, bloodied fist and the young man's pathetic and gory spitting. The spectators' eyes were squinted up, their faces white, their mouths hanging open in fascination; some of them were running their tongues over their own teeth as they stared. People in back stood on their benches and crowded to peer over shoulders at the cut fist and smashed mouth, which for the moment seemed to be the focal point of all existence. Elsewhere in the sprawling arena there were tens of thousands of people who were not even aware of this quick instant of bloody shock, and they just watched race cars whip by. But all who saw this had, for the moment, forgotten the race.

Then the young man with the bloody mouth evidently decided that vengeance would be worth any other disfigurement; his pained look vanished, his eyes flashed, and he threw a long, sweeping right-handed punch. Lloyd, his head seething with booziness, thinking he had won the Civil War once and for all, didn't move fast enough to avoid it, and the clout beside his left eye sent him sprawling across the bench. His feet sent beer cans skittering, and his arm bones and hipbone painfully whacked against the hard seats as he fell. But he was scrambling to get up even before he was all the way down. He had learned in tavern fights not to pause even an instant to appraise his hurts because somebody could gain on you in a pause. As he lifted himself out from between the seats, he saw the big youth climbing over the bench to get at him. The air was full of squeals, and men were yelling, "Get him, get him!" But before he had regained his stand, the youth swung another reaching right that caught him on the side of the chest and again sent him thumping down between the hard seats. As he tried to lift himself out, he felt a stabbing pain in his side. He had had a rib broken in a race once, and it felt like that. But again he came up fighting. The big youth charged at him again, eyes fierce, lower face red, bared broken teeth white in their bloody mass of lips and gums. Lloyd was sucking air, and every breath stabbed him sharply in the side. He kicked at the young man's crotch, but the youth caught his ankle and twisted it. There was a jolting pain in his hip, and he went down again on the concrete, this time on his right side, trapped again between the unyielding benches. This sumbitch wants to kill me, Lloyd thought. Billy Joe, where the fuck you at? In the rare times that Lloyd ever got this bad off, Billy Joe had always jumped in. But Billy Joe wasn't here. And now the big college boy had hold of Lloyd's legs and was dragging him between the benches. Lloyd felt his pants giving way at the waist. His shirttail had been dragged up. The concrete and beer cans scraped the skin of his back, and he couldn't get a purchase on anything to stop this. Suddenly his pants were down around his thighs, and his dirty gray underwear was showing, and people were laughing and yelling, "Get 'im! Get that crummy hillbilly son of a bitch out of here! Good boy, man!" Laughing faces loomed all around, looking.

Lloyd was dragged, lurching and cursing, out into the wide aisle. His shorts were torn, and his backside was scraping on the concrete. But he was out from between the seats now, and that had been the big boy's mistake. Now Lloyd had space where he could move. Spraddling, wriggling like a dying snake, he got his feet out of the young man's grasp. Gritting his teeth so he could bear to make all his hurting parts move, he somehow slithered around and under him and into the recoiling crowd on the other side of the aisle. Hauling up his pants, ducking behind yelling people, he kept getting distance between himself and the enraged young man with the bloody mouth. There was an elderly man nearby, standing as if paralyzed, holding a furled black umbrella with a long

steel tip. Lloyd snatched it from him. Then, clutching the
waistband of his pants with his left hand, pointing
the shiny tip of the umbrella at the eyes of his advancing
enemy with his right, he retreated down the aisle steps.
The young man followed a few steps, the people in the
crowd exclaiming in fright and astonishment, then his girl
friend in the yellow sweater darted out and held him by
the arm to keep him from getting too close. Lloyd's breath
rasped in and out as he edged down to the walkway at
the bottom of the steps. When he reached the bottom he
threw the umbrella up the steps and yelled at the top of
his lungs:

"YANKEE COCKSUCKER!"

But a race car went by and nobody heard him.

"eeeeeeeEEEEEEEYOWWWOOOOoooooooooooooooo-
ooom! WIBC—Ten-Seven-Oh in Indianapolis—"

*"Back in the Master Control Tower once again, this is
Sid Collins at Indianapolis, Indiana. After two frustrating
days we're making up for it today with a tremendous automobile race—with Gordon Johncock, Swede Savage,
and Al Unser, Mark Donohue, all in contention right now,
Bill Vukovich, and the positions changing all the time, due
to pit stops. And there are some cars out of the race. So
we have an opportunity here, I think, John DeCamp, we'll
call you in, and let you give a rundown of those cars out
of the race."*

*"Sid, just before I give you that, the leader, number
twenty, Gordon Johncock, turned the last two laps, the fif-
tieth lap at one-eighty-one-point-four and the fifty-first lap
at one-eighty-two-point-nine. So Gordon Johncock is going
along at a little bit faster pace than I was getting Bobby
Unser at in the mid-twenties in the laps. These are
the cars that are out of the race, so far: car fifteen,
Peter Revson, spun out in the fourth turn, hit the wall
lightly; car twenty-eight, Bob Harkey, went out with engine problems; car fourteen, A. J. Foyt, went out with
engine problems; car number nine, Sam Sessions, likewise;
the black flag, by the way, was just waved at one of those
cars that went by in a group of three, and we'll see who
comes in this next time for consultation. Other cars out of*

the race include car number eleven, Mario Andretti; car number twelve, Bobby Allison; and car number eighteen, Lloyd Ruby."

Kevin Cole was lost. Somehow he had been unable to find the biggest thing in Indianapolis: the Speedway traffic jam.

He kept driving his mother's car down streets that came to dead ends. He hated that. He hated it because a dead end meant a delay, and a delay meant he was missing more of the race. A dead end also made it necessary to back the car up, and he wasn't very good at that. He wasn't too bad at going forward, but he couldn't seem to back a car up very straight. He couldn't see to back up. He was too little. It infuriated him. He had had to back up several times, and in doing so he had heard the wheel grind against curbs, he had bumped a street sign, and he had backed into somebody's yard.

Now, furious and impatient, he backed out of a dead end street, went forward on another terribly bumpy street among ugly houses with scary black people sitting on their front porches, and then turned right on a wide street. He made right turns whenever he could because left turns required looking both ways and then starting at just the right time without killing the motor. Right turns were easier, and he did understand that if you made enough right turns you could end up going the same way as if you had made one left turn. Anyway, he thought, why risk making a left turn when you don't know where you're going, anyway?

A red light came on suddenly in front of him and he had to step on the brake very quickly, and it killed the motor. While he was making sure he had everything set right to start the motor again, a voice said, "Hey! Where you goin'?"

He looked up. There was a girl standing by the right car window. She was a little older than he was. Not quite so old as Pam. She was dirty. Very dirty. Her yellow hair was stringy. There was another girl standing behind her. That girl had brownish hair, and it was frizzy.

Kevin turned the ignition switch and gave the car a little

gas, and the motor raced. "I'm going to the Speedway," he said. "But I can't find it."

"We know where it is," said the yellow-haired girl. "We need a ride there. How about a lift?"

Kevin hesitated a moment. These girls looked terrible. But he sure wanted to get to that Speedway. "Get in, then," he said. The yellow-haired girl smiled and opened the door and sat beside him, and the other one got in beside her and pulled the door shut. They smelled awful.

"Turn left here," the yellow-haired girl said.

"I'd rather turn right," Kevin said.

The girl looked at him the way Pammy looked at him sometimes when she thought he had said something unbelievably dumb.

"Okay, okay! I'll turn left." He did it. He made a lurching, exciting left turn that caused several cars to put on their brakes nearby. The girls giggled. They acted silly, the way a girl had done in class one day at school before they took her to the principal's office.

"I'm Renee," said the yellow-haired girl. "This is Puggles."

"I'm Kevin."

"You're kinda little to be drivin', ain't you?"

"Oh, I don' know—"

"Oh, oh!"

The girls were looking back. Kevin heard a motor that sounded like a big motorcycle. Then a siren gave one whoop and died down.

"Oh, Jesus," said the girl called Puggles.

"Oh, shit," said the girl called Renee.

And Kevin just started crying.

Lloyd Skirvin wandered for a few minutes along the walkway, hugging his hurt rib, glaring wild-eyed at anybody who looked at him, yelling for Billy Joe Marshall. He was mad at Billy Joe for not being there when he needed him. But he really wanted to see Billy Joe, and he wouldn't give him any hell when he saw him because he just needed him now. He needed him because he hurt and he had been whipped and run off by a Yankee, and all his beer was still up there and he couldn't go back and get it, and he was just plain down and out and needed his friend.

"BILLY JOE!"

The skies were cloudy. The race cars kept going by and drowning out his voice, and coming into the pits and going out of the pits. There were so many people along the fence watching the work in the pits that it was hard for Lloyd to make his way along, feeling the way he did.

"BILLY JOE!" Shit, he thought. It hurt to yell, and he knew Billy Joe wouldn't hear him, anyway. Where th' fuck is he at, Lloyd wondered. That's a goddamn long piss. That sumbitch is doin' somethin' 'sides takin' a piss. Lloyd wondered if Billy Joe had maybe turned up a girl. Usually anytime he disappeared for a long time it meant he had found a girl and was talking to her. Sometimes he'd find one who had a friend, and then he'd show up with them both, happy as a retriever wagging its tail, and let Lloyd pretty much have his choice. Well, goddamn, I hope he ain't out on a pussy run now, Lloyd thought, wincing against his pains, which now seemed to be coming from everywhere. I don't have no use for no goddamn girl now, 'less she knows how to tape a rib.

Hell with him, he thought finally. I gotta git t' that goddamn car and lay down.

"Johnny Rutherford coming back to the pits—he was black-flagged once again to come in, and he comes back into the pits once again. At fifty-four laps, we have the leader, number forty, Swede Savage; number four, Al Unser, second; number sixty-six, Mark Donohue, third; number forty-eight, Grant, fourth; and they're changing the number on the Tower right now as to fifth position: number twenty, Johncock, running fifth."

"Sid, they're pulling the engine cowl on Johnny Rutherford's car; apparently something is a little bit askew there—and did an adjustment on it, and out he goes."

"That's him there," Becky said, her lips bitter, tight. She gave the binoculars to the nice white-haired woman.

"With the beard. In the corduroy jacket. See him, with the cameras, up there on the other side of that wall?"

"Oh, yes. Mhm. Nice-looking. But you can do better. My Bill was nice-looking like that. And he was a prick, too."

The white-haired woman was wonderful. She had sympathized with Becky, telling her that her own first husband had run away with another woman, but that she had found a much better one, her Ollie, who was an absolute dear. "And I wouldn't have Ollie now if Bill hadn't been such an s.o.b. So things do turn out for the best," she had said. "Why, right around the corner, I'll bet, there's a fine man just waiting for you. And you'll be free for him!"

"I hope so," Becky had said. "I'd be free for him if Nick was dead, and I wish he were." She had tried to envision the face of the next man, but it was always Nick's face. She raised her binoculars and looked across the track. Nick was still there, where he had turned up shortly after the wreck of Peter Revson's car. He was looking toward the fourth turn, standing just a little way behind the inside retaining wall, one hand on his hip, his thick dark hair blown by the wind.

Becky swept the glasses farther south. And suddenly she stopped and came back: there was that blond girl. She was walking toward the place where Nick was. She was making her way along the other side of a fence, very tall, very graceful. Becky recognized one of Nick's equipment bags, which the girl carried slung over her left shoulder. Bitterness flooded anew through Becky. Oh, so now *you're* his assistant, she thought.

It was getting to be very frustrating. Ella Rumple and Ivy Yarbrough were running out of old favorites to root for. After Mario Andretti had gone out of the race after the fourth lap, the big woman had helped Ella root for A. J. Foyt. Foyt had gone out of the race after his thirty-seventh lap. Ella would have switched her allegiance then to Lloyd Ruby, but he had already gone out after his twenty-first lap with engine trouble. She might also have rooted for Sam Sessions, but he had gone out after his seventeenth lap. Or she might have rooted for Bob

Harkey, who had been a Speedway racer for years, but he had lasted only twelve laps. After Foyt had gone out of the race, therefore, the only old-timer she still favored was Jim McElreath. So she had yelled "JIMMY!" for seventeen laps or so until, just a few minutes ago, he had gone into the pits and climbed out of his car. Now she was yelling for Bobby Unser, whom she didn't really like at all.

"You know," Ella yelled now over the roar of the cars, "that Joey Leonard really did a good job of recovering from that spin! He's really a fine driver, isn't he?"

"Guess he must be," Ivy yelled back, "He beat A.J. out of the 'Seventy-one National Championship!"

Ella remembered that and went glum. Obviously, she couldn't yell for Joey after that. So she decided on Roger McCluskey. "GET 'EM, ROG!" she yelled the next time his blue-and-white McLaren-Offy went by.

"RUN THEIR ASSES OFF, BOBBY!" shrilled Ivy Yarbrough.

After leaving the rest room, Billy Joe had gone back into the Tower Terrace. But instead of going to the seats, he had made his way along the fence that separated the pits from the crowd. He went along studying the pit setups: the tall stacks of smooth tires, the big fuel drums, compressed-air bottles, desks, stacks of equipment, tools, parts, fire extinguishers. He watched the pit crewmen in their overalls looking anxiously up the track, or stepping over the wall to service the cars when they rolled in, or just sitting and waiting. There had been a period of a few minutes when the yellow flag was out and all the cars had run slowly around the track. Many of the drivers had taken advantage of that time to come into the pits for service, and there was a lot of activity for Billy Joe to study. There seemed to be thousands of dollars' worth of stuff in every pit, everything a mechanic could think of needing. Man, he thought. That would be heaven.

Billy Joe wasn't very good at talking to new people, except girls—he always had an appropriate line when he saw a girl—but now he stayed on the fence and tried to talk to any crewman who didn't seem busy. They seemed pretty snobbish to him. Maybe it was because he looked so dirty. He knew he wasn't at his best. They were pretty clean-cut for the most part, these guys. Most of them looked more like college kids than grease monkeys. Maybe they're just too busy to talk, he thought. After all, when he was in the pits and Lloyd was out running the Merc, Billy Joe himself didn't feel much like talking to people, either; he was always listening for the Merc, and watching to see how it looked when it went by, and wanting to be ready whenever Lloyd had to bring it in.

Now and then, one of the pit crewman would talk to Billy Joe, once he got far enough to tell them he was a stock-racing mechanic. They'd keep looking up the track, or would have to go do something, but some of them didn't seem to look down on him, and they answered his questions. Now and then, one of them would recognize a name that Billy Joe would mention, and they'd talk a little about that. Then Billy Joe would ask whether the crew might need a new hand, maybe sometime soon. He wasn't having much luck so far, but there were still a lot of pits. He went on up, heading north. Billy Joe was amazed at all the attention these cars needed. It seemed that the pits were half-full all the time. Cars in, cars out. Their stops were just a few seconds' long. He watched the speed and teamwork with which these crews worked when a car came in. It would be good to work with people who were that good, he thought. Of course, he was used to being *the* mechanic, and maybe he wouldn't do too well in a bunch of guys. But then again, he might. Billy Joe had always been happy just in Lloyd Skirvin's company. But this trip— Well, he didn't know about ol' Lloyd, this trip.

Billy Joe remembered Lloyd coming down to the riverbank last night looking for him, lighting his cigarette for him. Billy Joe had gained a little bit on ol' Lloyd. Now he was even getting a little bit tired of nothing but Lloyd Skirvin all the time.

Maybe I'm jus' outgrowin' him, he thought. Now, they could be.

Becky watched the blond girl through the glasses. The girl had gotten as close as she could to the place where Nick was, and was standing behind the fence looking toward him. Her mouth opened and closed, opened and closed, her hand cupped beside it; obviously, she was trying to call him. Becky couldn't hear her voice above the noise of the race cars or the crowd. It was weird, unreal, to see so clear and close someone yelling, without being able to hear the voice.

Becky shuddered, remembering a spooky dream she had had many times, in which she tried to call Nick, but no voice came out.

"A fast race, exciting, and thus far—we're crossing our fingers—safe. Jerry Grant goes back out, and Rutherford is back in once again! Are we keeping track of the number of pit stops Rutherford has made, John, by any chance?"

"Yes, I was, Sid. I've got three pit stops for John Rutherford; it's possible he had that fourth one, but I've just recorded three. Swede Savage's last stop was nineteen and a half seconds, and about five laps ago the interval between first and second was just five seconds; the interval between first and fifth places was just twenty-six seconds. Sid?"

"Now to the south pit, Lou Palmer."

"All right. Johnny Rutherford is back out on the race track, but the Norris Eagle, number thirty-five, it is not. Jim McElreath, now with helmet off, is standing alongside. He hasn't deserted the car yet; they're looking it over; no decision has yet been made, but he's out of the cockpit, unstrapped, standing by it. Mark Donohue, meanwhile, is going very, very slowly, and I think you may have—"

"WE HAVE A CRASH ON THE FOURTH TURN!"

Becky smiled at the apparent futility of the blond girl's calls. She moved the binoculars to the left to see if Nick had responded yet. A white race car blurred through the foreground of the lenses' view, its sound enveloping her. And the glasses found Nick; there beyond the low wall was that contemptible son of a— But he was leaping into the air! Something enormous shot into the glasses' narrow view and burst right where Nick was. Then there was nothing but fire in the glasses' twin circles.

Becky dropped the glasses. There where Nick had

stood was just fire, a soaring curtain of fire. A terrible din of human screaming rose with the fire, as if it were the sound of the fire itself. The shrieks pulsated on and on, shredding Becky's fragile nerves like hands tearing cobwebs. And then she was a part of the scream.

I wished he was dead and he is.

Ella was looking into the fourth turn. "OH, GOD," she cried suddenly. In the turn, a red race car was doing something crazy. It was high in the turn where it should have been low, and sliding. Ella's heart leaped up, and a terrific shiver ran through her as the car darted down across the track as quick as a blink and exploded on the inside retaining wall. An enormous geyser of flame shot into the sky and something huge and aflame came screeching and bounding across to the outside of the track, struck the wall a few yards up the track, and came to rest in the middle of the pavement right before her eyes. She screamed in utter terror as the whole racetrack went up in whooshing flames and a hot wind sucked through the stands. A river of flame came sweeping down the track, following a white car. A tire seemed to be hanging a hundred feet in the air like a black moon. The air was full of pieces of junk. Red junk, black junk, silver junk. Ella felt heat on her face and threw her hand up to shield her eyes; before the hand blocked her vision she thought she saw two wrecked cars flipping along the track. There were several earth-jarring thuds and then only screaming, screaming from everywhere; she was in the center of a shriek storm, and her heart quailed.

There was a red race car coming straight at him. Nick was paralyzed. His brain told him to raise his camera, but it also told him to run. For an instant he could not do either. A bolt of energy shot through him then, and his legs suddenly propelled him five feet into the air. He was in the air when the red car exploded into a white mist against the wall a few yards in front of him. He was landing on his side in the grass when a holocaust of flame went up with a force that popped his eardrums. Little things stung his face like sleet. He scrambled to his feet, his heart walloping. Hot scraps were raining out of the sky. The grass was turning brown. Thousands of voices were beginning to scream. Nick's skin anticipated the cut and jolt of flying metal. SHOOT! his brain finally telegraphed to his muscles. And he started photographing. His eternity of jumping and falling and getting up had actually lasted two or three seconds. There were still great chunks of machinery and wreckage tumbling along the wall and through the air. Down the track with loud crunchings and thuddings there was one race car bouncing, flying to pieces, followed by a sheet of flame and heat-crinkled air. Along the inside wall Nick saw the motor and axle segments of a car tumbling. There seemed to be still another car cartwheeling beside the near wall. And inside the curtain of flame and smoke there were thumps and smashings and roars that made him think more cars were colliding. Crouching and running through the heat and mayhem, he aimed his camera at anything that moved. And everything was moving.

Diana screamed. A red race car was plunging toward the low wall directly in front of Nick; it was coming too fast for him to get out of the way. She felt the impact through the ground. She saw pieces of the car in the air, flames in the air, Nick in the air. She screamed again, her fingers over her mouth. "It hit him!" she screamed. He was on the ground. The air was hot. The sky was full of fragments. But Nick was getting up! He did a strange, awkward, disoriented sort of dance, then he began running down the wall. Diana gasped for air and held her hand over her hammering heart. There was a taste of copper in her mouth. But the car hadn't come through the wall. It hadn't hit Nick! He was out there running along the edge of the fire now, taking films of the sliding, bouncing wreckage.

"OH, GOD, NICK, GET AWAY FROM THERE," she shrieked. "YOU'LL GET KILLED!"

Members of David Earl Savage's pit crew were watching for him to come out of the fourth turn and down the main straight. They were exultant. Swede, the big, nice twenty-six-year-old guy with his long blond hair, their very own Swede, was doing a terrific job. This was only his second Indy "500," but he had led it from the forty-third to fifty-fourth lap and was moving on. He was leading Bobby Unser last time around.

Way up there now, they saw their red car flash into sight. Then it darted to the inside of the track, and there was suddenly a wall of flame all the way across the north end of the straightaway.

Swede's crewmen stood stunned. And then one of them, who was operating the two-way radio to Swede's car, heard Swede's voice come through a rush of static. It said:

"Holy Christ, what a mess!"

The screaming pulsated and shrilled in the air. All the people in the stands were on their feet. Some were running back from the heat; others were making their way closer down to the fence. Ella stood dumbstruck, clutching at Ivy Yarbrough's shoulder, staring at the ragged, twisted mass of metal that lay burning in the middle of the track a few feet away. The thing was wavy and indistinct with the heat of burning. Ella's heart felt as if it were in her throat. She wasn't sure she was seeing what she thought she saw. Maybe it was just the turbulence of the air fooling her.

No. It wasn't. She saw it clearly now. It *was* a man. He was hanging face-down in the wreckage. She saw his helmet moving as he struggled in the middle of the fire. She saw his arm and a white glove moving, jerking, pushing at the torn debris.

There was a man in there. Face-down. His face was almost on the concrete. He was burning. He couldn't get out.

Ella started crying. "Come on," she said. "Come on, get out. I've had enough. Won't you please get out of there?" Ella thought she was going to throw up.

"Jesus H. Christ!" Ivy Yarbrough repeated over and over, her eyes popping, leaning forward and clutching Ella's arm. "Jesus H. Christ! Look at that!"

"Wait," Ella cried. "He'll get out! He's all right! He'll

get out in a minute! You'll see! People don't just get killed and—and die!"

Gerald Rumple could endure only a few minutes at a time in the so-called Chapel of the funeral parlor: the people coming in, wearing their finest clothes and their gravest expressions, signing the register, then tilting their heads and going directly to the kids with arms outstretched and their faces saintly with sympathy and grief. Gerald didn't know how Allan and Janet could stand it, this endless parade of great, comforting bosoms and compassionate handshakes, but they were holding together well.

Near the two closed caskets, behind the mountains of redolent flowers, there was a small door leading into the back of the funeral home. Gerald slipped through the door and went down a short hallway, looking for someplace where he might get a drink of water. The hallway ended near a door that opened into a small back office. In the office there were three men in dark suits, evidently minor funeral directors and hearse drivers, listening to a radio and smoking. Gerald knew what it was, and he hung near the door. The announcer was saying:

"A CRASH ON THE FOURTH TURN! JIM, CAN YOU SEE IT? THE YELLOW IS OUT! JIM SHEL-TON!"

Oh, my God, not another one there, he thought. His skin prickled, and again he was afraid for Ella.

"IT WAS A VIOLENT CRASH—WITH MUCH—FLAME! BUT IT'S WAY DOWN THE TRACK FROM ME, SID! I CANNOT SEE REALLY WHO IT IS!"

Gerald looked at the three pink, smooth faces, still and intent, the dark suits. His heart was pounding.

"THE RED FLAG IS OUT, AND THE RACE IS BE-ING STOPPED! So we'll have to— There's a tremendous flame in the car— Tremendous flame, covering the race-track, all the way across—"

Fourth turn again, Gerald thought. Where Ella is. Where we were yesterday. Where Gene and Ruthie were Monday. He visualized it as it probably looked from those seats. Maybe there's fire in the seats, he thought, shuddering. No. Don't think that. Sid Collins's voice on the radio sounded sick and dispirited. Gerald had always thought Sid's voice sounded like Bob Hope's, with a throaty, round-mouthed resonance. Now he sounded tired, distraught.

"And unfortunately, after fifty-nine laps, a beautiful start and a smooth-running race, it is being stopped, has been stopped—and we have fire—"

And then in the background, beyond Collins's voice, Gerald heard the sound of an accelerating motor and then a yell and a massive outburst of hysterical shrieking.

"—all the way across—and—a—A MAN WAS HIT HERE BY AN OFFICIAL FIRE TRUCK! DIRECTLY IN FRONT OF US!"

In the depths of the radio beyond Collins's voice, it sounded as if a thousand women were screaming their lungs out; still farther in the background was the deep, distant voice of the track announcer booming. Collins's voice went on, distractedly:

"—trying to go up the pit area—around the track— and a man was hit—"

Billy Joe Marshall had been looking over the fence into another one of the pits, trying to start a conversation with a lean young mechanic with sideburns, when the crowd in the grandstands beyond the track suddenly murmured and rose up like the hair on a dog's back, all looking northward. The young mechanic leaped to the pit wall and stared up the track. Billy Joe looked and saw at the far end of the track a wall of flame and smoke. Then he heard a truck motor revving somewhere nearby, turned to look, heard a thud, heard a deep voice yell, "HOLD IT!" saw a pickup truck braking to a stop on the far side of the pit apron, and saw somebody in a white overall suit sailing through the air.

Hundreds of shrill voices were screaming all around when the body fell to the pavement like a broken doll twenty or thirty feet in front of the stopped truck.

Billy Joe's eyes almost popped out of his head.

*   *   *

*"—and we have a great amount—of confusion—out
here in the pit area waiting for a doctor to arrive—"*

Standing in the dim hallway of the funeral home in
Chicago, Gerald Rumple listened to these words, and in
his mind's eye he could see everything: in the foreground
of his image loomed Collins, big, urbane, well-groomed,
looking down through a picture window at the pavement
upon which a body lay, people running and hovering
around it; and in the right corner of his mind's eye, in a
corner of that oval-shaped microcosm, wreckage was
burning and probably someone was dead.

Gerald shuddered. All those people watching you die on
the pavement in broad daylight, he thought.

It *is* a Roman circus.

At the moment the screaming started in front of the
Tower, Harry Kuntz was wiping overnight sebum off his
forehead with a white handkerchief and looking at the
gray smudge on the white cloth, thinking over the alibis
he and Diana had agreed upon to explain their absence
the night before to his wife and her parents. On the phone
this morning he had brokenly given his wife a story that
he had stayed at the Athletic Club and that he hadn't
been able to call her because her phone had been busy
every time he had dialed. He would simply elaborate on
that, and if by any remote chance she had doubted him
enough to call the club and check, he would extempo-
rize, invent extenuating circumstances. Diana was going
to tell her parents she had stayed all night with a girl
friend, and would call the girl friend first and ask her to
corroborate the story if asked. Harry's story would be
harder to handle, but he thought he could do it because
his wife didn't like being upset and usually would believe
good and safe things if given half a chance.

Harry's thoughts were broken by ululating screams that
suddenly went up all around him, shocking him, making
his heart pound. He looked up from his handkerchief and
saw, a few feet in front of him, a dark-haired young man
lying on his back on the pavement near the starter's platform, his legs strangely spraddled out like those of a dead

frog. Men in white Speedway caps were running toward him. A few feet away, there was a pickup truck, steam pouring out of its bent grille and hood. Its door on the driver's side was opening, and a large man was scrambling out. There were hasty movements in the seats near Harry; he looked to his left and saw one of the Festival Princesses, a black girl, slumping in a faint.

He thought of Diana, who had left him a few minutes earlier. Dear God, he thought. I hope she didn't see this. He turned to his right, the direction she had gone, and only then did he notice that there was a huge fire at the upper end of the straightaway.

Harry Kuntz clapped his hand over his mouth and felt sick. First, all that about Diana; now this, he thought. I've had enough of the "500" Festival. Forever.

It was incredible, but whoever it was in there was still alive. Nick Alef got as close as the heat would permit and started taking pictures of the burning hulk of rubble with the moving man hanging out of it. He breathed fast through clenched teeth and aimed; the camera recorded everything. The dark-gray pavement covered with little bits of metal and thousands of chips of red paint. The man trying to crawl out from the mangled section of race car, which looked as if it had been blown open by a bomb. The light-colored suit and gloves beginning to burn. Still strapped onto the man's broad back, something that looked like a seat-back cushion, burning. All of this shimmering in the heat-troubled air. Beyond, the colorful clothing and intent faces of the spectators, watching the man try to crawl out. Medics in white suits now were running up as close to the chunk as they could, but the heat stood them off.

Talk about being in the right place at the right time, he thought. Heart racing, he bore in with the camera. Someone shoved him from behind and he almost fell, but he didn't take the lens off the burning man. "Get the fuck out of the way!" Men were yelling all around, and there were sirens, and firefighters running about. Nick dodged and kept filming. He was doing the best he possibly could do.

I wonder who this driver is, he thought.

*   *   *

"Come on!" yelled Ivy Yarbrough. She shoved past people and made her way as fast as she could go to the end of the row of seats and then down the aisle toward the fence. Ella watched her go. She couldn't move her feet. People who had fled from the blast of heat were moving back down toward the fence now, though a few were still moving higher among the seats, as if they feared something might still explode.

Something could, Ella thought in alarm. Jerry, she thought. I'm so sorry! She thought of Gerald and wished she were with him. She watched Ivy Yarbrough go as close as she could to the fence and peer through it at the struggling man on the track. Ivy turned and waved a beckoning arm to Ella, her face intent, fierce and hideous. Then there were firefighters there putting out the fire, surrounding the wreckage.

Ella turned away. Her tongue tasted bitter. There seemed to be a steady pressure in her chest. She was ashamed of Ivy. Ashamed. And she was trying not to be that ashamed of herself. She couldn't look anymore at the mayhem on the track. She looked up into the bleachers. There were people up there standing, gazing down past her at the smoke and foam. Their faces were bland with curiosity. One man was chewing gum. Another was lighting a cigar, looking at it all through the flame of his lighter. A girl was nibbling her nails, her eyes a blank stare. She took her fingers out of her mouth and inspected a nail, then looked back at the track and resumed her gnawing.

The last time Ella had noticed expressions like these, absorbed, lifeless, was when she had come into a room where Gerald and some neighbors were watching the telecast of the *Apollo 13* moon mission. They were sitting on sofas and chairs looking into the television screen, seeing the Manned Spacecraft Center at Houston, where technicians were sitting looking at television screens, while the announcer speculated on the chances of getting the astronauts in the damaged spacecraft back alive. That had seemed so strange at the time: people watching televised people watching television, while out in space, somebody in a machine was struggling to stay alive.

And nobody could do a thing. Just blank faces watching blank screens. Just waiting to see if there would be a picture.

"I KILLED HIM! I KILLED HIM!" Becky sobbed. She kept crying it, over and over. Inside she felt black, torn, turbulent, falling apart. She had wished Nick dead, prayed for him to be dead, and now he was dead. It would be ghastly to go on living with this on her conscience. Of all her prayers, none had ever been answered. Until this dreadful one. Her son— Oh, God! Davey would somehow know she had wished Nick dead, prayed for him to be dead! The boy didn't know how awful his father had been to her, but he would know somehow that his father was dead because she had wished him dead. "OH, GOD," she sobbed. "I KILLED NICKY!"

Her screaming and sobbing would have attracted attention, but everyone else was screaming and no one heard her except the white-haired woman. She held Becky's head to her shoulder and stroked her hair, her jaw muscles set firmly beneath her finely wrinkled cheeks, and stared toward the fire, looking for something. And then she saw it. She thought she did. Yes. The corduroy jacket. Better be sure, she thought. She lifted Becky's binoculars. Yes, there he was, stalking around like a Great White Hunter, calmly aiming his camera. The playboy husband of this distraught girl. She knew his type, and in her opinion the world would be better off if the fire *had* killed him. But—it hadn't.

"Honey," she said. "Honey, look over there. Look! Look! Shut up and LOOK! He isn't even hurt! LOOK! See him? He isn't even hurt! LOOK!" She had to push Becky's face in that direction because she hadn't yet comprehended the words. There were all kinds of awful things out there on the track, but this girl had to see that her husband was still out there, as alive as she was herself.

And then Becky did see.

Yes. There he was. Out there, working coldly, professionally, zeroing in on everything as he had learned so well to do, detached from what everyone else was feeling, caring only how it looked in a photograph.

"See? He's not dead."

Becky took a deep breath, then let it out in a long, shuddering exhalation, shutting her eyes again and shaking her head rapidly from side to side, hugging her arms across her waist. Then she looked up, opened her eyes, and watched Nick working for a few seconds.

She turned to the white-haired woman. She squeezed her wrist. "Listen," she said. "You've been wonderful. I've got to go over there if I can. Thank you. Thank you."

Billy Joe Marshall hung on the pit fence and watched them put the dark-haired young man on a stretcher table that had wheels on it. He looked like he was dead for sure, that one. They lifted the stretcher into the back of an ambulance, all those people looking very serious. Billy Joe could read the signs on the open back door of the ambulance. They said:

CONKLE "500" AMBULANCE

———

MILLER-METEOR
PACESETTER
AMBULANCES

The men shut the door, and the ambulance sped away. Billy Joe and lots of other people on the fence watched the young men of the pit crew stand around talking to each other and to some people with notebooks.

After a while, the lean pit crewman with the long sideburns came and sat down on a wheel close to the fence. He sat there just looking at the ground under his feet.

"Hey," Billy Joe said to him. "Hey, buddy."

The young man looked up without any expression.

"Hey," Billy Joe said. "Reckon ya'll could use another good mechanic?"

The young man got up and walked away.

"Well, this has been, uhm, one of the most disastrous months of May, all the way around— Getting the race

*under way— Getting it started—having a first-lap accident
yesterd—uh, on Monday—unable to start yesterday because of bad weather— Now we've had a man in the pits
being hit—by an official fire truck—and we have fire
being put out, as the race is stopped in the north end.
So, John, if you can—you've seen it, you can pick up
your microphone and give us what you have— But we,
of course, strive for accuracy; we'll take our time and be
certain that we stay calm."*

*"Sid, there is so much—fumes from chemical fire ex-
tinguishers down there that we can't see any of the cars
— We can see none of the action— We know that there
were two cars, at least, involved, because there was fire
inside—of the fourth turn, and outside of the fourth turn.
But I feel certain there were two cars involved— Now
the chemical fumes are clearing away, and Sid, if you'll
take over, I'll go back and put the glasses on them
again."*

Werner Dold heard the dejection in the radio announcer's voice and decided that by now Tony Hulman
would be approachable. It was midafternoon now, after
3:00 P.M.; obviously, it would be a long time before the
race could be resumed, if it could at all; the weather was
threatening again, and another forty-two laps would have
to be run before the race could be called half-finished, and
it had to be half-finished before the Speedway could be
free of its obligation to the raincheck holders. With a third
day ending like this, in carnage and confusion, Werner
doubted that any sane person would come back for a
fourth day. All factors considered, it seemed to Werner
that Tony Hulman should be just about at the nadir right
now, absolutely disgusted with his arena, and this would
be the time to go to see him to make an offer. Besides
that, the hilarity of his wife and the Air Force man in the
next room was becoming unbearable. They were laughing
like a couple of crazy people in there. He would have to
get rid of her, obviously. He would sit down and figure
that out after he had taken care of this matter of the
Speedway.

Werner straightened his ascot, put a raincoat over his arm, picked up his cap, and left the room.

When the firefighters and rescuers got the fire put out and began prying the sides of the cockpit open to extricate the driver, they had Nick's view blocked, so he turned his attention elsewhere on the track to see if there were other drivers strewn around. The whole track surface to the north was quivering with heat waves and adrift with fire-extinguisher foam. Firemen in safety suits were running about, turning their extinguisher nozzles on burning chunks and on the sheet of flaming fuel. Fire trucks and ambulances were parked all around, and others were arriving. Beyond the trembling haze, Nick could see the fleet of race cars stopped in and above the turn, a surrealistic pattern of colors distorted by the turbulent air. He photographed that, with the chunks of junk in the foreground, the white puffs of foam, the rescuers moving about.

As far as he could see, there were no other whole cars or even driver cockpits lying on the track. It dawned on him then that all these thousands of pieces might be from the same car, the one that had come toward him and exploded on the wall. It was hard to believe, but it was beginning to look like it. Near the wall there was a crumpled red wing with a number on it: 40. That would be— he searched his memory quickly—Savage. Swede Savage. Jesus. A kid. Nick had met him. His wife was pregnant. Swede Savage, he thought. That's who was burning over there, then.

Nick took a photograph of a hole in the middle of the track, where something heavy—the engine, he surmised —apparently had hit the asphalt.

They had Savage on a stretcher now and were taking him to an ambulance. Nick ran to the side of the stretcher-bearers, shouldered some other photographers aside, and, holding his camera high, quickly photographed the driver on the stretcher. He was a ghastly sight. His suit was scorched. His right hand was a tattered mess of burned skin with fragments of glove sticking to it. Both his legs were twisted out of shape, obviously broken in many places. His eyesockets were blackened, and his mouth and chin appeared to be swollen, skinned, and scorched. Yet he was conscious, trying to look around. Nick saw and photographed all this before he was thrown aside by other photographers. Then he was shoved still farther away by a grimacing fireman whose sooty face was streaked by tears and mucus, his eyes seeming to bulge with hatred. Nick suddenly felt a bolt of fear. But when the fireman moved on, Nick made one more effort to get near the stretcher. It was useless. The photographers were fighting and climbing each other's backs to get one last shot of this incredible survivor before the ambulance doors could seal him away.

And finally Nick was just standing there beside the track, panting, totally drained of energy. He knew he had done a fantastic job. Surely nobody had been able to get better film than he had. Dozens of angles. Prizewinners! He couldn't even remember all he had! All those plus the fabulous films of Diana naked from last night and this morning! Jesus! It was the greatest day's work he had ever done in this business.

And then suddenly, in the midst of his euphoria, he remembered the grimy face of the fireman, the contemptuous eyes glaring at him with the whites showing clear around the pupil. Nick's knees began to tremble. He could no longer hold his camera steady. He shook his head and clasped his hand over the back of his neck. That fireman's face haunted him. He couldn't get it out of his mind. No one had ever looked at him like that. It was the eyes.

He was afraid, but he didn't know what he feared.

Diana Scheckley watched Nick take pictures. She stood by the fence in the midst of people who were screaming and shoving and yelling and talking fast and retching, and she watched Nick. She saw him creeping as close as he could to the chunk of wreckage, aiming first his movie camera and then one of his others, standing tall to shoot down, kneeling, going to the right, going to the left. In his crouching and swaying body there was a powerful, somehow rhythmic intensity, an absolute concentration. He was the way he had been last night in the garage when she was naked in front of his camera, when she was— And now he was the same way, taking pictures of somebody dying, struggling, twitching. Diana felt an awful revulsion, an enervating sense of remorse, a feeling that some awful mistake had been made, that her soul had been violated.

She thought of Harry Kuntz and his vigil in the Hilton lobby and his pathetic plea for an alibi. Then she thought of her father, who worked for Harry, and she thought of her mother, and she envisioned them looking at the photographs this—this *monster* had taken— Yes, some kind of a monster, a Cyclops— It was strange, but she thought of Cyclops—and it was as if a sheet of glass came down between where she now stood and where Nick moved.

Diana stood there with no place to go, and watched Nick do his terrible work on the other side of that pane of nothingness. She watched him come back and fight to get his camera close to the man on the stretcher. After that, she didn't want to watch anymore. She turned away from the fence and made her way toward the Tower, wading through cellophane, paper, cans, bottles, chicken bones, hot-dog buns, paper plates. There were big trash drums along the fence, stenciled with the legend:

PITCH IN

Some of them were overturned, their contents spilled, blending into the refuse on the ground. As Diana went past an upright trash drum, she took Nick's photo bag off her shoulder, the bag containing all the rolls of film he had taken of her. Holding the bag by the strap, she raked some trash aside in the top of the barrel, dropped the bag in, and covered it up.

And then she walked on.

Werner Dold strode through ankle-deep trash. Somewhere in his papers he had figures that told how much it cost to clean up the Speedway each year after its fans had departed. Thousands of dollars. Thousands more to repair rest rooms, seats, and fences. Thousands more to repair the greens and fairways of the golf course inside the track. This year, after this three-day siege, it obviously would cost even more than usual. Much more than usual.

There was a strong, cold wind. Cars were still coming into the Speedway. Werner went around a forest of parked motorcycles. In the absence of the moaning race-car engines now, the prevailing noises were different: the snarl and belch of motorcycles creeping through the infield crowd, rock music and talking voices drifting up from transistor radios and out of car radios, shouts, laughter, curses, now and then the track announcer's subdued voice on the loudspeakers, the hysterical screaming and giggling of girls or squalling of babies coming from within parked vehicles. Werner walked past a large, shallow pond of liquid mud in which beer bottles floated and two cars sat abandoned. Nearby, a youth with dirty hair sat on the ground leaning against the wheel of a van, wearing an old-time editor's visor and a sheepskin vest, all alone, strumming an almost inaudible guitar; his strange, rapt solitude and moving hand oddly reminded Werner of someone masturbating. He looked away, embarrassed, then was embarrassed at being embarrassed by such a thing. He went past a group of dirty boys dressed alike in derby hats, kinky, shoulder-length hair, and faded blue cotton shirts torn off at the shoulder seams. The boys were coaxing a young, glassy-eyed girl to expose her breasts, which were very large. Werner paused there until, giggling hysterically, she did, and they were enormous, ugly things, already victims of gravity, hanging nearly to her waist. The boys laughed. Werner went on, thinking. There would always be hundreds of thousands wanting to come to this and to see famous drivers and be scared by spins, and some perhaps who really did come to see people hurt or dying. There would always be a few hundred who came not to see the race at all, but to impress each other with their expensive observation suites and penthouse seats and box seats and their familiarity with the famous drivers and celebrities. And there would always be thousands, like these, who came not to watch the race but to be absorbed in a mob, nameless, and do whatever they wanted to do without having to face censure or consequences.

Werner remembered his brief, anonymous, pleasant

encounter yesterday with that fellow Bixby who hadn't known who he was, and he could understand those who came here desiring anonymity. For their various reasons, there would always be hundreds of thousands wanting to come to this spectacle. Werner Dold knew that, and knew that Tony Hulman knew it better than anybody; and Werner knew that only this miraculous combination of bad weather, discomfort, frustration, deaths, and injuries could ever make Tony Hulman think of getting rid of it. But the miracle had occurred, and Werner knew, from his readings of biographies, that great men are great because they know how to strike while the iron is hot.

While the Master Control Tower announcers were waiting for more information on the fourth-turn crash, there was a commercial break, and this commercial was played:

"Anybody who's been to a championship auto race has seen STP Oil Treatment in action! But where does all that action lead? It leads to millions of cars, just like the one you're driving right now! STP Oil Treatment will help keep your car running smoother, cooler, quieter, longer! Have your service station add STP to your oil, and run —RACER SHARP!"

"S—T—P IS THE RACER'S EDGE!"

Sid Collins looked down through the glass of his broadcasting booth. It was hard to keep talking. This was his twenty-sixth broadcast of the 500-Mile Race, and though he had seen many terrible spectacles here, he was appalled by the carnage and confusion he had been seeing today.

Just below his window, the drivers' wives were seated in an area fronting on Victory Lane. Many of them held transistor radios and were listening to learn whose car or cars had been involved in the conflagration in the northwest turn. Others were trying to see their husbands in the cars that had been flagged down along the main straightaway.

When he heard the first reports that it was Swede Savage's car, he looked at Mrs. Savage. She was down there wearing a pink maternity outfit. She was listening to a radio. When he got official word that it was Savage, he had to announce it to the world—including Mrs. Savage, who now sat tense and vulnerable down there under his eyes.

When she heard it was her husband, Mrs. Savage gave a cry that Collins heard in his booth. She leaned over a rail in her pink dress, comforted by other drivers' wives, and cried hysterically.

A reporter for the *Indianapolis Star* saw an ambulance come to the Speedway field hospital at 3:10 P.M. A very young man, looking dead, was whisked from the ambulance to the hospital's treatment room.

Two minutes later, another ambulance arrived. Attendants transported a scorched, broken human figure from the ambulance to the emergency room.

The reporter learned that the first man was named Armando Moreno Teran. He was twenty-three years old. He was a member of the pit crew of Graham McRae, the rookie STP Team driver from New Zealand. The reporter learned that Teran had had three years of college in California and was planning to be married in the summer. The doctors were giving him heart massage and cardiac application. Teran had been handling the signboard for McRae during the race. After an STP-red race car vanished in flames in the fourth turn, Armando had left the pit wall and started running toward it along the pit apron. A Speedway fire truck going north toward the fire at an estimated sixty miles an hour had struck him from behind, and he never knew what hit him. He had fractures of the skull, left arm, shoulder, and all the ribs on his left side, as well as internal injuries.

The safety patrolman who had been driving the fire truck that hit Teran came to the hospital. His eyes were red. Tears came when he learned that Teran wasn't expected to live. The man waited there for a while with tears in his eyes. He did not want to talk to reporters.

The other young man was Swede Savage. The doctors in the emergency room were learning that, in addition to his severe burns, Savage had two legs all broken up, a fractured arm, internal injuries, and perhaps some damage to his eyes. The good news was that he had not inhaled flames and he was conscious. He had been able to mutter the word "Two" when a crewman held up two fingers before him.

A few minutes later, the race driver's wife came to the hospital. She looked as if she were having a hard time holding herself together. An STP crewman came out of the treatment room to talk to her. "Swede's injuries are bad," he said, "but not as bad as his other accident." Mrs. Savage managed a weak smile. The reporter remembered that Swede had been critically hurt in the 1971 Questor Grand Prix at Ontario Motor Speedway in California. That one had put him in a coma for a long time and kept him out of racing for a year.

At 3:36 P.M., Swede Savage was put in a helicopter. A doctor and two nurses got in. The helicopter rose over the heads of the staring fans in the infield, its rotor blades fluttering, and went away eastward to Methodist Hospital.

"For those who make films, they try to dream up a new title, Fred, as you know; the 'Fastest "500,"' the 'Most Thrilling "500,"' etc.; this should be the 'Most Frustrating "500,"' from every possible aspect."

"I don't know what they would name the film this time, Sid—uh, by golly, that's going to be a real tough—row to hoe for those people. They'll come up with something appropriate, I'm quite certain."

Crews were beginning to clean pieces of car off the racetrack now. Nick Alef sat on the wall with his hand over the back of his neck, still remembering the eyes and the tear-streaked face of the fireman. The noises all around him seemed to fade. He felt like a vacuum inside, a void. Then he started remembering images, camera images. He remembered Diana's face, full of ecstasy. He remembered the face of the Air Force captain, with its strained, vulnerable look. He remembered the haggard faces of Marine infantrymen in Vietnam. He remembered the face of a captured North Vietnamese in the moment before he was executed.

Suddenly Nick remembered something from seventeen or eighteen years back.

He had been a beginning police reporter then. A Southside gardener had unknowingly backed his pickup truck, loaded with garden soil, over his two-year-old grandson in the driveway of his home. Nick had been one of the reporters who went there to cover the incident. In the pathetic aftermath, there had been one quiet moment when the police and all the other reporters, the relatives, and television cameramen had gone outside. Carrying his Speed Graphic camera, Nick had walked into the kitchen to find himself confronting a hushed scene:

On a Formica-topped table backlighted by a window, the tiny corpse had been laid, wrapped in a white sheet, to await the hearse. The grandfather was sitting on a chair beside the table, in profile to Nick and unaware of his presence, looking uncomprehendingly at the swaddled body. There was no one else in the house at the moment. A clock ticked. The grandfather had slowly leaned forward, curved his arms around the body like parentheses, then pressed his face to the shroud and remained motionless.

Nick had recognized a prizewinning photograph in that moment. Breathless, stealthy, he had estimated the light, adjusted the lens setting and distance on the big camera, inserted a flashbulb, withdrawn the filmholder slide, raised the camera, and composed the scene in the viewfinder. Every element was perfect: the grief-stricken grandfather in his simple coveralls, his white hair backlighted by sunshine from the window. Outside the window, the police could be seen inspecting the fatal rear wheel of the pickup truck while the victim's young parents leaned against each other and watched the police. Trivets and Disneyland souvenirs flanked the window. And time seemed to have stood still to allow him to photograph it right. Holding the image in the viewfinder and fingering the shutter release, Nick had been able to envision the delight on his city editor's face, and his first-page news photograph. And there had been no other photographer in the house to capture the moment. Nick had had the perfect picture all to himself.

He had stood there for long seconds. And he had not been able to snap the shutter. His conscience had paralyzed his hand until, shaken with doubt about his suitability for the journalistic profession, he had lowered the camera and crept away to leave the old man alone with his tragedy.

Nick had never told anybody about that, especially his city editor, for fear of being called a fool. He had been ashamed of his inability to perform.

And yet, he had always felt right about it, somehow.

Imagine, he thought now, there was a time when you couldn't stand to take a picture of somebody suffering.

Maybe the old man wouldn't have noticed even if I had shot it, he had argued with himself after that day. I didn't notice anyone taking pictures of Becky and me and Davey in the street when Timmy was killed, but in every paper and newscast for the next twenty-four hours, there we were with our hearts hanging out and our faces all crumpled up. . . .

And then Nick understood what it was about the fireman's eyes:

In the photographs after Timmy was killed, there was Davey's face, dark with dirt as usual, with the white tear-tracks down across it. Davey, that timid, quiet little guy, had suddenly rushed, sobbing, at the photographers and tried to make them stop taking pictures of Timmy and the Alef family.

Nick raised his head finally. He took a deep, quaking breath and drew his middle fingers across his eyes and gazed across the track. Beyond the fence there were thousands of people standing, looking down at the littered track. And photographers going berserk with cameras.

Crowds watching, he thought. Everything here seems to have to do with crowds and cameras watching. Watching you get hurt or watching you screw or watching you make an ass of yourself or watching you die. Watching you do what they themselves would only want to do unseen.

He looked down at his cameras. Their blue-black, shining eyes stared up at him from the ground at his feet:

unblinking, unfeeling, mechanical, insect eyes, through which Nick Alef himself had been seeing and recording things from which human eyes should be averted.

He lifted the cameras up from the ground, staring at the hard, cold, flawless lenses.

And then in a sudden, sobbing fury he jumped to his feet, swung the expensive cameras by their straps, and bashed them to pieces on the concrete wall. Again and again, he smashed them against the wall.

"Ivy, can we go now?" Ella said.

"Go?"

"Can we go home? Will you drive me home now?"

"Are you outa your skull, honey?" the big woman exclaimed. "Leave now when only fifty-nine laps've been run? We're not leaving," she said firmly, looking back to the track. "I mean, I can't stop you if you wanna go, but damned if I'm leavin' yet. Jesus Christ, did I have you figured wrong? This is one *hell* of a race, honey."

Ella sat, disconsolate. She watched the work crews clean pieces of Swede Savage's race car off a quarter of a mile of the racetrack. She watched them drag its crumpled engine away in a tarpaulin. She watched the fleet of emergency vehicles go away. She watched them push the race cars from the fourth turn, where they had been stopped by the crash, down to the pits where they could be serviced while the red flag was out. Ella watched all this, let Ivy eat the rest of the fried chicken, bread and butter, and stuffed celery, and tried to keep from crying. She almost cried when she felt some sprinkles of rain beginning. I could kill myself for not going with Gerald, she thought.

But no real rains came, and a little after four o'clock Harlan Fengler told them to line the race cars up, single file, for a restart.

Then something happened that ordinarily would have rocketed Ella's spirits to the skies:

A. J. Foyt unseated George Snider, his Gilmore Racing Team teammate, from Snider's car 84, which Snider had worked forward from thirtieth position into the top ten before the red flag. So, when Harlan Fengler gave the order for the drivers to start their engines again, A.J. was back in the race. When she saw this, Ivy punched Ella in the side with her elbow, raised a fist in the air, and yelled, "RRRRRRRRUN 'EM DOWN, SUPER-TEX!" She winked at Ella and punched her in the ribs again. But Ella just sat, not looking at the track. She shifted her weight and sat leaning away from Ivy. Ivy looked at her, shrugged, and turned back to the track.

Then, paced this time by an electronic device called the Electro-Pacer, instead of the pace car, the big race cars once again roared down the straightaway. The crowd stood up—all but Ella Rumple.

"BLAST 'EM OFF, A.J.!" Ivy Yarbrough bellowed.

"What are you doing here, Kitty?"

"Oh, that out there." She swept her hand to indicate the great event, of which, in their joy, they had been almost unaware. "My husband's interested in it."

"Are you interested in it?"

"You can see how interested in it I am. Are you?"

Carl George sat crossed-legged on the bed and smoked and thought. He squinted. She hadn't seen him squint since they had begun laughing together. Then he said, "Did you see what happened Monday?"

"You mean the accident? No. I heard about it."

"A big ball of—a big ball of fire. It went right into the crowd. What do you think of that?"

"I don't like to think about it."

"I don't, either. It—it flipped me out. But I can now— You're a good person." Tears started in his eyes when he said that, but this time he felt good inside. He paused and sucked the smoke out of the last bit of his cigarette. "Will I see you anymore after this is over?"

"Do you want to?"

"If I could. I need to."

"So do I."

"You don't know how much. You don't—" He paused and cleared his throat. "You've about saved my life."

"You've about saved mine."

*   *   *

Becky Alef finally got through the teeming tunnel and
went toward the place where she had last seen Nick. She
didn't know what she was going to say to him. But it
wasn't going to be about the blonde or about divorce.
Not yet, anyway. She was confused. All she knew was
that she wanted to be near him.

When she got to the fourth turn, he was gone. She
couldn't find him.

At 4:23 P.M., the doctors officially pronounced Armando Teran dead.

At that same moment, the race cars were flying down
the straightaway for the fourth start of the 1973 Indianapolis 500-Mile Race.

*"This is Sid Collins at Indianapolis, Indiana, once again,
and just as we take the air, the race has just been restarted! Let's pick up the leader on turn two, HOWDY
BELL!"*

*"We see Al Unser coming through the short chute.
Brother Bobby is actually, uh, oh, about five car-lengths
behind as they head up the backstretch! They should be
to Doug Zing by now!"*

*"Thank you, Howdy, we've got 'em! Al Unser, then
Bobby Unser; he's not in second position. In second position, quite a distance back, is Gordon Johncock in car
number twenty! They're up to turn three and Ron Carrell!"*

*"I have them, Doug! And there's Al Unser, Bobby
Unser right behind him, and they're in turn four already
—Jim Shelton!"*

*"Well, it's the same way! It's four and eight! Al Unser,
being followed by his brother, Bobby Unser, and it looks
like Bobby is catching up with him! How about it, Sid?"*

*"They started in single file—their positions— Al is
ahead of Bobby Unser— Let's take 'em into turn number
one, Mike!"*

*"Okay, what Bobby Unser's trying to do is unlap him-
self there. He's a full lap behind. There they go! Al*

Unser, Bobby about three to four car-lengths behind, and Lee Kunzman! Turn two, and Howdy Bell!"

"Aaaaand we see them now! Here he comes! Two wheels below the yellow line, right by us! This is Al Unser, our leader, going by right now! There is your second-place car, and they're up to Doug Zink on the back-stretch."

And so on.

AND SO ON.

Until the drizzle started again about an hour later.

The yellow flag came out. On the 130th lap there were only nine cars still running. All the other cars had been damaged or had mechanical failures. A broken gearbox had forced A. J. Foyt's second car out of the race on the 101st lap. Gordon Johncock was leading, Billy Vukovich was in second place, Roger McCluskey was third, and Mel Kenyon was fourth. Umbrellas were going up. The cars were slowed to eighty miles an hour and ran under the Electro-Pacer while the officials tried to decide whether to continue under the yellow caution flag, stop the cars with a red flag with hopes of still another restart, or give Gordon Johncock the checkered victory flag. Some of the drivers were seen wiping their visors with the backs of their gloves as they went by, to get the fine spray off. The sky was very dark.

And then:

"The red flag is out now! The red flag comes out! At five-thirty-two! And the winner will be Gordon Johncock in—car number forty—I beg your pardon, twenty—the STP Double Oil Filter Special— What's the matter, Ray?"

"There is an indication that they may line them up again with the possibility of a restart. Now this final decision has not been made, and may be made in just the next few minutes—"

"There is no checker, just a red. So we do NOT have a win as yet. The race was stopped only with the red flag. And Ray Pashke tells us that we may have a restart and try to get the entire two hundred laps in. They're really trying very, very, very hard indeed, to get a full Five-Hundred-mile race in. Starting on Monday—Tuesday—

Wednesday—and now the rain is coming down and more umbrellas are going up, but it's not dark here yet, it's only five-thirty-three. So we have another brand-new thing occurring with the 1973 running of the 'Five Hundred.' "

Werner Dold stood in the shelter of the Tower, looking out at the track. It was becoming dark gray with water. The lighted numbers on the scoring pylon shone brightly in the gloom. Some of the fans were still in the seats, covering up, their tarps and umbrellas tugging in the wind. But many of them were getting up and filing out toward the exits. Out in front of the Tower in the rain, there were officials starting, hesitating, turning around, listening to each other, and talking with waving hands. Werner recognized Andy Granatelli, the sponsor of the STP Racing Team, who was arguing vehemently with Chief Steward Harlan Fengler and a Speedway official. Fengler walked away, and Granatelli then turned his bulk toward Victory Lane and walked off in that direction. The gates to the Victory Ramp were opened. The announcer called the end of the race. The crowd cheered. Starter Pat Vidan, who had waved a red flag but no checkered flag to stop the race, now opened a checkered umbrella over his head. Werner Dold squinted and grinned. There was something very appropriate about that checkered umbrella, he thought.

Werner Dold looked at the tired, shambling, dispirited people all around until he saw somebody he knew was a member of Hulman's staff. "Hey," he called, raising his left hand, snapping his fingers, and waving him over. "Tell Tony Hulman that Werner Dold wants to talk to him."

"Who—"

"He'll want to talk to me, I guarantee you."

Werner's manner caused the hurried man to pause and look at him seriously. "Your name was—"

"Werner Dold."

"Does he know you?"

"He should."

"I'm not sure where Mr. Hulman is."

"I'll wait here. Tell him it's one of the most important

conversations he'll ever have." Werner drew a cigar out of his silver case and lit it, flashing his enormous diamond ring, while the man paused and appraised him. Werner felt confident and powerful. He enjoyed this feeling; he enjoyed making people come to him. Anonymity might be a nice novelty now and then, but. . . .

The man nodded and went away.

Werner turned toward the track. The bright-red winning STP car was being moved into Victory Lane. The driver was standing up in it, his helmet off. Werner watched the familiar Winner's Circle celebration: the kiss from the Festival Queen, the drink of milk, the words into the microphone, the wreath of orchids and little checkered flags being placed over the driver's shoulders, the huge silver Borg-Warner Trophy, the photographers swarming. All this in sifting rain.

Sometimes Andy Granatelli, carried away by his Italian emotions, would kiss his winning drivers on the mouth. This time Andy was very subdued; his smile seemed forced. He shook hands with Johncock and patted him on the head. The STP Racing Team had won. But it had won an incomplete race, and it had lost a driver and a crewman.

Werner watched and thought. He smoked his cigar while he waited. Some very serious considerations were working inside his head.

If you bought this place, he suggested to himself, might you not be obtaining something similar to Kitty? Something you got because of your emotions and then might regret having attached to your name?

He tried to be objective, to remember what his impressions of the place had been before he had started wanting to buy it. What he was asking himself was whether any respectable financier would really want to be remembered as the man responsible for all this. How would it look in his biography, owning the Indianapolis Motor Speedway? A biography is a very serious thing, he reminded himself.

And then suddenly he understood something else. He remembered his own conversation three days ago with Doc Upton about what race fans really like. Tony Hulman must know a debacle like this would not keep fans away from next year's race; it would only add to the lure, the legend of the place. The crowds will get bigger every year, and Tony Hulman knows that as well as I do, Werner thought. I think I've been looking at this whole thing backward. If I really wanted this place, this probably would be the *worst* time to come for it.

When the man from Tony Hulman's staff came back to get Werner Dold, Werner Dold was no longer there.

Bob Collins of the *Star* was writing his "Sports Over Lightly" column for Thursday's morning paper.

Maybe we should call this the Vicente Blasco-Ibáñez almost 500-Mile Race. Blasco-Ibáñez' Four Horsemen ran amuck during the month of May in Indianapolis.

There was fire and, sadly, there was death.

And if I may continue along the lines of the grim humor in racing—there was famine: represented by the thousands who ran out of beer and stood in line all day Tuesday to discover the concession stands were fresh out of hotdogs. And pestilence: according to a reporter who had spent two days watching the celebrants wallowing in the mud in the "snake pit" on the first turn, "I don't want to go back. There must be disease down there by now."

A man whose telephone number was 546-5209 picked up his ringing phone. He was a priest in a Northeastside parish church. "Hello?" he said.

"Mr. Bixby," said the voice, "this is Werner Dold, the man you were talking with in the Speedway lounge yesterday. I'm in a hurry to get to my plane, but wanted to tell you our deal's off. Thank you for your company. I'd like to get in touch with you soon about helping me with my biography—"

"Uhm—perhaps you've got the wrong number," said the priest.

"Damn," said the voice. And the priest was left gazing blankly into the buzzing receiver.

"I'll tell you, young man," Marjorie Cole said, "we almost decided to let the police keep you all night. We may give you back to them as it is, if you step out of line one inch."

Kevin didn't say anything. He had had enough of police —and their endless questions. He dreaded the hearings that lay ahead. He never wanted to see another car or cycle. He sat slumped far down in the back seat, red-eyed, his chin on his chest. Pam sat on one side of him, and Keith on the other. They had been told to grab him if he tried to escape. Marjorie didn't trust her little boy at all now. She looked in the rearview mirror. The headlights of her Mustang were still right behind. Cliff was driving it home. Marjorie was amazed and thankful that Kevin hadn't wrecked it.

The reason they had decided to drive down to Indianapolis to get him instead of leaving him in the juvenile lockup all night was that they had read about perverts and drug users in jails. Besides that, Cliff had felt that, somehow, Kevin would be a genuine juvenile delinquent if the police kept him all night; if he stayed at home in his parents' custody, he might still pass for a mere bad kid.

Pam and Keith were afraid to say anything to Kevin, even to ask him about the girls with the marijuana. And they were afraid to offer any censure, even though they were brimful of smugness and self-righteousness. Their mother was too mad to put up with any kind of hassling. So Pam and Keith just sat silently as the darkness and headlights swept by. But Pam couldn't contain herself entirely. As they stopped for a traffic light on the outskirts of Kokomo, in the flooding light from a drive-in restaurant and a service station, she reached over Kevin and touched Keith to get his attention. Then she glanced at Kevin, withdrawn in his fetal position, and spelled out, in their sign language that he didn't comprehend:

T-H-E E-N-D
O-F T-H-E R-O-A-D

The director of the Girls' School interlaced her fingers on her desk and gazed at Renee and Puggles until they thought they couldn't stand it any longer. "Is there anything you want to say?"

The girls shook their heads, looking down at their hands.

"Don't you have anything to say? Why don't you just tell me all about it?"

They didn't look up at her. Heads down, they glanced at each other out of the corners of their eyes, and each tried to keep from giggling but hoped the other would start laughing. Renee crossed her legs quickly and put one arm across her midsection and the other over her mouth to hide her smile.

"We just wanted to go to the race," Puggles said finally.

"We had never been there before," Renee said.

"Well, I hope you enjoyed it."

"It was dumb," Renee said.

"Boring," said Puggles. "But we did see a man get burned up."

"The first day."

"Yeah. I mean, I guess he burned up."

"That must have been awful."

Renee shrugged. "It was yecky. Boring."

"Did my mom call here?" Puggles said.

"Yes, she did," said the director. "After you called her."

"How often did she call? Very often?"

"Several times a day."

Puggles thought about that and smiled.

"Do you want to call and tell her you're all right?" the director asked.

Puggles brightened up. "Uh, could I, I wonder? I think I could be pregnant."

"Prob'ly got VD, too," Renee said.

"Oh, yeah," Puggles said enthusiastically. "I might have VD. Please, I'd like to call Mom."

* * *

It was almost eight o'clock when Ella Rumple got home. She unlocked the door and dragged herself in, the picnic basket bumping against the doorjamb as she entered. She heard Ivy's car roar away. Its horn blasted out the rhythm of shave-and-a-haircut-two-bits.

Ella went to the kitchen. She sat down by the phone. She bit her lips. Then she braced herself and direct-dialed the Roepkes' number in Chicago. Gerald's voice answered.

"Gerald, do you—"

"Honey! Am I ever glad to hear from you!"

"You are?"

"You know I am. Ella, are you too tired to drive up here tonight?"

"No—"

"Then hop in that Olds and get up here. I'll wait up. Honey, we've got something to tell you. Something big, and—wonderful!"

"You—" she said in a small voice, "you don't sound like someone who's been to a—a funeral home."

"Well, never mind that. Just come up. And honey, don't drive too fast, but hurry. Okay?"

She gave a sad little laugh. "Don't worry," she said. "I'm—I'm, uh, through with speed."

"Good," he said after a pause. "Who needs it?"

It seemed to Diana that her parents believed her. She knew they would eventually because they wanted to. They talked with exaggerated cheerfulness and exclaimed again and again to the maid about how good the roast was. Diana looked at herself in the mirror above the sideboard. She always looked particularly good in this light from the twelve flame-shaped bulbs in the cut-glass chandelier, and had a habit of sneaking glances at herself in it while they dined. But she was so tired. So let down.

Then the telephone rang.

The maid's voice mumbled in the kitchen. Then she came to the dining-room door. "It's a feller for you, missy," she said.

"Who is it?" Diana was sure she knew.

"I don't know."

"Would you find out, please, Martha?"

The maid went back to the kitchen, mumbled, then returned. "It's a Mr. Alef, and he says he's just *got* to talk to you."

Mr. and Mrs. Scheckley pretended to be engrossed in their roast beef.

"Tell him—tell him I'm not here. No, wait. Just tell him I don't want to talk to him. Ever."

Mr. and Mrs. Scheckley looked at her and then at each other and then at their plates again. Martha went away, mumbled into the phone again, paused, spoke more loudly, then hung up.

Diana's mother looked at Diana searchingly. "Who was that, dear?" She finally had to ask.

"Oh, it was a—it was a guy at the Speedway who tried to get fresh with me."

Diana's mother looked at her, and moisture glinted in her eyes. A tremulous smile came onto her lips. "That's our *good* girl."

"That's right," Mr. Scheckley said emphatically, laying his knife and fork down beside his plate and swallowing. "You know, Diana," he said with a contrite smile, "we didn't really *think* you, uhm, were with, uhm, Harry last night. We just—you know—thought he might have, uhm, known where you were going or something."

"You must know I wouldn't ever do anything to upset you," Diana assured them.

"We know! We know! You're our good girl."

"You're our Princess. That's what you are. Our Princess!"

Lloyd Skirvin had finished off a pint of whiskey by the time Billy Joe Marshall came back, and his ribs and arms and head didn't hurt so much now, but he felt mean as a snake inside. Billy Joe was shitty. Yankees were shitty. Beer was shitty. Even Yankee tits were shitty. "Where the fuck you been, Worms?"

"I ain't Worms. I'm Billy Joe Marshall. Lemme have your keys."

"My keys, your ass."

"C'mon."

"Kiss my ass, you fuck-off. Where you been?"

"I'll tell you if you give me the keys. I'll give 'em back."

"What's goin' on?"

"Just gimme 'em and maybe I'll tell you." Billy Joe didn't want to tell Lloyd what he was going to do, because he knew he might never get the keys if he told him. "Come on. I jus' need t' git in th' trunk a minute."

"What fer?"

"Maybe I got somethin' good t' drink stashed away back there," Billy Joe hinted.

Lloyd looked skeptical but gave him the keys. He got out of the car painfully, and unsteadily followed Billy Joe around to the trunk. Theirs was the only car left within a hundred yards. In the evening gloom, the field was strewn with damp refuse. A newspaper tumbled by in the cold wind. Billy Joe unlocked the trunk. There were two big, battered suitcases in the trunk. There was a toolbox with the name WORMS painted across the top in red nail polish. A girl had painted it on there for him once, a girl in Tennessee. Billy Joe lifted out his toolbox and one of the suitcases. He set the toolbox down. Then he shut the trunk and gave the keys back to Lloyd. Now this would be the hard part. He took a deep breath.

"Lloyd, I be a-seein' ya."

"Huh?"

"I think I got me a job lined up."

"Huh?"

Billy Joe tilted his head toward Gasoline Alley. "I think I got me a job lined up." He stuck out his hand. Lloyd didn't take it. He stood there for a moment with his mouth open. Then he inhaled and spat on Billy Joe's hand.

"You crud," he said. "You suck-ass Yankee dawgshit."

Billy Joe set his jaw. He was quaking inside because of the way Lloyd was, but he wouldn't give him the satisfaction of saying he was sorry or anything like that. He stooped and picked up his toolbox, ready to dodge in case Lloyd tried to kick him in the face or the nuts. The spit on his hand was cold in the wind. He started walking away.

"Y'go one more step, y'better never come back!"
Lloyd snarled.

Billy Joe went on, making no reply.

"Y'fuckhead! Y'cunt-rag-chewin', shit-eatin' Yankee!"
Lloyd hurled the car keys to the ground in a fury.

Billy Joe kept walking.

"I'll get you, you son of a shit-eatin' nigger," Lloyd
began sobbing. "I'm gonna run y'r ass int' th' muthafuckin' ground." That's what he would do. Yeah. He'd
just fire up this ol' Merc and run that shit-eatin' bastard
quitter right into the mud. Sobbing, cursing, he looked for
the keys on the ground. It was all muddy here. The keys
were somewhere in the mud, and he couldn't see them.
Whimpering, he dropped to his hands and knees and
started raking his hands through the cold mud. "I'll git
you. Oh, man, I'll git you!" His nose was running, and
he sniffled and wiped it on his arm. He whined curses
and squished mud through his fingers trying to find
his keys. His eyes were swimming with tears, and he
couldn't see.

Billy Joe looked back once to see the Mercury. MOVIN'
MUTHA, it said on the front fender. Lloyd was there on
all fours behind the car, rooting like a pig.

Billy Joe couldn't stand to see that. So he didn't look
back anymore.

Nick Alef walked west in the dark along Twenty-fifth
Street. Wind-blown trash tumbled by. The big field
across the street was almost empty now. In the distance
the parking lights of some vehicle glowed, and there were
shouts, reminding Nick of someone breaking camp. Like
when we used to camp on the Ohio, he thought.

"She doesn't ever want to talk to you, sir," that housekeeper had said.

"Well," he sighed. "Well." He shivered with cold and
loneliness. There was no place to go but home.

When he came to his house and saw the lights on inside, he stopped. An invisible, impassable wall of dread
seemed to stand across the walkway. He stood, looking
at the lights, trying to swallow. His stone bench lay
broken in the yard.

Let's face it, he thought. You have to go in sooner or later.

Becky and Davey were at the table when he walked into the kitchen.

"Hi, Dad," Davey said. Then he looked quickly at his mother and dropped his eyes.

"Hi, Davey. Hi, Becky."

She nodded, staring at him. She didn't look angry, but she didn't say anything.

He stood until it was too awkward just to stand there any longer. He didn't know what to say; obviously, they didn't, either. He opened the basement door and turned on the light and went down to his office. He expected Becky to follow him down, but she didn't. It was ominous, somehow. He noticed that things had been changed on his desk. He went to it and looked. His publicity work and speech materials, usually in disorderly drifts all over the desk, had been made into a neat stack and set back near the wall. The rest of the desktop was clean—for the first time in perhaps three years—and in its center there was a deep stack of file folders and manuscript boxes. He recognized them. They were his books and stories and scenarios. Beside them there was a row of newly sharpened pencils.

He stood and looked at it for several minutes. He wasn't quite sure why she had done all this. He understood only that it was some kind of a message.

He trudged up the stairs. Becky and Davey were still at the table, under the hanging lamp, each with what appeared to be a glass of Coke. He stood and looked at them; they sat and looked at him.

"Do you want to talk?" he said.

"Do you?" she said.

"Right now?"

"Oh, whenever."

He bit a piece of dry skin off his upper lip. "Uhm, would you mind if I had a little run first—to clear my head?"

"If you want. Your sweat suit's in the dryer."

He looked at her for a moment. "It *is?*"

She nodded.

Davey moved. "Can I run with you, Dad?" He looked

at his mother. She nodded; he rose from his chair and paused, half-standing.

Nick swallowed and blinked. "Sure, Davey. Love— love to have you—" Then he turned and started down toward the dryer because he couldn't talk.

EPILOGUE:

July 3, 1973

NICK ALEF drank iced tea in a crowded restaurant in downtown Indianapolis. He had read in the newspapers that Swede Savage had succumbed to his massive injuries after a month, and had died in the hospital. Nick was thinking about that, and remembering his own traumatic experience of Savage's crash, when he saw his wife, Becky, and a tall young man pass through the front of the restaurant and go out, laughing. The man was one of the young account executives from the advertising agency where Becky was now working full-time; he was a man Nick had met before, a charming but shallow man who had a reputation as a seducer. As co-workers, of course, they had cause to be lunching together, but the sight of these two handsome people, one of them his wife, strolling affably together out onto a public street, struck Nick with an awful, poignant sense of his own failing as her mate. He knew he had taken her for granted, had been a poor provider and a negligent parent, had kept no promises, and had chosen to transfer his passions now and then to passing outsiders: Kitty, Diana, and a few lesser ones now all but forgotten. He knew that from this moment he would probably be suspicious of Becky's absences; he understood, though, that he deserved whatever anxiety he might have.

The waitress, a woman of big form, piercing voice, and dark-veined legs, came to his table and looked down at him over the rims of her spectacles.

"That be all, Mr. Alef?"

"Guess so, Ivy." He paused and stared at her. "You knew my name," he said.

"Well, I ought to, dearie. I been serving you for, what, fifteen years now?"

"About that, I guess."

"Sure is," she said. "I remember you used to come in at night. Clear back when we was across the street. You sat there and drunk rye and wrote in a notebook. I never saw anybody write so much. I asked you what it was, and you said a book."

He remembered. *Life as Foreplay* and *Hubris*. "That's right. I wrote two whole books here. At that last booth back by the kitchen, remember?"

"I remember."

"If another waitress came, I'd say, 'Send me Ivy.' "

"Ha-ha! That's baloney, but thanks. You'd try to get the young ones."

"No, I always wanted my Ivy."

"Ha! I love you, you liar." She shook her head, and he could see memory working behind her homely visage, and he wondered how anyone could do the kind of work she had done for fifteen years. I guess all you have to do is have to do it, he thought. Remember that the next time you don't think you can grind out another press release. He thought of the two book manuscripts, still sitting on his desk where Becky had put them. You could end up waiting tables yourself at the rate you're going, he suggested to himself. Maybe that wouldn't be so bad. To stop fighting and have the feeling of resignation must be a relief. Ivy doesn't seem to agonize.

"But I always wondered," she was saying, "why you'd write in a restaurant instead of a nice quiet place."

"Restaurants are perfect. There are people around, and that's good, but they don't want you for anything, which is even better."

"Well, that sure ain't my case," Ivy laughed. "They all want something from me. D'you still write books?"

"Sure," he lied.

"Good. Hang in there. Well, looks like you owe me about thirty-two cents."

"Here. Keep the change."

"Hey, wait. That's a five."

"It's for remembering who I am." But he thought: That was too extravagant a gesture.

"Shoot, I'll remember you in eternity for this! Ha-ha. Have a nice day now, hon."

He picked up his scuffed briefcase and went out into the bright heat of the street. For eternity, he thought. Maybe it wasn't too extravagant, at that. Five bucks is cheap for immortality.

Nick's briefcase was heavy at his side, full of materials he had been preparing for his downtown public-relations clients. He was catching up on it. With Becky gone all day at the ad agency, he got a lot done. He could get around better now that that Kokomo kid had adjusted his car. And having destroyed his cameras, he had all the time he used to spend on photography. He still didn't like his work, but he was working harder, working well. It was necessary.

He and Becky had never really had their talk. There had been no mention of the night he had stayed out. At home it was now like some sort of limbo, but it was more bearable. Maybe the marriage would last. For a change, he wanted it to.

But his public-relations work was a dead end. He was still looking for a way out of it. He had applied for positions at all of the radio and television stations in town, and at the newspapers. So far, all had said they had no place for him. Jobs were scarce. He was nearly forty. He would have welcomed a job in the work he had hastened to escape a few years before. At least, he thought now as he walked along Market Street, if you were writing news somewhere, you weren't obscure. There was always a chance of parlaying yourself into some degree of prominence. Look at— Well, he thought, look at Sid Collins. Worked his butt off, but he's known all over the world now. Got a thing going. Even if it's for something like the "500," he's the guy who's got it. But what can you do with a little homegrown flack firm? Besides fade into oblivion?

Hell, everybody fades into oblivion sooner or later, he thought. Swede Savage died yesterday; five years from now, who'll remember Swede Savage? You fade or you go out in a flash. What's the big deal?

It's just that some of us would choose the flash, he thought. At least a flash is noticeable.

In this same context he had been thinking recently of his strange, pointless encounter with Werner Dold. People who want to hire a flack are hoping to flash out instead of fade out, Nick thought. Wonder what became of his scheme to buy the Speedway? Haven't heard or read a word.

He thought of Kitty. And he thought of Diana. Or rather, Diana billowed through his mind in a series of tawny images.

But now Diana and Kitty and Werner Dold and the Speedway were in his mind again. His head was filling up irresistibly with impressions of those three rainy days. Those impressions had been brewing in him for a month. In the middle of the night he would awaken to wallow in recollections of that event. It had been like a world unto itself. He thought of it as a microcosm, somehow, of the world in the age of technology, with the machinery in charge. There was some connection between the race and the Vietnam War and *Playboy:* the filming and the watching, the fornicating and the dying, and the awful hunger for amusement. Suffering as a spectator sport, he thought. He remembered himself filming the agony of Swede Savage. How could I do it that way, I who once couldn't take a picture of a grieving grandfather, he asked himself. How could those people in the bleachers watch it that way, with their hands in their pockets or eating fried chicken or picking their noses? Maybe you see so much of it that it stops meaning anything.

It gets to a point where you have to think about it to be able to feel it.

Nick stood on a curb at Monument Circle. The lime-stone of the archaic monument and its statues was bone-white against the blue sky and the Hilton Hotel behind it. The waterfalls of the monument flowed with a steady rushing sound that was not quite drowned out by the susurrus of traffic that forever went counterclockwise around the Circle. He mused on the thought that the two main landmarks in Indianapolis featured automobiles going around and around in the counterclockwise direction.

He watched the cars go around, and remembered people and incidents. Diana and Dold and Kitty. Harry

Kuntz. A spectator kneeling at the site of Walther's crash with a woman's head in his lap. Scruffy kids fucking for an audience in the Snake Pit. A naked girl being tossed in a blanket. Sid Collins looking down from the Control Tower onto rain, fire, and death.

Suddenly Nick had a thought that was too big to handle standing up. He turned around twice and then walked back to the restaurant, his heartbeat accelerating.

"Forget something?" the waitress asked with an open-mouthed, surprised glance over her spectacles.

"No. Remembered something. Listen, Ivy. Give me that table in the corner. Bring me an Old Overholt neat every hour on the hour, and aside from that, leave me alone."

He gulped the first rye and sat looking at the blank sheet of a new legal pad. With a felt-tipped pen he printed:

SPECTATOR SPORT

He lit a Pall Mall and thought. The Muzak was playing an insipid rendition of "The Windmills of Your Mind." Meat flared on the grill nearby. Dishes clattered in the distant scullery. Voices receded to a murmur, and the world grew small and cozy. Nick put out his cigarette in the ashtray. He paused, then threw the rest of the pack onto a bus tray full of garbage and dirty dishes. For a moment he held the pen's point poised an inch above the virgin page.

Then he began to write:

At five o'clock on the wet and windy morning of Memorial Day, an aerial bomb exploded over a residential neighborhood four miles northwest of downtown Indianapolis. . . .

Made in the USA
Coppell, TX
14 May 2021

55453545R00263